A History of Russia

A History of Russia

Joel Carmichael

Hippocrene Books
New York

Copyright © 1990 Joel Carmichael.

For information, address:
Hippocrene Books, Inc.
171 Madison Ave.
New York, NY 10016

Library of Congress Cataloging-in-Publication Data

Carmichael, John.
    A history of Russia / Joel Carmichael.
      p.   cm.
    Includes bibliographical references.
    1. Soviet Union—History. I. Title.
DK40.C37   1990
947—dc20   90-31344
                                    CIP

Production by
Combined Books, Inc.
26 Summit Grove, Suite 207
Bryn Mawr, PA 19010

Printed in the United States of America

ISBN 0-87052-624-3 (hbk)
ISBN 0-87052-957-9 (pbk)

Contents

Foreword

*I*t is fashionable to distrust the sweep of generalization. Yet the temptation to extract a pattern from the thousand years of Russian history is irresistible.

Russia owes its germination to the vagaries of international trade: when Europe was barred from the Mediterranean by the expansion of Islam a thousand years ago, the Vikings—armed businessmen who had established a chain of trading posts between the Middle East and northern Europe—created the embryonic Russian State while bypassing the Middle East.

But this seminal contact was entirely exceptional: Russia generally remained isolated from contemporary influences. Cut off from Byzantium by the Tatars and Turks under the House of Chingis Khan, it was impinged on by a more advanced society only twice before the modern era—when Novgorod briefly led the Hanseatic League in the 13th to 15th century, and when English merchants found the North Sea route to Muscovy in 1553.

Urban growth, the groundwork of civilization, was inhibited in Russia by the interaction of two factors—remoteness from the international trade routes and the rural backwardness that prevented the accumulation of surpluses.

Russia's population remained small for centuries. In the mid-sixteenth century it numbered 9–11 million, at a time when France numbered 19 million, Spain 11, and Austria 20; in the following century Poland had about 11 million people.

As in Europe generally, but with a greater coefficient of

vii

increase, a demographic spurt began in Russia around 1750: in a single century the population quadrupled—from 17–18 million to 68. By 1897 it numbered 124 million; in 1914 170 million. Today the Soviet Union has more than 250,000,000 people.

Russian evolution was framed by its general backwardness, its scanty population, its great expanse, and the vulnerability of its frontiers.

The characteristic institutions of the West may be said to stem from a differentiation, originating in Rome, between two types of authority—over people and over objects. It was this fundamental cleavage of category that ultimately enabled Western society to distinguish between statecraft and the management of property.

In Russia this complex development, slow to start, remained unconsummated. The Vikings who had launched Russia never settled down within juridical structures based on territory, as they did in England and Sicily, but persisted as a merchant community rather like the English East India Company or the Hudson's Bay Company in Canada. Owning their territory collectively, they required no constitutional differentiations. Thus in the very genesis of Russian society the confusion between ownership and sovereignty suffocated the conception of political authority.

The "patrimonial" mentality of the Vikings laid the foundations of authoritarianism, whose essence consists of just this lumping together of two distinct relationships. Russia has in fact remained the patrimonial state *par excellence:* Russian rulers have been both sovereigns of the realm and its proprietors. There was no foundation for an institution that in Western Europe was basic—contractual vassalage, which, entailing a network of reciprocal rights and duties, is the foundation of personal liberty as well as constitutionality.

The natural consequence of the absence of reciprocity was arbitrary force. Just as the absence of contractual vassalage gave rise to pervasive lawlessness in Russian society, so the lawlessness of society, conversely, engendered extravagant measures of repression to cope with it.

This had a further corollary: the struggle for liberty, lacking an anchorage in the self-consciousness of real social groupings, could not depend on accepted social norms, but was obliged to invoke abstract ideals. Thus two abstractions collided—arbitrary force and intellectual idealism.

As Russia's contacts with the West began proliferating a couple of centuries ago, this polarization grew more and more difficult to sustain. Indeed, the conflict between authoritarianism and the desire for liberty has generated a pervasive internal tension down to our own day.

The Russian state inevitably remained oppressive: in the absence of an instinct, so to speak, for constitutionality, the conflict between force and freedom became the matrix of society. In the nineteenth century the tradition of police rule, especially concentrated since Ivan the Terrible and Peter the Great, was further institutionalized. From 1845 on all criminal codes contained an "omnibus" clause worded so vaguely that the government could imprison anyone for such crimes as "undermining" morale or "arousing doubts" and "disrespect."

Against an age-old background the repression that characterized the second half of the nineteenth century was particularly stimulated by the shake-up of the elite: the educated classes—especially, of course, their idealistic children—were permeated by "liberal" and "revolutionary" sentiments. As dissidence was organized in the seventies and eighties, the government was bound to react: after the celebrated Zasulich case in 1878—in which a militant dissident, given a jury trial for shooting a high functionary, was freed by the pressure of "public opinion"—juries were avoided altogether and administrative methods were resorted to in handling the population.

Thus, by the early eighties, all elements of a bureaucratic-police regime were present—the police were preoccupied with crimes against the state; politics was the business of high functionaries. The security organs, authorized to search, arrest, imprison and exile anyone suspected of political activity, had, in theory, practically limitless control of the population.

Nevertheless, administrative repression was already slackening substantially in the late nineteenth and early twentieth century. The vitality of free enterprise, energetically reinforced by capital from Western Europe, was transforming society. The first translation of Karl Marx's *Capital* was into Russian; Marx's notion that "capitalism" had to realize its full potential *before* it could be shaken, fitted in very appropriately with the large-scale organization of new industrial complexes: the railways alone were changing the face of Russia.

In addition, a powerful social force counterbalanced the administrative hangovers of the past. The Russian upper classes had sponged up European culture, especially in its French and German versions, with such avidity that by the end of the eighteenth century they were producing a first-rate intelligentsia, gifted and energetic in the arts and sciences, with able thinkers bestriding all horizons. In the nineteenth century cultivated Russians had become numerous enough to outweigh the patrimonial spirit infusing the regime's conception of itself.

The Tsarist administration never, for instance, violated property rights. Alexander Herzen, while in the midst of attacking the regime from the safety of London in his periodical *The Bell,* always had his personal revenues forwarded to him. Lenin's mother drew a government pension as a civil servant's widow even after one son had been executed for an attempt on the Tsar's life and two others had been jailed.

Upper class urbanity had even permeated the security organs, where cultivated gentlemen took a genuine interest in the ideas of the revolutionaries and treated them with remarkable indulgence. Life in Siberia was practically idyllic: revolutionaries could hunt, shoot, fish, read and write books, hold meetings, and escape at will.

Under the Tsars, Russian officialdom was rather small; moreover, the lack of funds, the size of the country, and the difficulties of communication combined to hamstring it. In the 1880s only 17 people were executed, all of them assassins or would-be assassins; during the repression under Alexander III that followed the assassination of his father, only 4,000 people were interrogated, in connection with genuine offenses.

With the Tsarist breakdown in 1917—from February to

October—repression vanished totally; for eight months Russia was freer than ever before.

In October the Bolshevik nucleus took over the patrimonial idea in its purest form—it expropriated the whole country. Giving the center a matchlessly tight control by modernizing both transport and communications, it solved the bureaucratic problem of allocating funds between government departments—repression was now the very essence of the regime.

The temporary restoration of capitalism in 1921 that the parvenu regime was obliged to resort to by the twin disasters of "War Communism" and the Civil War played out its role of reviving the economy within the tight embrace of the streamlined despotism: it was brought to an abrupt end in 1929 by the crash programs of collectivization and industrialization that constituted the true Russian revolution. It was then that totalitarianism truly flowered.

What had been a mere potentiality under Tsarism was endlessly realized by the Bolshevik apparatus. The omnibus clauses of the Tsarist criminal codes reached full fruition in the Bolshevik codes of 1927 and 1960. The apparatus foreshadowed under Alexander III achieved a scope and ferocity unprecedented in history, consolidating itself in the thirties: at least 20 percent of the population were destroyed. By mid-twentieth century the Bolshevik conspiratorial nucleus had grown into an elite comprising some 1 percent of the population.

The first political action taken by the Bolsheviks after the *putsch* was to dissolve the Constituent Assembly, a political goal they had shared beforehand with generations of Russians. Thus the neo-Bolshevik dictatorship was in full control of all the resources of the State.

In addition, though Marxism does not, in fact, contain any guidance for societies after their transition to socialism or communism, and even though the very seizure of power by a socialist party in a backward peasant country contradicted the main thesis of Marxism, this could not be admitted, since it would have detracted from the authority of the new government. In fact, Marxism was turned into a State cult and taken as the foundation of all education and discourse: though the problems facing the new regime could not be solved by Marxism, it was to remain the idiom of the government; the inherent flexibility of that idiom was to serve as a vehicle for explanation, justification, and exhortation from then on. Thus the ideas of Rousseau, Hegel and Marx may be said to have achieved, through contradiction, an institutional expression.

The control of the State, plus the cult of "Marxist-Leninist" orthodoxy devised by Stalin, brought about a mixture of autocracy and sectarianism buttressed by technology, the most massive police state in history.

Introduction

*T*he most obvious thing about Russia may also be the most illuminating: its sheer size. Encompassing one-sixth of the land surface of the earth, the equivalent of the whole of the North American continent, Russia is by far the largest country in the world.

Politically, modern Russia—since 1917 the Soviet Union—is all the more striking because it began only some six centuries ago with the five hundred square miles of the tiny principality of Moscow; a combination of territorial absorption and pervasive colonization has extended it from the Baltic Sea to the Pacific Coast, from the Arctic Ocean to the Black and Caspian Seas, and all along the northern borders of Persia, Afghanistan, India, and China.

But in spite of Russia's size and the wide variety of its climatic zones, from the barren tundra of the extreme north to the lush orchard groves of the Crimea and Caucasus and the cotton plantations of Turkestan, a certain monotony gives an essential unity to the Eurasian plain that stretches, undisturbed by any abrupt elevations, from Hungary to China.

The Urals, which in schoolbooks still separate Europe from Asia, are altogether negligible—a chain of dwarf hills rising no more than 1,500 feet above sea level, with any number of easy passages. There has never been any serious obstacle to movement back and forth across the great plain.

Extensive in space though Russia has been for so long, it

is to European Russia that one must look for an explanation of Russian history; there, basic communications have been ensured by a ramified waterway system. The low-lying watersheds of central Russia are the sources of a number of great rivers such as the Volga, the Dnieper, and the western Dvina. Even in pre-Russian history, the cluster of great waterways formed by the outlets of the main rivers and their numerous tributaries was used by a variety of drifting peoples, who settled and came into contact with other peoples, both Western and Eastern. The waterways also promoted the conquest of Siberia, since the Volga water system merges with the western Siberian system of the Ob.

The self-centered quality of Russian history, fostered by the vastness of the Eurasian plain, was accentuated by the contrast between Russia's internal capaciousness and the relative insignificance of its shoreline. The Arctic Ocean and the White Sea are for all practical purposes useless; the Caspian Sea for all its size is landlocked. As for the Black Sea and the Baltic, they played no role in Russian history until the eighteenth century, when the cardinal traits of the nation-state were already formed.

The importance of the steppe in Russia's formation should not deflect one's attention entirely from the role of the forest belt. Though the boundary line between the forests of the north and the steppes of the south is not definite, it was the forests that shaped the Russian people in their earliest days. Going much farther south than it does now, the wooded zone started along a line passing as far south as Kiev, below present-day Moscow and Kazan. The timber zone stretched parallel to the endless steppe to its south; after dipping slightly southward along the eastern slope of the Urals to the Sayan Mountains, it resumed its eastward sweep to the Pacific Ocean. The steppe of European Russia merged imperceptibly with the steppe of Siberian Russia, flowing through the broad passage between the Urals and the Caspian Sea.

Most of us think of Russia today as primarily agricultural because of its southern flatlands, but it was not until after the middle of the eighteenth century that the forest belts receded into the background of Russian history proper, as distinct from the history of the Asiatic invasions that influenced early Russia so profoundly via this Ural-Caspian gateway. It was, indeed, just these timberlands of north and central Russia that served the Russians as shelter whenever the steppe disgorged its burden on them. The invaders generally moved with cattle and horses, often in entire caravans; for them the forest zone was inhospitable.

The open steppe was an important factor in Russian history in a purely negative sense: not only was the steppe the natural stamping ground for the mounted Asiatic nomads, but it also served for centuries as a refuge for all sorts of malcontents in flight from the oppressive regimes that have been a permanent feature of Russian life. The southern steppe, for instance, incubated the turbulent Cossack communities.

The creation of the Russian state was thus hampered by a dual problem: on the one hand there was nothing to keep out periodic Asiatic invasions, and on the other there was no way of keeping the Russian people firmly tied to the land. The free steppe constituted a chronic leak in the state, and until the rise of modern technology and its application to the control of populations it could not be stopped up.

Isolated individuals gradually permeated the marshy, forested hinterland in northeastern and central Russia, but the broad streams of social life could only flow along rivers and roads. The steppe was the cardinal thoroughfare; because of its far-flung, unimpeded emptiness, it was a source of disintegration both inside and out.

This emptiness was the corollary of territorial space. The country was in fact too big to be occupied by a people till they grew numerous enough, and because of the constant incursions from without this was difficult.

But—more important—the spatial vacuum was the counterpart of a cultural vacuum. Civilization came to Russia only a little more than a thousand years ago, and it came heavily mortgaged.

Civilization came with Christianity, oddly enough through the failure of Christianity elsewhere. The introduction of

Christianity to Russia was a consequence of the Muslim Arab conquests of the seventh and eighth centuries. As the Muslims pushed toward the Caucasus, they thrust back a Turkic-speaking ally of Byzantium, the Khazars, into the steppe of the lower Volga and the Kuban, where the Khazars became powerful enough to maintain themselves for a couple of centuries.

Some of the Bulgar tribes whom the Khazars did not absorb emigrated north and west. One branch settled along the middle Volga, while another pushed into the lower Danube. After defeating the Byzantines, the Bulgars gradually came to dominate the whole of the eastern Balkan peninsula, adopting Slavic culture and language so thoroughly that they were to leave nothing but their name to the modern Bulgarians.

The Khazars were rather versatile for nomads; not only did they become farmers and fishermen, but they developed a great merchant empire centered on the Volga, spread out laterally between the Far East and the Black Sea and vertically between the Muslim South and the primitive forest dwellers of the North. Perhaps the Khazars' chief distinction was their conversion to Judaism, which became the official religion of the rulers and a substantial part of the population. The conversion was probably a way of fending off the Muslims on the one hand and the Byzantine Christians on the other.

The Khazars eventually were undone by the Muslim advance, and the primitive Slavs they had been patronizing found themselves adrift. It had been by way of the Khazars' pacific trading empire that the first seeds of Christianity reached the Slavs. But though Christianity acted as a cultural channel, the channel was turned into a bottleneck by the Byzantine form it took.

Through a quirk of circumstance Christianity was brought to the Slavs in their own language, not in Greek, so that the history of the Russian Church revolves around the poverty of Church Slavonic. Russian churchmen, to say nothing of their parishioners, had no need to learn Greek: the consequence was that with no Latin and no Greek, the Russians found themselves cut off on the one hand from the civilized world at large, and on the other from their own fellow-Slavs who had become Roman Catholics.

Byzantine Christianity thus had the paradoxical effect of depriving the Russians of a share of Greek civilization. While Islam avidly sponged up classical Greek thought and passed it on fruitfully to Latin Europe, and while Byzantium itself dispatched scholars and manuscripts to Italy, there was no such migration of learning to Russia.

What Russia received from Byzantium was what the court and the pious monks from Athos, Sinai, and the oriental churches could give her: a broad conception of sovereignty, in which the ruler's property was confounded with his authority; the canon law; an art that could only be religious; an ecclesiastical education (very meager); and the habit of secluding women (which lasted for centuries). The fact that Russian clerics learned neither Greek nor Latin meant in effect that Russia missed Rome twice: the Roman Empire itself, and the Roman Catholic Church, which inherited the values of classical civilization and the pagan-Christian compound that had emerged from it. For that matter Russia also missed the Renaissance, which owed so much to the rediscovery of Greek learning.

Russian Christianity also inherited from Byzantium the profoundly rooted tradition of a detestation of the Roman Catholic world. This insulated Russia against wider cultural influences for many centuries.

All this made the Russian Church deeply and intimately national, but at the same time condemned it to a windowless chamber, the origin of the backwardness endemic in Russian life down to our own generation.

A Russian churchman once said, rightly, that "the Russian Church knows no development." Because Russian religion developed outside the Roman Catholic Church, there was no occasion for a Reformation; church and state were too densely interwoven. Nor was there the Counter-Reformation that reformed the Roman Catholic clergy and made it a potent factor in Western progress.

Finally, the closing of the seas to Russia proved decisive.

Russia began with the cultural tradition of Byzantium, thinly filtered through Church Slavonic and reduced to a bagatelle in the process, but it lost even that cultural resource in the fifteenth century, when the Ottoman Turks entered the sphere of Islam and wiped out Byzantium at the very moment when Russia might have had most use for it. From the early sixteenth century on, Russia was almost closed to Roman Catholics, while Byzantium had vanished. Both Latin and Greek civilization were unavailable; Russia was cut loose in a sea of ignorance. Thus Russia's physical isolation achieved its historic significance because of the spiritual isolation that accompanied it.

Ultimately, of course, the gap between Russia and the rest of Europe was bridged, but it took so long that by the time it happened there was a yawning chasm between the upper-class recipients of European culture and the masses of the people.

By the last decades of the nineteenth century, nevertheless, the expanding educated classes swiftly reached the cultural level of Western Europe. The economy as a whole, moreover, surged forward within the free-enterprise system, with concomitant effects on the peasantry and the working class.

The autocracy itself began loosening up. In the wake of the Russian defeat in the Russo-Japanese War of 1904–5 and of a Marxist movement of agitation, the Duma, a parliamentary body with considerable powers, was set up by the Tsarist government. A constitutional monarchy seemed in the offing.

But the titanic upheavals of the First World War, which broke out in 1914, transformed Russian society. In February 1917, while Russia, alongside the Allies, was at war against the Central Powers led by Germany, the monarchy was unseated by an administrative break down in the capital. The Tsar's abdication was followed by eight months of "Dual Power"–a provisional government, made up of moderate upper- and middle-class elements, and the Soviet of workers' and soldiers' deputies, made up of parties led by more or less Marxist intellectuals claiming to represent the working class and peasantry.

This uneasy alliance lasted eight months: while half paralysed and still carrying on the war against Germany, it was terminated by a *putsch:* the Bolshevik branch of the Russian Social-Democratic Workers' Party established a totalitarian dictatorship that survived for generations.

CHAPTER I

THE BEGINNINGS TO THE DECLINE OF KIEV

*T*he mistiness of antiquity lasted much longer for Russia than for the rest of Europe. In fact nothing in any detail is known about the ancestors of the Russians until the tenth and eleventh centuries. Even the Slavs as such are not mentioned until the sixth century: before that we must be content with archeological traces of the Scythians, mentioned in the seventh century B.C. as trading with some Greek colonists north of the Black Sea.

But the Scythians vanished before the Christian era, to be succeeded by the Sarmatians, who also remain a mere name for us; they were overcome in the second and third centuries A.D. by the Teutonic Goths. It was after this that tradition began solidifying. The Goths, who spread throughout the eastern territories of the Roman Empire, were finally halted and turned back by the first of the periodic Asiatic invaders, the Huns, who expelled the Goths from the steppes north of the Black Sea and subsequently overran the Roman Empire.

The Huns were the first Asiatics to come within threatening

distance of Europe as a whole. In the fifth century their leader, Attila, moved into what is today Hungary; after him came the Avars, another obscure Turkic-speaking Asiatic tribe, who appeared in the southern steppes in the second half of the sixth century.

The Khazars, apparently a mixture of Turkic-speakers that included Huns and Bulgars, and their allies, the Magyars (another intangible name for us), took control of the steppe north of the Black Sea by the middle of the seventh century; this is where they doubtless first came in contact with the great family of Slavic tribes, at this time still undifferentiated and all speaking much the same Indo-European language, the ancestor of the various Slavic languages of today.

The Slavs are first mentioned by Latin and Greek writers as "Sclaveni, Sclavini, Sclavi"; they split up fairly early into the great divisions that have come down to us—the southern Slavs from the Balkans, the western Slavs, including the Czechs, Moravians, and Poles, and the eastern Slavs, later known as Russians. A dimness overhangs the movements of these vanished peoples, but it may have been the collapse of the Hunnish Empire and the later invasion of the Avars that dislodged the Slavs from the Carpathian Mountains and nudged the eastern Slavs into reaching the Dnieper some time during the seventh century and then infiltrating the Russian hinterland along the great rivers.

As the Slavs gradually advanced—doubtless as a slow drift— they occupied land formerly held by the Lithuanians, who by the ninth century were gradually pushed back to a stretch of land around the Baltic Sea, in the basin of the Niemen River and the lower western Dvina. The Slavs also seem to have pushed various Finnish tribes back into the North and the East; they were to come across the Finns again later, as we shall see, when the Slavs in their turn, under the impulsion of still other ethnic drifts, began penetrating the northeastern forests. The Finns and the Lithuanians are two of the very few peoples the Slavs excelled culturally: the first contact of the Finns and Lithuanians with the outside world, which gave them the rudiments of civilization, came about because of their gradual investment by the Slavs, who in their sluggish migrations dislodged them from the great waterway that led from the Baltic to the Black and Caspian Seas.

The history of the eastern Slavs, and hence of the Russians, may be linked to this great international waterway, which led both to Byzantium and to Baghdad, and thus could serve as the spawning ground for mercantile settlements.

The primitive Slavs conquered by the Khazars benefited a great deal by their subjugation. It brought them into contact with the commerce of the new great mercantile centers, engendered by the meteoric rise of Islam, that were open to the various peoples in Russia. Slavic traders are reported by a Muslim writer as having gone as far as Baghdad.

The Slavs had the raw products of the forest to sell: furs, honey, wax, and, above all, people. They sold both their own people and any others they could enslave. The Slav stock-in-trade consisted of the natives, who handed over both the tribute levied on them and their own persons.

The earliest cities recorded for the ancestors of the Russians were military strongholds that owed their existence to the dual aspect of this primitive commerce: they were storage points for goods and at the same time a rendezvous for merchants. Thus these ancient centers—Kiev, Novgorod, Liubech, Chernigov, Polotsk—were all established on the main trade routes and gradually gave rise to a Russian state or pseudostate.

The Khazar state collapsed during the tenth and eleventh centuries (it was extinguished in 1016). The Khazars succumbed to a combination of the Slavs and another Turkic-speaking people, the Patsinaks, who were instrumental in expelling the Magyars eastward. This drift had at least one important consequence: it cut off the southern Slavs from western and eastern Slavs alike. Some southern Slavs, soon after their settlement in the Balkan Peninsula, were converted to Byzantine orthodoxy. Then, when two Slavic-speaking Greek brothers from Salonika, Cyril and Methodius, were invited to Moravia in the ninth century, the formal conversion of the eastern Slavs to orthodoxy was systematized. The two Greek brothers adapted Greek capital letters to a Bulgarian dialect from Southern Macedonia, and since as late as the eleventh century the Slavonic languages were still sufficiently undifferentiated for this so-called Church Slavonic to sound to each one of them like a standardized form of itself, this dialect ultimately became the language of the Russian Church and for many centuries the only literary medium available to speakers of Russian.

The collapse of the Khazar State put the politically disorganized Slavic traders in a difficult position. Finding their commerce endangered, the Slavic merchants were obliged to organize their own defense, and to do this effectively they now turned to another people, the catalyst in the crystallization of the earliest Russian state.

These were the Vikings, businessmen and bandits simultaneously. A Swedish branch of the Vikings had long before established an important international trading center in the Isle of Gothland; by the eighth century they had come by way of the Caspian Sea and Persia to sell their slaves in the markets of Baghdad.

The Vikings had already made themselves felt elsewhere; they had rowed and sailed their small ships not only across the sea but up all the main rivers of Western Europe. In the eighth century they had raided Paris and London, and had, indeed, changed the history of France and England. Then the Vikings came upon the western Dvina and the Volga in the East and saw the commercial possibilities of a waterway that led from the Baltic, at their very doorstep, to the Caspian Sea. Soon they established a trade route between Western Europe and the Muslim East.

Curiously enough, it was the water route over the western Dvina and the Volga to Baghdad and the Middle East that was discovered first, before the other and equally fruitful tradeway along the Neva, Volkhov, and Dnieper planted the Vikings before the gates of Byzantium itself. The extent of the Vikings' trade is attested to by the great hoards of Muslim coins found in Sweden and on the Isle of Gothland; these are much more numerous than the similar treasure troves of Byzantine coins.

Ultimately the Vikings found Byzantium more attractive than Baghdad, perhaps simply because it was nearer. From their point of view the Dnieper was superior to the Volga because it emptied into a real sea, and they established the great "eastern route" by way of it; Kiev thus became one of the principal stages in the Viking encirclement of Europe.

Russian legend—i.e., the earliest chronicles—has it that the Vikings were invited by the ancestors of the Russians to rule over them. This must be an endearingly stylized account of something far more disordered, but whether the Vikings were summoned by the Slavs to rule over them, or whether the Vikings simply conquered the Slavs and the legend was later built up out of self-regarding motives, the Vikings were employed by the Slavs along the middle Dnieper as mercenary soldiers and commission brokers. In accordance with a fixed tariff, the Vikings were supposed to conduct the boat trains from Kiev to the Dnieper rapids, organize a portage from there, meanwhile protecting the merchandise against the Patsinaks, and then take the river again as far as the Black Sea to land ultimately at the Byzantine quays, where the goods and slaves were to be sold or bartered.

The Russian word for Viking that has come down to us (*Varyag* or Varangian in most accounts) has always had a connotation of merchant rather than warrior. In any case the same Vikings who had produced such turmoil in Western Europe launched the Russians in their state-making. Buccaneers, adventurers, and above all merchants, the Vikings founded the Russian state. They are personified in the figure of one Rurik.

According to the chronicles, Rurik established himself in Novgorod in 862. He is in all probability the same person as a Dane of the same name who ascended the Elbe and the Rhine with a band of Norsemen, obtained sections of Friesland in fief from Emperor Lothaire (a descendant of Charlemagne), and after betraying him was expelled by the Frisians to seek his fortune elsewhere.

The Vikings left scarcely anything in Russia beyond their names, including the word Russia itself, by which the country has been known for a millennium. The word comes from *Ros* or *Rhos;* whatever this might have meant, it seems to have referred first to the upper class, then to the people as a whole and their language, and finally to the country. It is an engaging illustration of the flux of human affairs that the biggest country in the world derives its name from some happy-go-lucky cutthroats and barterers from a tiny country known for little else. In any case, the naming of Russia is a close parallel to other Viking operations commemorated by the Franks in the Lutetia region, the Normans in Normandy, and the Lombards in the Po Valley of Italy.

The Vikings were assimilated so quickly that they left no other mark. They melted into the Slavic communities they were supposed to organize. They carried on the traditional activities of the merchant princes with the same twofold aim: to maintain commerce with the East and the South, and to defend the land and the waterways from the Turkish tribes. The continuous incursions of these tribes along the great steppe and their constant harassing of the sedentary populations gave them a paramount role.

Although little evidence of them remains, there is no doubt that there were a great many Vikings in the Russian northwest from very early times on. The date assigned Rurik's settlement in Novgorod doubtless indicates that they were well established in the topmost stratum of the military-mercantile communities along the Russian waterways. These military-mercantile cities were the nodules that collectively made up the primitive Russian state.

The first Russian state is traditionally supposed to have had Kiev as its base, though there is not much more that is worth saying about it. The available records, though of course indispensable as our sole source of information, are a theologically tinctured mixture of legend, fantasy, and apology. For that matter they were written down many generations after the events they are supposed to describe: the very term *Russian state* was not adopted officially until the fifteenth or sixteenth century. The extraordinary outburst of historiography and belles-lettres that was taking place in the Muslim East during the first few centuries of Russian self-consciousness gives us an arresting comparison with Russian backwardness.

The early Russian princes were not sovereigns in any national sense—they were simply adventurers in a vast, empty, and at first foreign country. We perceive them too dimly to make a personal description either possible or interesting. Perhaps the only one worth mentioning after Rurik, the forefather of the Russian aristocracy, is Vladimir I (978–1015), a pagan who was the first specifically Russian ruler to be converted to Christianity, which he imposed on the population by force. His choice of Greek Orthodox Christianity, which he is supposed to have made after weighing the claims of Judaism and Islam, was due to his love of strong drink, prohibited by Islam, and to the ornateness of the Byzantine Church services in Constantinople as reported to him by a visitor. Aside from his conviction that the Russian joy in drinking made Christianity indispensable, his religious conversion did not interfere with his maintenance of a harem of at least eight hundred concubines.

Vladimir's conversion was an echo of Viking influence, since during their trips to Constantinople the Vikings had been impressed by the splendor of the Byzantine Church ritual (at the Saint Sophia Cathedral). In addition, some compatriots of theirs serving in the imperial bodyguard had already been converted; it was in the interests of the Byzantine Empire to convert as many barbarians as possible in order to absorb them in peace.

Accordingly, the conversion of the Russian rulers by Byzantium was a decisive factor in Russian history. Whereas the Poles and Balts were converted by missionaries originating in Germany and Sweden, the Slavic peoples of the Dnieper, like those in the Balkans, were converted by Greek monks. The Byzantine Empire exported the religion of the Eastern Church together with its wines and brocades. The imposition of Christianity, in Russia even more than elsewhere, was accomplished by fiat from above.

It would be far-fetched to call Kievan Russia a genuine state. Not only were its boundaries uncertain, but the Slavs themselves were still partly nomadic. What the cluster of rulers descended from the legendary Rurik did was to bring together under an increasingly complicated, confused, and weakening family rule the variety of elements that populated the Russian plain. Their rule revolved around the combination of war and commerce that was the hallmark of the first few centuries of Russian history. The warfare carried on intermittently by the various Viking-Slav princelings was the source of their principal article of commerce—slaves, which is, of course, why the word for slave in most European languages is derived from the word *Slav*.

The sole objective of the Kievan princelings was the collection of tribute; the country was treated both then and later as a milchcow. The more primitive form of tribute was paid in kind, though it was also collected in the Muslim coins widely current in Russia during the Kievan period. By this time the Muslim conquests had established a great network of markets throughout the Middle East and as far afield as Khorezm in Central Asia.

The Kievan state was no more than a loosely articulated federation of city-states, each one in its turn essentially amorphous. A lasting accomplishment of Vladimir was the setting up of his twelve sons as governors. This linked each member of the ruling family to some specific, territorially defined headquarters, and created a material basis for future dynastic claims by Rurik's descendants. But this apportioning of the land among Vladimir's sons did not regulate affairs in a simple, incontestable way. It was itself a source of constant strife, chiefly because of the absence of any principle of succession, a confusion that exacerbated the amorphousness of the Kievan confederation. The moment Vladimir died, his sons fell out, beginning the uninterrupted clan feuds that were to plague Russian life till the establishment of the Moscow autocracy centuries later.

Vladimir had held the title of Grand Duke of Kiev, which, since Kiev was the most important city in the region, was tantamount to acknowledging his senior authority in the Rurik clan. But the looseness of governmental relationships, as well as the sparsely settled state of the country and the continuous nomadic incursions along the ill-defined periphery of Kievan Russia, made the falling out between his sons inevitable. Vladimir's son Yaroslav was the last Grand Duke of Kiev to exercise any direct control over the whole of the realm that in theory belonged to the Rurik clan and hence to its senior member.

This whole question of imprecision in the principle of succession had its roots in the primitive concept of state authority that Rurik's descendants—the "Rurikoviches"—developed as a guide to administration. During the early period of Kievan Russia, the legal supremacy of the Grand Duke of Kiev was conceived of as an aspect of property law. Legality involved the recognition of paternal authority, plus the notion of the indivisibility of clan property. The whole area of Russia in the hands of the Rurikoviches was considered the joint property of the whole family, headed by the Grand Duke. The combination of these two notions of paternal authority and the indivisibility of property inevitably generated feuds between the princes.

Before Yaroslav died he made an attempt to circumvent this baffling principle of succession by willing his eldest son more authority than his other sons, while simultaneously partitioning the state. After his death his sons and their descendants were to consider the principalities and cities they ruled not as elements in an abstract entity known as Kievan Russia but as their personal property, and the property of their issue, to the exclusion of the other branches of the clan.

This notion of the primacy of actual property relationships symbolized the profound change taking place in the character of the formerly adventurous Vikings—they were becoming squires and administrators.

Europe was so backward at the time that Yaroslav (1019–54) was one of its greatest sovereigns. He believed in ramifying his family connections as much as possible. He married his sister to King Casimir I of Poland, whom he helped in the latter's own internal struggles; his daughter Elizabeth to King Harald Hardrada of Norway; his daughter Anastasia to King Andrew I of Hungary; and his daughter Anne to Henry I of France, which makes him an ancestor of the reigning English house. His favorite son Vsevolod married the daughter of the Byzantine Emperor Constantine Monomachus.

Though the principle of seniority established by Yaroslav in an attempt to settle the succession in Kievan Russia seemed clear at the time, it led to even greater confusion. He had wanted every death of a prince to be succeeded by a movement of princes, each being promoted to a senior district. That is, the seniority of princes throughout the clan and the order of importance of the districts were correlated. Since the clan was very large and kept increasing at a great rate, what with early marriages, numerous wives, and the general high spirits of the princes, both individuals and branches multiplied so rapidly that it soon became impossible to say whether or not a nephew in one line, for instance, was junior to the uncle in another.

Hence the fundamental notion of patrimony had to be reinterpreted. It came to acquire the meaning settled on at a princely conclave convoked in Liubech by Vladimir Monomakh, Vsevolod's son; patrimony finally meant the right to succeed to one's own father's property, i.e., territory.

This modification in the original idea, though it merely acknowledged an existing state of affairs, eliminated the pretence of unity that had been the goal of Kievan Russia: it was a copious source of feuds.

By the twelfth century the composition of Russian society was far more complicated than it had been before the advent of the Vikings, when as far as we know the people were simply divided into freemen and slaves, the slaves being the spoils of war. After the Vikings, the slaves continued to be the dregs of society: though they were normally made up of prisoners of war, anyone could become a slave by birth, bankruptcy, or voluntary agreement.

The princely clans, though the apex of society, were essentially mobile and rootless. Each prince had his own retinue, which was the source of his power: a retinue might have as many as two thousand men. By the time the princes came to number a hundred, the drain on the countryside the clan lived off must have been very substantial.

At first the princely retinue seems to have had a Scandinavian core. Its duties were those of adjutants in each prince's military, commercial, administrative, and judicial activities. This retinue was quickly swallowed up by the native population, as well as by other foreign elements that drifted in, such as Poles or Lithuanians. The princely retinue was the germ of the later aristocracy or quasi-aristocracy that was initially a military-mercantile caste depending for its position on the princes' favors, on the holding of high offices, or on its own wealth.

In the early days each prince was the source of his retinue's subsistence; at the same time the retinue was indispensable for collecting his own revenue. Members of the retinue were sometimes paid off directly in money, though sometimes they were sent as satraps to the more remote parts of the country, where they were supposed to live by milking the population. This widespread practice was known, rather juicily, as "feeding." It lasted for centuries.

The retinue was not tied to its prince hand and foot. On the contrary, though it was customary for it to follow him about, it was not a legal duty; the custom depended on personal loyalty or egotistic interest and was prevalent before society became stratified and developed a corresponding juridical structure.

As the original Viking bands settled down, the proto-aristocracy constituted by the princely retinue began splitting up in its turn. Though a class known as *boyars*—who were to play a role in Russian life for centuries—became the most influential group, there was no clear-cut line of demarcation between them and the other free elements of society. What was to fix the aristocracy in one place as society developed was the ownership of land, which became a criterion of position as society grew more sedentary.

The power of the aristocracy was greatest in southwest Russia, in the principalities of Galicia and Volynia, where political life was dominated by the Boyar Council and the prince was compelled to submit. He could impose his will on the boyars only by combat.

The boyars and other segments of the ruling groups were superimposed on the free townspeople—merchants and small artisans—and on the free peasantry. It was possible even in the earliest days for a merchant to accumulate very considerable wealth, since it was the mercantile factor that was paramount in primitive Russian society and was proportionally far better developed than crafts and farming. The international markets based on the Muslim Caliphate and the Byzantine Empire were lush enough for traders to prosper even in the basin of the remote Dnieper.

The real hallmark of the period was precisely this economic dependence not on agriculture but on the market: it was not the farming community that was politically influential during the eleventh and twelfth centuries, but the cities, based on commerce. The merchants, consequently, were far too important to be helpless vis-à-vis their princes.

The institution of the *vyeche,* or popular assembly, constituted one of the three foci of authority in Kievan Russia. It had a democratic principle, in contradistinction to the monarchical principle represented by the princes and the aristocratic principle represented by the princely retinue and its offshoots. The popular assembly spoke for the urban population. It was an effective element of government in early Russia, though neither its composition nor jurisdiction was defined with any precision.

This popular assembly was not supposed to be representative—it simply consisted of all the adult males in any given town. Decisions had to be unanimous. There was no formal way of resolving a dispute: if an agreement couldn't be reached, a free-for-all would break out and settle the question. In Novgorod, for instance, where because of the lengthy history of that city as an international trading center the popular assembly had reached the zenith of its power, brawls became tremendously violent; they would be settled on the bridge over the Volkhov River, with the losers being tossed into the freezing water.

The popular assembly was the closest approximation to democratic government in Russian history down to our own time. As the great commercial cities declined, the popular assembly declined with them; by the thirteenth century it was, except in Novgorod and Pskov, already extinct.

Kiev has come down to us as the symbol of early Russian statehood, but though it was the most magnificent Russian city of the period, as well as the seat of the head of the church and the target of the incessant intrigues and feuds among the princes, it had no real foundation. In an attempt to retroject the concept of unification as far back to the beginnings of national self-consciousness as possible, Russian piety has over-emphasized the primacy of Kiev, which was never, after all, anything more than the largest center of an essentially informal federation of regional units, whose real demands were far stronger than the chimera of allegiance to a national capital.

During the eleventh and twelfth centuries Russia was split up in a number of substantial territorial subdivisions—Novgorod, Rostov, Suzdal, Smolensk, Chernigov, Volynia, Galicia, Murom-Ryazan—that had grown up from the city-states deposited along the great waterways in the earliest historical times. None of the early Kievan princes had ever managed to impose any unity on these principalities; all of them, for that matter, with the exception of Kiev and Novgorod, had their own dynasties from the middle of the eleventh century on. But though a princely conference would occasionally take place, and though there was a striking similarity in basic institutions and social conditions, perhaps even a general recognition of the need for unity, these principalities of Kievan Russia were in a state of perpetual bickering and warfare. One might say that the nation had acquired its essential character only in depth; tempests kept agitating its surface.

In comparing Kievan Russia with Western Europe of the period, perhaps the most striking difference is just this rootlessness of the early rulers; that is, the absence of hierarchical social relations based on territorial attachments. Western feudalism was a rigid pyramid: everyone from the king down occupied a fixed place by birthright. A network of customs and contracts underlay the formation of classes and also welded these classes into a social organism called a state.

The hierarchical motionlessness of Western feudalism was based on a territorial theory: status depended on the connection between an individual and his *place*. The peasant was attached to his plot of land, the artisan to his guild, the bourgeois to his commune, the lord to his fief. Each one of the classes formed a sort of building block; all together made up the state.

The emptiness of Kievan Russia made this impossible. The country was too sparsely settled to be broken up into precise segments. With their economic life subject to the commerce of a great waterway, the people were accustomed to moving back and forth, looking for opportunities to trade. Without natural frontiers the armed force had to be constantly prepared to move as quickly as possible to any point that was threatened. Consequently, an individual was expected to perform the services required of him anywhere at all. In early Russia the criterion of status was thus function, not situation. This essentially horizontal character of society became even more evident when the roving, fluid Kievan society was overlaid centuries later by the evolving Moscow state, rooted firmly in land relationships.

In Kievan Russia, for instance, when a prince changed residence he took along his retinue, whose motives were nothing more than good wages or an occasion for trade or loot. The retainers at first had no links with the soil, since they were constantly on the move, nor with their lord, since they were perfectly free to leave him at will. They were functionaries more than vassals; that is, they were not vassals of the lord of a fief who was in his turn the subordinate of a sovereign. Kievan society was not compartmentalized, as it was in feudal Europe.

The emptiness of the country and its low cultural level were also reflected in its intellectual life. The chief source of culture in Kievan Russia was the church, which was responsible for the introduction of letters and the arts. The hierarchy of the church sprang up the moment the population of the big cities was either forced or cajoled into baptism, and in spite of the total illiteracy of the overwhelming mass of the people, clerical schools managed to mold preachers, primarily monks, with a smattering of knowledge.

For the first few centuries, to be sure, the conversion of

Russia to Christianity was nominal: very often the higher clergy—to say nothing of the lower—knew nothing about Christian dogma at all. The primitive Slavs retained an essentially magical interest in their religion, which was facilitated by the unintelligibility of the Church Slavonic that was its medium. Linguistically, of course, it might have been considered a standard form of the local speech, but no one actually understood it, not even the scattering of educated people. It was perhaps just this obscure and unintelligible ritual, as well as the flowing robes and sacred vestments of the clergy, plus the threat of eternal damnation, that gave the church its prestige.

Of course this general backwardness of the population did not prevent individual artists from achieving work of great distinction. There were many talented mosaists, painters of frescoes and ikons, and jewelers, who while adhering to their conception of the Byzantine tradition that inspired them gave their handiwork a national flavor. The enamelists in particular showed considerable originality. It is true that though the church introduced these activities, it also quickly came to control them and standardize them into the lifelessness that later became their hallmark. But Russia's golden age of painting took place under the influence of Greek and Italian models; it was only later that ecclesiastical conformity standardized the ikons.

It must be recalled that the ikons, perhaps the primary form of artistic expression in Russia, were intended not as portraits but as semimagical objects of veneration. Their existence as objects of art at all was only made possible after the anti-iconoclastic party in Byzantium was defeated in the middle of the ninth century.

The type of architecture that was indigenous to Russia still can be seen in the wooden churches of the northeast and the brick churches influenced by them, though Byzantium set a characteristic stamp on the architecture as well as on the painting and mosaics of Kievan Russia. Most of the churches built of wood have not survived, though there are some distinguished stone churches in Kiev and Chernigov. After the middle of the twelfth century, the architecture of Suzdal and Novgorod began to strike an original note; some of the finest examples of Old Russian art are to be found in churches there, which unaccountably show a great many foreign affinities, oddly enough with the Perigueux group of churches in southwestern France. Suzdal imported German masons, considered master craftsmen.

Much later, Russia acquired impressive architectural landscapes in its big cities. Though the building was done by Italians, the results looked entirely at home on Russian soil. Sculpture, on the other hand, was practically nonexistent, perhaps because the church, though it allowed saints to be represented in the flat, forbade them in the round.

As for literature, there was no question of this at all. Russian literature, like Russian art in general, was an offshoot of a Greek transplant. But the use of Church Slavonic cut off Russia from the Greek language; the resulting literature was completely sterile—chronicles and lives of saints. There was no acquaintance in Russia with any secular Greek literature, and the pre-Christian classical tradition was utterly unknown. Consequently, though Old Russian literature goes back to the middle of the eleventh century, its interest for us is largely anthropological. The sole exception for the period, the *Saga of Igor's Host* (a prose-poem from about 1186, recording a campaign against some Turks), is completely isolated; there is no continuity between it and later Russian literature. The *Saga* was in fact not discovered until the end of the eighteenth century.

Thus, from its inception in the beginning or middle of the eleventh century to the end of the seventeenth century, Russian literature was meager and sterile. Modern Russian literature arose only after Western European influences of one sort or another began flowing into Russia in the seventeenth century.

Music seems to have been even more meager. Unison singing was the chief musical form, aside from the wealth of folk songs that must have existed and developed entirely outside the formulae of the church and so have come down to us very skimpily. Harmony did not develop until the fifteenth and sixteenth centuries.

The Kievan period is generally thought to have ended in 1169, when Andrew Bogolyubsky, the son of Yuri Dolgoruki, Prince of Rostov and Suzdal, stormed Kiev and pulverized it. This was the first time a Russian prince had given Kiev the treatment reserved for non-Russian cities. Kiev was plundered and sacked, churches and monasteries were burned, and the people slaughtered, expelled, and enslaved. The sack of Kiev represents the triumph of the disruptive forces in early Russia, which the competition of the grand dukes, unbridled by any constitutional regime, had sorely aggravated.

Actually, the primacy of Kiev had already been declining because the city was dependent on its superb position along the great waterway from the Baltic to the Caspian Sea and on its commercial ties with Byzantium. Not only were new commercial links being forged between northern Russian and Western Europe that bypassed Kiev altogether, but the Russian area as a whole was becoming increasingly vulnerable to Asiatic attacks. The Patsinaks had been succeeded by another Turkish people, the Qypchap Turks—the "Cumans"—who were both more numerous and better organized than their predecessors, and who from the middle of the eleventh century on had been exerting more and more pressure on the Dnieper. The Cumans raided Russia annually, killing farmers, burning their barns, and carting their wives and children off to slavery. They had made the great waterway "from the Varangians to the Greeks" unsafe. Kiev was very close to the steppe, and the Kievan princes were incapable of organizing any defense against the Cumans. To make matters worse, several Kievan princes married daughters of the Cuman Khans, who thus entered into the complex network of clan strife characteristic of early Russian history. The princely feuds were interminable; the Cumans were merely another element of discord.

From the beginning of the eleventh century on, the sufferings of the Kievan Russians made them turn to an expedient that has been a leitmotif of Russian history—they took to their heels. There was no sudden exodus, but very gradually a migration began that cut into the population along the Dnieper. Rich and poor began drifting westward and northward to elude the immediate prospect of being robbed, raped, slaughtered, or enslaved.

The stream of migration along what was called the "straight road" from Kiev to the Volga—along a Dnieper tributary, the Desna—ultimately led to the establishment of Moscow. It was another example of the characteristic phenomenon of Russian colonization via a river; the banks of the Desna, passing through dense thickets infested by robbers, were quite underpopulated.

The decline of Kiev meant that after the middle of the twelfth century the "Mother of Russian Cities" was no longer capable even of defending its inhabitants. The former principalities began regrouping into different political formations: the Moscow state in the northeast, and the Lithuanian-White Russian-Ukrainian state in the southwest, where the Russian territories were gradually absorbed by the Grand Duchy of Lithuania, which at the end of the fourteenth century fused with the Kingdom of Poland.

In short, the eastern Slavic community that we call Kievan Russia was parcelled out to its immediate neighbors—Finns, Lithuanians, Poles, and a number of Turkish peoples. In the west, the eastern Slavs were to develop into the White Russians within the frontiers of a Lithuanian-Polish state. In the south, the Ukrainian grouping came into being as a partial reflection of the powerful influence of Lithuanian Poland. In the north, the territory of what was to become Muscovy served as the spawning ground for the Great Russians with whose history we are concerned. This division was not consummated, to be sure, until between the fourteenth and sixteenth centuries.

After Kiev's political submergence, its western neighbors, Galicia and Volynia, grew in importance, only to find themselves outflanked by two different movements. First the Mongols appeared; I shall speak of them in a moment. Then, in the marshy forested region of the Niemen Basin, the Lithuanians, an ancient race still pagan, who had withstood the movement of proselytization launched by the German military monks, suddenly and surprisingly claimed the attention of history by embarking on a program of conquest under some able rulers. They extended their power to the Dnieper, turned Kiev into a Lithuanian city, and subjected Western Russia to Vilna, their capital. Greek Orthodox Christians found themselves in thrall to pagans in the west just as they were being politically effaced by Mongols in the east.

By the beginning of the fifteenth century, the Grand Duchy of Lithuania embraced a large area, including the basin of the upper and the middle-western Dvina, the Niemen, the southern Bug, the Dnieper, and the upper Oka.

These Russian lands were to remain outside of the Russian orbit for a long time. The harassed Russian princes in the southwest were absorbed by the Lithuanian-Polish combination chiefly because many of their economic interests were in the west, such as their trade with Germany, which used waterways under Lithuanian and Polish control, and also because the core of Russian society had been substantially disintegrated during the thirteenth and fourteenth centuries by both internal dissension and the pressure of the Tatars. Also, both Lithuania and southwestern Russia had a common enemy in the form of the Teutonic monk knights in the north.

Because of all this, what was to become the Russian state began to form only when Muscovy emerged during the thirteenth and fourteenth centuries.

Kiev's place was taken at first not by Moscow, which, first mentioned in 1147, was wholly negligible in the twelfth century, but by Vladimir, in the Principality of Rostov-Suzdal, not far from Moscow. Vladimir was taken by Andrew Bogolyubsky after he ravaged Kiev. In Vladimir, Andrew could do as he pleased. He would have had more trouble in Rostov and Suzdal, which were older than Vladimir, with relatively independent boyars and popular assemblies.

The great migration that had drawn the Russians away from Kiev and the Dnieper basin densed the population of northeastern Russia very considerably. The bulk of the migrants concentrated in the triangle formed by the upper Volga and the Oka, that is, the Principality of Rostov-Suzdal. It seems to have been the influx of these more or less fugitive Russians, steadily drifting away from Kiev into the new area, formerly inhabited by Finnish tribes, that changed the ethnic complexion of the region. Part of the Great Russian people's ancestry is Finnish.

The forests, immune to the caravans and hordes of the nomads, gave the fleeing Russians a natural shelter, and since Russian peasants were pacific by nature and the Finns even more so, the Finns met by the Russian farmers in the forests of the northeast completely accepted them and intermingled with them. It was a typical frontier situation. The topography of northeastern Russia militated against the creation of large villages such as those common in southern Russia; the country was covered by virgin timber and marshes that were difficult to cultivate.

As for the princes, they too changed swiftly in response to the contrast between this environment and Kievan Russia. The new combination engendered a different social structure. The northeastern princes became similar to the American pioneers who went west to carve their own estates out of the new lands. Contemplating the land they had laid their hands on, they regarded it as personal property, theirs by virtue of their own toil and sweat and disposable as they saw fit.

The boyars themselves began turning into a squirearchy, since the established tradition of princely rewards for services now took the form of land-grants. This practice broke up the territory into innumerable tiny principalities, and thus, by accentuating the fragmentation of the region, enabled the future Moscow dynasty to impose on the atomized principalities a degree of centralization that has characterized Russian affairs ever since.

The atomization of northeastern Russia, combined as it was with the principle of allocating land to the boyars in the service of some particular prince, led to a clash of interests between princes and boyars. The boyars were bound to be hostile to any change in their rulers. A change meant that a new prince, accompanied by new boyars, would be coming along to oust them. The selfish interests of the boyars tended to make them support their prince's dynastic ambitions insofar as these princes were determined to maintain the local dynasty. But since the princes had inherited the tradition of looking on the principality they ruled as a piece of family real estate, and since they tended to divide the land among their heirs, they not only collided with the economic interest of the boyars, but they constantly generated clan warfare, which exasperated the boyars, who by now had their roots in the soil. We shall see how the interplay of these factors led to the emergence of the Russian autocracy some centuries later.

The boyar aristocracy was an element of stability; it was the boyars' interest to establish order, which at that time could be accomplished only by the emergence of a strong house, in this case the Grand Duchy of Vladimir.

To sum up the period politically, the main tendency was a growth in the strength of both princes and boyars, with consequent collisions, while the popular assemblies declined rapidly. This process, so full of meaning for all subsequent Russian history, throughout which we see the chasm widening between the summits of society and the people, was consummated on the eve of the Mongol invasion.

Moreover, though the seniority of the Grand Duke of Vladimir was accepted, more or less theoretically, and the holders of the Vladimir office tended to act as though they were advancing the interests of the northeastern territory as a whole, this very process worked against the interests of lesser principalities, with the upshot that the traditional concept of the Russian princes as brothers became an empty fiction.

Russia was pulverized by ferocious strife. The princes detested each other and were incapable of cooperating with the boyar aristocracy they depended on. Also, the decline of the popular assembly reflected the growing oppression of the rural population as well as the growth of the landed estates of the boyars and princes. Rural Russia had in fact been launched on the course that was to lead to bondage.

But peace was about to be forced on the country for a time by the last of the Asiatic invaders, and the ablest—the Mongols.

CHAPTER II

THE MONGOLS

*W*ith the advent of the Mongols, who became known to the Russians and thence to the world as Tatars, Russian history encounters a factor qualitatively different from any others.

To give impartial consideration to the Mongols, who exacted tribute from the Russians for 240 years, we must change our perspective altogether. There is no point in looking at the Mongols through Russian eyes; the Russians must be seen through Mongol eyes. From the Mongol point of view, the Russian adventure was simply an episode, on the whole a minor one, in a campaign of conquest that included China and Central Asia; the campaign failed in Russia not through Russian action but because the Mongol realm began to decompose from within.

Around 1300, the Mongol Empire extended from China to Poland, occupying the whole of Asia except India, Burma, and Cambodia. When we consider that the Mongol people numbered possibly a million, while the peoples they controlled amounted to some 100 million, and that at their zenith the

Mongols had fewer than 150,000 troops, it is obvious that the leadership of this small group of nomads was based on something special.

Russian history between the thirteenth and fifteenth centuries is incomprehensible without the Mongol background. Fundamental decisions were made by the Great Khan of the Mongols, who held his residence in Mongolia or in China. This meant that the Russian vassals of the Khan of the Golden Horde—the Mongol unit encamped in Russia—were really governed by the ruler of Peking. The structure and function of the Golden Horde itself, and hence of Russia, was established by the founder of the Mongol Empire, Chingis Khan, whose followers considered him enjoined by heaven to rule the world. It was Chingis's "Great Yasa"—actually a constitution—that was the legal foundation of the whole Mongol Empire, including Russia.

Conversely, Russia made a substantial contribution to the power both of the Golden Horde and of the Mongol Empire of which it was a part. Russians drafted into the Mongol armies played an important role in the campaigns of the Khans of the Golden Horde as well as of the Great Khans themselves. During the 1330s, there was a Russian division of guards stationed in Peking; the division was an important pillar of the imperial regime in China. Russia was milked for craftsmen and artisans of all kinds, who worked both in the Golden Horde and as far east as Mongolia.

In short, though Russian historians have generally had a biased view of Mongol influence, either pretending that it was on the whole negligible, or on the contrary magnifying its negative effects and blaming the Mongols for Russian backwardness, their perhaps understandable nationalistic bias cannot obscure the fact that Russian political life was molded by Mongol politics for two centuries and more.

The Grand Dukes of Vladimir and Moscow, as well as all other princes, were only rulers by the grace of the Khan, who was both the *de facto* and the *de jure* source of power throughout Russia. The church, too, exercised its functions by virtue of Mongol authority. From a religious point of view this was quite benign, since the Mongols were wholly tolerant of religious differences and, though at first apparently Shamanists themselves, had no objection to following Russian customary law. This, to be sure, did not eliminate discords, since "immemorial tradition" in Russia was a tissue of confusion, but at any rate it made for quiet.

The Mongols were unknown in Europe and the Middle East before their sudden appearance in the thirteenth century. They were the last of the long line of invaders of the western steppe—the proto-Persians (Scythians and Sarmatians), and the Turkic-speaking Huns, Avars, Khazars, Patsinaks, and Cumans. The interaction between Turks and Mongols was always intimate; a substantial portion of the Mongol armies were Turks under Mongol officers. Among the Russians the world *Tatar,* originally the name of one of the Mongol tribes, came to encompass some of the Turks who settled in Russia later (the Kazan and Crimean Tatars).

To organize this confusion by giving it a name, modern Russian Orientalists sometimes use the word "Turco-Tatar" to take in these various related peoples, whose features vary from an out-and-out "Mongolian" look in northern Central Asia to an entirely "Caucasian" look in southern Central Asia.

In the part of the Golden Horde that occupied the lands west of the Volga, the Turkish element consisted of Cumans, who as a people were absorbed once they had been defeated; there were also remnants of Khazars and Patsinaks.

Turkish elements predominated in the Golden Horde to such an extent that the Mongols lost their language rapidly; even the ruling classes gradually began speaking Turkish. Documents of internal administration during the late fourteenth and fifteenth centuries were kept in Chagatay Turkish.

The Mongols had an extraordinarily efficient striking force based on a swift coordination of light and heavy cavalry that was far superior to anything else at the time. It was not, to be sure, an innovation, but rather the perfecting of the traditional mounted steppe warfare. The horses, like their riders, had immense stamina. The Mongol light cavalry was armed with bow and arrow; their heavy cavalry carried sabre,

lance, a battleaxe or mace, and a lasso, with a helmet of leather
(later of iron) and a leather cuirass or coat of mail.

But perhaps the most effective thing about the Mongol armies was their strategy: they succeeded by applying the principles of a hunt—the Great Battue—that they held every year
at the beginning of the winter. It was a basic rite in the training
of adult warriors. During the Great Battue, hunters would
be deployed around an area comprising thousands of square
miles. There was a center and a right and left wing, each
with its special commander. After the columns had been deployed, the Great Khan himself, together with his concubines
and his commissariat, set up camp in the center of the Battue.
The lines would then gradually converge—it took from one
to three months—and drive the game into the presence of
the Great Khan. Couriers kept the Khan informed of the location and quantity of the game. If any of the game slipped
out through a badly manned section of the ring, the commanding officer would be personally liable to severe penalties.

After the game had been driven into a circle about ten miles
in circumference, which would be marked off by lines of ropes,
the ring was sealed. While huge numbers of panicky animals
milled about inside, the Great Khan would go inside the inner
ring and begin the shooting, followed in turn by princes of
the blood, army commanders, and then ordinary soldiers, all
slaughtering the animals for a number of days.

Now, when the Mongols were about to launch a military
campaign, the Great Council—the Kuriltai—would convene as
a staff headquarters. Operations and targets would be laid
down, with the captains of all the major army units present
to be given their orders. Special agents had already been sent
to spy on the land to be attacked; as much information as
possible about the people and the countryside was collected
in advance. The marshalling grounds and take-off area for
the army were designated, and appropriate pasturing grounds
were reserved along the route to be taken by the troops.

This procedure was not a mere matter of information gather-
ing; secret agents, who were sent out long before the troops
were to start marching, carried on systematic propaganda and

psychological warfare. The Mongol approach was to persuade the religious minorities that the Mongols tolerated all religions, the poor that the Mongols would be against the rich—and for that matter they actually were against the rich, i.e., the enemy rich—and the merchants that the Mongol peace would make the routes safe for business. Everyone was promised safety if he surrendered and frightful vengeance if he did not.

The Mongols believed in carrying on their war *à outrance*—their goal was the encirclement and physical extirpation of their opponents' armies. This was where the Great Battue came in. The Mongols first would envelop a vast area and then tighten the ring around it. The columns operated with astonishing coordination, communication between them being kept up by couriers or smoke signals. If by some chance the enemy was too strong at first for the Mongols to burst through his lines, they would pretend to retreat; as a rule the enemy would then break ranks and rush forward in hot pursuit, thinking the Mongols had been routed. The Mongols then would pivot quickly on their agile little horses, reform their ring, and this time finish things off.

Though at first the Mongols lacked siege machinery, after their first Turkestan campaign they developed an effective technique for taking fortified cities by storm. A wooden wall would be set up around the city some distance away to stop supplies and cut off the besieged garrison from any contact with their kinsmen outside. Then captives picked up in prior campaigns, or natives drafted on the spot, would fill in the moat with stones and earth; siege engines would be drawn up to bombard the city with rocks, containers of naphtha, and javelins, while battering rams would be turned against the gates.

Because the army was supposed to live off the conquered area and was followed by a camel caravan with only a minimum of supplies, the Mongol strategy worked on the assumption that the seizure of huge enemy territories was not only feasible, but lucrative: thus, the smaller the Mongol armies were the better. The Mongol army kept growing as it advanced through enemy territory by levies made on the native population. The peasants would be drafted to besiege fortresses and drive carts, while urban craftsmen were drafted into the engineering corps or manufacturing units to make weapons and tools. The Mongol army often would be stronger at the end of a campaign than at the beginning. When Chingis died the Mongol army proper numbered only 129,000, probably its zenith.

All this of course sounds strikingly modern—both the practice of living off the land and the principle of extreme mobility in warfare. Consequently, though military historians traditionally have disregarded Mongol strategy and tactics, interest in them has now revived, precisely in the era of tanks and airplanes: the fast, far-flung Mongol columns of horsemen are startlingly reminiscent of the most effective techniques of the Second World War.

As far as we can see, the architect of the Mongol Empire, Chingis Khan, seems to have made an arbitrary decision to conquer the world, though he was doubtless motivated by one of those intangible though pervasive geopolitical factors such as the gradual desiccation of Central Asia. In any case, the initial stage in his program of world conquest—China—was quickly attained. Chingis's first China campaign, in 1211, ended with the surrender of Peking in 1215. His seizure of northern China and Manchuria gave him not only a corps of army engineers but a body of cultivated bureaucrats who proved indispensable to the organization of the Mongol forces.

From the Mongol point of view Russia was an unknown country lying vaguely to the west. When Chingis had conquered the ancient, cultivated state of Khorezm in western Turkestan, he gave one of his generals, Subudey, permission to reconnoiter "the western lands." Coming first upon the Cumans, allied by now to the Russian princes by marriage and other ties, Subudey routed both together at the celebrated battle of Kalka in 1222. The Mongols are reported to have celebrated their victory by a tremendous feast on a wooden floor, under which their Russian and Cuman captives were slowly crushed to death.

After destroying or enslaving the Cumans and Russians wholesale and driving the remnants off to Galicia, the Balkans,

Asia Minor, and even Egypt, the Mongols vanished again, to the complete bewilderment of the Russians. Nothing was seen of them for fourteen years, until a Turco-Mongol army headed by one of Chingis's grandsons, Batu, who had been appointed commander-in-chief of one prong of the Mongol drive westward, crossed the Volga; Subudey acted as chief-of-staff.

About 50,000 Mongols made up the backbone of Batu's armies, which together with his Turks and various auxiliaries may have come to 120,000 or more. The territories to be governed and garrisoned by Batu were vast, yet his field army was probably never more than 50,000 in any given phase. Batu's troops were accompanied by whole caravans, including women and children. It was a real migration.

The Mongols' preliminary raid in 1222–23 had been aimed at southern Russia, but Subudey now thought it more prudent to reduce northeastern Russia first, perhaps because he thought his success at Kalka fourteen years before had been facilitated by the inertia of the Grand Duke of Vladimir, the strongest of the Russian princes. Since Subudey contemplated, it seems, a campaign ranging as far west as Hungary, he had to secure his northern flank.

In thinking of warfare in Russia, our point of view is dominated by literary recollections of "General Frost" and the undoing of Napoleon and Hitler. But Subudey thought winter the best time for making war in northern Russia. Since the Mongols felt at home in the cold, what with their furs and general hardiness, and the Mongol horses were quite capable of foraging beneath the snow for leaves or stubble, the freezing of the numerous rivers and lakes made their task much easier.

By 1240 Kiev was stormed and taken, after the Mongol envoys sent to demand its submission had been killed; there is an account of the city's being deafened by the rattle of wagons, the neighing of horses, and the bellowing of camels. The people of Kiev had built new wooden walls in the center of the town; when these were stormed there was the usual massacre, especially in the churches the townsfolk had crowded into. Six years after the destruction of Kiev, a Minorite friar

(Plano Carpini), journeying eastward to visit the Mongols, described the city as having only 200 houses left, with nothing but skulls and bones around the countryside. In Russia this was a common sight.

The Mongols were anxious to get to Hungary, which was the farthest extremity of the great Eurasian steppe and thus useful as a base for their cavalry in Central European operations, just as it had been for Attila 800 years before. Also, the Magyars, because of their origins, were excellent candidates for the Turco-Mongol alliance now in mid-ascent.

The Mongols seem to have been all set for a further advance into Central Europe until the spring of 1242, when Batu, who had reached Vienna and was camped in Klosterneuburg, heard that his uncle Ugudey, the Great Khan since Chingis's death in 1226, had died, leaving the succession problematic.

Batu cancelled his offensive—the Mongols were now in Hungary and Croatia—and withdrew via northern Serbia and Bulgaria to jockey for position in the new elections for the Great Khan, for which as a descendant of Chingis he was eligible. His campaign of 1237-41 had brought immense areas under Mongol control; not only the southern Russian steppe and the northern Russian forests, but also the lower Danube, Bulgaria, and Moldavia were part of the Mongol Empire for a century.

By 1242 the Mongol Empire, centered in Karakorum, was consolidated. In one generation an entirely new and hitherto unknown people had emerged with a claim to universal dominion. After having seized immense areas in Asia and Europe, the Mongols, as lords of the Eurasian steppe, were strategically capable of controlling both the northern half of Asia and the eastern half of Europe.

At least so it seemed. Yet, though the Mongols acquired more territories, their conquest had now achieved what turned out to be its natural limits. From then on, their Empire was to digest what it had swallowed, settle down, and begin decaying.

The cardinal event of Ugudey's reign was the establishment by his nephew Batu of the Qypchak Khanate in southern Russia, centered in the new city of Saray on the lower Volga. This became known as the Golden Horde, which for the first century of its existence was an *ulus,* or satrapy, of the Mongol Empire. The Golden Horde, in which the Mongol aristocracy was the topmost stratum, was ruled even after the Mongol Empire disintegrated by the descendants of Chingis, who also ruled its successor states.

Russia was only one of the departments of the Golden Horde's affairs. From the very beginning it governed an immensely complex variety of peoples, more so even than the Mongol satraps in China and Persia. Most of the Cumans were still pagans, as they had been when the Mongols first burst into the southeastern Russian steppe, while the people of Khorezm and the Bulgars along the Volga were Muslims.

The Mongol dominion annihilated Russian sovereignty. The Russian princes were ordered to Saray in order to be licensed to rule; even after being confirmed in office by the Khan of the Golden Horde, they often had to go all the way to Mongolia to get the ultimate sanction of the Great Khan himself.

The helplessness of the Russian princes is amply demonstrated by the nine voyages to Saray made by Ivan I of Moscow (1325–1341), and the five made by his son Simeon (1341–1353). The granting of the executive license, which took the form of a ceremony of enthronement, was carried out in the name of the Khan and in the presence of his ambassador: it was a dramatic illustration of the peremptory nature of Mongol rule. All in all, between 1242 and 1430, some 130 Russian princes journeyed to the Khans and to the Great Khans, sometimes for purely personal objectives.

Saray became a hotbed of princely intrigues aimed at the Mongols' favor; a considerable number of Russians were killed by their own people. Though the native Russian chronicles do their best to gloss over this fact, so distasteful to the national myth, enough traces remain to indicate that mutual denunciations to the Mongol rulers were commonplace.

The interests of the Mongol rulers were simple: they wanted revenue and recruits, the basic requirements of their Empire. The Russian princes became tax collectors; by the fourteenth century they had replaced the Mongol officials who, supported by a police force, had originally been posted in charge of taxation all over the country.

The license to govern a grand duchy or principality was auctioned off by the Mongols. The most effective way of getting a Khan's executive license for a desirable territory was to offer to increase its tax yield; this meant, of course, that the prince had to grind more out of it.

Thus the constant intrigues at Saray all tended in the same direction, toward extracting as much as possible from the Russian subjects of the princely sub-vassals of the Khans. This naturally increased the friction between the princes and the communities they governed; it turned the princes into active sponsors of Mongol interests.

The clashes between princes did not take place merely around the Khan's court in Saray; the Mongols were invited to make punitive expeditions inside Russia again and again in order to help one of their favorites, i.e., a prince who could offer more revenue. There are supposed to have been some 48 Mongol invasions of Russia between 1236 and 1462, some of which were merely punitive, but many of which came about at the invitation of the Russian princes themselves. The Russian national hero, Alexander Nevsky, famous for having repulsed a Swedish army on the ice of the river Neva (whence his surname), who was canonized by the Russian Church, denounced his own brother Andrew to the Khan for having been remiss in his duty to the Golden Horde. It was in fact the Tatars (as I shall hereafter call the Mongols) who, after ousting his brother, installed Nevsky as Grand Duke of Vladimir in 1252.

The Russians cooperated closely with the Tatars even in the earliest times. Not only did the Russians take part in the military adventures of their conquerors, as indicated above, but the Tatars gave the Russian princes great support in the struggle against their enemies on Russia's southern and western borders. The symbiosis between Tatars and Russians was very close.

Economically, the Golden Horde itself was a symbiosis between nomadic and sedentary populations. The Tatars found pasturage for their cattle and horses in the steppes of southern Russia and the northern Caucasus, while the edges of the steppe were also used for crops.

In addition, the Tatars had a great interest in commerce, which was aided by the location of Saray on the lower Volga. This was the ancient trade route to the east, which enabled the Tatars to create a system of commercial exchange points between east and west. These commercial settlements stimulated exchange between merchants from many countries, and the Tatars themselves played a part in it, contributing horses, hides, and leather goods.

The Russo-Tatar symbiosis was particularly intense at the summit of Russian society, that is, the princes and boyars, who often married Tatar princesses. Oddly enough, Tatar influence in Russian domestic affairs began to increase *after* the decline of the Golden Horde, which began about the middle of the fourteenth century and culminated in the collapse of the Tatar state a century later. After this collapse, numerous detachments of Tatar princes and high functionaries poured into Russia, accompanied by throngs of servants and armed troops. As Moscow began to ascend, it attracted them into service; it could offer them more than could the crumbling Golden Horde.

This migration took on mass proportions after 1445, when Basil II of Moscow lost a battle to the Tatars and was taken prisoner. He seems to have bought himself off by a huge ransom and by undertaking a great many obligations delicately glossed over by the chroniclers. He went back to Moscow with a vast number of Tatar soldiers and grandees.

By the end of the seventeenth century, the Moscow upper class is estimated to have been about 17 percent Tatar or oriental. But the Tatar influence was far more than a question of bloodlines: the state that evolved during the sixteenth century and lasted some 400 years was an offshoot of the monolithic rule of the Tatars. The Tatars, once feared, then mingled with and imitated, were the prototype of the Tsarist autocracy. They had reduced the relatively independent squirearchy to subservi-

ence, first to the Grand Dukes of Moscow and later to the
Tsars. The popular assembly, which had been declining rapidly
even before the Tatars' appearance, lost its most important
function under the Golden Horde—the right it had once had
to choose and oust its princes. The Khans took over this prerog-
ative. The popular assembly vanished, leaving the bulk of the
people to sink still further under the twofold burden of domestic and Tatar exactions.

There is an aspect of the Tatar expansion that is of general
interest. The Tatar experiment in dominion, in spite of its
immense initial success, finally failed. Perhaps this was because
the technology of the time made it impossible to maintain
a centralized empire spread so thin over such a vast territory.
It represents a curious embryonic parallel to the still more
brilliant nomadic attempt to rule a sedentary civilization that
was embodied in the Slave Household of the Ottoman Empire
during the period of its efflorescence (roughly 1365–1565).

Nomads in general all face the same problem with respect
to the sedentary peoples they have overrun: unless they want
to give up their nomadic ways and settle down themselves,
intermingling with their subjects and sooner or later vanishing,
they must apply to men the methods that have been successful
with their flocks and herds: they become shepherds of men.
What the Tatars did (though only partially, as we can see
by the far more extensive system of their Ottoman cousins)
was to use the Russian princes to ride herd. This failed eventually because the fabric of Russian life was not transformed
or even changed substantially, so that when the Tatar Empire
began to crumble under its own internal tensions, Russian
society was still vigorous enough to take advantage of this
enfeeblement of Tatar authority and resume its autonomous
evolution.

The Ottoman Turks perfected a far more efficient device,
which enabled their empire to survive into the modern era.
Not content with training their human auxiliaries, they made
a point of uprooting them in such a way as to cut them off
from their origins entirely, thus making them far more mallea-
ble for the executive intentions of their masters. The Slave

Household of the Ottoman Turks gave a career only to those born *outside* the Muslim Turkish fold, i.e., to the children of infidels. Seized when young, these were then brought up in accordance with a program, organized in minute detail, that opened up to them the most influential posts in the empire while keeping them subordinate as the Sultan's watchdogs.

The social atomization of such slaves was evidently essential since a new loyalty had to replace the old. This was why the children of the Ottoman Turkish Pashas were excluded from running the Ottoman Empire when it was at its height. The children of free Muslim feudal lords, full of race pride, with local and family connections, were obviously far from suited to run the empire on behalf of a centralized regime.

When the ban was rescinded on the admission of free Muslims, in contrast with the children of Christians and pagans forcibly enslaved and converted to Islam while in a state of bondage, the Ottoman Turkish regime began decaying with great rapidity.

The charm of slavery, from an administrative and military point of view, lies in the purity of the executive relationship between ruler and ruled: in effect the rulers commanded their slaves, do our ruling for us!

The Ottoman Slave Household represented the perfection of what other Turks—the Tatars—tried in Russia, and which in its turn was a superior application of the same principles of human herdsmanship tried out before the Tatars by the Avars and other nomads from Asia, as well as the Muslim Arabs in the initial phase of their expansion. The comparison is the more illuminating because in many ways the westward drive of the Ottoman Turks during the fourteenth and fifteenth centuries was an after-effect of the Tatar overflow. The sinister impression made on Western Europe by the Tatar sack of Kiev in the thirteenth century was completely overshadowed by the Ottoman conquest of Constantinople in 1453. Though the Tatars threatened Vienna for a while, they soon went away, whereas the Ottoman menace to Vienna lasted until the late seventeenth century.

The slaughter wrought by the Tatar conquests amounted

to several million dead; few other periods before our own have seen so much killing. Still, the *Pax Mongolica,* by unifying most of Eurasia under a single regime and thus protecting the overland trade route from China to the Mediterranean, established a network of cultural exchange between Europe, the Middle East, and China that over the long run bore fruit.

The influence of the Tatars on Russian life during the 240 years the Russians paid them tribute was substantial. It must be remembered that of the many peoples the Tatars conquered, the Russians were one of the few they could learn nothing from. Although they had borrowed many elements of civilization from others, notably the Chinese, Persians, and Muslims, in Russia they found nothing at all to imitate. Saray was an industrial center with construction yards that ran on hydraulic power; the Tatars' palaces were very luxurious, and even had central heating; as indicated above, their army engineering units had machines capable of reducing fortresses.

The Tatars have sometimes been held responsible for traits of cruelty characteristic of Russian life, especially in the treatment of criminals. It may have been under Tatar influence that Russians took with such enthusiasm to torture, flogging, mutilation, and execution. In the Muscovy that slowly took shape beneath the shell of Tatar rule, it was commonplace for criminals to have their noses, ears, hands, or feet lopped off, to be impaled, quartered, racked on the wheel, and whipped to death. Heretics and sorcerers were burnt alive; counterfeiters had molten lead poured down their throats. Great ingenuity was employed in the interrogation of suspects.

The Russians thought the Tatars glamorous. Though one side of Russian secular literature expressed a conventional feeling of hatred for the national oppressor, and the heroic folk-sagas recording the conflict with the previous enemy, the Cumans, were recast to fit the Tatars, a contrary fascination also rooted itself in literature. It has, indeed, remained a permanent motif in Russian literature to this day. Tatar chivalry in warfare was much admired, as was the life of the steppe, with its free nomadic ways, which during the nineteenth century were very attractive to Russian writers.

In the fifteenth century the Tatar-Russian union in the upper classes was so intimate that the court of Basil II of Moscow actually spoke Turkish, the general language of the Golden Horde. Indeed, many Russian noblemen in the fifteenth, sixteenth, and seventeenth centuries even adopted Tatar surnames, perhaps the best known examples being the Velyaminovs, of Viking ancestry, who took the Turkish name of Aksakov. A descendant of the Tatars was to become a famous propagandist for the Slavophile viewpoint of the nineteenth century, and the philosopher Shaadayev, a zealous pro-Westerner, was a descendant of Chingis's son Chagatay. Many well-known Russian families are of Tatar descent, including the Yusupovs, Kutuzovs, and Urusovs. The Tatars even produced a Russian Tsar, Boris Godunov.

Intimate association with the military adventures of the Khans familiarized a great many Russians with the Tatar army system: it was natural for Tatar methods to be introduced into the Russian army. The Russians adopted the Tatar tactic of enveloping the enemy on both flanks and also introduced Tatar armor and weapons. The articulation of the Russian army into five large units—center, right and left arms, vanguard, rear guard—was also modeled on the Tatar cavalry.

The Tatars gave the Russian language a great many terms, filtered through from Mongol and Turkish, or from Persian and Arabic through Turkish, not only for the vocabulary of trade and commerce, but for clothing, household objects, food and drink, fruit and vegetables, metals, and gems, and so on. They gave the Russians a census and a postal system.

The Tatar age also stimulated a religious revival: there was a blossoming of religious painting both in frescoes and ikons. Though until the middle of the fourteenth century Russian painting remains obscure, while Greek artists seem to have executed most of the better surviving ikons, neo-Byzantine influence streamed in during the second half of the fourteenth century and gave birth to some remarkable painting, both in Moscow and Novgorod. Theophanes the Greek (florebat 1370–1410) played a stellar role in this artistic renaissance: he lived in Russia some thirty years before his death, working first in Novgorod, then in Moscow. Theophanes's influence was limited to his free brush-stroke technique, but his expertise was carried on by Andrew Rublyov, the only Russian master whose name is embodied in a continuous native tradition. Rublyov's work is contemporary with Fra Angelico's; it is thought to resemble it. His most famous painting, distinguished by the serenity of the composition and the delicacy of the colors, is the ikon of the "Old Testament Trinity" in the great Church of the Trinity Monastery. The scarcity of the names of individual painters reflects the characteristically collective, impersonal spirit of the Russian Church.

As in so many other arts, the origin of Old Russian painting was wholly Byzantine; this is surely the explanation of the curious contrast between Russian talent and its background of unrelieved barbarism. Russian artists were not outdone by the finest Byzantine painting, though the Russians lacked its emotional picturesqueness and realism. While conserving Byzantine grace and mobility, the stylization of Russian painting was wholly static—a counterpart of the liturgical formality of the Russian Church. The congealed adoration of rows of saints turned toward Christ expressed the motionless transcendence of the church-sponsored autocracy.

The devastation wrought by the Tatars, on the other hand, was tremendous. Ancient centers of Russian civilization—Kiev, Chernigov, Pereyaslavl, Ryazan—were laid waste; the first three mentioned did not recover for centuries. Russian casualties were immense; also, the number of civilians of both sexes enslaved by the Tatars must have come to at least 10 percent of the population.

Perhaps even more important for Russian civilization, the cultural demands of the Tatars accentuated the intellectual impoverishment of the Russians. The best jewelers and craftsmen, as well as artisans of various kinds such as smiths, armorers, and saddlers, were sent to work for the Great Khan or assigned to various Mongol hordes. This dispersion of Russia's best craftsmen for a time exhausted her reservoir of skills and interrupted the continuity of industrial traditions. When the enamel shops of Kiev were destroyed in 1240 and the artisans were either killed or kidnapped, the Russian art of making cloisonné enamel, which had achieved such distinction in Kievan Russia, vanished altogether.

It took a long time to recover from this; it was not until late in the fourteenth century that champlevé enamels were made in Moscow again. In the sixteenth century native craftsmen resumed the making of cloisonné enamels, but their handiwork was quite inferior to what had been produced in Kiev centuries before. There was a halt in the making of filigree: when it was finally taken up again it was visibly modified by the use of models from Central Asia. The niello technique also vanished with the Tatar invasion; it was not until the sixteenth century that it came into vogue again. Glazed polychrome ceramics, as well as decorative tiles, also seem to have stopped being made until the fifteenth century. The art of masonry and fretwork, as well as construction crafts in general, was halted or impaired by the consequences of the Tatar occupation. The last masterpiece of stone-cutting was the reliefs in the Cathedral of St. George in Yuriev-Polsky in Suzdalia, finished just before the Tatars struck. This depression lasted for a whole century in eastern Russia, and it was not until the middle of the fourteenth century, when Tatar control began weakening, that some branches of industry, especially metallurgical, began reviving.

The disappearance of urban crafts during the first century of Tatar control indirectly accentuated the growth of the manorial system. Since the absence of trained people to satisfy consumers' demands made the villages and upper classes depend on themselves, the princes, boyars, and monasteries were obliged to sponsor crafts on their own estates. Ultimately, after the princes and monasteries managed to redeem some captive craftsmen (others came back from Tatar captivity), a large number of smiths, potters, carpenters, and tailors settled on princely and monastic estates. When the grand ducal manor became a major center, as it did in Moscow, they continued to work for the local prince or grand duke instead of for the market. This led to a marked growth of manorial industries during the fourteenth to sixteenth centuries.

This process paralleled the growing importance of the large landed estates. To be sure, the manor as a socio-political institution had been extending its role even before the arrival of the Tatars, and in the twelfth century both princes and boyars owned huge estates that were sources of basic revenue, but the cities were still the hub of political life. The princes spent more time playing politics than attending to business.

But as the Tatars curtailed the political rights of their subjects, the princes were reduced to the management of their estates; and as the cities declined, the natural resources of the country—its forests and agriculture—became more important. Consequently, the domains of the Grand Duke ultimately became the chief foundation of both his economic power and his administration. His estates not only gave him an income, but they became the axis of his material power. In this way patrimonial habits were to modify the very concept of princely power.

This same process happened to the boyars, too. Since the princes, as former pretenders to sovereignty, were the ones most affected by the Tatar power, the boyars actually had greater relative influence on state affairs under the Tatars than before. Until the Tatar invasion, it had been only the Galician boyars who had successfully opposed the princes and who were actually responsible for the drawing in of first Lithuanian and then Polish rulers. In eastern Russia, on the other hand, the boyars became eager to sponsor the expansion of the grand duchy or principality they were counselors of, since this expansion benefited them both socially and individually. As the Tatar dominion waned, and it became clear that among the numerous petty Russian rulers it was the Moscow princes who were in the forefront, this supremacy itself attracted more and more boyars to offer the Moscow princes their support. Thus the natural desire for self-aggrandizement on the part of the prince merged in this early period with the spontaneous collaboration of the boyars.

Hence, though Russian political life was not wiped out but merely distorted, the relationships between its constituent elements were completely upset. The paramount process in political life, as well as in economics, was the decline of the role of the cities.

Since most of the major cities of eastern Russia were destroyed during the Tatar invasion, the urban democratic institutions represented by the popular assembly, which had prospered variously throughout Russia, were wiped out. The few cities that either escaped destruction or managed to revive gave the Tatars their only serious resistance during the first century of their rule. There was no basis for accommodation between the Tatars and the urban population: the townspeople, especially the craftsmen, were constantly threatened by conscription, and unlike the princes and boyars, who swiftly interacted and often intermingled with the Tatars, the city dwellers were in a state of continuous turbulence at each oppressive Tatar measure.

The Tatars were eager to stamp out the popular resistance rooted in the nature of city life. Their eagerness led them to extend their dynastic or oligarchic combinations with the Russian princes to the repression of urban opposition. The alliance was all the more organic because the Russian prince were also inherently opposed to the unsettling tendencies of the popular assembly. Both Tatars and Russian princes, in fact, had a joint interest in combating the popular assembly, and thus, as in so many other alliances concluded on the surface of Russian life against the stirrings beneath, for a long time the factions were welded together. The cooperation between Tatars and princes forestalled the spread of urban mutiny during the second half of the thirteenth century and stamped out the isolated rebellions that flared up now and then.

The authority of the popular assembly thus dwindled sharply. By the middle of the fourteenth century it no longer meant anything as an element of government. It is true that during the latter part of the fourteenth century, as the alliance between the Russian princes and the Tatars began to break up with the decomposition of the Tatar Empire and the growing boldness of the Russian princes, the consequent alienation of the princes from the Tatars eliminated at least one cause of friction with the popular assembly. But even then the princes and boyars remained suspicious of its inherent unruliness. Even while appealing to the townsfolk for their cooperation against the Tatars, the princes had no intention of allowing the popular assembly as an institution to take shape again. Hence, though the popular assembly kept springing up in times of crisis, it never resumed its role as a permanent source of authority.

The Tatars had always been extremely tolerant—or indifferent—in religious matters. Chingis had admitted to his court every sort of religious persuasion—Buddhist monks, Nestorian and Franciscan Christians, Taoists, and Muslims. A grandson, Guyuk, wrote his "son" St. Louis of France that his aim was to protect all Christians regardless of denomination; another Great Khan, Mongka, said all religions were like the five fingers of a hand. According to Marco Polo, Kubilay, the ruler of China, kissed the Gospels presented to him by a Nestorian priest. In the West, however, while remaining broadminded, the Tatars gradually yielded to Islam. The most important cultural development within the Golden Horde during its efflorescence in the reign of Uzbeg (1313-1341) was the Muslim conversion that took place on a large scale. Batu himself had been a sky-worshiper; his son had accepted Christianity; though his brother Berke became a Muslim, it was not until Uzbeg's reign that Islam became the official religion of the Khan's court and was adopted by most of his Turco-Mongol subjects.

Since Tatars were actually a small minority of the Golden Horde, most of which consisted of Turks, the spread of Islam among both groups, already so closely intertwined, fused them still further; Muslim institutions gradually grew up alongside Mongol institutions.

The international trade underlying the Golden Horde probably stimulated its conversion to Islam because of the central role played in finance and trade by the Muslims of Central Asia and the Middle East. It was probably this conversion to Islam that, in splitting the area ruled by the Golden Horde into Muslim and Christian cultures, postponed the unification of the Russian state.

Though the Golden Horde finally declined through a series

of crises, splits, and defeats, the dominion of Saray did not collapse completely until two new Tatar states sprang up over its ruins. The Kazan Turks, on the Volga, seceded in 1445, while the Crimean Turks set up a state of their own in Crimea with the support of the Poles. The Russian contribution to the shattering of the Golden Horde was minor; the Horde was in fact eliminated in 1502 by the Crimean Tatars.

The Golden Horde declined primarily because of something again outside the purview of Russian history—the rise of Timur (Tamerlane), born in Transoxania in 1336. Timur was one of the most devastating of Chingis's successors, though, while a Mongol, he was not a direct descendant. He ruined the Golden Horde both economically and politically by his contest with its Khan Tokhtamysh. All the great trading centers in which the power of the Golden Horde was rooted were destroyed. Timur apparently intended not merely to defeat his rival in the field, but to reroute Western trade with China and India from the North Caspian and Black Sea regions to Persia and Syria, in this way starving out the Golden Horde and diverting its profits to himself. Timur, in fact, did to the Golden Horde what Batu had done to the Russians: he destroyed the major cities, which were centers of crafts and industries as well as of trade, and thus eliminated their social elite. This victory of Timur's Central Asian empire, and the consequent crumbling of the Golden Horde, constituted a favorable medium for Russia's revival.

Generally speaking, the Russians were incapable of coping with the Tatars militarily; they relied chiefly on inertia and guile. The celebrated victory won by Dmitri, Grand Duke of Moscow (1359–1389), over the Tatars at Kulikovo in 1380, which flabbergasted the Russians themselves, was not only the first but the only major setback they imposed on the Golden Horde.

It is fashionable for historians, looking for crucial "turning-points" and other props for thought, to regard this battle as a pivotal event marking the definitive turning of the Asiatic tide from the heart of Europe. But in fact the Russian victory inflicted no serious damage on the Tatar power. For a century afterward the Russian princes remained in thralldom, and probably never more so than during the first half of the fifteenth century. Even when the Tatar overlordship was definitely sloughed off in 1480, tribute to the Tatars was unchallenged for decades afterwards.

CHAPTER III

THE RISE OF THE MOSCOW STATE:
Ivan the Terrible

*D*espite the Tatars' heavy hand, Russian life developed forms of its own.

In some ways Russian feudalism resembled that of Western Europe. Government was still only feebly centralized; there were great estates and a hierarchy among landlords; the landlords were delegated judicial and fiscal powers; the reciprocal services of boyars and tenants were governed by contract. But the principle paramount in Western Europe—the hereditariness of relationships and their objective, i.e., impersonal, foundation—was generally absent.

Feudalism never crystallized as it did in Europe. Aside from the fact that the Russian princes did not embody different dynastic claims, as did the great feudal houses in France and Germany, the people themselves had no regional characteristics. In a curious way the Russian nationality was formed long before the Russian nation-state. This was partly due to the abovementioned social fluidity. A Frenchman would be far more Burgundian than French, and a German would be much more a Bavarian than a German, but the two would have a basic allegiance, both spiritual and material, to an aristocratic house that was absent in Russia.

More important, as I have pointed out before, property symbolized nothing. A principality, in accordance with the ancient Viking attitude, was simply a piece of real estate. At bottom this notion is profoundly antifeudal. The wills left by Suzdalian and Muscovite princes treated cities, villages, jewels, and furs on exactly the same level. Russian feudalism was thus essentially different from Western European feudalism—contracts were absolutely revocable: this was primarily because relations were not between things, but between people. Vassaldom in the West, for instance, was theoretically quite independent of the person of the vassal. A baron of such and such a place was a vassal of the count of such and such a place not because of any personal ties, of sympathy or material interest, but because the baron's land was part of the count's fief. The squires in Western Europe had their claims rooted in the land (that is why their titles contained the particle *de*). The Russian boyar custom of retaining family names is illuminating because it indicates the absence of a basic attachment to land. A Morozov or a Romanov might be a lord or a serf: the lineage of Russian nobles was purely genealogical and independent of the land.

This also meant the absence of a fixed hierarchy. There was no question of "great vassals" as in France. Russia was divided up between the members of what was theoretically a single family who were all equal in terms of lineage and might go up or down in life in accordance with nothing but their luck. This also applied to the lords owning their land outright: whether they were descendants of the old princely retinues, or favorites of the moment, or people performing services for a prince and rewarded by land, their material and spiritual status was a function of a contract they had concluded with him. As far as the prince was concerned, what they had was not a title of nobility but a function.

Consequently, there was not even a clear line between plebeians and nobility. The basest villein could be elevated by receiving a charter of immunity from a prince, as could a boyar or the head of a convent.

In a word, the whole complex of relations revolving around the notions of privilege, status, and immunity was based on an economic, not a political, concept. Thus all functionaries of the state, however exalted, were mere employees who could be sacked at will.

In a way, of course, this system was democratic, in the sense that status did not depend on a concept of the person but on a relationship between functions. Boyars were not obliged to acknowledge a more powerful boyar; their domain was not attached to a domain that was larger but directly to the person of a prince. Thus there was no question in Russia of that vertical ladder of status that distinguished the Middle Ages in the West. The Russian functional, democratic, plebeian system might be called a horizontal checkerboard, in which the criterion of status remained what it had been in Kievan Russia—function, not situation.

Perhaps the contrast is best illustrated in the absence among the Russians of any concept of honor: chivalry was an alien idea. The success of the Roman Catholic Church in moralizing combat by creating the concept of the knight "without fear and without reproach" had no counterpart in the Russian Church, which was indifferent to the organization of society. Everything in Western Europe to do with honor, whether of the class, family, or individual—chivalric orders, duels, tournaments, heraldry—was completely absent in Russia.

When boyars and princes spoke of "honor," what they meant was a rank they claimed in a genealogical hierarchy; it involved no duties. The extraordinary unscrupulousness of the society thus was unbridled even by lip service: neither lying, perjury, nor assassination was regarded as something beneath a prince's dignity. Deceit was not only commonplace, but admired; treachery aimed at securing a brother's or cousin's death was entirely acceptable. In this as in other things the customs of Russia seem an echo of a more ancient past, of France, for instance, under the Merovingians and Carolingians, before the rise of a moral ethos humanized manners.

It seems clear that in a regime where vassaldom was a link between individuals regardless of land, where aristocratic hierarchy was inherently indefinite, where there was no genuine nobility, no chivalry, no knighthood, and no concept of honor, there is no point in referring to feudalism. It would be better to say that Russia missed the Middle Ages, just as it missed the influence of Rome and the Renaissance. If the Middle Ages are taken to span the end of Roman civilization and the beginning of the Renaissance, then Russia, unacquainted with either one, simply remained unarticulated throughout this period. It remained submerged in the religious conception of individual and social life until the reign of Peter the Great and, if the masses of the people are kept in mind, for generations afterwards.

Russian backwardness is not a mere epithet but for historical purposes a structural concept. Dante's composition of the *Divine Comedy* some one hundred and fifty years before the unification of Russia by Moscow is a useful point of comparison, as is the fact that five centuries after its conversion to Christianity Russia remained strongly pagan and almost a hundred percent illiterate.

This general background affected everything. Even below the level of state politics, for instance, there was no genuine concept of hierarchy. Of the three social groups dependent on the prince—the boyars, the prince's administrative personnel, i.e., the "courtiers," and the taxpayers who cultivated his land—relationships were governed by contract. The slaves, who were outside all this, were possessions and were in any case a minor factor in the growth of Muscovy. The prince's governmental apparatus was not directed at the maintenance of society, but had been engendered for the sole purpose of aggrandizing his treasury.

A dependent prince, i.e., one invested by so-called patrimonial princes with an appanage, had the same sort of court on a smaller scale. He too had his "courtiers," functionaries, and domestics, either free or slave. A large part of his land would be rented to tenant farmers. His land would form a universe to itself, separated from others by vast forests or impassable marshes. Whenever it rained, or the snows melted, the roads would dissolve in a vast sea of mush; when communications were made easier by the big winter freeze, he would be more vulnerable to attacks by marauders, usually Tatars.

The point about such princes is that they were essentially landowners and not gentlemen. Their point of view was materialistic. If things went badly on a prince's land and he found himself ruined, there was nothing in his habit of mind that would prevent his hiring himself out, to some luckier landowner, as a farmer or even a voluntary slave.

Foreign trade had long since vanished with the retirement of the Russians into the nooks and crannies of the vast timbered northeast; there was no merchant class to carry on the role it had played in Kievan Russia. Muscovy slumped into the squirearchal, peasant life that was to be its hallmark for centuries. There was a sort of middle class, made up of the prince's functionaries, who took up taxes and collected the tributes for the Tatars, and the scribes who coped with the administrative red tape that was the forerunner of the bureaucratic jungle of a later day. Every individual was enmeshed in a network of liabilities: everything had to be paid for—crossing a bridge, hunting beavers, tolls for the marketplace, being tried, acquitted, or condemned. The most trivial transactions of daily life were grist for the prince.

In Muscovy, with production negligible and commerce sharply reduced, land relations formed the matrix of society. The concepts underlying them were to evolve rapidly and to exercise a profound effect on politics.

At the very beginning of Russian society the original ownership of land had doubtless derived from occupation or purchase. Land acquired in this way was the absolute property of the owner, whose only obligation to the authorities was paying taxes. A landowner might be granted all sorts of exemptions and privileges by the prince controlling his land, such as the right to act as judge over those living on it. He might also be designated tax collector for the prince; also, the estate, for one reason or another, might be exempt from taxation altogether. These privileges were all defined in some detail in actual letters patent issued by the prince to a landowner; it was the lands held in outright possession under such conditions that were known as patrimonial or hereditary estates.

The patrimonial domain was distinct from another source of land ownership—service tenure—that became widespread during the thirteenth and fourteenth centuries, when the problem afflicting the country as a whole was still the scarcity of manpower. Land was very abundant, but without development it meant nothing. The princes' revenues would be magnified immensely if waste or fallow lands were converted into agricultural settlements, which they might secure by granting individuals and monasteries estates, and they did so.

But they did not always do so unconditionally; they would make the land-grant, unlike the patrimonial estates, dependent on the performance of various duties, primarily military service. Though its actual point of origin is obscure, service tenure in land became very common, especially during the second half of the fifteenth century, and was the general rule in the sixteenth, when the line of demarcation between patrimonial and service estates became altogether blurred and all landlords were subject to government service.

The upper class grew more stratified. The boyars, who owned land that they exploited with servile or semi-servile labor, depended for their economic independence on the size of their estates, though their independence as individuals still benefited by the custom inherited from the ancient retinues of the Viking princes and their successors, according to which they were under no obligation to serve their prince simply because they lived or held land within his political sphere. This privilege was always paid lip service to in agreements between boyars and princes; since this was the only guarantee of the landed aristocracy's independence, it was highly cherished. Boyars never showed the slightest hesitation in changing sides at their convenience, nor was there ever any legal impediment to this. The princes were in no position to challenge this privilege since they were often weak and found the boyars indispensable; for that matter the custom often worked in their favor.

To be sure, if a prince lost his own boyars, a *de facto* question of retaliation would arise regardless of theoretical rights. Boyars who left their prince would find that their traditional immunity would be laughed at; they found themselves ruined by having their estates taxed beyond endurance, pillaged, or confiscated outright. With the consolidation of princely authority in the rise of the Moscow dynasty, the ancient right that had been breached more and more frequently was forgotten. By the second half of the fifteenth century it was a dead letter, though never abolished by any edict. By the sixteenth century, when all landlords found themselves burdened by compulsory service, the independence of the former landed aristocracy had vanished; as the Moscow state consolidated itself, it turned the former aristocrats into its servants.

This gradual imposition on the population of the duty of service was even more important in the case of the farmers, who had formerly been free and were now gradually slipping into a network of obligations to the owner of the land they worked as well as to the state. Though the process in its early phases is obscure, it seems that the formerly independent farmers eventually became tenants on land owned variously by princes, boyars, or the Church. In some cases big landlords, both secular and ecclesiastical, would simply seize land belonging to weaker neighbors, but more generally the privileges the princes could bestow on estates both of boyars and of the church, especially in taxation, were a great inducement for the farmer to exchange his nominal independence for the protection of a powerful lord. This inducement grew during the Tatar occupation; since both before and after this landlords had a vital interest in manpower, the farmer might well come to think it better to have a protector interposed between himself and the voracious treasury official.

In any case, by the fourteenth century tenant farming seems to have been far more common than independent small farming. Slavery had meanwhile become a negligible factor, especially since prisoners of war, its chief source, had vanished with the pacification of the national territory.

Relations between tenants and landlords and between princes and boyars evolved in the same direction. At first the tenant could theoretically leave his landlord and work for whomever he pleased whenever his contract had expired, while the landlord, contrariwise, could also dismiss his tenants. But the tenant's right to go wherever he wished was soon encroached on. The prince had a fundamental interest in keeping his taxpaying population within his reach, and the farmers' freedom of movement began to be hampered, initially through agreements made by the Grand Dukes of Moscow with the other princes binding each other not to accept free peasants leaving each other's domains.

At first such restrictions did not touch the actual freedom of the tenant; they merely increased the difficulty of finding a new landlord by limiting the freedom of the landlords themselves in this respect. But this was only the first step; a further restriction, applied by the middle of the fifteenth century, made it impossible for the tenant to leave whenever he chose during the year, which had formerly been his right, and restricted him to the fortnight preceding and following St. George's Day (26 November). This restriction was the beginning of a trend.

Quite apart from these administrative restrictions, what ultimately bound the tenant to his landlord was the burden of indebtedness he incurred for purely economic reasons. Since farmers, then as always, needed help to carry on from one season to another, they were bound to turn for aid to their landlords, both secular and ecclesiastical. They paid heavy interest on their loans, and though at first a debt outstanding between tenant and landlord did not of itself stop a farmer from leaving, eventually it came to much the same thing, since a debt could be enforced. The debtor was compelled to work for his creditor until the debt was paid. In practice this was tantamount to bondage for life; even by the thirteenth century indebtedness had become a substantial force for the enslavement in fact of people who were free in law.

It was against this complex background that the Moscow dynasty emerged, a powerful centralizing and state-making factor that in the space of a few generations began playing a positive role abroad as well as at home. The components of the new Moscow state were not themselves new—if only to judge by their churches, Rostov, Suzdal, and Vladimir had a substantial history behind them—but in fact the collapse of Kiev turned out to have marked the end of an epoch, the rise of Moscow the beginning.

Moscow was to achieve the unification of the diverse Russian-speaking territories and ultimately of the vast country in existence today precisely because of their fragmentation by the disruptive tendencies in Russian life that antedated even the Tatar invasion. By reaction, the Tatars gave Russia an attitude of collective identity, on the one hand, and on the other magnified the relative position of specific rulers by the pressure of their demands.

Moscow was the focus of three groups of water-routes: the western group to Northern Europe via the Baltic; the Volga-Middle East route it acquired in 1552–56; and the northeastern route to Siberia, where the precious furs came from that have always produced so much foreign revenue for Russia. The first two routes, which were a basic transit route from northern Europe to Persia, connected Moscow with the world market; Moscow became firmly embedded in the rapidly developing commercial revolution then sweeping Europe as a whole, especially after the English discovered the White Sea route to Russia in 1553.

In addition, Moscow was a natural goal for immigrants fleeing northeastward from the chaos of southwest Russia; thus it benefited by an influx of population as well as by the growing commerce based on its far-flung river-complex.

Politically, the emergence of Moscow was conditioned by its relationship to the Tatars, who may, indeed, have given this emergence its initial stimulus. An example of the interaction between Russian domestic and foreign policy is the career of Alexander Nevsky, whom I have mentioned as a shrewd maneuverer between Tatars and Russians. Nevsky, though in some sense representing the collective interests of northeastern Russia on the western frontier vis-à-vis Swedes and Germans, was in domestic affairs a mere tool of the Khan. Having won his surname from his victory over the Swedes on the Neva River in 1240, he beat the German knights in 1242, after their entry into Pskov, and the Lithuanians three years later with a motley army from all over the country. All the while he was taking his orders in domestic affairs from the Tatars. Alexander's position as Grand Duke of Vladimir by grace of the Khan illustrates the subtle dynamic in the evolution of Russian national interests.

Nevsky's son Daniel was the first ruler who was definitely Prince of Moscow as such: before him no Russian prince had been pre-eminent. The history of Vladimir during the last quarter of the thirteenth and the beginning of the fourteenth century had been chaotic; the feuds between princes with equal claims, making coalitions and freely using Tatar troops, precluded the emergence of a paramount prince. Moscow suddenly emerged from parochialism at the beginning of the fourteenth century, about a hundred and fifty years after its first mention in 1147.

The expansion of the Moscow ruling house may have been stimulated psychologically by the ineligibility of the Moscow rulers, as a younger branch of the Rurik line, for the Grand Dukedom of Vladimir. When Ivan I (Ivan "Moneybags"), Nevsky's grandson, the first to launch the territorial aggrandizement of Moscow, was licensed by the Tatar Khan, he was repaid for his subservience by being appointed Grand Duke of Vladimir as well as Prince of Moscow. This helped ensure the primacy of the Moscow line over various other princelings.

The fact that Ivan I was the chief revenue agent increased his prestige among the Russian princes, on the one hand, and on the other gave him an effective instrument for the exercise of pressure. Since none of the Russian princes had any better claims to legitimacy, this was at least a negative factor in the growth of the Moscow dynasty. Dmitri's substantial, though ephemeral, victory over the Tatars at Kulikovo also enabled the Moscow ruler to present himself as the spearhead of an eventual emancipation from Tatar rule.

Ivan Moneybags, who died in 1341, began a custom among the Moscow Grand Dukes of leaving a constantly increasing share of the family patrimony to the son who actually inherited the title, which enabled him constantly to increase his material primacy among the Princes of Muscovy, which around this time, like the other Grand Duchies in Russia, consisted of a group of tiny and theoretically independent principalities that were actually a form of appanage controlled by the princes. This control included the right of testamentary disposition: thus, though theoretically independent, or semi-independent, a principality could be bequeathed at will by the Grand Duke. This combination of circumstances was the lever used by the Moscow Grand Duke to eliminate the very appanage order that gave him these advantages.

Moscow focused all the forces hostile to the permanent dismemberment of the country: its chief rival at the time, Tver, was preoccupied by complex affairs in the west, while Moscow's interests were simultaneously more comprehensive and because of its central position more "national." In the west Moscow's interests took in Novgorod, Tver, Lithuania, and the Baltic countries; in the south and east, the Golden Horde; and, as a permanent accompaniment to all this, the currents of colonization and commerce along the Volga.

It is impossible to discern any actual *movement* for Russian union. Perhaps the most important single factor amidst the endless internecine clashes that enabled Moscow to emerge as the unifying element in Russian history was the concurrent sponsorship of unification by the boyars and by the Church, each group for its own reasons.

The boyars were unconscious, to be sure, of any altruistic goals. The aggrandizement of the Grand Duke they served naturally offered them lucrative opportunities, especially in the form of land-grants, that might very well be scattered throughout several principalities. The landed aristocracy had the most to lose from the bloodshed and sacrifices attendant on feuds between princes: not only was their land subject to confiscation, but they were the first to be slaughtered by the prince's enemies.

As a great landowner, the Church shared these material preoccupations of the landed aristocracy; at the same time it had the further goal, as heir to the Byzantine claims to universality, of having one Russian metropolitan (or bishop) as the sole head of the Church. This naturally made the Church a strong supporter of union as against princely strife.

Ivan Moneybags' name refers to his supposed methods of acquiring territory, but this may be a misunderstanding, since the growth of the Muscovite State did not arise out of the acquisition of land as much as out of the accumulation of political authority by the Moscow Grand Dukes. Ivan Moneybags actually increased his power not merely by thrift, as the historical legend has it, but by his skill in acting as a Tatar agent—docile toward the Tatars, ruthless toward the Russians.

Russian unification may be summed up as the consequence of two interwoven processes: the unification of the Principality of Moscow under its "senior" Princes, their fusion with the Grand Dukes of Vladimir, and the establishment as a result of the "Grand Duchy of Moscow, of Vladimir, and all Russia"—the forerunner of the Muscovite Tsardom.

The extension of Muscovite authority to other Russian territories took place with the full sanction of the Tatars; from their point of view it was just another, more efficient way of running their herds. But the process, though promoted by the Tatars for their own reasons, had to overcome the conflict between two principles I have mentioned before: the contradiction between the idea of patrimonial succession, or the right of a descendant to share in his father's principality, conceived in accordance with traditional Russian law as a piece of real estate, and the other principle, just accepted, that called for unification under the rule of a senior prince. Russian unification, in fact, had to overcome serious obstacles.

Basil II may be said to have laid the foundations of the Muscovite autocracy. The first genuinely energetic, strong-willed, and rapacious ruler in his line, he managed to concentrate in his own hands all the fragments of political power scattered among the hodge-podge of Russian principalities. Leaning even more heavily than his forerunners on a hired Tatar force, he became famous, even in this blood-drenched country, for cruelty to his enemies, both past and potential.

But though he was an effective man of action, he was fuzzy-minded in a way characteristic of early Russian political thought—he failed to recognize or formulate any change of principle in what he was doing. Without discarding the outmoded dogma of the patriarchal family, and while retaining the same traditional formulae in his testament as other princes, he paved the way for a new source of authority by disregarding the former distinction between the Grand Duchy of Vladimir and the portion of the senior Moscow Prince. Thus, the Grand Duchy he bequeathed to his eldest son as his patrimony left the way clear, by virtue of its geographical redefinition, for the aggrandizement of the territory comprised in the new patrimony and the eventual investment of the growing region with an evolving concept of autocracy, which in effect fused Vladimir and Moscow both territorially and constitutionally. The Muscovite State had now been born.

When Basil II died, he controlled some 15,000 square miles. The reigns of his son and grandson added at least 40,000 square miles. The Tatar rule, already declining toward the end of Basil II's reign was officially terminated in 1480, while the Golden Horde was liquidated in 1502 by the Crimean Tatars.

Both Muscovy and America were discovered by Western Europe at about the same time. With the growth of Muscovy, it gradually became evident that Europe did not end, as had been thought, on the northeastern frontier of Lithuania and Poland.

The increasing importance of Muscovy led to a momentous development in the Russian Church. When Moscow became a sovereign state in 1480, in the wake of the Golden Horde's dissolution, it grew into a situation in which it found itself the only independent Greek Orthodox community. Byzantium had been conquered and suppressed by the Ottoman Turks in 1453, only five years after Russia had acquired the right to elect and consecrate her own metropolitans as a by-product of the council of Roman Catholic and Greek Orthodox dignitaries that had met in Ferrara and Florence in 1438 to bridge the great schism.

The Russian Church no longer could look to Byzantium on the one hand or the Tatars on the other to protect it against the growing power of the Grand Dukes. Weak, primitive, utterly unlettered, the Church not only tacitly submitted to the primacy of the grand ducal power but actively promoted the expansion of Muscovy by expounding a theory of allegiance that made of Moscow a "third Rome."

This theory was engagingly simple: since the first Rome had fallen because it had betrayed true (i.e., Greek Orthodox) Christianity, and Constantinople, the second Rome, had been taken by the infidel for the same reason, Moscow was the natural heir of these two other backsliding Romes and would, moreover, continue forever. This theory was actually an adaptation of earlier theories commonly held in other Slavic and Balkan countries, especially Bulgaria, but it lacked the element of a definite material link between Constantinople and Moscow. Logic required some factual support to enable Ivan III and Basil III to assume the mantle of Byzantium.

Ivan III had married Sophie Paleologue, niece of the last Byzantine emperor, who had been killed by the Turks when they took Constantinople. The fact of this marriage was now supplemented by a brilliant lyrical invention that made the Moscow house not only the direct descendant of a so-called Pruss, supposed to be a brother of Caesar Augustus, but also traced the transmission of Christianity not to Byzantium but directly back to Andrew, a (putative) brother of the Apostle Peter.

With these additions, the old theory was enough to give the Moscow Grand Dukes the most splendid genealogy imaginable and make them leaders of Greek Orthodoxy in their own right. This theoretical cornerstone of the growing Muscovite absolutism was then reinforced by some further apologetics buttressing the alliance between the Church and the State by stating that blind, obedient faith was the only road to salvation and proscribing the use of reason altogether. The slightest show of independent thought was heresy and blasphemy *per se;* the only acceptable arguments were scriptural quotations. This school is associated with the name of Joseph Sanin, the founder of the Volokolam Monastery and a contemporary of Ivan III. His fanaticism, put to the service of Muscovite absolutism, was summed up in his remark that though the Tsar physically resembled other human beings, "in his power he was similar to God in Heaven."

The fanatical Sanin school started some counter-reactions. A sect of dissenters called "Judaizers" had been discovered in Novgorod about 1470, just about the time Novgorod was carrying on its final, losing battle against absorption by the Muscovite state. These Judaizers seem to have denied the Holy Trinity, claimed that the Messiah had not yet come, that Christ was only a man, and consequently that Christianity could not be the true religion. They also denounced monasticism, repudiated the need for the Church and for Church services, denounced the ecclesiastical hierarchy for simony, and went so far as to claim that reason was paramount, not faith.

Of course these views, which are known only from the opponents of the Judaizers, seem to imply not a heresy but a secession from Christianity altogether. The sect naturally irritated the Church authorities, since by denouncing monasticism and prayers for the dead the Judaizers were undermining the foundations of the Church's wealth.

Now, this dissenting sect was looked upon with a kindly eye, oddly enough, by Ivan III because it advocated the one thing the official Church was reluctant to concede the Moscow state it otherwise supported with such zeal. This was the secularization of the vast Church estates, which had grown very substantially toward the end of the fifteenth century, enjoying the protection of Russian princes and Tartar Khans alike. When the Moscow government under Ivan III needed land-grants for its retainers, the tradition was broken; when he incorporated Novgorod, Ivan III confiscated a great many Church lands.

Thus on this one point Sanin and his followers were at odds with the Muscovite regime. Since the Judaizers advocated secularization for their own reasons, the Moscow government handled them with unusual leniency.

The Judaizers were especially annoying to the church because they were much better theologians. The name Judaizer itself may be an epithet, but it is also possible that it originated with three Jews who had come to Novgorod in the fifteenth century; their teachings seem to have some connection, also, with the small sect of the *Strigolniki,* which had appeared even earlier in Novgorod and Pskov and repudiated the ecclesiastical hierarchy, its sacraments, and prayers for the dead. The leaders of this sect had all been executed, but their followers survived as a seedbed for other dissenters.

The simple-mindedness of the Orthodox Church theologians was to give the Judaizers a first-rate polemical victory. The year 1492 was officially considered the 7,000th year from creation; for some reason it was thought certain that the Second Coming of Christ and the Last Judgment were at hand. These forecasts were supported by an endless array of incontrovertible proofs drawn from Scriptures, especially Revelations and the Apocrypha. The Judaizers held the same theory, but since they used the Jewish calendar, they were sure that the world still had another 1,747 years to go before it hit 7,000.

Consequently, when the Last Judgment missed its cue, the Judaizers derived a great polemical advantage over their adversaries by claiming that if the official church had flubbed on a matter of such primordial importance as the end of the world, it might be wrong on other things, too. This argument was persuasive; after 1492 the Judaizing movement forged ahead for a time.

Another dissenting movement, which was to keep producing ripples and crosscurrents in Russian life for generations, was that of the so-called Volga hermits, whose leader was one of the few outstanding personalities of the fifteenth century— Nil Sorsky (1433–1508). This movement also took a strong line for the secularization of the Church lands; hence it also fell foul of the official churchmen. On the religious side, Sorsky was a mystic, persuaded that inner conviction, not external observance, was the core of Christianity. He also thought that inner conviction could be arrived at by a diligent, though critical, study of the Scriptures. Sorsky was a monastic reformer; he had spent some time at Mount Athos, and when he came back to Russia after extensive travels in the eastern Christian communities, he tried to reform monastic life by founding a hermitage east of the Volga, on the very rim of the Russian sphere. This accentuated the drift into the woods on the part of individual seekers after salvation; hermitages were scattered everywhere throughout the woods of northeastern Russia.

When the Sorskyites, who believed that the Church must never use violence but must confine itself to moral persuasion and prayer, were attacked by the official hierarchy, they were, oddly enough, backed by a group of boyars, who for their own reasons favored the Church's independence so that there might be some check on the Grand Dukes. They also wanted the monastic estates secularized, to stop the state from encroaching any further on their own privileges.

But the Church won out, over the hesitations of both Ivan III and Basil III, at the price of becoming utterly subservient to the state power. It is illuminating to read the kernel of Joseph of Volokolam's argument concerning relations between church and state:

> If the monasteries are deprived of the villages they own, how would it be possible for an honorable and noble man to take orders? And if there are no honorable monks, where shall we find candidates for the metropolitanate, the archbishopric, the bishopric, and other honorable offices? It there are no honorable and noble monks, faith itself will be undermined.

The net effect was that the Church and the landed aristocracy, which had both sponsored the rise of absolutism, found themselves engulfed by the jaws of the beast they had unleashed. The ancient privilege of the landed aristocracy—the acceptance of service on its own terms and under its chosen princes—was outmoded the moment Ivan III and Basil III acquired a monopoly of political authority. By the end of Basil's reign, boyar malcontents could no longer find any independent princes to serve. The only alternative was leaving the Russian sphere and entering the service of a foreign state outright, such as Lithuania or Poland, but the new rulers of Muscovy found what was now explicitly called treason a convenient pretext for confiscating the culprits' estates.

The allocation of service land was widely applied by Ivan III and Basil III. This practice counterbalanced the second source of the landed aristocracy's authority—its right to the absolute ownership of its own estates. The expenses involved in the expansion of Muscovy could be met only by the lavish distribution of land under service tenure. The former juridical distinction between hereditary estates and those held on service tenure simply vanished. This was actually part of the disappearance of the ancient right of a boyar to opt for any prince at will while retaining title to his estates wherever located. Thus, just as failure in allegiance to Moscow ultimately brought about the confiscation of the offender's estates, so the corollary was equally valid—the holder of an estate in Muscovy was bound to serve the ruler of Muscovy, the Grand Duke.

This too was never actually formulated as a principle; it simply evolved during the fifteenth and sixteenth centuries. It affected minor princes and boyars in basically the same way. The traditional privileges of princes, who had previously been sovereign on their own territories, were gradually curtailed as the Moscow Grand Dukes extended their control. Meanwhile, the old practice of defining the privileges of monastic and secular landlords in letters patent issued by the sovereign came to be the source *in law* of the actual ownership of the land itself, as the formerly unambiguous distinction between hereditary and service estates was blurred.

In this way the custom gradually developed of allowing a given estate to be enjoyed only on condition that the crown was served. Though introduced haphazardly and pragmatically, the change-over—from tenure derived from purchase to tenure derived from service—ultimately revolutionized the basis of relations between the sovereign and the upper classes. The change, in spite of the failure to formulate it juridically, was unmistakable—the new principle underlying the regime was shown in the mass deportations of landlords to remote parts of the country, where they received land in service tenure, while their own estates were allocated to others on the same principle.

Nor was the aristocracy capable of defending itself. Despite the general discontent, there was no solidarity of any kind. In the fifteenth and sixteenth centuries the Moscow aristocracy was a mere hodge-podge that included all sorts of newcomers, adventurers, dispossessed princes and princelets, and boyars. The diversity of the origins of the aristocracy produced a scramble for cushy jobs handed out by the court. This primordial process of socio-political maneuvering was congealed in a special institution called by the Russian equivalent of *placement*. This involved the fixation of the aristocratic families in hierarchical order, based primarily on their genealogical standing in terms of government offices previously held. Special books had to be kept in special government departments to handle this confused system, which was arrived at in an attempt to counteract the mass of nondescripts thronging into Moscow. Unlike the feudal system in Europe, the placement system did not establish hereditary rights. It was the relative position of the officeholder that mattered rather than the office itself.

The system was so cumbersome that it was a permanent source of dissension among the boyar families and achieved nothing beyond curbing the efficiency of the official hierarchy. It lasted until the end of the seventeenth century only because in order to get anything done at all, various pockets were created in the higher military offices that were exempt from the so-called placement arithmetic.

The boyars spent an immense amount of time and energy in litigation designed to protect their positions in the placement system. They even fought each other physically to defend what was thought of as their honor. The ethos of the time made death itself preferable to serving in the army or sitting at the Grand Duke's table below someone whose ancestors lacked a sufficiently distinguished record.

The concentration of power in the Muscovite autocracy, on such a great and novel scale, changed life in Moscow and at court. The new status of the crown had to be made manifest by the embellishment of the city; both Ivan III and Basil III exerted themselves to do this. Italian architects were imported for the building of cathedrals and churches; the palaces of the Grand Dukes were built of stone, instead of the wood that had been used in the much less pretentious houses they had been living in; the Kremlin was given a ring of stone walls and towers. The court developed an elaborate ceremonial, possibly under the influence of Sophie Paleologue. Ivan III, who often used the title of "Sovereign of all Russia by the Grace of God," was occasionally also referred to as "Tsar and Autocrat," thought the Russian connotation of this was simply that he was independent of the Tatars. The unification of the realm was symbolized by the adoption of the two-headed eagle of Byzantium.

The development of a strong centralized monarchy at the time was not at all peculiar to Russia. Ivan III (1462–1505) was contemporary with the English War of the Roses and the rise of the Tudor dynasty; strong monarchies were pushing forward in other countries in Europe.

But the growth of the Muscovite autocracy far outstripped the parallel development of monarchy elsewhere in Europe. In 1517, when an envoy from the Holy Roman Empire (the Austrian Baron Sigismund von Herberstein) visited Moscow, he felt as though he were entering an entirely different political atmosphere, and that Basil III had completely outdone any other monarch in the degree of his power over his subjects.

The Muscovite Tsardom of the sixteenth and seventeenth centuries was in fact based on a different concept of society and state. Whereas Kievan society may be called with all due qualification a free or semi-free society, the Muscovite Tsardom was based on the principle that all classes from top to bottom except, curiously, the slaves themselves, were yoked to the state.

Basil II had laid the foundations of the autocracy; Ivan III and Basil III set it up. Though the emancipation of northeastern Russia from the Tatars was the result of a combined national effort involving the Moscow Grand Dukes, the Church, the gentry, and the commoners, the new monarchy that now anchored itself in Russian society was based on a principle that would have seemed alien to the Kievan Russians—the subordination to the state of society *in toto*. The profundity of this process is indicated by the fact that the regimentation of the social classes that had begun under the Tatars grew progressively afterwards, and in fact reached its peak about 1650, two whole centuries after Tatar rule had dissolved.

This is far from paradoxical: the new monarchy grew up under the aegis of unceasing warfare on its borders as well as the suppression of elements contending for power at home.

In the southeast and south, there was still a Tatar threat; in the west, there was a constant struggle for power going on between Moscow and Lithuania (after 1569 between Moscow and Poland); in the northwest, the absorption of Novgorod by Moscow meant that Moscow was now thrust into the forefront of a struggle to contain the Teutonic Knights and the Swedes around the Gulf of Finland. The defiance of the Golden Horde by Moscow did not mean peace, since even after the collapse of the Golden Horde several Tatar successor states continued making almost annual raids on the southern and eastern provinces of Muscovy, pillaging systematically and capturing thousands of people.

The Tatars remained an exceptionally difficult problem since in the absence of any natural boundaries on the broad highway of the steppe the Moscow government had to keep the whole border under constant guard. The Moscow regime, reversing the historic process, had set up a vassal Tatar state of its own, the Kasimov Khanate, around 1450; while the Kasimov Tatars and the Cossacks hired by the Moscow regime as irregulars were very useful, regular army troops were needed as well. The Tatars kept piercing the complex and expensive systems of fortified defense lines the Muscovites set up, and poured into the country beyond.

Thus Moscow had to control the steppe lands, either by conquest or diplomacy, a problem that was duplicated by its harassment in the west, where the struggle, though not so relentless as against the Tatars, cost just as much money because whenever a genuine crisis broke out, stronger and better equipped armies had to be put in the field. Armaments made taxation heavier; in its turn this called for increasing centralization to tighten the government screw.

The whole process was a vicious circle. The struggle against the west called for recruits, which was what the land-grants held in service tenure were supposed to supply; the provision of recruits meant a crisis in manpower to till the soil, with the further consequence that the peasants had to be tied down to the land they had originally been free to leave on the expiration of their contract with the landowner.

In this complex fashion, the regimentation of the social classes that had begun under the Tatars in response to the Tatar principle of centralized administration was developed still further by the Muscovite regime. A chain reaction was started that lasted for centuries; it was signalized by the spiralling interaction of autocracy and serfdom. Social chaos was the other side of the autocratic coin. It was doubtless because Russian society was so backward and chaotically organized that it was possible for the Moscow autocracy to suppress rival elements of authority and monopolize the whole country.

And it was during the reign of Ivan the Terrible, the longest in Russian history (1533–1584), that this autocratic complex was streamlined and formulated.

Ivan was the first to rule Russia as a wholly autocratic Tsar in theory as well as in practice. Three years old at the death of his father Basil III, he grew up in a period when the savagery of the princely and boyar cliques and clans kept lapsing into the violence that, while largely repressed under the thumb of Basil III, had kept breaking out under the regency of Ivan's mother. Deportations, confiscations of estates, tortures, assassinations, and executions were commonplace.

Ivan's nickname seems well deserved, though in Russian it properly denotes menace and has sometimes been translated as "Dread." He became known for an extreme kind of sadism while still a boy, and grew up with a combination of extreme piety of the Russian type—obsessive devotion to the external observances of the Church and utter indifference to the inner meaning of the religion, to say nothing of its ethics—and extravagant sexual license.

He had himself crowned "Tsar of all the Russias" at the age of seventeen and thus made official a title that had been used only casually during the preceding century. The word had meant nothing characteristic beforehand: it was also used to refer to the Khan of the Golden Horde.

The new title set an official stamp on the uncontested primacy of the Moscow regime; its resonant comprehensiveness reflected Ivan's view of his role. A talented though erratic writer, unquestionably the only articulate Russian ruler (except possibly Catherine the Great), Ivan was the first Russian ruler who openly gave principled support to monarchical absolutism as a philosophy. In contrast to his predecessors, who with all their ruthlessness had been land-grabbers, Ivan articulated a rough but comprehensive theory; he regarded himself as the actual vicar of God on earth, consequently a completely unhampered ruler in both theory and practice. Since his legitimacy was based on heredity, he not only emphasized descent from Rurik but took over the theory of the Third Rome mentioned above. In his negotiations with foreign powers, Ivan and his envoys made great play of his descent from Augustus Caesar's brother, Pruss.

Ivan seems to have been a paranoiac. His mistrustfulness made him kill almost anyone who came into contact with him. Executions by him were commonplace on all levels of society, generally accompanied by the most ingeniously contrived tortures. After 1560 especially, when Ivan decided he had been a mere tool of his counselors during his early days, he conducted a wholesale massacre among members of his family, Church dignitaries, princes, boyars, and commoners.

During an expedition Ivan undertook against Novgorod in

1570 to punish it for remissness, churches were desecrated, pillaged, and burnt; priests were flogged, tortured and executed in public. But it was rare for Ivan to miss mass; he spent a great deal of his time composing monastic rules or contriving complicated ceremonies for the consecration of the metropolitan. This did not stop him from treating his metropolitans with the utmost ferocity. An archbishop of Novgorod is said to have been sewn into a bear's skin and thrown to the dogs.

Ivan's prey generally met their deaths in churches, quite often during the mass. In the midst of the most extravagant bloodbaths, Ivan kept lists of the people he had murdered; he distributed money to monasteries to pay for the victims' eternal repose. Some 4,000 names of those killed were listed; the true number is thought to have been much larger. Obsessed, doubtless rightly, by terror of plots and general catastrophe, he wrote Queen Elizabeth in 1569 asking for asylum should he be ejected from Russia. He offered to make the arrangement reciprocal; she declined.

Ivan's rule may be summed up as the elevation of state authority to institutional as well as practical supremacy. To some extent this involved the apparent magnification of local authorities, since Ivan curtailed the highhandedness of some of the provincial governors still battening off the local populations. Socially, Ivan's contribution to the centralization of state authority took the form of destroying the power of the landed aristocracy, whom his wrath, generally quite indiscriminate in its choice of targets, eventually fixed on and blighted.

The isolation and annihilation of the landed gentry was begun by Ivan's suddenly and unexpectedly leaving Moscow in what seems to have been a clumsy but successful piece of guile. In December 1564 he left with his family and a huge retinue carrying treasure, jewels, and household goods. At first the caravan seemed to be heading into the unknown, but then it stopped a short distance from Moscow at Alexandrovskaya Sloboda, which remained a sort of second capital throughout his reign. A month later Ivan sent two messages back to Moscow. One was a bitter denunciation of the landed gentry and clergy as traitors and thieves. The second was addressed to the merchants, artisans, and commoners, who were cleared of any responsibility for the others' misdeeds. The whole maneuver, doubtless intended to sound like an abdication, was a trick to facilitate his setting up a new regime; Ivan was invited back to Moscow by a delegation that persuaded him to reconsider.

He came back on his own terms, celebrating his return by the slaughter of some leading boyars. The most significant change he instituted was the so-called *oprichnina,* a curious old word meaning an entailed domain, generally the portion of a sovereign prince's widow. He split up his entire realm into two parts. The first, the *oprichnina,* was to be Ivan's personal realm, whose cardinal function was the wiping out of treason in the other half of the realm, which was to be run by the normal administration.

The *oprichnina* was autocracy institutionalized. It was an omnipotent security police that raised the Tsar's personal authority far beyond any other institution in the country. Dressed in black, the members of the *oprichnina* rode black horses, carrying a dog's head and a broom attached to their saddles.

The *oprichnina* finally pulverized the political power of the landed gentry. The *oprichnina* had a spatial location: provinces, cities, and even a number of streets in Moscow were cleared of their gentry and landowners, who were deported to other parts of their country while their estates were distributed among the officials of the *oprichnina.* The provinces handed over to the *oprichnina* eventually took in almost half the country; the distribution was calculated so as to dislodge the former princely families, whose estates were granted to newcomers whose title to the land derived solely from Ivan's caprice.

Though the *oprichnina* and the rest of the country were theoretically to remain separate, the *oprichnina* gradually took over the chief trade routes and markets; ultimately it dominated the country completely. Thus, in addition to destroying the aristocracy's political influence and changing its composition, it brought about a transfer of land on a huge scale.

The very fact that the personnel of the *oprichnina* included some of the oldest names in the country, such as Trubetskoy and Shuisky, indicates that it was a novelty only institutionally. The *oprichnina* officers were not, of course, immune from Ivan's sadism; he put some of them to death in a particularly gruesome manner.

The imaginative ferocity of the tortures that became commonplace under Ivan blurred the institutional significance of the *oprichnina:* observers both in Russia and abroad were so struck by the incredible ritualism and fantasy in the activities of Ivan and the *oprichnina* that the long-range effects were only gradually perceived. The new capital, for instance, was transformed into a sort of semi-monastic fortress run by rules Ivan wrote himself; he and his favorites of the moment would dress like monks and divide their time between lengthy church services and extravagant orgies, punctuated by long sojourns in the torture chamber.

Aside from these long-range sociological innovations, Ivan's reign was marked by the decisive beginning of the protracted eastward expansion of the Russian state. Strife between the Tatar states of Kazan and Astrakhan on the Volga enabled Ivan to conquer and annex them both, Kazan in 1552 and Astrakhan in 1556. This eastward movement led to the absorption of western Siberia, which was carried on by purely private initiative as a result of the trading operations of the Stroganov family, which had been assigned large estates near the Urals and given permission to extract metals and salt and to extend its domain beyond the mountains. The Stroganovs had a private army, formed of Cossacks and the haphazard bands of Lithuanian and Muscovite fugitives who roamed the southern Russian steppe. One of these Cossacks, Yermak, who was under sentence of death for rebellion, led about one hundred fifty freebooters into Siberia in September 1581. By 1582 he had a hold on two great Siberian rivers, the Irtysh and the Obi. In return for a full pardon and a few presents, he handed over his conquests to the Moscow crown. This marked the beginning of the long Russian advance to the Pacific Ocean, which was reached by 1643, mainly through a process of permeation, with very few armed conflicts and scarcely any government help at all.

The annexation of Kazan and Astrakhan did not end the Tatar danger, since the southern border was still subject to invasion at will by the Tatars impregnably ensconced in the Crimea. These Crimean Tatars were not interested in territorial acquisition but in booty, primarily in the form of prisoners of war. They flooded the slave markets of Europe, Africa, and Asia with people dragged from Muscovy, Lithuania, and Poland. Their raids were endless. In 1571 they laid siege to Moscow, burnt its suburbs, and carried off some 150,000 captives; the next year they followed this up by sending in an army of 120,000 to invade Russia, this time being stopped before getting to Moscow.

Moscow in fact remained in a state of permanent tension because of the Tatars, with an added element of danger in the Tatars' willingness to ally themselves with Russia's enemies in the west.

Under Ivan it was only in the east that Russia began expanding; it never broke through to the Baltic Sea. This was made up for to some extent by the unexpected discovery by some Englishmen of a new maritime route to Western Europe in 1553; but the route involved crossing the White Sea, and so was much inferior to a warm-water route. It had the odd by-product of anchoring British tradesmen in Russian life for a long time to come; the leader of the expedition, Richard Chancellor, was treated very well by Ivan, who developed a great fancy for the English and gave the Muscovy Company of London very valuable monopolistic privileges. Characteristically, this did not stop Ivan from arresting all the English merchants and confiscating their goods after his failure to secure an English alliance. He expressed his irritation in a letter to Queen Elizabeth, calling her a "common slut."

Apart from the territorial expansion he encouraged, Ivan's main achievement was the creation of a complete vacuum around the Moscow autocracy, consummating the process of suppressing all other sources of power and many old institutions in favor of the unification of the realm set in motion by Ivan the Great and Basil III. Ivan the Terrible, however, by elevating the executive power above the melee, did not devise an instrument for quieting the turmoil; on the contrary, he ruled out any but an explosive solution.

By the end of Ivan's reign the whole country had been churned up. The older aristocracy found itself expelled from its ancestral lands, deprived of most of its influence, and forcibly dragooned into the service of the state. Many individual aristocrats had been tortured to death or executed. Landowners, both boyars and the descendants of former ruling princes, were staring ruin in the face because of the dearth of manpower on their estates. In addition, the military expenditures involved in Ivan's ruinous wars constituted an intolerable burden.

Nor was there any compensation to be looked for in the parvenu class, the rapidly increasing service people—those with land-grants subject to military service. In the sixteenth century this was a very motley group drawn from every social element, including slaves. The size of the land-grant might have been a mere parcel of land with only one peasant household on it; it might even have been farmed by the service-noble. The diversification of elements in the parvenu nobility precluded any solidarity.

The dearth of manpower, especially in the central and western areas, led to tremendous competition among the landlords for available hands. The country, never densely inhabited in any case, was now depopulated because of the general state of disorder, the military defeats caused by Ivan's abortive attempts to break through to the Baltic, and the repeated raids of the Tatars, especially the invasions of 1571 and 1572 mentioned above. Also, the combination of the expansion eastward plus the spread of service tenure, with its creation of a new class of agricultural overseers in the shape of the motley beneficiaries of the land-grants, emptied out the country eastward to some extent and also to the southern steppe, where the free life of the Cossacks attracted many. As in Kievan Russia, huge numbers of people simply began drifting away.

The regime had a twofold reason to halt this migratory movement: not only was it deprived of potential taxpayers by the mass exodus, but the very foundations of the military class it depended on were undermined. It was essential to find a way out of the cul-de-sac inherent in the worthlessness of a service-holding without manpower; the measures developed to solve this problem were, as we shall see, the source of the gradual imposition of bondage on the bulk of the population that became known as serfdom.

The competition for manpower was particularly burdensome for the smaller service-nobles since the greater lords, both secular and ecclesiastical, could secure tax exemptions from the state that enabled them in their turn to promise their tenants lower taxation. Such tax exemptions were given most often to the big landlords, especially to the Church. In the long run, of course, these promises did the tenant no good, since the additional burdens would more than counterbalance the slight, though immediate, tax savings. But it goes without saying that few tenants were in a position to think of the long run.

Now, a tenant could leave the land he worked if he settled his debt to his landlord, and since he was scarcely ever able to find the money he needed, he would have to turn for help to a prospective landlord. This increased the advantage of the wealthy landlords even more; on top of all this, the devastation likely to befall a service-holding with no tenants made it easy for a big landlord, particularly a monastery, to take it over. The service-nobles were thus in frightful straits; there was a tremendous clamor for relief that was never given.

On the other hand, while the smaller landlords were squeezed by the bigger, the landed class as a whole was bound to benefit by the peasants' indebtedness. Hence it was to their interest to halt the flight of the tenants with the support of the state. An illustration of the tenants' plight is a provision in the Code of 1550 that canceled the usual restrictions on giving up tenancy if the tenant sold himself into slavery.

Thus, since an indebted tenant could be bought off as a rule only by some other landlord, and since there was keen competition for manpower, whenever the time came for tenants to be transferred—during the fortnight before and after

St. George's Day—the violent outbursts accompanying the transfer would reach their height. Petty landowners would often take up arms to resist the big landlords' recruiting agent, sack the houses of tenants who wanted to leave them, and actually shackle the tenants.

It was these two roots, the combination of the fiscal regime of the Moscow state and the burden of peasant indebtedness, that gradually gave rise to serfdom, which evolved in a spasmodic, piecemeal, but relentless fashion, to be consummated in the middle of the seventeenth century. During Ivan the Terrible's reign the circumstances referred to above accelerated this process of tenant enslavement.

This process was eased only slightly by the opening up of the lands to the east. The newly acquired territories were soon distributed as service land in their turn; fugitives from the steady march of serfdom kept finding the same system catching up with them. The other refuge, the southern steppe that separated Muscovy from the Crimean Tatars, also attracted many. In the sixteenth century the entire area north of the Black Sea was teeming with fugitives from Muscovy, Poland, and Lithuania. A Turkish word, Cossack, was applied to them; with a loose, semi-military organization under an elected leader, they lived by banditry and mercenary soldiering.

There was a parallel pattern to this in the cities, which in general were very slow in developing. Throughout Russia's history, especially the early history, its cities were generally trading-posts or military establishments; production was the last thing to develop. Primarily interested in collecting taxes, the government tried to centralize commercial activities in a restricted number of localities, thus hindering the growth of commerce. The richer merchants would be appointed revenue agents by the state; without direct payment for their services they had to depend on exemption from taxes and on the jurisdiction of ordinary courts. Thus they had to be rich in order to ensure the carrying out of their duties. With such privileges being granted the richest merchants, the other burghers had to make up for the gap in the tax yield. In the social stratification promoted by this process, the underprivileged burghers found themselves struggling for existence. Their situation was made still more difficult by the thronging into the cities of military officials who, since they were not supposed to be in trade, were exempt from burghers' taxes, though in fact they took advantage of their immunity to compete with the burghers on more favorable terms. Big landlords, especially the monasteries, would start competitive businesses run by their tenants or slaves on their estates next to the trading centers.

Because of all this the cities began expiring slowly; the urban population also began drifting away, and the government was compelled to nail down the urban burghers to their shops and trades just as it had tried to do with the peasants in the countryside.

The Moscow regime thus found itself caught in a situation that was inherently contradictory: in order to be able to benefit fiscally from the labor of the population, it had to tie people down, and when it tied people down the exacerbated conditions led to even greater distress. The state's reaction to the immense turbulence it was itself responsible for throughout the country was a ruthless straitjacketing that wiped out all vestiges of freedom.

The Russians are the only people in recorded history who have been completely enslaved by themselves. Slaves have generally been people uprooted by brute force and transported elsewhere, as a rule in the wake of wars. But Russian history so worked out that almost the whole of the population was enslaved by its own leaders.

The ruthless concentration of authority in the Moscow state, consummated during the reign of Ivan the Terrible, plus the disastrous evolution of socio-economic conditions throughout the rapidly growing country, soon led to an extraordinary upheaval, which, though prepared for over many decades, was launched by a dynastic crisis.

In 1581, Ivan, in a fit of rage, killed his son and heir, personally, with a metal-tipped staff he used to carry; the young man had apparently been trying to shield his pregnant wife against his father's brutality. Ivan spent a good deal of time repenting, but when he died in 1584—characteristically after taking monastic vows on his death-bed—the only heir to the throne was his remaining feebleminded son, Theodore, who died in 1598. His death extinguished the Muscovite dynasty and led directly to the "Time of Troubles."

CHAPTER IV

PETER THE GREAT

*T*he years that followed Ivan's death were full of ungoverna-
ble turbulence. Since Ivan's successor, Tsar Theodore,
was feebleminded (wholly concentrated on the ringing of
churchbells), his brother-in-law, Boris Godunov, who had been
a favorite of Ivan the Terrible's, took advantage of his sister's
influence over the sickly Tsar and made himself the *de facto*
ruler of the country. Boris was thus the temporary victor
in the dense swarm of palace intrigues and internecine boyar
conflicts that had broken out upon Ivan the Terrible's death.
These intrigues, far too complex for even a brief summation,
were rooted in the bitterness between the ancient nobility—
Shuiskys, Vorotynskys, Golitsyns, Kurakins—and the less distinguished families that may be referred to as the nobility based
on court influence, such as the Romanovs and Godunovs.

Godunov established himself so thoroughly that, on Tsar
Theodore's death without issue, he easily arranged to have
himself elected Tsar by a so-called Territorial Assembly; the
election did no more than inflame the old intrigues all over
again. Godunov, formerly considered charming and amiable,

soon lost his appeal. The upper classes found themselves in much the same situation as under Ivan the Terrible, with deportations, confiscations, and executions everyday events.

All this was climaxed by a great famine that lasted from 1601 to 1603. Both merchants and landlords became profiteers; confiscations were accompanied by the release of slaves, who were forbidden to find another master, while many other slaves were merely turned out to forage for themselves. Banditry grew rife; the flood of peasants already drifting away from the encroachments of serfdom was increased by a torrent of famished and dislocated refugees.

The general disaffection crystallized in the False Dmitri, a pretender to the throne—the first of many—who with the assistance of the Polish government led a movement against Godunov. Dmitri claimed to be a son of Ivan the Terrible, who in his account was supposed to have died in 1591 under enigmatic circumstances. Dmitri's actual identity seems irremediably obscure. In any case, in 1603 the False Dmitri took up headquarters with Mniszek, an adventurous Polish nobleman. Dmitri had numerous Polish connections—he even married his host's daughter, Marina—but his emergence was mostly a reflection of the disaffection among the boyar groups, primarily, no doubt, the Romanovs, who ultimately benefited by his enterprise. The whole Romanov clan had been accused by Godunov of having used witchcraft in an attempt to usurp Godunov's crown; the head of the family, Theodore Romanov, father of the future Tsar Michael, had been forced to become a monk, under the name of Philaret, in a distant monastery where he was kept imprisoned.

Dmitri assembled an army of some 3,500 to 4,000 men—a random assortment of Polish knights, soldiers of fortune, and runaway Russian peasants. Polish complicity enabled Dmitri to organize this group on Polish terrain, but the army's quick successes were due not to Polish support but to the feebleness of the Moscow regime. The unruly Cossacks and discontented small landowners of the southern regions went over to Dmitri in a body, as did many of the petty nobles and burghers; the Russians in fact engulfed the small Polish core of his army.

When Godunov died unexpectedly in 1605, the pretender made a triumphal entry into Moscow.

But the False Dmitri's anti-Godunov coalition fell apart at once because of its contradictory composition. The boyars hoped for a restoration of their ancient privileges; the petty nobles wanted bigger land-grants, more money, and a tighter grip on the peasants working their estates; the peasants, especially the Cossacks, longed for land and freedom; the foreign mercenaries clamored for their pay; the Jesuits and Polish clericals intrigued for a reunion of the two churches under the Vatican.

These conflicting currents undid the pretender, who was murdered by May 1606, as they ruined the next Tsar, Basil Shuisky, who was appointed by the aristocracy without even a pretense of formality. A scion of the senior branch of the house of Rurik, with no reservations about absolutism, Basil represented, socially speaking, the people who had appointed him, which immediately made him the target of the radically inclined Cossack masses and small landowners.

For the first time in Russian history, a movement of disaffection was launched that injected a social element into the dynastic conflicts. A runaway slave, Ivan Bolotnikov, rallied the fugitive peasants and slaves who made up the main body of the Cossacks, and under the guise of restoring Dmitri he proclaimed a program of social revolution, which included the slaughter of the upper classes, the incitement of the poor against the rich and of the peasants and slaves against their masters, and the redistribution of the land, wealth, and women held by the oppressors.

This movement, which fought, oddly enough, together with a detachment of some of the petty service-nobility, came within sight of Moscow by October 1606; here, as it turned out, the very extremism of Bolotnikov's movement enabled Tsar Boris Shuisky to rally round himself the proprietary and conservative groups appalled by Bolotnikov's aims. Bolotnikov quickly lost his allies among the nobility; his movement was suppressed by the most savage means. The rebel provinces, about a third of the country, were flung open to plunder;

thousands of prisoners were executed, a great many by slow drowning, a peculiarly cruel form of torture.

Pretenders sprang up like mushrooms in 1607–8. A score of rebels took the name of Tsarevich: imaginations were strained to provide the flimsiest of connections with the Moscow dynasty. The most effective of these pretenders became famous as the Tushino Bandit, so called from the location of his headquarters, set up in the spring of 1608, in Tushino, a few miles from Moscow. Even less is known about this second False Dmitri, as he was also known, than about the first. In his case there was not even a pretense of belief in his dynastic claims. To be sure, the names taken by all the impostors were merely a pretext for attacking the official regime.

Shuisky appealed to foreign governments for help, as well as to the Russian cities whose support he could depend on. But perhaps the chief reason for the failure of the Tushino Bandit's rebellion was its invasion of the northern provinces, which were not so disaffected as the southern and had continued to enjoy a slight degree of self-government, which was disregarded entirely by the Polish mercenaries, Russian gentry, and Cossacks in the Bandit's entourage. Even the northern peasants resented the bandit's savagery; by 1610 the siege of Moscow had fallen apart.

For two years Tushino played the role of a second capital because of the radical instability of Shuisky's regime. An unusual number of boyars, churchmen, nobles, functionaries, merchants, and commoners kept switching back and forth between Tushino and Moscow, hoping for the best. As the price of their slippery support, they traded the grants and promotions they managed to secure from Shuisky for still greater benefits from the Bandit, and the other way round. It was the desperation of both camps and the country's exhaustion that made this situation possible. One of the chief notables in the Bandit's camp, for instance, was Philaret Romanov, who while presumably a prisoner was revered by the insurgents as their patriarch.

When things looked black for the Bandit, Philaret Romanov

and the Tushino aristocracy turned to Poland and signed an agreement in February 1610 that made the Polish King's son Tsar of Muscovy while ensuring the inviolability of the existing Russian state and the Orthodox Church.

Shuisky finally had to abdicate. Polish troops occupied Moscow and the Kremlin, whereupon Sigismund, the King of Poland, made an attempt to get the throne for himself, not his son. This infuriated everyone; in addition it aroused the anti-Catholic mood of the masses, and for that matter irritated the Swedes, who had joined the Polish-led anti-Shuisky coalition while at the same time becoming rivals of the Poles on the Baltic coast. (The Swedes actually launched a False Dmitri of their own.)

From the Russian point of view, the Protestant Swedes in Novgorod, the Catholic Poles in Moscow, and the huge bands of brigands roaming about the country were a sign of utter political devastation. This chaos was finally ended by a popular uprising, instigated, curiously enough, by a wealthy butcher, Kuzma Minin, who together with a Prince Pozharsky defeated the Poles. Russia was confronted by the urgent need of settling once and for all on a Tsar who would be genuinely accepted.

A Territorial Assembly began forming in Moscow in January 1613; though there is hardly any information about it, this may be the first representative group ever to have convened there. The numerous candidates for the throne included many foreigners, among them some Habsburgs, but eventually Michael Romanov, a quite unknown boy of sixteen, was elected in February and proclaimed Tsar.

Michael was chosen as a compromise between conservative and radical elements. He was favored partly because of his family status, since the Romanovs were related to the house of Rurik and had been immersed in Moscow court affairs for a few hundred years; he was also a nephew of Ivan the Terrible's son, Theodore: both factors made him attractive to the legitimists. From a different angle, since his father Philaret had been made Metropolitan of Rostov by the first False Dmitri and Patriarch by the second, the Romanovs were ensured the backing of the Cossacks.

But perhaps what promoted Michael's candidacy most was his insignificance. This was taken by many of his backers at the Territorial Assembly to mean pliability. He was so little known that the delegation sent by the Assembly to offer him the crown had no idea where he was.

In spite of all the social turmoil that had been going on for fifteen years, the new Tsar ascended the throne with no limitation whatsoever on his power. He was invested with all the traditional absolutism of the autocracy developed by Ivan the Terrible and his forebears.

For that matter, the country had not changed in the slightest during the preceding period of anarchy; it was the same, only more exhausted. It had had a social upheaval expressed in various ways and under various leaders with an unmistakable element of revolutionary unrest; dynasties had changed kaleidoscopically, foreign powers had invaded the country, there had been the devastation, impoverishment, and slaughter typical of civil wars, but nothing had been changed in the state structure. Indeed, though it was undoubtedly the revolutionary nature of the Time of Troubles, both comprehensive and profound, that accounts for the extravagant churning up of the whole country, the strangest thing about it is the total subsidence of the whole movement. The masses of peasants and slaves were given back to their masters; the institution of serfdom emerged from the chaos rejuvenated and stronger than ever—the foundation of the Muscovite state.

Nor did the number of parvenus represent a change in the state's structure. On the contrary, the Time of Troubles, which had accelerated the political decomposition of the old boyar and princely families, merely replaced them with a different group of service-nobles who owed their wealth and power to the Tsar's favor. This rounded off a process begun with the unification of the realm under Ivan the Terrible's immediate forebears and consummated by his *oprichnina*.

The formation of this new social group, distinct from the old families, had been well advanced during the sixteenth century; the Time of Troubles made the process irrevocable. For that matter the parvenus who had rocketed to the surface wanted to make themselves respectable as quickly as possible; they had no interest in overhauling society. As for the Church, throughout the storm and stress of the civil war, neither its vast estates nor its old privileges were touched.

The primordial chaos of the Time of Troubles is another illustration of Russia's political inarticulateness—none of the currents of unrest was capable of creating a new idea or even a new slogan to symbolize its dissidence. The peasants followed only leaders who claimed the authority of the Tsarist tradition; the royal principle was indispensable as the theoretical justification of any movement, however lawless in essence. It was the contradictory combination of royalist legalism, organizational incapacity, and the leaders' shortsightedness that was responsible for the inherent sterility of all the dissident movements; they inevitably slumped back into the old forms.

When Michael ascended the throne, the first of a line that was to last three hundred years, the country was ruined. Foreign travelers reported that to stop for the night in abandoned villages they had to sleep on their sledges—the stench of rotting corpses still filled the huts. The collapse of the country was almost total: villages and towns were abandoned wholesale, fields were rapidly becoming woods again, and the commercial communities had deteriorated completely.

The classic answer to this desperate situation was flight. The mass desertion of taxpayers undermined the treasury and dried up the manpower reserves needed for the army and the fields; it also increased the tax burden of those remaining. The only solution that occurred to the Moscow regime remained one of strict regimentation. A police-state gradually formed, the institutional expression of absolutist theory.

During the sixteenth century, the growth of serfdom was accentuated by some other factors. The practice, formerly permitted, of serving a lord personally without losing one's personal liberty—distinct from tenancy, since it had nothing to do with the use of land—was drastically reduced. The celebrated Code of Laws *(Ulozhenie)* of 1649 laid down that anyone who served a lord even for three months renounced his status as a freeman. It also became usual during the second quarter of the seventeenth century for a tenant to give his landlord a written promise to live on the land assigned him until his death: this amounted to a renunciation of his former right to give up his tenancy, which meant that the tenant's dependence on his landlord, formerly based on his indebtedness, now assumed the character of a contract.

This was a reflection of the government's need to pin down its taxpayers, since peasants still paid taxes and did so even after becoming serfs.

But the peasants could still run away; the government constricted them still further, in the Code of 1649, by abolishing any limit on the time runaways could be searched for. This enabled squires to recover runaway peasants whenever they found them and riveted the tenant to his landlord even more strongly than before. What had been a contractual relation now became a hereditary one backed by law.

The situation, though altogether incoherent in its juridical formulation, ultimately boiled down to forging a link between the servile population and the person of the landlord. The tendency developed for bondsmen no longer to be attached to the land itself, but to be bound over to the landlord as *individuals*. The Code of 1649 and other legislation never defined the personal services the landlord was entitled to, nor did it define the property rights of the bondsmen.

In fact, from the middle of the seventeenth century on, what had once been a clear-cut line of division between former peasant tenants and slaves tended to vanish, despite the survival of some technicalities that were not wiped out until a decree of January 1723 laid a poll-tax on the whole servile population.

For generations the service-nobility exhausted itself in cantankerous disputes about fugitive serfs. They were so preoccupied by the problem of keeping the serfs tied down that they were quite unable to curb the powers of the autocracy; indeed, since they derived their privileges only from the whim of the sovereign, they had no desire to. Relations between master and man were dominated by a hunt for runaway serfs, in which churchmen and monasteries vied with secular landlords in ferocity and imaginativeness.

This hunt was naturally taken up by the peasants themselves: landlords were assassinated right and left, manor houses burnt. The situation reached an extreme point in the revolt, still celebrated in folk-songs today, of Stenka Razin, who started a campaign against Moscow in the summer of 1670. Once again this campaign was not aimed at the Tsar but at the boyars and landlords. Peasants rushed to slaughter their masters and joined Razin *en masse,* but despite his initial successes, which gave him control of the Volga River from its mouth to Simbirsk, and after exterminating landlords wholesale he was defeated and executed in 1671.

Razin's movement had been typically spontaneous and shapelessly ferocious. Its persistence as a motif in the folk imagination doubtless reflects the permanence of conditions underlying Razin's career; the legend has it that he miraculously escaped death, eluded his executioners, and turned up a century later during the reign of Catherine the Great. The paradox of Razin's career was characteristic of Russian society of the time—while even the most extremist elements of society vehemently proclaimed their devotion to the crown, the Tsar himself was in terror of his own people.

The Time of Troubles had given vent to so many different kinds of social pressure that in the seventeenth century, for the first time in its history, the unity of the Russian Church itself was destroyed, and in a way that was far more radical than the relative pinpricks of the Judaizing and rationalist heresies of two centuries before. The piety of the people had been shaken by Russia's afflictions—wholesale impoverishment, devastations of war, treacheries of boyars and princes, bogus Tsars, and heretics ruling in the very heart of Russia. The Russian Church was feeble in every way: politically because of its total subjection to the state power, morally in its indifference to the secular order amidst its material self-aggrandizement, and intellectually in the inability of its authorities to contrive moral or mystical content for the rigidly maintained superstructure of rites and dogmas.

The repercussions of the Protestant Reformation had penetrated as far as Moscow, to some extent via the influence of

Kiev, which finally re-entered the Russian orbit as a result of a peace treaty made by Muscovy with Poland and Turkey in the aftermath of a war that had gone on intermittently from 1672 to 1681. The Ukrainians also brought a Western influence to Moscow. Finally, there was an influx of outright foreigners into Muscovy. Catholics, Lutherans, Calvinists, all sorts of heterodox elements seemed to be corroding the one true faith of the Russian Church. At Narva, Swedes were attacking Orthodoxy in works printed in Russian; foreign Protestants had a temple in the Foreign Suburb of Moscow; Poles had planted some Roman Catholic seeds during the Time of Troubles. Some boyars had stopped wearing their long robes and were even cutting their beards to the scandal of the right-thinking. Tobacco had penetrated the customs of the people in spite of the punishment smokers were subject to—the slashing away of their nostrils.

The Patriarch Nikon, who was venerated by Michael Romanov's son, the pious Tsar Alexis, undertook a reform of the Church, actually no reform at all but simply a return to some ancient usages of the Byzantine Church that involved minute changes in the phrasing of certain texts retranslated from the Greek, a slightly altered spelling of Jesus's name, the use of three instead of two fingers in making the sign of the cross, saying *hallelujah* three times instead of twice during church services, and having religious processions walk in the direction of the sun instead of against it.

The contrast between the triviality of these reforms and the incredible violence with which they were opposed indicates the degree of Russian insulation against humanizing influences. The virulent concentration on such bagatelles, unconnected with any dogmatic changes, illustrated the purely magical value of the rites and formulae of the Russian Church. For example, Tsar Alexis was so pious that he often stood in church for five or six hours on end; at the great festivals he would prostrate himself fifteen hundred times; his library contained six notebooks of religious music, copied in his own hand. His chief counselor was Basil Barefoot, an "innocent," i.e., one of the psychopathic mystics the country had always been full of.

Nikon's enterprise sprang, of course, out of a broad cultural context, but the narrowmindedness of the Russian clergy made them regard any deviation whatever from established custom as heresy and blasphemy. Their underlying reasoning was that the credit of the Byzantine Church had been gravely impaired by its having accepted the notion of union with the Vatican at the Council of Florence. In spite of its later repudiation of Rome, the Byzantine Church's debased status under Muslim rule in Turkey was taken to be a sign of divine wrath, reflected by its inability to keep the purity of the ancient faith.

Nikon himself, completely fanatical, eventually brought about a breach with Tsar Alexis, despite the latter's veneration, by proclaiming the primacy of the ecclesiastical power over the secular and by repudiating the limitations in the Code of 1649 on the Church's traditional privileges in jurisdiction and landownership. Nikon's high-handedness created enemies everywhere; in the upshot, the dispute about details broadened into an actual schism. The dissenters rejected Nikon's trivial alterations as heresy and called themselves the "Old Believers"; they were anathematized in 1677.

The Old Believers' heresy was handled by the government, which backed the church reform despite Nikon's falling out with the Tsar, the same way Christianity had been introduced into Russia—by fire and sword. In 1681 Avvakum, the most famous of the dissenters, a talented, fanatical priest and the only gifted writer of the period, was burned at the stake. His party regarded the changes in spelling and the number of fingers used in making the sign of the cross as cardinal criteria of Christianity itself. Meanwhile, the masses of the peasantry, the burghers, and many of the nobility felt desperate at the prospect of being deprived by the state of the hope of eternal salvation.

Avvakum and his disciples thought Nikon's changes in spelling heralded the advent of the Anti-Christ; the ardor of the movement expressed itself in an epidemic of mass suicide by burning. The dissenters considered this martyr's death preferable to being burned forever in the eternal flames. They thought the end of the world was on them once again. In any case

it was supposed to take place in 1666 or 1669. When it failed
to turn up, new calculations were made, fixing the date at
1698. Between 1672 and 1691, when the movement slacked
off, 20,000 people immolated themselves, sometimes as many
as 2,500 at a time, especially after a ukaze of 1684 threatened
heretics with burning at the stake. Groups of people would
lock themselves into huts filled with hay or tar and burn themselves to death.

The dissenting movement, nourished by political and social
factors, proved indestructible. Its stronghold was in the remote
and almost unapproachable timbered wilderness of the north
and northeast, spreading to Siberia along the Volga to the
regions of the Don and Dnieper. The Old Believers also found
a good deal of Cossack support, which gave this religious
controversy a revolutionary tinge, since the schism provided
an axis for the expression of discontent. The Church lost some
of its most pious followers, since the loyalty of those who
stayed in the official fold was a reflection only of fear, and
it found itself still more dependent on the state, the police,
and the army.

The intellectual level on which these profound internal
stresses of Russian society expressed themselves was remarkably low. The movement of the Old Believers might, hyperbol-
ically, be called a counter-reformation, if Nikon's reforms could
legitimately be compared with the Reformation. When the
Protestants of the West shook loose of the Roman Catholic
Church, they turned upside down the whole universe of
thought and usage; the struggle was waged in the name of
definite and peremptory principles. Protestantism also induced
a counter-reaction within the Catholic Church itself, actually
reinvigorating it. But for all its blind violence, the Russian
dispute produced nothing but dissident sects mouldering in
a dogmatic and intellectual penury that could resist the official
Church only because that was more penurious still.

No new prospects were opened up either by the official
churchmen or by the Old Believers. The intellectual isolation
of Russia is demonstrated most dramatically by this mindless
schism; Muscovy had not been touched by a single movement

of the European Middle Ages. In the period of Louis XIV, Muscovy had the look of eleventh-century France. Europe had been utterly transformed, with a religious civilization succeeded by a secular civilization and a substance economy succeeded by the money economy that gave rise to modern capitalism; in such a Europe, Muscovy was an anachronism. In France, for instance, the bourgeoisie had enriched itself, and while still outside the administration of the state was immensely powerful socially. Europe had been set in ferment intellectually by the Reformation, by the Renaissance, by the invention of printing, and by the discovery of America. Muscovy remained practically untouched.

With rare exceptions, the Russian upper classes had no education at all. If the boyar could read, he read nothing but works of piety or a romance translated from some foreign language; there were no native writers. The rich folk-lore and folk-literature of the peasants, an immense cultural treasurehouse, was completely outside the interests or knowledge of the upper classes. Both Nikonians and Old Believers had the same attitude: while the latter rejected any changes at all, however trivial, the Nikonians themselves believed solely in a return to the Greek source of the religion. Both parties were incapable of intellectualizing their positions by devising new ideas; thus both clung to the dead letter of essentially unintelligible doctrines.

The Church in Russia lacked the strength to stamp out heresy, as the Inquisition had succeeded in doing in Spain and Italy. The fervor of the dissidents kept generating new sects, and once this process of breaking away from the mother Church was launched with no intellectual inspiration to guide the wanderers, there was nothing to act as a curb on fantasy.

At the very beginning of the schism there was a fission between the "moderates," who accepted priests ordained before Nikon, and the extremists, who preferred to live with no sacraments at all rather than be tainted by Nikonianism. The latter came to be known as the "priestless": they spread chiefly in the northern wilderness, where the custom, rooted in necessity, of dispensing with priests had already been prevalent; settlers had to baptize their children themselves and confess to each other.

The knotty question of whether marriage was possible without an official blessing was given a special answer by the sect of the White Doves; they thought the simplest way out of the dilemma was to castrate themselves. The flagellants, on the other hand, would dress in long white blouses and whip themselves while chanting hymns; when they had reached a climax of ecstasy, they would have a collective orgy. Other sects were quieter, such as the Milk-Drinkers and the celebrated Spirit-Wrestlers, or Dukhobors, who eventually moved to their present location in Canada.

Regardless of the absence of intellectual content in all this sectarianism, the schism was the first time Russian peasants and burghers were infected by an emotion tinged with social protest, an emotion they were willing to sacrifice their lives for. In this sense the schism, infused by a substantial element of non-egotistic rebelliousness, takes its place by the side of the persistent rebellions of the peasant masses after Bolotnikov.

It may not be far-fetched to think that this deep-rooted, anti-intellectual spirit of sectarianism has remained a persistent trait of Russian life into the modern era, culminating in the endlessly casuistical political discussions during the nineteenth and twentieth centuries in the most intellectual of the sectarian groups—the revolutionaries.

For centuries Russia was a unique combination of dreariness, coarseness, and brutality. Debauchery, drunkenness, and illiteracy were universal. The courtiers around the sovereign were not courtiers in any European sense; there was nothing sociable about the life of the court. Upper-class women, including the Tsarina, were secluded in a Byzantine type of harem: they never went out unless heavily veiled; they looked on at palace ceremonies from behind a gallery grillwork. The Kremlin had the aspect of a convent, night-club, and shop simultaneously. Church services were frequent and long, drinking on feast-days was tremendous, and Russian noblemen spent most of their time discussing sales of hemp, furs, and tar.

Ignorance was profound. Secular reading was out of the

question, nor was any foreign language known. Even in the highest clergy, those who knew Greek were rare exceptions. At a Territorial Assembly in 1648, 141 of the 292 delegates were quite illiterate—and the Assembly was supposed to be of the "best people in the Russian land." When the Patriarch Philaret, father of Michael, the first Romanov Tsar, wanted to learn Latin, he had to ask an Englishman who happened to be passing through Moscow to write down a few words for him in Russian characters.

Nobody learned to read or write at all except the Tsar, future priests, and children of the wealthiest boyars. It was not until 1696 that Latin was made part of the curriculum at the Ecclesiastical Academy newly opened in Moscow. At the end of the sixteenth century, when the Papal Legate Possevinus spent some time in Moscow, only one member of the Boyar Duma knew any Latin. Though a few people knew Polish, they were nearly all clergymen; a great many of the boyars could not read or write at all.

Business preoccupied the Muscovite gentry. Possevinus was astounded at seeing Russian envoys, supposed to be negotiating peace with Poland, set up shop on the side in order to sell some goods they had brought from Moscow. The Tsar himself set the example: he was the country's chief businessman, monopolizing the sale of vodka and furs as well as the sale abroad of caviar and cod liver oil. He actually rented out from his personal wardrobe festive garments for marriages.

The extraordinarily low standard of culture obliterated any serious differentiation between the classes. The boyar, merchant, and peasant, even the priest, were all equally boorish. There was a vacuum between the aristocracy and the plebeians, since there was no genuine middle class. The bourgeoisie was not marked either by education or by social function; both aristocrats and plebeians had the same manners.

Moral standards were equally primitive. In the arranged marriages, a trick was commonly played on the bridegroom by switching a less attractive daughter on him at the last moment. Homosexuality was widespread and a favorite topic of comedy; few pains were taken to conceal it.

Though there was a trickle of learning in spite of all this, and though printing gradually increased the amount of reading material for the few who could read, there was scarcely any progress. Mathematics, for instance, made none at all. Arabic numerals were not used generally until the eighteenth century; because of the use of Slavonic characters, hardly anyone could go beyond addition and subtraction. The only textbook used in the seventeenth century was an adaptation of something more than a hundred years old. Euclid, who had been rediscovered by Western Europe during the twelfth century, was not given the Russians until 1719. Algebra and trigonometry were not available until 1730, when the first textbooks were published. Copernicus, Kepler, Galileo, and Newton might never have existed. Ideas concerning medicine and natural history were still taken from the scholastic handbooks of the thirteenth and fourteenth centuries.

Though the schism gave some impetus, paradoxically, to the advancement of theological studies because of the Church's excommunication of the Old Believers, who damned Western science and thus made the Church in its turn relatively more indulgent toward learning, obscurantism remained widespread. No one was allowed to have a teacher of any foreign language, including Greek and Latin, without the permission of the Slavonic-Greek-Latin Academy. Only the graduates of this Academy were allowed to own foreign language books or to discuss religious questions even in private. Foreign scholars could come to Russia only with this Academy's permission, and they had to be supervised. Anyone expressing any doubt whatever concerning Greek Orthodoxy was liable to Siberian exile. Conversion to any other faith, or any slighting remarks about orthodoxy, ikons, or holy relics were punished by the stake.

But this apparently solid wall of parochial self-centeredness had too many chinks and crevices to keep Old Russia watertight. By the end of the seventeenth century, in spite of everything, a small stream of foreign culture had seeped through that linked Russia with Western thought. Physical contact with Europeans had of course long since been established. Ever since the end of the fifteenth century foreigners had been trick-ling into Moscow looking for gain; Chancellor had counted three hundred of them at Ivan the Terrible's court. Popular xenophobia had kept foreigners confined in a sort of ghetto called the Foreign Suburb, which after a lengthy interruption during the Time of Troubles was restored in 1652, to survive well into the eighteenth century.

Even the first Romanovs, historically speaking all nonenti-ties, had had to use foreigners to develop Russia's much needed natural resources. It was plain to the few thoughtful members of the upper class that something had to be done to reform Russia, if only technically. Out of the seventy years between the first Romanov's accession and the death of Peter the Great's father, the Muscovite autocracy was at war for about thirty, sometimes fighting on several fronts at once. It had focussed the attention of both the rebellious masses and liberally minded upper-class individuals on its slovenliness. A change of pace and direction was needed, a serious effort to catch up with and pass the West, to use a phrase put forward by the Soviet government more than two hundred years later.

This change was begun by Peter the Great; by the time he appeared, Russia had fallen so far behind that the whole of society seemed to need recasting. Peter was to encounter opposition, but it must be recalled that he was backed by the bulk of the service-nobility and a small but active minority of the mercantile community. The conventional picture of Peter as a titan fighting against terrible odds on behalf of civilization, or conversely of a tyrant obliged to overcome universal recalci-trance, is highly misleading.

Peter was born in 1672, the fourteenth child of the pious Tsar Alexis by his second wife, a member of the Naryshkin clan. Alexis's first wife had been a Miloslavsky, by whom he had three sons and six daughters; the resulting situation was so confused, when Alexis's first son died in 1682 after a brief reign, that it triggered a flare-up of intrigues between the two clans.

In the Russia of his time Peter might have come from another planet, or even from nineteenth-century America. He had an altogether secular, democratic view of life. Physically huge, with fabulous energy and stamina, he grew up completely outside of and indifferent to the traditional life of Muscovy. He was self-made; he never learned any grammar or spelling, and had scarcely any formal education.

He was soon enthralled by the purely material achievements of European civilization in the form of the scraps of technical information he picked up hanging about the motley assortment of expatriates in the Foreign Suburb, which he became familiar with before he was twenty. He made his first contact with Western civilization, in fact, through a friendship with a Dutch seaman; throughout his life he retained the dress, speech, and bearing of his first Western tutor. Western Europe, as represented in the Foreign Suburb, dominated his mind as long as he lived.

As a boy Peter lived most of his life in a small village, where he collected a large group of young men of the lowest social origins to drill with. Beginning when he was only eleven years old, though exceptionally well developed, he turned them into the nucleus of a military force. His taste for low companions continued throughout his life; one of the "stable-boys," a childhood friend he seems to have been in love with, the illiterate, unscrupulous, ambitious, and beautiful Menshikov, who had started life as a street-peddler, was one of the most powerful figures in the state even after Peter's death.

Peter's inner circle was bound together by liquor and debauchery. Their orgies were distinguished by a complicated and imaginative ceremonial devised by Peter. Unlike other interests, erratic and fleeting, these orgies remained a constant preoccupation.

When he was eighteen he organized his disreputable associates in a sort of satirical society called "The Most Drunken Assembly of Fools and Jesters," sworn to the worship of Venus and Bacchus and with an elaborate ceremonial parodying both the Roman Catholic and the Greek Orthodox Churches. In this drunken hierarchy, Peter was a mere deacon. This ostentatious humbling of himself was characteristic. In the procession celebrating his first signal military success, the capture of Azov on the Black Sea, he marched in the ranks himself, dressed as a naval captain.

There are voluminous records in Peter's own hand describing the structure and activities of this Assembly. People had to take part in public celebrations in which a stellar role was assigned the Assembly, or else they would be liable to severe punishment. Parades and masquerades that lasted for days on end had to be attended by the royal family and court and state functionaries, as well as by diplomats, all playing peculiar musical instruments and all in costume. Peter would be present dressed as a Dutch seaman and pounding away at his favorite instrument, the drums. Toward the end of his reign these enforced celebrations became more and more common.

He had a weakness for arranging pseudo-weddings for which he would contrive fantastic and obscene rituals. When one of the two heads of the Assembly, Zotov, a septuagenarian drunkard, formerly Peter's tutor, who had been given the mock title of Pope or Patriarch of the Assembly, was "married," the preparations for the mock ceremony kept everyone at court and in the government busy for months; Peter himself supervised every detail. In the thick of his war with Sweden, Peter never neglected his ribald, silly correspondence with his drunken friends.

Historians have naturally devoted a good deal of effort to extracting some point from this curious rigmarole. It is a futile enterprise; the Assembly was exactly what it sounds like.

Peter was very free-and-easy in his manner, with a peculiar sense of humor. On noticing his friends' disgust during a visit to an anatomical laboratory in Holland, he made them tear a corpse to shreds with their bare teeth. Once, on overhearing a maid-in-waiting to the Tsarina complain of a wasted youth, he gave her a lesson at first hand, in front of the whole court, in the sexual experience she had missed.

At the age of twenty-four Peter decided to see Western Europe for himself. After imposing himself on the attention of European governments by defeating the Turks in an impromptu campaign, he set out on his own idea of a grand tour. He had already shown his interest in foreign countries by resuming the practice of Boris Godunov of sending young Russians abroad for study, but he was the first Russian sovereign to leave his country on a peaceful mission since the legendary Princess Olga's trip to Constantinople in the tenth century.

At the European courts he visited, he struck everyone as most peculiar: his behavior was bizarre, his anger volcanic, his person sloppy, his manners nonexistent, and his attitude toward knives and forks hostile.

Of course he had a certain air. The Duke of Saint-Simon, who saw him in 1717, when Peter was forty-five years old, portrays him vividly:

> He was a very big man, well built and fairly thin, with a rather round face. He had a large forehead, fine eyebrows, and a moderately small nose fleshy at the tip. His lips were rather thick; his complexion ruddy and brown. He had large, fine black eyes, well traced, lively and piercing. His look, when he was aware of it, was majestic and charming; when not, it was stern and fierce, with a tic that, though not recurring often, convulsed his eyes and his whole face: it was terrifying. It lasted only a moment, giving him a distraught and frightful look, then vanished at once. His whole bearing attested intellect, thoughtfulness, and majesty, and was not without a certain grace. He wore only a linen collar, a round wig, brown and seemingly unpowdered, which fell short of his shoulders, a brown jacket, a tunic with gold buttons, a waistcoat, breeches, stockings; no gloves and no cuffs, the star of his order on his coat with the loop below; his coat often completely unbuttoned, his hat on a table and never on his head, even out-of-doors. This simplicity, however plain his coach or attendants, was unmistakable for the majestic air that was native to him.
>
> The amount of food and drink he consumed at two regular meals is inconceivable, disregarding the quantities of beer, lemonade, and other drinks he swallowed between meals. His whole retinue drank even more: a bottle or two of beer, as much and sometimes more of wine, followed by liqueur wines, and, at the end of the meal, blended whiskies, a pint and sometimes a quart: this was more or less the usual fare at every meal.

On his first trip, to be sure, Peter had no intention of spending too much time at stuffy court functions; he wanted to learn shipbuilding, navigation, and warfare. His visit to Holland was enough to start a legend, still alive, about the "royal carpenter of Zaandam," though he stayed there no more than a few days. He traveled around looking at factories, shipyards, museums, and hospitals; he studied architecture, engineering, book-printing, anatomy, drawing, and even dentistry.

Then, having heard that the English knew more than the Dutch about building ships, he did much the same thing in England, where he also spent a great deal of time carousing. (He left a house lent him as though a tornado had struck it.)

Peter had upset enough people in Russia for a dissident movement to spring up. Shortly before he left for Western Europe, in March 1697, a conspiracy against him was discovered. It involved the "Archers" *(Streltsy)* and the Cossacks, and was aimed at reinstating Peter's older half-sister Sophie, who had been enabled to rule as regent while Peter had still been a boy.

The Archers were a peculiar semi-military formation of seventeenth-century Muscovy. Though organized as regiments in reserved areas in Moscow, they actually plied a variety of trades and were highly accessible to political currents. Many of them sympathized strongly with the Old Believers, and as an armed and mutinous group they were a constant menace to the government. They had been used before by Sophie and the Miloslavskys, who made them all sorts of promises. The Archers had installed Sophie in power with great bloodshed, slaughtering a number of young Peter's relatives, including his uncles, in full view of Peter and his mother, and then erupting throughout the city, killing anyone in their bad books.

After Peter's unexpected return to Moscow he started a reign of terror unheard of since Ivan the Terrible. He personally kept fourteen torture chambers busy twenty-four hours a day; in an attempt to involve Sophie and his other half-sisters in the plot he personally, together with his intimates and henchmen, tortured more than seventeen hundred people. But in spite of great imaginativeness, he failed to get enough evidence.

The tortures were followed by mass executions, hundreds of people being killed. Peter led his friends in the head-lopping. The corpses were left to rot in public for five months. One hundred and ninety-seven were hanged in the convent where Sophie was imprisoned, three in front of her window, their dead hands clinging to letters allegedly written her by the Archers.

Peter then left Moscow for a few days; when he came back in January 1699 the slaughter was resumed with equal savagery, preceded by a riotous celebration of the Most Drunken Assembly, including a particularly obscene masquerade, to open a new and luxurious mansion Peter had had built for one of his oldest friends, Lefort, a Swiss. After paying their respects to Venus and Bacchus, the merrymakers surged back to the torture chambers, execution blocks, and gallows. By the end of February, more than a thousand mutilated bodies had been taken away. The Archers were shattered.

This extravaganza of ferocity was accompanied, typically enough, by Peter's first spectacular attempt to Westernize Russia, or at least the shaving customs of the upper classes. The day after his return, Peter showed himself in Western dress in public and took a pair of shears to the flowing beards of the court dignitaries. This was bound to inflame sentiment. A beard was of the utmost importance to pious Muscovites; the Russian Church taught that it was indispensable to the "image of God" in which man was made. Its loss therefore meant that people were no better than cats and dogs. That led to eternal damnation.

This was only one of the many shocks reserved for Peter's generation. His effort to transform Russia sprang out of his preoccupation with warfare. When he found himself confronted by better organized armies in the West, he was led, shortsightedly and planlessly, into an assault on the whole social structure. Out of the thirty-five years of his reign, only the last year, 1724, was free of war; the rest of the time Russia was at peace for only thirteen months. These wars were not imposed on him in any way; he launched them arbitrarily, with no clear view of their aims.

His most demonstrative attempt at catching up with the West had to do with changing the way Russians looked. His cutting the beards of the court functionaries in 1698, after coming back from Western Europe, turned out to be not merely one of the pranks the young Tsar was famous for, but the beginning of a systematic regime of savagely enforced modernization in the dress and appearance of the boyars, the nobility, and for that matter the entire city population. Decrees in 1700 and 1701 ordered all these classes to adopt "Hungarian" dress, and all men and women, except the clergy and peasants, to wear "German, Saxon, or French" clothes on pain of "cruel punishments." By 1705 most of the upper classes had yielded, though for a time the aristocracy preferred its traditional high bonnets and long robes with flowing sleeves.

A special tax was laid on beards, graduated according to the social status of their owners. The peasants' beards were tax-free, as long as they were kept in their villages, but every time a beard came into a city or left its owner was charged a kopeck.

Peter also forced the Russians to start mingling socially like Western Europeans, or at any rate like the patrons of a Dutch tavern. A decree of 1718 gave precise instructions for informal parties to be held in private houses, attended not only by officers and noblemen, but by merchants and artisans. Women were forced to attend; this broke up the tradition of Byzantine seclusion they had still been subject to at the beginning of the century.

Peter launched an immense series of cultural reforms, beginning with the reform of the calendar, which reckoned time since the beginning of the world and started the year with September. This calendar, an object of veneration, especially to the Old Believers, was changed in 1699 to the Julian calendar. The first Russian newspaper appeared in 1703, and in 1708 the alphabet was simplified. But the retention of the ancient Slavonic alphabet for the Church accentuated the alienation between the Church and other educated groups that was to leave its stamp on intellectual evolution.

Peter thought geometry the key to all knowledge; since his

interests in general had a narrowly practical tinge, there was a steady output of dictionaries and translations of textbooks on arithmetic, geometry, fortification, etc. No literature was published to speak of. The light side of life was coped with in a book on etiquette translated from German; since the Russians had been commanded to behave according to Peter's view of polite society, the book was very popular.

Peter hired a troupe of German actors to come to Russia, both to act and to teach young Muscovites the trade. In 1702–3 they played fifteen tragedies and comedies, mostly translations of current German plays about mythological and celebrated personages. Though Molière was also played, the defectiveness of the Russian translation made his *Précieuses Ridicules* as well as most of the other plays utterly incomprehensible, not so much because of the translators' incompetence as because the Russians of the period were nonplussed by the basic situations of the German and French plays; their bafflement was reflected in the lack of any language to express such themes.

Peter made a tremendous effort to launch higher education, at least his own version of it, which was formed largely by his obsession with navigation and related studies, but he kept colliding with a currently irremediable absence of textbooks and properly trained teachers and the equally marked absence of pupils. School discipline was grotesquely harsh even for the period; most parents were reluctant to allow their children to get an education. The student quota, laid down by fiat, was difficult to fill; the schools were ignored by the potential students *en masse*.

The entire conception of an educational program was lopsided. At a time when the country had no schools worth mentioning, either elementary or secondary, Peter, apparently inspired by Leibniz, arranged to launch a Russian Academy of Science. Seventeen professors were imported from Germany, but since no Russians were qualified to take the courses, some eight students had to be scraped up in Germany too, and as this number was not enough to listen to the seventeen professors' lectures, the professors were obliged to attend each other's. The oddity is that in spite of everything the scholarly ability of the first fellows was quite respectable; after Peter's death the capital benefited by this novel note of intellectual life.

Peter's alienation from the parochialism of the Russian milieu he was born into constituted a chasm that could be bridged only by willpower; institutionally expressed, Peter's social ideal was the police-state. The police were given the most diversified duties. They were not only supposed to make everyone work at an honorable trade, but to "prohibit excessive domestic expenditures," "bring satisfaction of all human needs," and "educate the young in . . . moral purity and train them in honorable sciences." These statements, from statutes enacted in 1721, conclude by proclaiming the police the "very soul of citizenship." The Church itself was subordinated even more than before to Peter's police notions. A civil body, the Holy Synod, was substituted for the Patriarchate; it was organized in just the same way as other administrative units of the government, except that the members were clerics. The following year the Holy Synod came under the rule of a Chief Procurator, who was to be invariably a layman. This office grew steadily in importance until the Chief Procurator was finally made a Minister of the crown. The office lasted until the upsets of 1917; it nullified any political influence the Church had.

Peter, while making a point of attending church services, was personally irreverent. This indifference of his to religion made for some slight tolerance, and though all forms of dissent were still persecuted—he resumed the hounding of the Old Believers—the driving force behind the persecution was now not so much a fanatical desire to stamp out heresy as a campaign against political opposition. This was part of Peter's secularization of life in general. During his reign and after, Swedes and Turks were no longer hated as heretics or infidels but simply as national enemies. He thus consummated the end of the Church's role as a symbol of national unity, which in any case had been shattered by the schism.

The combination of Peter's wars and the military-administrative reforms they necessitated had the most far-reaching effects on the social structure, especially on the organization of the nobility. The growing bureaucratization of the government and its intensified meddling in all social life made the burden on the nobility much heavier. The nobility were supposed to give the army its officers and the civil service its functionaries; since the government was taking on an immense variety of novel industrial and construction activities, it required numerous superintendents to run the masses of drafted workmen. Peter made it impossible for the nobles to go on stewing quietly on their estates. They were obliged to fit themselves into the evolving bureaucratic machine as best they could.

Peter did not abolish the privileges of the aristocracy; he simply formalized the old Russian concept of state service. The originally clear distinction between patrimonial estates, owned outright by the nobles, and estates subject to service had been confounded for some time; Peter wiped it out altogether. A decree of 1721 made every army officer an hereditary noble regardless of origin; the concept was developed and ramified in a decree of the following year that established the celebrated Table of Ranks. This included an attribution of personal lifetime nobility, a notion curiously at variance with any Western European concept. The upshot was that you were no longer an officer because you were noble, but noble because you were an officer. All landowners became nobles with the same obligations to the state; the distinction between the great and the petty nobility vanished.

The Table of Ranks drew a clear line, for the first time, between civilian and military service. All officers in each of these two branches were put into a hierarchical order of fourteen classes, each of which had to be passed through, beginning from the bottom. The Table of Ranks extended the privilege of hereditary ennoblement to civil servants who had attained a certain rank.

In this way government service, regardless of its particular facet, was formally acknowledged to be the source of nobility. The basic decrees establishing the Table of Ranks sound like an attempt at democratization, but the Table did not have that effect at all. The facts of life—status, connections, wealth—

still made opportunity accessible chiefly to those already on the summits of society. What it did do, however, was weaken the notion of an hereditary aristocracy even more than before by making the bureaucratic function of an individual the source of his status. A bureaucracy dependent on a sovereign's favor is obviously more pliable than an aristocracy with autonomous pretensions.

The Table of Ranks was one of Peter's must durable reforms. It gave a sharp outline to the bureaucratic state that had begun developing in Muscovy even before him, and it created a bureaucratic tradition that was to survive the upheaval of 1917. Peter replaced the easy-going sloppiness of patriarchal Muscovy by a ramified system of protocol and etiquette, ranks, titles, emblems of obsequiousness, and above all of uniforms. These became compulsory for anyone even remotely connected with the state; they were worn by civil servants as well as by army officers, and later on by students, including secondary-school students of both sexes. On its upper levels the country became a sort of gigantic barrack-house. Though the pervasive regimentation was relaxed to some extent during the liberalization of the upper classes in the nineteenth century, it never entirely disappeared.

The regimentation of the landlords was naturally passed on to their serfs: the poll-tax not only added to the burden of the servile population, but extended serfdom to groups that had formerly been relatively free. Discontent seethed, with mass desertions to the southern steppe and northeastern wilderness, and rebellions, all of them drowned in blood, flaring up at one point after another, especially along the Volga and to the south.

Peasant discontent was heightened by grotesque, though well-founded, rumors about Peter's personal life as well as that of his entourage. From reports in the files of the security police, which had become all-powerful, a nightmarish picture emerges, especially after the Old Believers began being persecuted again. The universal denunciations led to torture chambers that were in constant operation. From the records it seems that a very large number of people caught up in the police network thought Peter the living incarnation of the Apocalyptic Beast, an opinion shared by many besides the Old Believers.

Peter concretized the autocratic principle already expressed theoretically by Ivan the Terrible. He proclaimed himself Emperor for the first time in 1711; in 1716 the army regulations he had drawn up gave this notion legislative form. This was the formula he used: "His Majesty is an absolute monarch who is not responsible to anyone in the world for his deeds; he has the right and power to govern his realm and his lands as a Christian sovereign, according to his will." A church statute of 1721 said the same thing in a form that was to be retained with slight modifications until 1917: "The power of monarchs is autocratic; conscientious obedience to it is ordained by God Himself."

This of course had nothing to do, as it were functionally, with his "democratic" feelings: his second wife, Catherine, was a Latvian peasant. She had first been a servant-girl at a Protestant pastor's, then mistress of a Swedish dragoon. Imprisoned by the Russians at the sack of Marienburg in 1702, she soared aloft amazingly. She passed through a great many hands before becoming the mistress of Peter's boyhood friend Menshikov, who passed her on to Peter in 1703, whereupon she was converted to Greek Orthodoxy. Though plain, quite illiterate, and completely vulgar in manner, she had a very lively mind; she and Peter were devoted to each other. She actually followed him to war, slept outdoors with him, and ate soldiers' food. She was the only one who could soothe what seem to have been his epileptic crises. He had four bastards by her before marrying her in 1711. Muscovite public opinion, of a pre-medieval strictness in such matters, had to swallow the peasant Empress. It is entertaining to recall that Louis XIV required years of persistent effort to secure the legitimization of his bastards by Mme. de Montespan, who was, after all, the daughter of a duke.

Since Peter's basic motive had been the assimilation of Western technology in order to wage war, his indefatigable energies were flung into the substitution of factories for the tawdry workshops of the Russian economy. The objective was dual:

the army had to be equipped, and the country had to be enriched. Peter attempted to organize the production of saltpeter,
silk, wine, and so forth. He imported foreign engineers and
foremen, as well as machines and technical handbooks. He
tried to create an entire industrial structure by fiat, both by
offering premiums to private initiative and by flogging delin-
quents and recalcitrants. The factories were all built at the
treasury's expense and leased to individuals with varying degrees of competence. It was the first effort at the creation
of a state-economy. But it remained inherently unviable: as
Peter once exclaimed in despair, "There are no people!" There
was not enough experience or education in the country for
such an enterprise, and though government-fostered Russian
industry finally became capable of supplying uniforms to the
army at an extravagant cost, it was never able to withstand
the flood of foreign imports.

The founding of St. Petersburg may have been Peter's most
successful, and surely his most dramatic and expensive, enterprise in human as well as material terms. The new capital
was situated at the farthermost reach of the empire merely
to allow Peter to be near his navy. The terrain he chose was
so watery—at the point where the Neva, the shortest and wid-
est river in Europe, pours into the Gulf of Karelia in four
arms—that the mud had to be fortified by means of buoys
and piles. Hundreds of thousands of workers died in the freezing marshlands. St. Petersburg, which was to become one
of the finest cities in Europe, was at first built out of wood.
Great palaces along concrete quays were to grow up later. The
new capital, which Peter referred to as his paradise, was not
only a sepulchre for masses of people, but a bottomless well
for an inestimable loss of wealth.

Despite his fabulous energy Peter's mind was elementary.
Utterly "practical," he had no grasp of general ideas. Though
he has gone down in history as the great Reformer (or rather
Transformer), he never had any real plan. He was merely obsessed by a desire to catch up with the West technologically;
it was because of his determination to combine this general
obsession with his other obsession for warmaking that he had

to initiate an immense variety of changes in government and taxation to carry on his wars. Though he was quick and inquisitive, his ignorance was fatal. Since his obsession was always with a practical goal, and since he was incapable of formulating general principles, his method was inevitably one of trial and error, nearly always error. His practical policies generally cancelled each other out.

Both the imposition of industrialization from on top and the growth of the bureaucratic apparatus as a means of organizing society may be looked on as the inevitable response to the gigantic gap between Russia and Europe that had been allowed to develop as the material counterpart of Russia's spiritual isolation. Just as Russia disregarded the cultivation of Latin Europe for seven hundred years while deriving a thin trickle of culture from Byzantium, so now, when Peter, like a newborn child, determined to cultivate his country, he turned to Germany and Holland for techniques. But since it was only techniques he was looking for, he could never clarify to himself what made techniques possible. He thought he could convert sleepy, paternalistic Russians into energetic businessmen and engineers by changing their clothes and thrusting into their hands technical handbooks, largely unintelligible.

Peter was a combination of vast energy, practicality, and intellectual limitation; his reforms were both artificial and fragmentary. By failing to perceive that civilization underlies technology, not vice-versa, and that traditional Russian institutions eluded the superficial control of his administrative improvisations, he ran head-on into an almost solid wall of resistance.

His reforms were fragmentary in any case; they touched only a minute class. Not only did the Russian masses remain inert and lethargic as before, since in their vast numbers Peter could conceive of them only as targets of the knout, but Peter alienated the upper classes from the masses far more completely than occurred elsewhere by forcing Russia into the forms of Western culture. The comfortable national identity of ignorance, squalor, and coarseness, based on an identity of customs and beliefs, yielded to a society divided by a broader chasm than before. In order to live up to Peter's demands the landed nobility had to extract even more from their serfs; the functionaries of the more streamlined bureaucracy were tamer than ever. Together they constituted the summit of society. Underneath them lay the people, groaning.

Despite the conventional eulogies addressed to Peter even by Russians who disliked his methods, the fact is that the population of the country was more than decimated by Peter's ruinous wars. Hosts of Russian soldiers, badly dressed, badly armed, and badly trained, died on countless battlefields. Many thousands of conscripted workmen died of hunger, cold, and disease in Peter's vast enterprises, which included the construction of a canal, the waterway system, and Petersburg itself. It is enough to recall that during Peter's reign Russia's population, in spite of a proverbial fecundity, decreased by 20 percent. Russia was devastated, as it had been during the Time of Troubles and was to be so often again.

A vivid expression of popular bile may be more appropriate than a lofty summing-up of Peter the Great's career. An instance of cheap lithography, one of the few artistic media accessible to the masses, has survived in a poster showing a cat being buried by mice. It is a bitter satire on Peter, his court and his reforms, and on the extravagant display of official grief at his death. The poster itself is thought to have been the work of Old Believers, but it surely reflects an opinion widespread in practically every social group. It is in sharp contrast to the dithyrambs of professional historians.

CHAPTER V

CATHERINE THE GREAT

*D*uring the thirty-seven years between the reigns of Peter the Great and Catherine the Great, the Russian throne was occupied by a grotesque assembly of ignorant sluts, feeble-minded German princes, and children, a total of seven rulers in all, each representing the power of the Guards regiments founded by Peter, which remained a decisive factor throughout this period.

Having tortured his heir Alexis to death, with the only remaining heir a grandson he wanted to eliminate, Peter had formally decreed the Emperor's right to appoint his successor. Thus he projected the autocrat's power beyond the very principle of monarchy, and after a life spent magnifying the power of the throne left Russia without a ruler, since he died before he could nominate one.

The feverish instability of the regime may be traced to two acts of Peter's: his arbitrary negation of the monarchical principle, and the immense importance he bestowed on the Guards regiments. These factors came into play against the background of the dynastic alliances Peter had zealously entered into with a number of German princely houses.

With no stable principle of authority, and with a variety of contending elements of power, policy in St. Petersburg increasingly became a football of competing cliques, especially since the country had acquired international consequence. The political horizon was no longer confined to parochial disputes with Turkey, Poland, and Sweden; St. Petersburg was now a factor in Western Europe as well.

What may be called the regimental principle in the Russian state was launched in a very natural way. Peter's social upheaval, which had struck at the very heart of the old-line aristocracy, inevitably produced a cleavage between the parvenu clique that had prospered under his wing and the victims of his various persecutions.

This latter group, fortified by the general revulsion at Peter's extravagant personal behavior and especially at the murder of his son Alexis, considered Peter's grandson a legitimate successor ready to sweep away the plebeian adventurers who under Peter had been battening off the state.

These adventurers, naturally enough, were vitally interested in preserving the status quo. None of Peter's favorites, especially his peasant Empress, Menshikov, and Theophanes Prokopovich, his tame Metropolitan and professional eulogizer, could expect anything from a change of regime but death, imprisonment, exile, or confiscation of property.

It must have been obvious that the Guards would have the last word in deciding who was to ascend the throne; during Peter's last illness they were sounded out to see whether they would help keep his widow Catherine on the throne. Catherine, who had accompanied Peter on so many campaigns, was popular with the army, both officers and men; troops thought to favor her were rushed to the capital. Their approval of Catherine was stimulated by the simple device of giving them their pay, by now almost a year and a half in arrears, and promising them future rewards with understandable generosity.

This simple procedure established a mold for the palace revolutions that characterized the eighteenth century. During the forty years after Peter the Great's death, the throne was claimed by his grandson Peter; his two daughters by Catherine, Anne and Elizabeth, born out of wedlock; and his three nieces, Catherine, Anne, and Praskovie (the last of whom played no political role). The success of one or another depended on the decision, enforced by the Guards regiments, of a clique of fortuitously organized higher officials.

The justification given of making Catherine Empress of Russia in her own right, which took place even before Peter's death, was that she had been crowned a year before by Peter himself; this extraordinary innovation failed to create any serious disturbance. Some stick-in-the-muds, to be sure, at first felt there was something wrong about taking an oath of allegiance to a woman who on top of being a Latvian peasant had been the mistress of so many people and borne Peter so many bastards, but these traditionalists were soon shown the light by the security police.

Since Catherine did not pretend to rule but simply devoted herself to debauchery of one kind or'another, Menshikov, who had been instrumental in putting her on the throne, remained the chief power in the land. He managed to consolidate his power still further after Catherine's death in May 1727 by marrying his daughter to Peter's young grandson. A document signed by Catherine (now regarded as a forgery) provided for still another bizarre departure from the monarchical principle— the throne was to pass to the grandson, Peter II, and his line, or in case of its extinction to Catherine's two daughters, Anne of Holstein and her line or Elizabeth and her line. The daughters of the senior line, by Peter the Great's feebleminded brother and short-lived co-Tsar, Ivan V, were passed over in silence. On Catherine's death, Menshikov's prospective son-in-law, Peter II, was hailed at the age of eleven as Emperor.

But Menshikov's career, seemingly at its peak, failed to live up to its prospects. The arrogance of the "overbearing Goliath," as he was called, had multiplied his enemies beyond control. He had alienated the young Emperor and even lost his hold over the Guards in whose ranks he had started out. Only three months later, after a short illness, he was banished with his whole family, ultimately to Siberia. He died in exile a couple of years later.

For a short time the fall of Menshikov cleared the way for a restoration of Moscow as capital and a return to the traditional life Peter the Great had upset. Young Peter was crowned there in January 1728; that summer some major departments of the government were shifted to the old capital. Many observers thought that everything symbolized by St. Petersburg was done for.

Peter II's career was very brief, though full of fun. Very tall and sexually precocious, like his grandfather, he spent most of his time with some young friends; life was one long round of parties, hunting, and lovemaking. His festive career was ended by smallpox: he died in January 1730, leaving Russia without a ruler for the third time in five years and the male Romanov line a thing of the past.

The dynastic situation remained as amorphous as ever. After considering the various candidates mentioned above, the Supreme Privy Council, plus a number of other highly placed people, arbitrarily selected Anne, Duchess of Courland, second daughter of Ivan V, Peter's brother and former co-Tsar, apparently because she was considered a model of submissiveness. The throne was offered her on the basis of certain conditions that substantially curtailed her power as sovereign. These conditions were intended to ensure the influence of the great Dolgoruki clan; thus they were construed at the time as an attempt to replace the monarchy with an oligarchy. But the resistance to the novel scheme of curbed autocracy on the part of the noblemen who were even more against the oligarchy than against the autocracy, and their confusion as to any alternative to these two types of government, facilitated the restoration of an autocracy proper.

The Guards and noblemen outside the inner circle of the would-be oligarchy insisted on the restoration of absolutism; Anne literally tore up the restrictive conditions in front of a large group of army officers and notables. Thus, what might have been an experiment in monarchy based on an aristocratic oligarchy came to an end less than a fortnight after Anne's entrance into Moscow in February 1730.

Anne was thirty-seven at the time. Married at the age of seventeen to the Duke of Courland, she was widowed only a few weeks after the marriage; she had been obliged to spend nineteen years in the eccentric position of a duchess without a duchy. A bigoted, highly sensual ignoramus, she was dependent on the niggardly subsidies of the Russian court, whose agent was in charge of the duchy. All this time she had been writing humble, illiterate notes to her imperial relatives and to the favorites in power. When she finally found herself on the throne after this lengthy and generally hopeless-looking exile, she quickly made up for lost time.

She had been involved in a liaison with Ernst Johann Biron (Bühren), a minor functionary of German descent, who was supposed to be dropped on her return to Russia; like the other conditions, however, this was also disregarded. Biron became the real ruler of Russia during her reign (actually known in Russian history as the *Bironovshchina*—the Biron era).

The moment she became Empress, Anne flung aside the docile impersonation she had been forced to carry on for so long and plunged into an unflagging series of splendid palace and church festivities. She had inherited Peter the Great's predilection for peculiar people: she filled the imperial residences not only with animals, especially those that could perform amusing tricks, but with all sorts of giants, midgets, cripples, beggars, and clowns. She kept a large corps of women on hand who did nothing but entertain her by telling stories. Anne also had Peter the Great's liking for practical jokes and satirical rites: she celebrated a "marriage" between two princes, a Golitsyn and a Volkonsky; years later she made this Golitsyn the bridegroom of a famously repulsive Kalmyk woman in a grotesque ceremony performed in a palace made of ice.

In accordance with Anne's often proclaimed motto of ruling in the "spirit of Peter the Great," she moved the court and government back to St. Petersburg the year after her accession, putting an end to the short-lived experiment of reviving Moscow as capital.

As part of a campaign to crush the Dolgorukis, Golitsyns, and other great clans who had attempted to curb the autocracy in their own interests, Anne intensified the police terror. Once again the torture chambers began ingesting their quota of people, often on the mere suspicion of disapproval of Anne's regime; thousands were sent to Siberia, often to vanish completely.

Anne remained childless; as she began to fall ill toward the end of her reign, the regime was again confronted by a dynastic muddle. This was given a stop-gap solution by the birth of an heir to Anne's niece, Princess Anna Leopoldovna of Mecklenburg, the only descendant of the senior Romanov branch. Biron had attempted to anchor himself more firmly in the ruling circle by marrying his son to young Anna Leopoldovna, but he was unable to withstand the opposition of his rivals and the unwillingness of the bride herself, who chose to marry a German prince (Anthony of Brunswick-Bevern-Luneburg) for whom also she had no liking. This match produced a boy in August 1740; before Anne died a few months later, she appointed the infant her heir. The best Biron managed out of this was his appointment as regent until the baby, called Ivan VI, reached the age of seventeen. This arrangement was so private that this time no one was consulted at all, not even the Guards.

But in the uncurbed flux of interests around the Russian throne, the arrangement lasted only thirteen months. Biron had incurred much hostility; more particularly, he had failed to secure the support of the Guards. He was arrested only a few weeks later and deported to Siberia with his family. He was to languish in exile for more than twenty years.

Biron was replaced as regent by Ivan VI's mother, Anna Leopoldovna, possibly the most muddle-headed ruler of the confused interregnum that followed Peter the Great's death. She spent days at a time closeted in her bedroom seeing no one but her lady-in-waiting and her lover, Count Lynar, whom she was planning, curiously enough, to marry to her lady-in-waiting, to whom she was passionately attached. Throughout Princess Anna's regency, the contention for the helm of Russia between various German cliques and individuals was incessant; it was brought to an end only by a palace revolution at the end of 1741 that resulted in the arrest of the Brunswick family, the deposition of the infant Ivan VI, and the accession to the throne of Peter the Great's daughter Elizabeth, thirty years old.

Elizabeth was to reign for twenty years, until her death in 1762. Peter the Great, hoping to fit her for a major role at the court of Versailles, had taught her German, French, and dancing; otherwise she was uneducated.

Contemporaries considered her beauty and charm irresistible. Gay and amorous, she concentrated exclusively and with a disconcerting lack of inhibition on carnal amusements. The Spanish ambassador, the Duke de Liria, said she "shamelessly indulged in practices that would have made even the least modest person blush." It was indeed the amorous nature and the taste for low company that she had inherited from her parents, and that took the form of a weakness for handsome Guardsmen, that was to give her the throne. Lightminded and irresponsible, she seems to have frequented the Guards' barracks for simple pleasure rather than in pursuit of any elaborate political objectives, but her charming accessibility nevertheless created a faithful following for her among the Guardsmen, who were used to regarding the throne as their private preserve. Those who were against the Brunswick family and the German connection generally took advantage of her entourage. St. Petersburg, now deeply involved in European affairs, was an arena for power politics; it suited France and Sweden to use Elizabeth and her Guardsmen as a means of getting rid of politicians whom they could easily claim to be alien to Russia's interests without harping unnecessarily on their own.

Elizabeth's rule brought life in St. Petersburg much nearer to the European model the elite were longing for so ardently. The festivities were far more conventional. The relays of masquerades, spectacles, and hunts were no longer marred by the grotesqueries of Empress Anne's reign. The cripples and clowns had vanished, while Elizabeth's beloved Guardsmen did much to elevate the standard of looks if not urbanity around the court.

Elizabeth's agreeable frivolity was reinforced by her imperial status. The wobbly Russian treasury was completely outdistanced by her quest for amusement. Though she thought it politic to recommend thriftiness in dress to everyone else, when she died she left behind some 15,000 gowns, as well as many things needed for the masculine attire she was attached to.

Elizabeth also like traveling. On her frequent trips to Moscow and other cities, as well as to monasteries, she was escorted not only by the court but by various government agencies. The huge governmental caravan required thousands of horses and carts for all the officials, including their servants, furniture, and household utensils. The imperial residences even in Moscow were unprepared for the massive descents of the sovereign's entourage and administration.

Caprice was elevated to a state principle during Elizabeth's reign. The merry Empress was generally inaccessible to anyone but her private chancery, which was not even acknowledged as a state institution. Both Russian statesmen and foreign diplomats were reduced to lurking about in the hope of catching the Empress in an off moment and making her sign indispensable state papers that otherwise might lie about for months or be shelved altogether.

The German element in Russian society, so influential since the acquisition of the Baltic lands, was given permanent roots through Elizabeth's importation of her nephew, the Duke of Holstein-Gottorp, to St. Petersburg after her accession. On his conversion to Greek Orthodoxy, he took the name of Grand Duke Peter; in November 1742 he was proclaimed heir. His marriage to a German princess, the future Catherine the Great, was to put a German stamp on the Russian monarchy that remained fundamental until its extinction.

But with all the changes of regime during the period of turmoil that followed the death of Peter the Great, with all the personal corruption of the series of backstage favorites, with all the capriciousness of the policies that emerged through the complex filtering-chamber of the alliances with German houses, there was, nevertheless, a certain unity of development. Serfdom progressed steadily; not only did it become more comprehensive, but it also became a hallmark of class privilege.

A number of laws passed between 1730 and 1759 limited the right of anyone but a member of the nobility to own serfs; concomitantly, the peasantry grew progressively more desperate. Impoverished and decimated by the cost of Peter the Great's imperial expansion and the exorbitant exactions of its owners, the peasantry did what it always did—it ran away and revolted. The monarchs who succeeded Peter the Great, especially his daughter Elizabeth, confronted one peasant rebellion after another. These uprisings were especially frequent and savage on the monasteries' estates and in the industrial enterprises worked by serfs. It was a common occurrence for great bands of armed peasants, numbering sometimes several thousand, to wage pitched battles with the punitive expeditions sent against them. The private soldiers, who were subject to a life term of service, often joined them, only to be overcome ultimately by still other government troops. Every uprising was crushed; its leaders were all killed on the wheel, the gallows, or the whipping post, or deported to the Siberian wilderness.

The harshness of peasant life had its counterpart in the insecurity arising from the arbitrariness underlying the government. The rulers themselves, placed on the throne by capricious combinations of palace officials and guardsmen, never knew what was going to happen next. This arbitrariness applied to the nobility as well. Though the nobles as a class were more and more solidly anchored in their privileges, the personal security of any individual nobleman was much the same as that of his serfs. The greatest personages in the country were subject to the most abrupt changes of fortune.

Thus, while the official policy was savage repression of the peasantry plus the conciliation of the nobility as a class, there was at the same time a pervasive disaffection that showed itself in palace conspiracies, the evasion by the nobility of its obligations, mass desertion, and peasant revolts.

A palace revolution put Catherine the Great on the throne for thirty-four years. Born Princess of Anhalt-Zerbst, she ascended the throne over her murdered husband Peter III, with the support of the Preobrazhensky Regiment. Peter III has a peculiarly bad reputation (chiefly because of Catherine's tire-less literary energies), having come down in history as a de-praved and drunken moron, but his chief political shortcoming seems to have been that he was one of the few Russian monarchs in the eighteenth century to mount the throne legally; hence he had no effective support at all. Catherine herself was wholly a usurper: she could at most have claimed to hold the throne as regent for her son Paul. But after Peter III was murdered, apparently with Catherine's at least tacit approval, Catherine, though nothing whatever was known about her outside the court, clung successfully to the throne.

Paul's claim to the throne was incontestable; since his only obstacle to power was Catherine's determination, there was a profound estrangement between the two. When Paul visited Vienna in 1781, it was considered prudent to cancel a perform-ance of *Hamlet;* a license to put it on in St. Petersburg was cancelled when the authorities found out what the play was about. By titillating the curiosity of the reading public, this decision greatly stimulated Russian interest in Shakespeare.

Catherine II has come down as one of the most glamorous monarchs in history. This is largely due to her talent and zeal for press agentry. Also her position enabled her to hire the services of still more talented press agents such as Voltaire. One of her cardinal objectives was to be on friendly terms with Voltaire, Diderot, and d'Alembert, not only through snobbery but because she saw clearly how useful such indefati-gable writers and opinion-molders could be in singing her praises. As Frederick II said, she was "very proud, very ambi-tious, and very vain."

Voltaire, unusually available, became a completely pliant in-strument of her wishes. He praised her at all times and endorsed everything she did, lauding the first partition of Poland as a victory of "tolerance" over "fanaticism." Much the same was done by his colleagues and the growing band of their Russian followers. By acquiring the public support of interna-tionally known French writers and thinkers, Catherine thus secured her position at home.

The moment Catherine took power—nine days later, to be precise—she invited Diderot to shift to Russia the publication of the *Encyclopédie,* suspended in France. A few years later she bought Diderot's library, allowing him to keep the books and draw a pension of 1,000 livres as Her Majesty's Librarian. This openhanded policy paid off richly; such acts are the underpinnings of Catherine's reputation for enlightenment. After Diderot's visit to Russia in 1773, he gave Catherine *carte blanche* in the way of moral support and praised her as combining "the soul of Brutus with the charm of Cleopatra."

Besides Voltaire, Diderot, and d'Alembert, Catherine corresponded copiously with Frederick II, Joseph II, Prince de Ligne, Falconet, and a great many others. Mme. Geoffrin, who had a celebrated literary and political salon in Paris, and Frau Bielke, her counterpart in Hamburg, were particularly effective mouthpieces.

Catherine showed an engaging effrontery in what she wrote Voltaire about Russia. In 1769 she told him that since taxes were very low, "there was not a single peasant in Russia who could not eat chicken whenever he pleased, though he had recently preferred turkey to chicken." Some months later she assured him that Russia had always profited from wars. The Turkish war then going on was just the same: "There are no shortages of any kind; people spend their time in singing thanksgiving masses, dancing, and rejoicing." Voltaire may have believed these droll comments on the Russian scene or merely pretended to. Even those who thought them nonsense were flattered at being in the confidence of such a powerful sovereign. This kind of personal propaganda was fairly effective in securing the proper attitude on the part of Catherine's correspondents.

Favoritism had always had a lush growth at the Russian court; Catherine made it a semi-official institution. Her ten chief favorites, in succession, were given apartments next to hers and treated magnificently: titles, lucrative estates, and vast fortunes were the index of her affections. An oddity of hers was an absence of vindictiveness toward her lovers for straying;

nor did she persecute the lovers she sacked. Among her lovers, Orlov, Potyomkin, and Zubov were powerful influences on government policy, both domestic and foreign.

Potyomkin's power outlived his love affair; he influenced Catherine until his death. He was mysteriously skillful in influencing the choice of his successors, who were nearly all his tools. For years he was an all-powerful counselor of Catherine's; he was one of the inspirers of her ambitious project for the expulsion of the Turks from Europe.

In spite of her frivolous early education, Catherine became a voracious reader during the seclusion forced on her under the reign of her aunt-in-law, the Empress Elizabeth. She was also an indefatigable, thoroughly mediocre writer of tragedies, comedies, polemical works, musical comedy librettos, treatises on pedagogy, allegorical tales, and historical writings, as well as her memoirs, which have become celebrated. Her collected works, apart from her vast correspondence and her celebrated *Instruction*—a philosophical draft constitution for Russia—fill a dozen bulky volumes. Though her Russian was good enough for speaking, it was scarcely a literary medium—her ideas about grammar and spelling were vague. (In a very common Russian word of only three letters, she made four mistakes in spelling.) As for what she wrote in French, it was all thoroughly processed and corrected in the most modern manner before being released.

Under Catherine, Russian life—social, economic, and political—continued much as before. The gulf between her aping of French liberalism and the facts of life in Russia was unbridgeable. The above-mentioned *Instruction,* for instance— one more in a long series of abortive governmental attempts to cope with the chaos, corruption, and wastefulness of Russian society—was not a specific program for legislation but mere plagiarism of Montesquieu's and Beccaria's philosophical generalities. Catherine's throne was too shaky, aside from the shallow confusion of her ideas, for her to undertake surmounting the massive obstacles in the way of any genuine reform, to say nothing of her grandiose projects, equally abortive, for the remapping of Europe and Asia.

During her reign, Russia added some 200,000 square miles to its area; it was firmly established on the shores of the Baltic and the Black seas. Russia's population increased substantially, partly through these territorial acquisitions, from 19 million in 1762 to 36 million in 1796, the year of Catherine's death. This expansion cost a good deal both in lives and wealth and led to the assimilation of some peoples, such as the Tatars and Poles, who remained constant sources of disaffection. The Poles especially were a permanent target of bloody repressions.

Russian annexations seem particularly pointless if we recall that the Empire as a whole was scarcely exploited at all. Catherine shared Louis XIV's view—"to aggrandize oneself is the worthiest and most agreeable occupation of a sovereign." The actual driving force of most of the warfare carried on during Catherine's reign was nothing more than a powerful imagination, abetted by the flights of fancy of various lovers, principally, again, Orlov, Potyomkin, and Zubov.

As a matter of fact, not only did Russia's wars during the second half of the eighteenth century delay her economic development, but by extending her rule to the Polish provinces, which were never reconciled to it and in fact combated it stubbornly, these wars set up a source of disaffection very close to home. It is true that Catherine extended the boundaries of the Empire more than any other sovereign since Ivan the Terrible, but this merely heightened the contrast between the size of the realm and its underdevelopment, Russia's leitmotif for centuries.

There is a celebrated anecdote about Potyomkin's building some cheery bungalows, surrounded by merry peasants dressed in their Sunday best, in order to regale Catherine and her suite, plus some foreign diplomats, who were sailing down the Dnieper to witness the conquest of the Turks. The territory was still uninhabited, and since Potyomkin wanted to show the visitors a going concern, both the scenery and the extras were transported downstream at night and the spectacle duplicated. The story seems to be apocryphal, but its meaning is splendidly apt—all Russia was a vast Potyomkin village. It was like a brilliantly illuminated comic opera stage, with elegantly costumed lords and ladies strolling back and forth exchanging duets and witticisms in French while the mangling-machines were busily grinding away backstage.

Because Catherine was such a voluminous correspondent and gave such free expression to the loftiest ideas she could lay her hands on, the contrast between what she said and what she did is all the more striking. Despite the vast territorial expansion she is best known for, the acquisition of the littoral of the Black Sea and of new outlets on the Baltic, she failed in her attempt to undo the Ottoman Empire, not to mention her really extravagant schemes. She is reported to have said, "If I could live for 200 years, the whole of Europe would be brought under Russian rule." Also: "I shall not die before I have ejected the Turks from Europe, broken the insolence of China, and established trade relations with India."

Though the autocracy she believed in so firmly was kept unchanged, Catherine's attempts at administrative reform impaired the efficiency of the central government, while her attempt to multiply expensive local agencies of self-government failed to bring about any self-government, or even to curb the corruption of government officials. The much-publicized Legislative Commission that had occasioned her *Instruction* failed to produce even a draft of the exemplary code she had been hoping for.

Even in the sphere of abstract thought, the moment Catherine's freely professed ideas were put to the acid test of the French Revolution, she reacted like a conventional European ruler of the period and recoiled in horror, repudiating the superficial liberalism of her whole life. The French Republic was boycotted, and even individual French nationals who refused to take an oath to monarchism were expelled from Russia, while on the contrary the most reactionary French aristocrats were received with open arms. After the French Revolution, French education, which remained fashionable, took the form of education by "Monsieur l'Abbé," even at the risk of the children's being seduced by Roman Catholic propaganda.

It is true that in areas of activity where there was no danger,

Catherine did try to apply some of her liberal principles as well as talk about them. She let up to some extent on the persecution of dissenters, though the question of eliminating their legal disabilities was never raised. As for the Jews, who had always been subject to a great variety of legal disabilities in addition to outright oppression on the part of the populace as well as the government, they now found their position legalized, with some negligible exceptions: they were allowed to settle in what became known as the Jewish Pale, though even there they were more heavily taxed than others. With modifications, this remained characteristic of Russia until 1917.

The shakiness of Catherine's throne made her counteract the dragooning of the nobility into state service that previous sovereigns, particularly Peter the Great, had tried to accomplish. The dynastic upheaval following Peter's death had given the landed gentry a headlock on the sovereign, who though in theory absolutely autocratic had in practice arrived at a *modus vivendi* with the landed aristocrats that made them relatively more powerful than the boyars of old Muscovy. Since in this agricultural country the land was held by the aristocrats, they were *ipso facto* a vital economic force, and since they provided the army's officers the military strength of the regime was organizationally dependent on them. Because of this, as well as because of the vacuum surrounding the sovereign, it was now necessary to bribe the landed nobility with lavish concessions in the exploitation of the manpower that was the source of its wealth.

In fact, the second half of the eighteenth century put the landed nobility in a better position than ever. Catherine's consort had freed them from the obligation of service in 1762, and Catherine sustained this concession. Until 1785, when a new Charter of the Nobility was published, the nobles did not have to enroll in government service. They resumed life on their country estates, this time not as idlers, however, but as a group with privileges that included the direction of rural affairs. The Charter was very wordy and somewhat incoherent; it extended the privileges of the nobility and set up a framework for its corporate existence. The Charter protected the noble against deprivation of his "honor," life, property, and title (except for personal and non-hereditary titles) without a trial by his peers. Nobles could leave government service whenever they wanted to, travel abroad as much as they liked, and serve friendly foreign states. They were exempt from corporal punishment and the poll-tax, and could own houses in cities and estates with people, trade in the produce of their estates, and own industries.

The notion of service that had underlain the social structure of Russia was altered by lightening the nobility's obligations to the state. The theory, so to speak, of serfdom, or in any case its historical dynamics, had been rooted in its having enabled the nobility to serve the state by forcing the serfs to carry on the nation's economic activities. But with the concessions made by both Catherine II and her consort Peter III as formulated in the 1785 Charter of the Nobility, a social group was now created for the first time that had many privileges but no direct personal duties to the state. This was a continuation and amplification of the characteristically Russian conception of the aristocracy as a class with privileges but no duties. It was essentially an institution of profiteering, in contrast with the Western view of aristocracy as involving an ideal of service to something beyond individual gain.

This basically materialist view of the aristocracy was given a functional component by rooting the source of nobility in bureaucratic service. Individuals would acquire a coveted title by serving the government as functionaries, while the influence of the nobility as a class would be secured not by anything it did within the realm of its class privileges but because it was the ultimate reservoir of bureaucratic manpower.

Thus the emancipation of the nobility from its previous dependence on the state made the primacy of the bureaucratic machine more unambiguous; indeed, it reinforced the vast and ramified bureaucracy that survived even the upheaval of 1917 and left its stamp on the Soviet Union.

Catherine was not merely the tool of the nobility's shortsightedness. Many landowners were aware of the dangers inherent in the plight of the peasants. On various occasions even very conservative noblemen recommended alleviations of serfdom without suggesting abolition, while the records of the abortive Legislative Commission of 1767–68 show some support for a more liberal policy on the peasant question even among the rank-and-file of the nobility. Catherine was obdurate; in her defense of what she conceived to be the interests of the class to which she owed her throne, she invariably took the most narrowminded and reactionary conception of those interests, consistently disregarding all counsels of common sense as well as of humanity. By the end of her reign, serfdom was more solidly rooted in Russian life and more grinding than ever before. Voltaire's and Montesquieu's theories were confined to the elegant conversation of a tiny circle around Empress Catherine in the opulent mansions and graceful gardens of her entourage; they were quite irrelevant to the social legislation of "the age of enlightenment."

Serfdom, though not formulated in specific legislation, was established by the end of the eighteenth century; Catherine's legislation, piecemeal though it was, consolidated it completely. Noble landowners had gradually acquired the power, not unambiguously given them by law, to dispose of their serfs as they chose. They could transport them at will, sell them with land or without, mortgage them, or settle debts with them. The sale of serfs often led to the break-up of families, condemned in principle as far back as 1721 by Peter the Great. The only legal regulation of this practice came half a century later, when Catherine stipulated that the transaction must not take place at a public auction, presumably so as not to shock her French friends. The treatment of serfs as chattels was to continue until the emancipation of 1861.

A rich landowner might have a vast number of what were called household serfs, consisting of stableboys, cooks, tailors, artists, actors, musicians, and even astronomers. The master had complete judicial authority over them except for murder and theft. The rights of possessing land and of litigation had already been taken away from the serfs by two of Catherine's predecessors; now Catherine denied them even the right to lay a complaint against their owner.

Announcements such as the following were common in contemporary newspapers: "For sale: Two domestic servants, one a leatherstitcher who can also repair shoes. Thirty years of age, married: his wife is a laundress and can tend cattle; twenty-five years old. The other is a musician and singer, seventeen years of age, plays the bassoon, with a bass voice. Also for sale at same place: a Hungarian horse, three years old, very tall, English-bred, not yet ridden."

The price of serfs varied considerably; a girl might be sold for 10 rubles and a good cook for 2,500. As for their treatment, there was nothing to prevent a landowner from running a torture chamber: one master in Orel had thirty professional torturers and assistants. Other landowners had full-fledged penal codes applied on their estates. In some cases the cruelty that was common enough throughout Russia assumed psychopathic forms. A noblewoman, Darya Saltykov, was accused of having tortured to death some seventy-five of her serfs; it amused her to pass a red-hot iron over her servant-girls' breasts. This caused such a scandal that she was deprived of her title and imprisoned for life in the prison cell of a convent, where she incidentally had a child by one of the guards. But this case, which was unsuccessfully brought before a court twenty-one times before it was finally settled after six years (1768), was quite exceptional. The law said nothing about the punishment of landlords who killed their serfs. There are only twenty such cases, nine of them involving women, known throughout Catherine's reign. Of the twenty, six received sentences of forced labor and two were deported to Siberia. The others were imprisoned in convents or monasteries for terms varying between one week and a year.

The only recourse the serfs had was to petition the crown, but this often boomeranged. While Catherine was making a trip along the Volga in the spring of 1767, she was approached by some delegations of serfs asking her help against their masters. This produced a decree of the same year forbidding any complaint *at all* by a serf against his master; a breach of this decree made a serf liable to flogging and penal servitude for life.

Serfs were the index of wealth: a nobleman's status was calculated in terms of the number of "registered" serfs in his possession, i.e., the number of male serfs allocated him by the preceding census.

The following figures do not include the Ukraine and may not be precise, but they are illuminating: in the second half of the eighteenth century 59 percent of the landowners owned fewer than 21 male serfs each, 25 percent from 21 to 100, and 16 percent over 100. By 1834, however, 80 percent of the male serfs belonged to the big landowners with over 100. The concentration was actually much greater: in 1834 the 3 percent of the landowners who owned over 500 each together owned 45 percent of all the serfs, while only 870 magnates (about 1 percent of the landowners) owned some 2,038,000 male serfs, or 30 percent of the total. At the beginning of Catherine's reign about 34 percent of her people were serfs.

Serfdom was not only for life but was hereditary; it could only be brought to an end by army enrollment, Siberian deportation, or emancipation voluntarily granted by the owner. The first two remedies were dependent on the owner, the superintendent of the estate, or the village council, and were probably worse than serfdom itself; the third was very rare.

One of the anomalies of the period was in the serfs' economic position. Movable property, though not immune to expropriation by their masters, could be enjoyed by them as long as they owed nothing to them or to the state, and though they were forbidden to own real estate outright, there were many serfs who had *de facto* possession of town houses, populated estates, and even industrial enterprises registered in their owners' names. Serfs belonging to a great landowner, Count Sheremetiev, founded and owned many cotton mills technically belonging to him. Some serfs even accumulated large fortunes and could do as they pleased with them if they got their owners' formal agreement.

But these were of course exceptional instances. By and large there was no escape from the network of rules and customs that imprisoned most of the serfs, and when serfdom was formally introduced in the Ukraine and southeastern Russia, there was no longer any refuge from bondage.

It is this plain and simple fact that made Catherine's copy of Montesquieu's ideas in her *Instruction* a mere quip—she was repaying the landed nobility for their support by giving them free rein with their human cattle. The minor measures she passed mitigating grosser abuses, such as forbidding the enslavement of peasants once emancipated, or liberating some peasants upon the promotion of a village to a city, were more or less cancelled out by the wholesale distribution of vast troops of peasants to her favorites and generals. In fact the Russian peasantry was at the very nadir of its long and miserable existence during the reign of the Philosophers' Friend.

In reaction to this situation, the classical flight of the peasants continued without let-up; attempts to curb it, both by threats and cajolement, met with little success. Poland was one of the favorite refuges of runaway serfs until it was wiped out as a sovereign state. Catherine's foreign policy, which led to the partition of Poland and extended serfdom to the Ukraine and southeastern Russia, was welcomed with pleasure by the serf-owners. Though her regime could not remedy the conditions that provoked mass flight, it could at least block the escape hatches.

Mass flight and desertion aggravated the situation. The owner was vitally preoccupied by desertion since it not only cut into the revenues represented by the serfs' labor, but it increased the burdens of those remaining by making them bear the taxes and furnish the contingents of recruits that the runaways would have had to meet. This added burden naturally increased discontent, which incited the serfs to further flight or rebellion.

The growing mood of rebellion, exacerbated by the tightening of serfdom and in consequence of the relative emancipation of the nobility, culminated in the Peasant War of 1773–74, led by one more obscure, illiterate, and adventurous Cossack, Pugachov. This revolt, begun by Pugachov with an initial following of only eighty men, mushroomed so rapidly that it approximated the upheaval of the Time of Troubles. It actually endangered the throne.

The widely publicized Legislative Commission for which Catherine had written her equally publicized *Instruction* had fortified long-standing rumors about an emancipation of the serfs. When this hope was dashed by repressive measures, such as the above mentioned decree of August 1767 forbidding the serfs to complain against their masters, and the Commission itself was dissolved, an ugly mood struck root throughout the country. This, combined with the damaged prestige of the throne itself as a result of the constant series of palace revolutions since the reign of Peter the Great, accentuated by the murders of both Catherine's husband, Peter III, in 1762 and another claimant, Ivan VI, in 1764, generated the usual flock of imposters claiming to be one miraculously escaped Tsar or another. There were at least half a dozen pretenders in the decade after Catherine's seizure of power.

Pugachov was the most effective of these pretenders. After an extraordinary saga of adventure—commonplace for a Russian frontiersman of the time—he escaped from a jail in Kazan in 1773 and passed himself off as Peter III, a name he had been using intermittently for some months.

Pugachov's program was immensely effective among the numerous dissident elements of the population; it was also vague and contradictory. He promised an end to the landowners' regime, the restoration of the Old Faith and old-fashioned dress, a prohibition on the shaving of beards, and happiness for everyone. He said he would not rule the country himself but would simply depose Catherine as a usurper and install his son the Grand Duke Paul on the throne. His entourage was a clumsy burlesque of the Petersburg court. Once again a peasant revolt was presenting itself as a demand for the restoration of the rightful Tsar.

Pugachov unleashed a reign of terror. Though the noble landowners were the natural targets of his revolutionary program, the Cossacks and peasants did not do very well either. The same sort of situation developed as the one that would later turn Russia into a shambles during the civil war that followed the Bolshevik seizure of power in 1917—if the people rejected Pugachov, they were flogged to death or hanged; if they yielded, the punitive troops the government sent to put Pugachov down would do the same thing.

Pugachov was helped by the enthusiasm of the nomadic Turkic-speaking tribes such as the Bashkirs, Kirghizes, and Tatars, the forced laborers in the mines and workshops of the Urals, and the runaway serfs the provinces of Orienburg and Kazan were teeming with. On the negative side, he was favored by the feebleness of the local authorities, the shortage of reliable troops, and the incompetence of the central government. He occasionally assembled as many as twenty and even thirty thousand troops, or rather large groups of guerrillas incapable of any sustained *élan*. Whenever these casual stragglers encountered even a semblance of organized action from government troops, they melted away again; the regime was still capable of coping with an essentially anarchic uprising.

In 1775 Pugachov was executed in Moscow: his head was flaunted on a pole, and sections of his dismembered body were broken on the wheel in public and then burned. The authorities had been so alarmed by the success of the movement, and especially by the obvious fact that it was due not to any positive qualities but simply to a pervasive state of discontent, that the Holy Synod actually anathematized Pugachov's followers. Both his house and the whole of his native village were levelled to the ground; the village was transported to the opposite bank of the Don River and given a different name. The government's retaliation was as ferocious as the movement itself.

The Pugachov revolt enabled the bureaucratic arm of the absolutist regime to justify itself: it had defended the nobility—incompetently but in the long run effectively—against a common enemy. The peasants, acting alone before the development of a middle class and an industrial working class, had proved incapable of summoning up the technical capacities needed for an assault on the existing order.

Despite its aggravation of social and economic problems,

Catherine's regime, by flinging open the gates of at least upper-class Russia to the fructifying influences of French civilization, was another crucial stage in Russia's evolution. This time Russia, after having learned from Dutch and German technology, was thrust into the schoolrooms of France. French culture, which had been very much in vogue even under Peter's daughter, Elizabeth, now had the field to itself, except for a period of intense interest in German ideas that affected intellectuals and the "official" class in the nineteenth century.

Catherine's reign marked the beginning of the French tutelage of Russian society as a whole that lasted till 1917. The French language and a smattering of French literature became an emblem of social status and the precondition of a successful career. French tutors and private schools run by foreigners became astonishingly fashionable, so much so that any number of French barbers, coachmen from Marseilles, and often downright criminals would guide budding Russian nobles in the arts of civilization. All this took place, of course, in the summits of society. Catherine was far too taken up with expensive foreign wars and the repression of peasant uprisings to cope with the project of popular education. There were practically no schools at all. The upper classes had not yet swallowed their aversion to schools sponsored by the government; the few schools in existence could scarcely find the quota of pupils laid down for them. (Throughout Catherine's reign only one M.D. was conferred by the University of Moscow.)

The influx of influences of all kinds into Russia was matched by the exodus of noblemen abroad: their right to travel, granted by Peter III and confirmed by Catherine, for the first time gave them a chance to see Western Europe for themselves. There was a stampede to Paris, which, while offering the conventional nobleman an opportunity to ruin himself in gambling-dens, brothels, cafés, restaurants, and dress-shops, also opened the eyes of many others to Western European life, which began to change the artistic life of Russia at an increasing pace and initiated a ferment that for the next few generations was to churn up the Russian educated classes.

The effects on architecture were perhaps the most obvious.

St. Petersburg, an icy quagmire in 1703, was a celebrated me-
tropolis a century later; it had grown much more swiftly than
any other eighteenth-century city. Since Peter the Great had
been determined to make St. Petersburg an arresting symbol
of Russia's new orientation—a "window to the West"—and
thus a complete contrast to the ancient capital, it was the
chief focus of the innovations initiated by him and carried
on by his successors. The europeanization of the new capital
symbolized the growing cleavage between Russia's elite and
the rest of the population that was the outcome of Peter's
determination to overhaul Russia.

About 1713 Peter the Great had begun employing great numbers of European artists, architects, and engineers, more or
less indiscriminately. A Frenchman, Le Blond, and a Swiss
Italian, Tressini, were the only men of real distinction he found.
His urgency set them all to work helter-skelter, often side
by side on buildings standing next to each other. It was common for a building to be designed by an Italian or Frenchman,
started by a German or Dutchman, and finished by still another
architect.

A certain unity was given the city by the domination of
the baroque then in international vogue, though each architect
interpreted the general style in his own terms. In Peter's time,
accordingly, the city was a curious mixture of German, French,
Dutch, and Italian baroque that had not yet been fused into
a Russian harmony.

The first thirty-five years of the city's existence were marked
by a certain planless groping; the final establishment of its
center on the land side instead of on the islands during the
1730s ended an era of purely utilitarian construction, signalized
by the Empress Anne's building of the Winter Palace.

Elizabeth's unrestrained love of amusement laid its imprint
on what may be considered the second phase in the integration
of Petersburg. The city added the attributes of an imperial residence to its commercial, maritime, and military establishments.

Under Catherine the Great the capital was given its definitive
character as a center of government, transcending its use as

a port, military outpost, or imperial seat. The center was devoted to government offices and ministries; new palaces were erected primarily in the suburbs.

In spite of the disparate sources of the new architecture, a fusion was finally effected between the foreign architects and their Russian environment that established a characteristically Russian monumental style, partly because of the increasing familiarity of Russians with foreign countries, and even more because of the gradual melting together of specific national traditions into a more or less unitary international style, promoted by the growing influence of the European academies and of the numerous architectural publications, all tending toward a unification of theory and practice.

Perhaps the primary unifying factor was the revival of an interest in antiquity, which proved a magnet for the most widely differing political and social tendencies. The excavations of Herculaneum and Pompeii, accompanied by the assumption of the superiority of classical art that became fashionable, established a concert of opinion unknown since the Middle Ages. A supranational point of view came to be accepted as a matter of course; the similarities between contemporary public buildings in Russia, England, and America are striking. Since symbols are inherently plastic, American republicanism, English aristocratic romanticism, and Russian absolutism could derive equal inspiration from the admiration of the rediscovered beauties of the classical world.

Though the merry Tsarina Elizabeth's tastes were quite different from Catherine the Great's, Elizabeth left Catherine far more to build on than is generally recognized. Elizabeth's favorite architect, Count Bartolommeo Rastrelli (1700–71), was the son of an Italian sculptor (the title was papal) who had come to Russia in 1715 with Le Blond. During the formative years of St. Petersburg, Rastrelli showed such talent that he was sent abroad to study, once to Paris, where he worked under Robert de Cotte, and the second time on a lengthy visit to Saxony, Bohemia, Austria, and Italy. Empress Anne had been the first to recognize his gifts; in 1752 she commissioned him to rebuild the Winter Palace designed by Tressini and another Italian architect, Niccolò Michetti.

But it was under Elizabeth that Rastrelli established his authority. He not only designed the major government buildings for twenty years but acted as general supervisor of all architectural construction in the country. Since the younger generation gradually came under his sway, his talents became embedded in the mid-century Russian style.

Both in the magnificent Summer Palace (torn down at the end of the century) and in the Anichkov Palace (extensively rebuilt) as well as in a variety of other palaces, churches, and town houses for the nobility, Rastrelli demonstrated eclecticism at its best. While not wholly derivative, nor on the other hand completely untraditional, his work combined the best elements of a variety of styles in something that somehow looked Russian. In his churches especially he went beyond Peter the Great's tastes to a recollection of the older Orthodox style; in his Cathedral of St. Andrew in Kiev and the Smolny Convent in Petersburg, he achieved an extraordinary combination of spontaneity and sensitivity of balance. These buildings are considered to be rococo in the broadest sense: they manifest a highly personal attitude toward the baroque, infused with a worldly lightheartedness.

The Catherine Palace in Tsarskoe Selo and the Winter Palace in St. Petersburg, which Rastrelli reconstructed, were the chief imperial palaces. They were the last great works he undertook for Elizabeth. They gave formal expression to the symbolism embodied in the residences of the autocracy.

Rastrelli's achievement may be summed up as the creation of a Russian baroque that was both consistent and distinguished, by its scale, its use of colors, and its protean lushness of contrivance. It has a peculiarly theatrical quality that makes it a bridge between the life of spectacle, exemplified in Elizabeth's passion for masquerade balls, and the grandeur of official institutions.

Catherine's accession put an abrupt end to Rastrelli's influence. Perhaps partly because of her contempt for Elizabeth,

Catherine did her best during the 1760s to obliterate in one way or another the rococo inherited from her aunt.

Full of ideas, of her own and of others, and set on making Russia fittingly European in order to deserve the admiration of her foreign friends, Catherine introduced a novel point of view that stimulated a branching out of the revival of classical architecture in two different directions. For the first time in Russian history a sovereign made a distinction between public life and private. In ancient Muscovy this would have been unthinkable, and the distinction was quite alien to the interests of Peter the Great and Elizabeth, but since Catherine was, after all, thoroughly European, it was natural for her to carry on a private life while establishing the external symbols of an imperial apparatus.

Thus two types of buildings came into vogue during her reign: public buildings of unprecedented scope, and dwellings for private, though of course regal, use. An intermediate category might be considered to be those buildings erected for her lovers or buildings she inspired the wealthier nobility to undertake. As Empress, Catherine was powerful enough to indulge a desire for privacy, while the greater nobility, who owned vast estates and troops of serfs, had to be content with indulging an addiction to magnificence.

Turning away abruptly from Elizabeth's fancies, Catherine spent the first two decades of her reign in stimulating innovation through the work of three architects: Velten, a German, Rinaldi, an Italian, and Bazhenov, a Russian. These three may be taken as a transition between the baroque and the later classical influence generally associated with Catherine; each was responsible for at least one major building that, while baroque in design or elevation, marked a definite shift toward the classical in detail.

Catherine also made use of a talented Frenchman, Jean-Baptiste de la Mothe, who was summoned to Russia in 1759 and made a professor in the newly established Academy of Fine Arts in Moscow. Catherine, who must have been impressed by the Academy, commissioned de la Mothe to build

the first Hermitage as a private residence for her to retire
to from the wind-swept splendors of the Winter Palace. De
la Mothe skillfully grafted a characteristic annex of his own
onto Rastrelli's ornate structure. He also gave St. Petersburg
its Markets (Gostinny Dvor) on the Nevsky Prospect.

In the third and last phase of Catherine's patronage of architecture, the character of St. Petersburg, and thus of so much
of eighteenth-century Russian architecture, was consummated:
classicism, in a fusion of ancient Roman architecture and the
revival of Palladio, the sixteenth-century master, carried the
day. This classical efflorescence under Catherine, who had a
weakness for the mere activity of building as well as for ancient
Rome, was executed by another trio of gifted architects: the
Scotsman Cameron, the Italian Quarenghi, and the Russian
Starov.

Starov's most distinguished work was perhaps his design
for the Tauride Palace that Catherine gave her lover Potyomkin;
it was remodeled again and again(ultimately it became the
seat of government during the 1917 upheaval). Its splendid
colonnade became a favorite object of imitation in numerous
palaces and private houses. Indeed, its style infected all Russia: the aristocratic islets scattered throughout the countryside
began sprouting manors based on Starov's imitation of patrician Roman architecture. Somehow they blended intimately
with the birch-copses and rolling hills of the Russian woodlands
and plains.

Cameron, a Scottish Jacobite, came to Russia at Catherine's
invitation in 1779; he stayed on as her favorite architect until
her death in 1796. There is some mystery about his antecedents
and the circumstances of his arrival in Russia. He was known
for his admiration of classical art and of Palladio as well as
for his interest in eastern Europe. He may have had a fancy
for Russia because of the likelihood of his being regarded in
England as a rival of the famous Adam brothers, while on
the continent his being a Jacobite would not be a disadvantage.

Cameron's talent, formed by a study of Palladio, had been
refined by the French architect Charles-Louis Clérisseau, an-

other foreigner Catherine liked. His style was modeled on Roman patterns as popularized by the Adam brothers. It combined classical forms with comfort and made flexible use of scale to provide for both intimacy and austere dignity as required. It also displayed a novel opulence in accordance with Catherine's taste for luxurious materials, in contrast with the old St. Petersburg custom of using brick and plaster. Cameron was particularly fond of the exotic; he specialized in intricate ornamentation and a subtle use of color, in contrast with the strong primary colors characteristic of Tsarskoe Selo under Elizabeth.

By carrying on the tradition of the Adam brothers, Cameron was important as a link in the preparation of the style that came to fruition under Catherine's grandson, Alexander I. More immediately, his influence is visible in the Pantheon of the Tauride Palace. His talent was characteristically expressed in Tsarskoe Selo and Pavlovsk, indissolubly associated with him, and also in the provinces.

Giacomo Quarenghi arrived in Russia only about a year after Cameron. He was perhaps the most distinguished architect of Catherine's reign as well as one of the most prominent architects of the later eighteenth century. Catherine, apparently displeased, unaccountably, with most of her architects except Cameron, had asked a friend, Grimm, to send her "two good architects, Italian by nationality and skilled at their trade." Grimm sent her Trombara, of whom little was heard, and Quarenghi.

Quarenghi remained classical without ever becoming merely archeological, and majestic while retaining human dimensions. It was this deft combination of elements that made Catherine continually refer to his work as "charming." His first commission, the English Palace, which was to remain typical of his work, uniquely mingled classical quality, Palladian design, and Russian dimensions.

Quarenghi's talent extended beyond the buildings he designed: he was used as an advisor to such an extent that he influenced the last twenty years of the eighteenth century more than any other architect in Russia, though during the confusion of Catherine's son Paul's reign he was reduced to designing utilitarian structures (barracks and riding-halls).

Catherine's lavish spending on public buildings, private palaces, and churches, emulated by her favorites and the wealthier nobles, established the huge art collections for which Russia was to become famous. De la Mothe's Hermitage sheltered a vast collection of cameos, statues, drawings, and paintings by Raphael, Murillo, Poussin, Van Dyke, Rembrandt, and many others. The Hermitage collection had been based on the acquisition of a small number of valuable collections, notably those of Baron de Thiers, Sir Robert Walpole, and Count Heinrich Brühl, but it was soon substantially augmented. By the end of the century, St. Petersburg had become one of the major art centers in Europe.

Catherine dutifully devoted herself to music, too, in spite of her being practically tone deaf; she seemed to like the opera, the theater, and the lighter forms of music. Paisiello conducted his own works at the Hermitage, but no native Russian composer worth mentioning appeared until the nineteenth century.

Russian society, that is, the tiny upper-class elite accessible to European influences, was flooded by secular music from the West, both instrumental and vocal. It became fashionable to use music for entertainment of all kinds—banquets, balls, performances. The court was imitated by wealthy squires who organized orchestras and choirs among the serfs. The Italian Opera came to Petersburg in 1835; it gave rise to a few only moderately successful attempts to write Russian operas in the Italian manner.

In the continuing blight that afflicted Russian literature throughout the seventeenth century, leaving scarcely any names worth reminding the unpedantic of, there were nevertheless two figures whose influence was disproportionate. They may be thought of as the precursors of the intelligentsia that was to play a cardinal role during the nineteenth and twentieth centuries.

Alexander Radishchev (1749–1802), who had come under

the influence of French philosophy at the University of Leipzig before becoming a deceptively demure civil servant in Russia, wrote a bitter and effective castigation of serfdom in *A Journey from St. Petersburg to Moscow* (modeled on Laurence Sterne's *Sentimental Journey*). It attacked both bureaucratic incompetence and, even more important, the very principle of monarchical absolutism. After slipping past the censorship in 1790, it was shown to Catherine, who was consumed by rage. Radishchev was sentenced to death but finally exiled to Eastern Siberia for ten years. His book scarcely deserves any literary attention—it is altogether rhetorical, and despite its fury it is perhaps no more than an exercise on a set theme. But the factual background and its free and extravagant expression of the stimulus of the French Revolution, which was to have such a sweeping effect on Russian intellectual life, were to make the later intelligentsia consider Radishchev one of its first martyrs and spokesmen.

Radishchev was released by Catherine's son Paul in 1797, rehabilitated by Alexander I in 1801, and taken back into the civil service. But he seems to have become a melancholiac in exile; he committed suicide the following year.

Nicholas Novikov (1744–1818) became the leader of Russian Freemasonry, which had been introduced into Russia in about 1730 and had considerable success among the upper classes; it was to remain an influence of varying importance for generations. Novikov became a figure in publishing. Because of Catherine's mistrust of Freemasonry and Novikov's acquisition of a huge following, he was sentenced in 1792 to fifteen years in the Schlüsselburg Fortress, only to be pardoned, when already broken in health and spirit, by Emperor Paul.

These are only two examples of the infiltration of new ideas that marked the life of the Russian upper classes during the second half of the eighteenth century. These ideas, though confined to the tiny social elite, generated an intense fermentation. But just because the upper classes had adopted French language, thought, and various exotic theories, the gulf between them and their totally ignorant serfs was made even wider. The divergence grew progressively with the succeeding generations, as education, while encompassing more and more people in the upper strata, failed to penetrate any further. It was to have a decisive effect on the intelligentsia that developed during the nineteenth century.

CHAPTER VI

TSARISM MODERNIZED

*F*or a generation following Catherine's death, nothing
changed much in Russian society, though during the reign
of her grandson, Alexander I, Russia broadened the scope of
her influence from mere territorial expansion in Eastern Europe
and Asia and began to exercise an important, in many ways
decisive, influence on all continental questions, both during
and after the agitation of the Napoleonic wars. Nevertheless,
things had been changing behind the smooth and lustrous fa-
cade of the Empire. An awareness of the shortcomings of absolutism began to affect even the sovereigns.

In a preamble he wrote to a plan for constitutional reform
in the beginning of the nineteenth century, Speransky, one
of Russia's few imaginative statesmen, wrote that there were
only two classes in Russia: "the slaves of the autocrat and
the slaves of the landowners. The former are free merely by
comparison with the latter; in actual fact there are no free
men in Russia except beggars and philosophers. The relationship between these two classes of slaves destroys the energy
of the Russian people."

This thought had been expressed before, but it was now put into words by one of the Tsar's ministers. Though Speransky was ultimately undone by the clarity of his insight into the tangle of Russia's problems, the cleavage between illusion and fact was at last becoming unmistakable even to the topmost officials of the country.

Alexander I's father, Paul I (1796–1801), had been cooling his heels with growing bitterness in the antechambers of the power wielded by his mother Catherine. He ascended the throne at the age of forty-three to rule a mere five years. His German-trained rigidity, and above all the drillmaster's discipline he wished to apply to the nobility as well as to the people at large, left him dangling in a vacuum, exposed to the rancor incurred by his martinet's view of the nobility's privileges.

Paul I had no intention of undertaking anything like a radical solution of the peasant question, though he seems to have had some thought of alleviating their burdens, but he had reverted to the eccentric view that the aristocracy was supposed to serve as well as be served. Without repealing the 1785 Charter of the Nobility, he reinstated service, especially military service, for every nobleman; moreover, he laid a tax on their estates. Even more annoying, and symptomatic of his drillmaster's attitude, he regarded any nobleman convicted of a crime as having forfeited his noble title, thus laying himself open to the corporal punishment from which the nobility was theoretically shielded. Under Paul's reign the loss of a title, rare under Catherine, became more common; once again the nobility was bound to feel a certain insecurity in its relations with the sovereign. By adopting the same disciplinarian attitude toward the officers' corps and a genuinely paternal attitude toward private soldiers, as well as insisting on the fulfillment of all forms of discipline, including court etiquette, Paul gradually made himself so unpopular that his assassination created no ripple of resentment. Like his father before him, he had been guided too exclusively by an abstract view of his absolutist power, disregarding the practical consideration that even abstract views must be sustained by some vested interest.

In fact, regardless of his theories, which revolved around the institution of a rule of law, Paul's political regime became more and more arbitrary. His hatred of republican France, one of the few tastes he shared with his deceased mother, made him heighten the oppressiveness of his regime in the wake of his declaration of war on France. Foreign books, newspapers, and even music were forbidden; foreign travel was prohibited; the censorship became even more severe and was extended even to private correspondence; functionaries were sometimes deported and degraded. In 1801, when he was murdered in his bedchamber through a plot launched by three of his intimates, undoubtedly with Alexander's consent, there was no opposition and a great deal of rejoicing. This was the last palace revolution in Russian history.

When Alexander came to the throne, all still seemed well. Despite the somewhat bizarre circumstances of his accession—his connivance at his father's murder—there was no question of his legitimacy. Full of the French philosophy that had made his grandmother Catherine's conversation such an ornament of her salons, he had imbibed the most grandiose ideas from La Harpe, his Swiss tutor.

Born in 1777, Alexander I was brought up away from his parents under Catherine's direct supervision. A characteristic trait, his ambiguously sphinxlike charm of manner, was due doubtless to his early training. His formal schooling was ended when he was only seventeen; his teacher, La Harpe, was a fervent revolutionary in the fashion of his time, full of French radical ideas yet willing to trim his sail to the wind of autocracy. Alexander was brought up in two entirely conflicting atmospheres, the rhetorical liberalism of Catherine's court on the one hand, and the Prussian atmosphere of his father's entourage in Gatchina, where he was allowed to visit often toward the end of Catherine's reign.

Alexander, having learned at an early age to navigate between two conflicting winds, exemplified throughout his life the two attitudes taught him as a youth: liberalism in rhetoric and in practice devotion to the barrack-room regimentation identified with his father. It may have been the need he felt to plaster over the basic difference in these points of view that led to his charm of manner, which was successful with almost everyone and which in combination with his personal appearance—he was tall, fair, handsome, and limped a little from a horseback fall while young—lent him a peculiar aura of attractiveness.

Alexander's character, indeed, embodied the same contrast as his grandmother Catherine's—extravagant lip-service to the ideals of the French education they had been nurtured on, and in practical affairs an iron hand. This contrast may underlie his reputation as the "Sphinx," the "enigmatic Tsar." The French Ambassador at St. Petersburg, Count de La Ferronays, summed it up in 1820. "He talks of the rights of man, of those of peoples, and of the duties of a monarch as the disciple of a philosopher can and should talk, but at the same time he enforces his most arbitrary wishes with a greater despotism and ruthlessness than Peter the Great."

Speransky's rapid rise may be explained by his ability at grasping the general principles involved in Alexander's essentially declamatory view of affairs, while his even more abrupt decline was due to exactly the same thing—the moment Speransky approached the nub of the conclusions liberal principles inevitably led to in the Russia of his time, the very exactitude in their realization inevitably dispelled the mysterious enchantment due to gushing verbiage and left Alexander confronted by a chill reality.

It is significant that the most powerful personality associated with Alexander I was Arakcheyev (1769–1834), whose name is a synonym in Russian for ruthlessness. Arakcheyev's ascendancy coincided with that of the liberal Speransky, a coincidence that must be taken as a tribute to Alexander's simultaneously adroit and strong-willed maneuvering, since both Speransky and Arakcheyev were disliked by court and bureaucratic circles. For that matter, despite great personal differences, the universally charming Alexander and the universally loathed Arakcheyev had a great deal in common: they were both obsessed by the sort of orderliness and external symmetry achieved by close-order regimental drilling. This obsession of theirs underlay a common religiosity.

Alexander's piety may have been responsible for a growing detachment from practical affairs that began around 1812. It was made up of many elements, focussed on the study of the Bible, which Alexander interpreted in terms of his highly capricious association with Swedenborgians, Quakers, Freemasons, Russian dissenters, and individual visionaries.

Despite Alexander's supple charm in public, there can be no doubt of his firm, though capricious, will. In foreign policy, for instance, the alliance he contracted with Bonaparte in 1807, and his leadership in the anti-Napoleonic coalition of 1813–15, crowned by Waterloo, the Russian entry into Paris, and especially the Holy Alliance itself, were actually pushed through against domestic opposition.

Since the condition of the peasants remained unchanged throughout Alexander's reign, the uprisings endemic in Russian life kept breaking out. When Napoleon invaded Russia in 1812, rumors sprang up as usual about the imminent liberation of the serfs, a minority of them believing that Napoleon would free them, while most thought the Tsar would reward them for fighting off the invaders. Despite Napoleon's generally liberal influence throughout Central Europe, he seems never even to have considered improving his military position by emancipating the serfs.

Alexander's death created a slight mystery, well in keeping with his enigmatic character: a legend sprang up to the effect that he had not died at Taganrog on the Black Sea in 1825 but had vanished and taken up the guise of a holy monk, Theodore Kuzmich, dying at last in Siberia in 1864. Though this seems to be no more than a legend, there are so many convincing details about it that many knowledgeable people have believed it (including Tolstoy, who wrote an affecting story about it, published posthumously).

It was during Alexander I's reign that Russia for the first time achieved a position of international primacy, as a result of its decisive role in the undoing of Napoleon. Throughout the Napoleonic epoch and its aftermath, Russia, despite her sustained and savage defeats because of the shifting imbalance of the remainder of the continent, occupied a focal position.

Alexander's public gifts played a great role and gave him the nickname of the Blessed. During his reign, extensive new territories fell to the Russian crown: Finland, Bessarabia, and spacious territories in Poland and the Caucasus were added to the vast, relatively uninhabited Empire, creating in the case of Finland and Poland additional centers of disaffection.

The War of 1812, which has received so much publicity from nationally minded Russian historians as well as from the popularity of Tolstoy's *War and Peace,* had far less importance than it has been given. Napoleon's invasion lasted only six months, and it took the Grand Army a mere seven weeks to get out of the country: indeed, the whole invasion was both preceded and followed by far more ruinous Russian invasions of a score of countries.

As for the Holy Alliance, with which Alexander's name is associated, though he seems to have had sincerely idealistic or mystical ambitions for it, it never achieved the status of the "universal union" Alexander had dreamed of for it. Its influence, to some extent because of Metternich's skill in playing on Alexander's illusions, remained negative, a bulwark against revolutionary movements in Germany, Italy, and Spain.

By and large Russian society remained as lopsided as ever. The cities continued growing very slowly. Though domestic trade increased somewhat, the small and socially declassed bourgeoisie still had no say in public affairs. Despite his increasing administrative harshness, Alexander had not continued his assassinated father's attempt to discipline the nobility as well as the rest of the country, but though still in possession of its privileges the nobility was becoming increasingly restive. Its more alert or cosmopolitan members were chafing more and more at the very principle of autocracy. The alliance between the crown and its mainstay was beginning to crack.

There were still no elementary schools in Russia when Alexander's reign began, practically no state-sponsored secondary schools except military academies, and only three universities. An attempt was made to overhaul this skimpy educational system in 1803, but it collided with the same difficulties as all such previous attempts throughout the eighteenth century:

the absence of funds, the profound mistrust of state-sponsored schools, and the dearth of teachers. The 1803 plan had pathetic results: in 1824 only some 4,465 pupils attended lower schools throughout the vast St. Petersburg region: enrollment in secondary school had risen from 5,600 in 1809 to 7,700 in 1825. There were only 820 students attending Moscow University in 1824, almost half the total number of students in Russia.

This was in sharp contrast with the private schools of the nobility, which emphasized such useful accomplishments as French and dancing. In 1824 there were over 2,000 students attending these private schools in the St. Petersburg region, as against the 450 in the state-sponsored secondary schools and the 51 in the University of St. Petersburg.

The disproportion between the ideas of the enlightened summit of society and the material institutions of Russia, an imbalance that characterized Alexander's reign as much as Catherine's, remained the source of a growing tension that was to be pregnant with consequence. Western liberal and revolutionary ideas had played a great role in the drawing-room talk under Catherine, but toward the second decade of the nineteenth century they finally began to acquire flesh and blood. While the bulk of the nobility—those settled on and living off their own estates—were inherently conservative for fear of disturbing the serfdom that was the source of their wealth, the young officers who had been floating about Western and Central Europe during the Napoleonic turmoil had been brought into close contact both with the turbulent intellectual currents released by the French Revolution and with the moral and material superiority of the Western masses over the Russian.

The simple fact that so many European peasants, however heavy their burdens, were free men who were not subject to corporal punishment was an arresting example of the abyss that separated Russia from the West even in a period of general agitation and breakdown. The contrast between the backwardness of the Russian masses and the military prowess of the Russian armies had a stimulating effect; when these young officers got back to Russia aflame with enthusiasm for the new ideas they had encountered, their renewed contact with the obscurantist regime of Arakcheyev and Alexander kindled the spark of political opposition.

European influence had a dual effect. The tiny minority influenced by liberal ideas was disappointed by the course of events after the settlement of the Napoleonic turmoil: the growth of the security police, the harshness of the censorship, the promotion of the military colonies—a peculiarly silly idea, both oppressive and futile, that was one of Alexander's quirks—as well as the general ascendancy of religiosity, both mystical and orthodox, in the Tsar's entourage, all gave the ardent liberal aristocrats a feeling of suffocation. In addition, the evolution of Alexander's Holy Alliance into an agency for the suppression of the liberty and national independence he had so often praised was inherently unpopular—Russian liberals found it both pointless and reprehensible for Russian troops to intervene in Spain and in Italy. Contrariwise, the more radical of the liberal aristocrats were excited by the upheavals that had become commonplace in Southern Europe as well as in Central and South America.

The aristocratic opposition to the existing order came together in secret societies, a natural consequence of the concealment of strongly felt ideas. The opposition was expressed solely by the most aristocratic segment of society under the leadership of some of the greatest names in Russia. These secret societies, themselves the reflection of the great European current of thought aimed at "reaction," with parallels in the Italian *Carbonari,* the French *charbonnerie,* and the German *Tugêndbund,* had a specific political character; some aristocrats even accepted the assassination of the Tsar as a means to their goal. These societies were in sharp contrast with the somewhat dreamily humanitarian Masonic Lodges that after a long period of suppression under Catherine the Great and Paul I had returned to Russia under Alexander I.

The aristocratic mutineers had any number of reasons for disaffection: the corruption of the courts, the deplorable condition of the armed forces, to which as officers they were particularly sensitive, the abysmally low salaries of government officials and the resulting corruption, the savage conditions in the packed prisons, the economic stagnation, and the staggering burden of taxation, which oppressed all strata of the population, including the nobility. Above all, the condition of the peasantry was particularly upsetting to liberal Russians, who saw in the reform of serfdom not merely the fulfillment of abstract considerations of compassion but the furthering of their self-interest.

The general malaise was doubtless heightened by the widespread impression made by Alexander's personal brand of liberalism. There was an inherent tendency toward action in the theoretical liberalism of eighteenth-century Russia; Alexander's liking for constitutional government and detestation of serfdom were taken seriously in aristocratic and military circles. For that matter something had actually been done about it—constitutions had really been given Finland and Poland; there was perennial hope for a constitutional reform in Russia itself.

In December 1825 all these factors culminated in an insurrection, the first in Russian history to be engendered by an attitude based on principle in contrast with the play of selfish interests. The enterprise was halted instantly.

Only a handful of people were involved in the preparations, but they were in a state of hopeless disagreement on all practical points. For that matter they were split from the very outset into factions with basically differing perspectives. The great aristocrats and Guards officers from Petersburg, while agreeing that representative government and the emancipation of the serfs would be good things, were entirely in favor of property rights. They leaned toward a constitutional monarchy. The lesser nobles, who served in line regiments, were far more radical. Paul Pestel, for instance, a founder of the Union of Salvation, was a republican: he envisaged a centralized, egalitarian, and democratic republic that would exclude all privileges arising out of status or wealth. He was also a Great Russian expansionist: he wanted to expel the Jews from Russia wholesale and conquer various territories still inhabited by Mongols. Prince Trubetskoy, on the other hand, thought that the dynasty could be retained by forcing it to grant a few reforms. It was the inherent irreconcilability between these differing aims that doubtless explains the extraordinary slovenliness in the preparations for the insurrection. In the event it was a complete fiasco.

Alexander's unexpected death in November 1825 forced the conspirators to advance the date that in spite of all internal friction had been settled on. Alexander's death and the attendant uncertainty about the succession because of the ambiguous position of his brother Constantine, the heir-apparent, were a great opportunity for the conspirators, but all they could demonstrate was their unripeness. Trubetskoy's primary anxiety was to forestall popular intervention; he believed that the insurrection had to be kept strictly within the bounds of an action by the armed forces under the closest possible control of their officers. What he actually wanted was an orderly upheaval. But the membership of the secret societies involved was minute; more important, it consisted of almost nothing but junior officers. It was obvious that their effect on the rank-and-file, unaware of the broader implications of the insurrection, would be less effective than the authority of their superiors. There was no question of any solidarity between the junior officers and the soldiery.

The fiasco was grotesque. Trubetskoy vanished from the Senate square, where the actual seizure of power was to take place, and Prince Eugene Obolensky, who took charge, had no idea what orders to give. Everyone stood around doing nothing at all, while government troops under the personal command of Nicholas, who had succeeded his brother Alexander, thronged into the square and the adjacent streets. The insurgents, though listless and unled, refused to surrender; since their resistance was encouraged by a great many civilians who mingled with them and occasionally attacked the government troops with stones and logs, Nicholas decided on firmer action to forestall the transformation of the army mutiny into a popular rebellion. A few field guns were brought up; after the third volley, the insurgents were routed. By the time darkness set in, the Senate square was cleared except for seventy or eighty corpses, including some civilians.

Nicholas also supervised the subsequent commission of en-
quiry, demonstrating a love for interrogation that was to remain
one of his traits. Most of the insurgent leaders hurried to
surrender, and with the exception of Pestel and a few others
they made an embarrassing spectacle of extravagant remorse.
In pouring out their hearts, they freely implicated innocent
people. Of the almost six hundred people interrogated, one
hundred and twenty-one were finally tried, and in such a way
that some of them did not realize that their hearing had been
before a court. Five of them were sentenced to death, including
Pestel, while more than a hundred were deported to prison
in Siberia.

The Decembrist revolt was futile. On the one hand, the
people were utterly uninvolved, with no social group between
the peasantry and the aristocracy-bureaucracy to provide the
pseudorevolt with any social support. On the other hand, the
revolt could not have been successful in the manner of the
traditional palace revolutions because its makers had gone beyond such considerations, though not far enough. They tried
to ideologize and socialize a mutiny in an ambience that had
no foundations for it. They were blinded by a form of sentimental confusion about what they represented. Fundamentally,
they represented only themselves, but since their education
had projected them beyond the sphere of vulgar egotistic or
cliquish ambitions and provided them with an arsenal of ideas,
they failed to see through these ideas to the brute fact that
socially they were in a void. They were in effect championing
a nation that had never heard of them, nor could have.

The rebels' sincere desire to restrain the autocracy foundered
on their reluctance to give up their own social primacy, itself
dependent on the services of the peasantry they were consequently afraid to risk arousing. Thus, however brilliant the
individuals among these aristocratic officers, their isolated position was doubtless responsible for their most characteristic
collective trait—indecisiveness.

Of course, it is only too easy to produce such *post facto*
generalizations. In fact, if the insurgents had not been so slack
and had been more practical in concrete preparations, the De-

cembrist enterprise might have produced an altogether different result. Aside from Nicholas's personal unpopularity, the sympathies of a whole section of the population were obviously with the movement. It was doubtless a case in which a practicable scheme was wrecked by its executors.

Despite the lackadaisical, inept, and to some extent cowardly character of the Decembrist uprising, it became a symbol for future generations of dissident Russians. It is true that the crushing of the insurrection itself for a time pulverized Russian liberal thought. Since the Decembrists, with rare exceptions, had no desire to undo the existing order, they had no motive to sustain a revolutionary attitude. Most of the former liberals melted back into their milieu. Some members of the secret societies who had escaped Siberia covered themselves with distinction in the service of Nicholas; the exceptions, whose personal convictions made such surrender impossible, thrust themselves into what was to become the underground.

The fact is that while the secret societies were eliminated as a result of the Decembrist failure, the conditions that had spawned them continued and kept their ideals alive. These ideals were a negative reflection of the various imbalances in Russia; their survival was ensured by the failure of the regime to right them.

Perhaps one of the chief effects of the Decembrist mutiny was its reinforcement of the repressive party in court circles. The dilemma facing authority in a situation of disaffection may be said to be universal: it is bound to turn toward either mollification or repression.

Nicholas, a drillmaster like his predecessors, was profoundly moved by the abortive mutiny. It remained a constant preoccupation of his, all the more so because it had involved the Guards, the flower of the army he regarded as the bulwark of the autocracy. He showed a keen interest in the Decembrists he had exiled to Siberia; even more, he was far from blind to the cause of their rebelliousness. Indeed, Nicholas wa quite aware throughout his life of the necessity of some kind of reform, even though nothing was ever attempted during his reign. His attitude toward the master institution, serfdom, a suppurating wound in Russian society, sums up the contradictoriness and paralysis inherent in this dilemma: "There is no doubt that in its present form serfdom is a flagrant evil everyone is aware of, yet to attempt to remedy it now would be, of course, an evil still more disastrous." (He said this at a State Council meeting in March 1842.)

It was doubtless the awareness of the deep-rootedness of serfdom, as well as of its inherent perniciousness, that paralyzed Nicholas's willpower and intelligence, and throughout his reign this gave Russia a look of frozen immobility—an immobility that, as events were to show, was deceptive.

The twenty-year reign of Nicholas I saw absolutism at its apogee. He had received a good education, at any rate in languages, though like Alexander's it ended at age seventeen, but he showed no interest in such things as political economy and government, subjects he sneered at as "abstractions." His chief interest was warfare, particularly military engineering. Nicholas gave the classical principle of Russian autocracy a slight twist of his own by emphasizing dynastic and religious elements, the supreme virtue of duty and discipline, and national tradition. His view of the state was essentially that of a smoothly running regiment, based on a detailed hierarchy, rigid specification of duties, and the unquestionable authority of the head. This lucid outlook was summed up by his Minister of Eduction, Uvarov, in a formula that was to become famous: "Orthodoxy, autocracy, and nationality." (There is reason to believe the slightly ambiguous final word of the formula was actually a euphemism tactfully substituted for the more downright—and accurate—word, *serfdom*.)

"Nationality" never actually meant anything definite; it was generally used to convey the notion of "official patriotism," which is how Uvarov's slogan is generally referred to in Russian literature. Uvarov's obsequious inflation of Russia's past and present was particularly engaging because he himself had never read a Russian book in his life; he was at home only in French and German.

In education this slogan meant that the existing order had to be preserved by eliminating subversive, i.e., liberal, influences. The goal of the authorities was to discourage students from studying anything beyond their station and to concentrate in the government's hands the control of all intellectual life. But the authorities were, inevitably, disappointed. In fact, Nicholas's regime somehow coincided with one of the greatest bursts of literacy as well as of intellectual activity. Not only were some of the greatest Russian literary masterpieces produced, but the seeds of almost the whole subsequent cultural development were contained in the geyser of creativity that burst out in the intellectual vanguard, constricted though it was.

Nicholas had close ties to the Hohenzollerns: at the age of twenty-seven he married King Frederick William III's daughter, sister of the future King Frederick William IV, and had seven children by her. He admired his father-in-law enormously, especially since the Prussian monarchy was an ideal of his. It was during Nicholas's reign that Russia, which had always aped one European country or another, turned its face toward Germany. In Peter the Great's time, advanced Russians chiefly admired techniques and the economic life as exemplified by Holland, Germany, and Sweden; France had been the magnet for the elegant thinkers of the eighteenth century; and England had a short period of tutorship after 1815, when the utilitarians, the Byronic movement, and the economists were looked up to. During Nicholas's reign Germany became once again a lodestone for the official classes because of her absolutism and bureaucratic organization, while at the other pole the intellectuals looked to her for philosophy and rounded *Weltanschaungen*.

German blood poured into the upper classes and the ruling dynasty itself. Germans had first become prominent in Russia because of Peter's personal taste for ability and accuracy, and in mass terms through his Baltic acquisitions, which had a broad upper segment of German landowners and townspeople. The ruling dynasty itself was completely submerged in German blood as a result of the union of Catherine the Great, a German princess, with Peter III, the son of Peter the Great's daughter Anne and the Duke of Holstein-Gottorp. It is curious to reflect that every Russian sovereign since Catherine the Great married a German, so that even if her son Paul was not Peter III's son but was, as is likely, the son of a lover of hers called Saltykov, the amount of Russian blood to be attributed to any Romanov after Catherine is infinitesimal. If Paul was indeed Peter III's son, the blood of Nicholas II, the last Romanov sovereign, was only $\frac{1}{128}$ Russian.

Thus German influence had an altogether sweeping effect both on Russian officialdom and on the Russian intelligentsia. Because of the force of ideas, it was to be much more far-reaching in the intellectual sphere; ultimately, because of Marxism and kindred philosophies, it was of cardinal consequence.

Nicholas's political rigidity, his fear of popular discontent and of the principle of national self-determination that was making such headway in Europe during the nineteenth century, and his natural concern with the interests of the landed aristocracy made reform at home impossible. It also spurred him on to an aggressive and universally irritating policy abroad. Thus, while his theoretically paternalistic regime was in fact a police state, his foreign policy, though relatively successful at first—laying the foundations for the conquest of the Caucasus and making some Asiatic acquisitions while definitely enfeebling Turkey—ultimately led to the Russian catastrophe in the Crimean War of 1853–56. A major factor in the confusion that led up to this war was another reflection of Nicholas's dynastic obsessions and his lack of any conception of either abstract law or the conduct of states: he believed in the settlement of all questions by direct negotiations between heads of states. This produced a curious sort of personal diplomacy that in the Crimean calamity ended up by impairing the prestige of the regime and pulverizing the myth of Russian military power.

Despite the bitterness that had exploded in the December revolt, the throne and the landed aristocracy were bound to each other by common interests. Nicholas I liked referring to the aristocracy as the "mainstay of the throne;" sometimes he even described himself as "the first nobleman." For their part, the bulk of the noble landowners, blinded by a narrow view of their class interests and desperately anxious about losing their privileges, were in fact solidly behind the throne and the stability it stood for.

Nicholas was at one time obliged to abandon his policy of nonintervention between landowners and serfs in the Polish provinces he annexed after crushing a Polish insurrection in 1830–31; he also took some measures designed to weaken the position of Polish landowners *vis-à-vis* their Russian serfs. All that was, however, part of a general campaign of russification: it had nothing to do with emancipation and amounted to a mere definition of mutual rights and duties.

A way out of the impasse created by serfdom would have been an improvement in farming technique, but only a small minority of the more open-minded nobles took to this. Except in the case of some sugar refineries, most attempts to rationalize the farms took place against a background of backwardness; they were almost uniformly fiascoes. The basic difficulty was pervasive: rationalization could be done only with capital investments, but since the only capital most of the landowners had was their serfs, any attempt to modernize technique collided with the unwillingness or ineptitude of the uneducated and traditionally minded servile population. This interacted with the fluctuating international prices for produce and the limited capacity of the market, both foreign and domestic, which made the profitability of even a major capital investment dubious. It was this combination of circumstances that forced some of the more progressive landowners into a blanket condemnation of serfdom as the source of evil in and for itself.

But most landowners were reluctant to take such a leap into the unknown. The alternative to the emancipation and technical progress that they inclined toward was squeezing their serfs still further. There was a tendency on the part of many landowners, especially where the land was rich, to start extending the areas farmed by themselves directly, so that increasing numbers of serfs were forced both to pay an annual tribute and to perform services for their owners.

The fact is that both peasants and landowners were being squeezed. The position of the aristocracy was only powerful from an external point of view. Though some 102,870 nobles owned about a third of the territory of Russia in 1859, the great majority of the landowners were impoverished. Of the above total, for instance, more than 75 percent was made up of estates of fewer than 100 male serfs, while those of over 500 male serfs made up only 3.6 percent. The landowners were heavily mortgaged; their debts kept running up, and it was quite common for them to be foreclosed. It was just those proprietors who had the least capital who needed it most, and it was they who were in the greatest of difficulties.

The uneven pace of development that now began to be more and more marked in Russia also, oddly enough, brought about an increase in workers' wages. Industrialization, though still primitive, was progressing rapidly. The relative shortage of labor, due to serfdom and the prevalence of cottage industry, gave the workers a favorable position. Before the emancipation of the serfs, indeed, cottage industry could compete successfully with big industrial plants. Until the widespread use of machinery simple manufacturing processes could be done just as well by craftsmen as by big enterprises.

The number of manufacturing workers more than doubled during Nicholas I's reign, from 210, 000 in 1825 to 483,000 in 1855. In 1860 they numbered some 565,000. It seems likely that servile labor was being forced out by paid labor between 1825 and 1860. The situation was different in the development of mining and metallurgy, most of which enterprises were located in remote provinces. By 1860 the number of workers in mining and metallurgy was about 245,000, of which hired as distinct from servile labor amounted to 30 percent.

By 1860 the total number of industrial workers, accordingly, came to about 800,000, or a little more than 1 percent of the population, with servile labor accounting for about a third of the total. This was four times as many as there had been at the beginning of the century.

Mechanization began to become a substantial factor toward the end of the 1840s; it first made itself felt in textiles, where the technical processes were particularly adaptable to machinery.

As for education, it continued to be restricted to a small

elite. Nevertheless, Russian scholarship was finally launched; in the first part of his reign, Nicholas had sent some gifted Russian students abroad to be trained as scholars. This created a core of professors who were often very distinguished and who were able to arouse the zeal of their abler students. But the number of students remained small: after an increase from 1,700 in 1825 to 4,600 in 1848, it declined to 3,600 in 1854, when Petersburg had only 379 and Moscow 1,061. Nicholas I, who remained hypersensitive to all signs of popular disaffection, turned against education because of the French revolution of 1848 and its European repercussions. In March 1848 officers of the Ministry of Education, including teachers, were forbidden to leave the country. The number of independent students was severely limited. The teaching of the constitutional law of European states, and even of philosophy, was stopped; logic and psychology were put in the hands of theological professors to make sure they fitted in with Orthodox views.

The standards of instruction in lower schools were exceptionally debased, to say nothing of the infinitesimal number of pupils involved. Literacy among the peasants was practically unknown: a peasant child could only attend informal classes where unqualified teachers, often retired soldiers with only glimmerings of literacy themselves, would teach the rudiments of reading and writing.

Jews, a target of Nicholas's special dislike, were under special restrictions: in Russian schools their number was very small. Out of 15,000 students enrolled in 58 high schools (lycées) in 1853, only 155 were Jews. Nicholas wanted to have the Jews completely assimilated after the elimination of their "religious fanaticism and racial exclusiveness." His anti-Jewish policy was part of an intensified persecution of all forms of Russian dissenters as well; religious particularism was taken as a pretext for purely political persecution. But in the case of the Jews as well as in the case of the Old Believers, the policy of russification failed. What happened was that the draconian regime applied to the Jews—including compulsory army service of 25 years, prohibition against employing Gentiles, the dissolution of Jewish autonomous communities, and the compulsory wearing of Jewish traditional dress—was often evaded, furnishing the police and other government officials with an occasion to thrive on the intensified misery.

During Nicholas's reign, foreign policy revolved around a question that was considered to have become cardinal for Russia—the survival of the Ottoman Empire. The Russian attitude toward this question was expressed by Nicholas with a combination of insolence and ambiguity that exasperated the British and French and ultimately led to the Crimean War. Historians are of course fond of demonstrating the inevitability of past events; here, however, it seems likely that it was the incalculable element of personal capriciousness that led to this preposterous and futile war.

Generally speaking, Nicholas's seemed to believe that the maintenance of the status quo in Turkey was to Russia's interest, but at the same time he made no secret of his view that the collapse of the "sick man of Europe" was inevitable. Since not many people agreed with him about this, his making pacific statements while preparing to bury the Ottoman corpse was considered mere hypocrisy. Further, as a legitimist he was indifferent or hostile to the claims of the Greeks and the Balkan Slavs—he regarded them as disloyal subjects of their legitimate rulers—but at the same time he kept encroaching on the Ottoman power in Moldavia and Wallachia. This was naturally taken as another sign of deceit.

Also, Nicholas's irrepressible loathing for France made it difficult for him to secure the working agreement he desired with the British. His dealings with Great Britain were complicated still further by a congenital inability to grasp the dynamics of the British constitution, and hence of the powers of the Queen and her ministers. Of course these limitations of Nicholas's found a counterpart in Napoleon's desire for showy military triumphs, and especially in the obsessive British hatred of Russia shown by Palmerston and by Canning, the British ambassador at Constantinople.

For Nicholas, the Crimean War was a crushing blow: not

only did it mark the checkmate of the international diplomacy he had specialized in, but the army he had been so proud of was defeated.

The Crimean defeat had, as usual, an advantage. Because Russia was so humiliated and the autocracy's shortcomings were dramatically displayed, even conservatives were forced to face the necessity of a serious reform, a widespread feeling that came to a head after Nicholas's death in 1855 and the accession to the throne of his eldest son, Alexander II.

It is difficult to perceive the personal element in most of Alexander's behavior; like his uncle Alexander I, he remains immune to analysis. His practice of keeping people of irreconcilably opposed views simultaneously in office alone makes him elusive. Also, a curious streak of well-publicized sentimentality, perhaps acquired as a boy from his chief tutor Zhukovsky, an emotional humanitarian, blurs the outlines of his character (during the war with Turkey in 1877–78 he proposed attending the wounded in person as a male nurse).

Alexander was just as conservative as his father; he remained true to the autocratic traditions he had inherited by maintaining a very harsh police regime, exiling thousands of people without a trial of any kind. The traditional division of his reign into a liberal part ending with the Era of Great Reforms in 1866, when the first attempt at assassinating him was made, and the reaction afterwards, is wishful thinking: haphazardly mingled reactionary and liberal elements characterized his whole reign.

Alexander II is known as the Tsar-Emancipator, the inspirer of the Era of Great Reforms. His reign spans a general, though far from systematic, overhauling of Russian society, in addition to a number of far-reaching changes in public life. One of the most notable of these was a sweeping reform of the judiciary in 1864, which finally, though hesitantly and imperfectly, introduced the accepted principles of Western European jurisprudence—equality of individuals before the law, the impartiality and accessibility of courts, trial by jury, public proceedings, immunity of judges to removal except for misconduct in office. These new measures gradually eliminated or softened many of the abuses that had given Russian courts a well-deserved reputation for corruption and inequity, though against the background of Russian society as a whole the effects of the judicial reform were superficial.

The most far-reaching reform was the abolition of serfdom. After generations of social and individual malaise, this basic Russian institution was finally sloughed off. But it was done half-heartedly. The procedure was cumbersome and the results defective. The upshot was a regime of elusive complexity socially, administratively, and economically. While giving the peasants something, it did not give them enough to satisfy them; it left profound grievances. In the event, indeed, it satisfied no one, though it did, of course, transform society.

Alexander's decision to emancipate the serfs was doubtless due to the revelation of Russia's ineptitude in the Crimean War as well as to the widespread conviction that emancipation was the only way to forestall a major peasant upheaval. Emancipation was first hinted at in a royal manifesto of March 1856 announcing the end of the Crimean War. In order to enable the public to swallow the depressing terms of the Treaty of Paris, the manifesto alluded significantly to all the benefits peace was supposed to bring Russia, but since its wording was so indefinite it was taken to be merely another sop to piety. Even after emancipation was decided on by Alexander, the government proceeded with as much caution as possible to avoid frightening the landowners. Alexander had tried to persuade them to collaborate in preparing the reform, but since they naturally dragged their feet, the reform had to be prepared, typically enough, by the bureaucratic agencies, a traditional resource of Russian governments in the absence of any genuine public opinion.

In 1857 the landowners were called upon to set up provincial committees to recommend practical steps. Since the landed aristocracy was at heart against the emancipation, they did this as slowly as they could. They saw that serfdom was doomed, but they were determined to hold out for as high a ransom as possible for the liberation of their serfs. The great variety in their recommendations had nothing to do with degrees of conservatism, but was rooted in the diversity of conditions throughout Russia. The chief factors that weighed with the serf-owners were the quality of the soil, the type of estate management, and the density of the population. In the celebrated "black soil" belt, where the land itself made the estate valuable, the serf-owners were prepared not to be reimbursed for liberating their serfs as long as they were not obliged to surrender too much land. Contrariwise, in the less fertile, more industrialized central and northern provinces, where the landlords were often absentees and lived principally off the annual cash tribute paid by their serfs, they were quite willing to be openhanded with their land as long as they were compensated by high indemnities. The provincial committees were at one in recommending that the landed aristocracy keep a tight hold on the peasant population through police and judicial powers: it was natural for them to cling at least to their position in the social hierarchy.

The provincial committees finished their work by the end of 1859; the statutes agreed on were finally enacted in February 1861, and the end of serfdom was solemnly proclaimed (typically enough by a well-known enemy of emancipation, the Metropolitan Philaret). The statutes were originally published in a volume of 360 pages, which had to be amended over and over again. The vagueness and discrepancies in the official text were due to a conflict of opinion in the agencies supposed to formulate the emancipation legislation to their inadequate legal training, and to the pressure they had been working under.

The enactments of February 1861 gave personal freedom to 47 million peasants, of whom the 21 million belonging to the country squires were for all practical purposes slaves. The 20 million who had been crown dependents were in somewhat better circumstances; the remaining 6 million were artisans, industrial workers, or the household personnel of the squires.

But the problem remained that personal liberty was not accompanied by outright ownership of individual property. The entire discussion of emancipation had, after all, revolved around a complex question: should the serfs be freed with or without land? Also, how could the serf-owners be indemnified for the loss of their human property? In the event a complex regime of "more or less" had been instituted.

The reform was to take place in three stages, in the first of which, after the substitution of government agencies to perform the administrative functions formerly exercised by the noble landowners, the serfs were to be freed of their personal dependence on their masters. They were free to marry, own property, engage in commerce, and litigate. This was considered a temporary regime—though no time limit was laid down for it—after which land was supposed to be allotted to former serfs by a cumbersome system of redemption payments. The government handled the redemption debt, intended to make the serfs small farmers, by capitalizing at 6 percent the yearly charges the peasant allotments were assessed at and advancing to the landowners interest-bearing securities amounting to 75–80 percent of the total indemnification due them, the peasants usually providing the remainder. The government was supposed to be repaid by the peasants for the advances to the former owners. At first the peasants were given 49 years to repay the sum; the annual installments were supposed to come to the equivalent of the advance on each allotment, plus interest. Only after this obligation was settled could the serf regard himself as emancipated with a clear title to his allotment.

The hitch was that the redemption payments were assessed far in excess of the value of the allotments, so the plan simply broke down. Arrears kept accumulating over and over; ultimately all redemption payments had to be cancelled in the wake of the upheaval of 1905.

The procedural complications of the reform were overshadowed by even more basic questions. How big was the allotment to be? How much had to be paid for it? What was the legal status of the emancipated serfs?

The 1861 reformers agreed that the former serfs should be given their homesteads and an "adequate" allotment of farming land. "Adequacy" is of course a slippery concept: the expedient was adopted that allotments worked by the serfs before the reform should be considered adequate. This was dubious since under serfdom the peasants had had to spend at least half their time laboring for their masters. An attempt was made to compensate for the known disparity in the size of the pre-reform holdings by splitting Russia up into zones, with maximum and minimum norms for each zone's allotments. The maximum varied from a little more than 32 acres to about 7½ acres; the minimum was one-third of the maximum. However, in most places the landowners were entitled to hold one-third (in some places one-half) of their arable land regardless of what this might do to the size of the allotment.

The cumbersomeness of the arrangements could not conceal the fact that in a great many cases, even though the maximum norms were from 100 to 300 percent bigger than the allotments actually proposed, they were still substantially less than what the peasants had been holding before the reform.

The government repeatedly declared that there could be no question of the landowners' being indemnified for the loss of their service labor, as distinct from the loss of their land, but this principle was constantly infringed upon. It is obvious that many landowners would have been seriously embarrassed if they were to receive no indemnification for their serfs, especially in the less fertile regions of the country where labor and not land constituted the value of an estate. The reform acts of 1861 set up an elaborately graded schedule of charges on land that in effect gave the landowners the ransom it was distasteful to discuss openly. In Great Russia, for instance, the charges were levied in inverse proportion to the size of the allotment: the smaller the allotment, the bigger the charge. This is, of course, the converse of the principle of the modern income tax; its explanation is that the heavier charge on the smaller holdings was a way of indemnifying the former serf-owner for the loss of his serfs. Because of the system of capitalization embodied in the 1861 statutes, the redemption payments were often more than the rental value of the allotments.

But perhaps the chief irritation in the new regime from the peasants' point of view was that the land allocated the peasants was not handed over to the peasants individually but to the Mir, or village commune, which the peasants were compelled to belong to. Since the commune was basically in the hands of government functionaries, the emancipated serfs, though euphemistically described in the statutes of 1861 as "free village dwellers," were actually under the control of the commune. In this way, despite the ending of the peasants' personal dependence on their former masters, the commune nevertheless exercised a quasi-dictatorial power over them. Thus the property relations in a family, for instance the rights of inheritance, were not under a regime of law, but depended on the working out of old unwritten local customs.

The sponsorship of the village commune was based primarily on the theory, supported by both bureaucrats and sentimental theoreticians, that Russian peasants were instinctively cooperative and would remain immune to the charms of materialistic Western socialism by clinging firmly to the land while mollified by having their own institution to guide them. Thus they would not float into the cities to swell the new and dangerously uprooted working class.

The peasants remained subject to corporal punishment (abolished for other members of society in 1863); they paid a poll tax, gave recruits to the army, and had a number of other duties the privileged classes were exempt from. Some of these restrictions were, to be sure, removed soon enough: liability to recruitment in 1874, the poll tax in 1885, corporal punishment in 1904, while between 1906 and 1911 an attempt was made to loosen the network of communal organization in rural Russia as a whole.

Broadly speaking, what the reform had failed to do was to free the peasant either materially or juridically, and most important of all to provide him with an economically viable situation.

It was not the mere size of the allotments that irritated the peasants. Actually, they had been given the use of quite a lot of land: more than 300 million acres were transferred to the peasants between 1861 and 1870. In European Russia (not counting Poland, Finland, and the Caucasus) the peasant allotments amounted to 31 percent of the country in 1877, private owners holding almost a quarter and the state and various public bodies the rest. Much of the vast state domain consisted of forests and land unfit for cultivation; the Church held only some 5.67 million acres.

It was accordingly not so much a question of the absolute size of the land as the inability of the allotments to provide for a family, with the prevailing agriculture methods, or to give it enough work.

The difficulty of alleviating the plight of the peasants even after the reform was once again rooted in the general backwardness of the country, accentuated by the deadening influence of the village commune and the obtuseness of the government.

There was neither the capital nor the knowledge required for the introduction of a rational agriculture. Intensive cultivation was prevented by the absence of technical knowledge, by the lack of capital and credit, and by the communal organization, which subdivided the fields assigned peasant households into thin strips mixed together so that it was necessary to rotate the crops in a uniform way. This meant that one-third of the plough land lay fallow every year. This was common well into the twentieth century. there was no increase in crop yields: the grain plantings scarcely increased, and they failed to keep pace with the growth of the rural population, a large portion of which, moreover, remained idle, since freedom of movement was still inhibited by restrictions of one kind or another. Poverty, the tutelage of the commune (i.e., the government), and the natural conservatism of the illiterate peasant community in effect prolonged the existence of serfdom. The peasants were forced to lease land to make ends meet; since they could never accomplish this, they remained crushed by indebtedness.

In short, though the element of legal constraint involved in the juridical status of serfdom had disappeared, it had been replaced by economic necessity; from this economic point of view, the relations between landowners and former serfs were in some ways not changed at all by the 1861 reforms.

Thus the peasants remained impoverished, with few prospects of betterment. A cliché for the general situation was "rural overpopulation," or conversely, "shortage of land." The oddity of this in such a vast, relatively uninhabited country is of course just another way of referring to the contrast between the number of people and the inadequate means of subsistence available, but in the minds of the peasants the feeling that it was the land that was somehow in short supply became a fixed idea. They came to look on the seizure of the lands held by the state and the nobility as the only cure for the "shortage of land," and of course as a primordial act of justice that should long since have been accomplished. This basic economic fact, combined with the bitterness caused by the execution of the 1861 reform, led to a tenacious belief in the inevitability of a "second emancipation."

The Russian peasants' reaction to emancipation, in short, was one of bitter disappointment. The emancipation procedure was so complicated that it baffled professional historians and economists for decades; the peasants themselves, of course, were totally at a loss to understand it, but their common sense told them that the land and freedom they had been longing for had somehow eluded them. The extension of the redemption process over forty-nine years, for instance, was met with widespread mockery. A legend, usual in Russia, sprang up that the emancipation of 1861 was somehow not the real emancipation, but that the well-meaning Tsar had once again been thwarted by the wily landowners and bureaucrats—the peasants had been tricked once again. The execution of the reform thus encountered a great deal of resistance, both active and passive; spasmodic peasant revolts sprang up in many places.

Parallels with the American emancipation of the slaves in 1863 have often been noted; they are, indeed, obvious enough. An entertaining sidelight on social psychology is afforded by the recollection that both American Blacks and Russian serfs were uniformly thought of by their owners—before emancipation!—as childlike, musical, simple-hearted, lazy, and shiftless. But the American Black community could never escape from its ghetto, nor was it large enough to kick the lid off the cauldron it was simmering in, while the Russian peasantry, on the other hand, as part of a homogeneous society, was to prove capable of providing a powerful lever for change.

An irony of the emancipation was its failure to benefit even the nobility. Proportionately, the big estates suffered most from the general absence of technical competence, lack of capital, and the lackadaisical inefficiency that characterized the rural nobility. The nobility was mortgaged to the hilt, and even though it received substantial sums for lands transferred to former serfs—nearly 600 million rubles the first decade after emancipation—almost half had to be handed over to the treasury at once to settle mortgage loans, while only a small part of the remainder was invested in the land again. At the same time, of course, the nobles went on borrowing in order to live as they had been accustomed to. The employment of hired labor that could use machinery and livestock furnished by the owners—the transition to free-enterprise—was very difficult. Since most of the nobles could not or would not spend the necessary money to run their estates on a capitalist basis, they continued working the land under prereform conditions: they would rent the land to the peasants, who would use their own horses and machines as they had under serfdom. The average yield per acre on the nobility's estates remained much lower than almost anywhere else in Europe.

The recurrent famines at home were in contrast with the rapid increase in Russian grain exports, which the building of railways promoted substantially. This was made possible not by any greater yields but, on the contrary, by extending the cultivated land still further. Here, too, the nobles were inefficient: most of the profits were appropriated by middle-men.

Thus the nobility was badly squeezed in European Russia: it lost more than half its land between 1862 and 1911, chiefly to merchants, burghers, and well-to-do peasants. (A graphic description of this process, from the point of view of the nobility, is given in personal terms by Tolstoy in *Anna Karenina*.)

The reign of Alexander II thus marked the end of noble Russia. Gradually constricted by the newly evolving class of merchants, burghers, financiers, and industrialists brought into existence by the expansion of foreign trade, the construction of railways and of new ports, and the establishment of mines and factories, the nobility gradually began declining both economically and politically. It came to have little to depend on but the personal benevolence of the sovereign. The Russian nobility was finally eclipsed; aristocratic Russia had in fact become an external sheath under which new social forces gradually took shape.

This process was promoted by some of Alexander II's administrative reforms. The abolition of serfdom made it impossible for the squirearchy to play a cardinal role in administrative and judicial life. The local institution set up in the provinces by Catherine the Great had to yield to the 1861 reform. The village commune, which inherited the proprietary functions of the squires in the land cultivated by the peasants, also assumed their supervision of the rural population.

Principles of local self-government were extended to the administration of the provinces and districts Russia was divided into. The economic and administrative interests of both were assigned to an assembly composed of all classes of the population with a president who was, however, invariably a Marshal of the Nobility. The complex of these institutions was called a Rural Council *(zemstvo)*; it administered schools, hospitals, sanitation, outbreaks of animal disease, etc.

These Rural Councils were probably Alexander II's most effective innovation. They created a channel for the most idealistic feelings, which inflamed not only the evolving intelligentsia, as we shall see, but also those provincial nobles who prided themselves on their liberal opinions. The feeling that it was high time things were accomplished, which had marked the accession of Alexander II to the throne, engaged the most energetic elements in thinking Russia in the labor of overhauling the countryside. Liberal squires often became diligent, benign tutors of their former serfs, furnishing them with doctors, nurses, and veterinarians; they taught them new methods of cultivation that they themselves had learned with difficulty and that their own class often found no use for.

Defective though the emancipation was, it nevertheless levelled to a large extent the dam that had been keeping the nineteenth century out of rural Russia. This newfound enthusiasm of the liberal and "penitent" nobility, to be sure, waned gradually as the country, once caught up in the millstream of Russia's Industrial Revolution, began to develop new turbulences, and as the intelligentsia, with more sharply defined and less exclusively humanitarian ideals, began to encompass the newly emerging conscious elements of the peasantry and working class.

For an industrial proletariat was gradually forming. Lenin, restricting the term *factory* to enterprises employing at least 16 workers, was to calculate that Russia had 2,500 to 3,000 factories in 1866, 4,500 in 1879, 6,000 in 1890, and 9,000 in 1903. The gradual introduction of the industrial revolution to Russia was accompanied by abuses usual in every country: long hours, disagreeable working conditions, low wages, and the exploitation of women and children. In Russia, of course, such conditions were not noticeably different from the general situation, though they were sometimes worse. The working day was 12 hours as a rule, occasionally going as high as 18. Women and children as well as men commonly worked at night; workers were often crowded into dirty barracks, sleeping on the floor or on tiers of bare bunks.

Many cottage industries were gradually shut down by the gradual growth of cheap, mass-produced articles. This shutdown, while increasing the flow of cheap manpower into the factories gradually being built, exacerbated conditions still further: the development of industry, while rapid enough to squeeze people out of cottage trades, was not rapid enough to absorb them all. This depressed wages and living conditions still further. It was not until the great industrial boom toward the end of the nineteenth century that real wages resumed an upward rise, after a substantial depression (20–30 percent) between the 1860s and the 1890s.

One of the factors that enabled the newly forming class of Russian workers to endure the low wages was the very fact of their newness: most of them were peasants still tied to their native villages, with an interest in the farm homesteads still being maintained by their families. Thus they did not have to maintain a family near where they worked; before they could abandon the land completely, they had to receive higher wages.

But this, of course, was only a transitional phenomenon. It was just this emergence of an industrial working class, which paralleled the appearance of the familiar modern complex of entrepreneurial and financial groups, that is surely the most significant phenomenon of the post-emancipation era.

Perhaps the cardinal factor in Russian economic progress was the great increase in railway construction mentioned above, again a result of the Crimean War, which had demonstrated the need of good communications for modern armies. In 1860, curiously enough, railways had been denounced as a pernicious luxury. In 1855 Russia had had less than 660 miles of railways, with another 330 added by 1860, when they began to boom. By 1885 mileage came to 21,780, a substantial increase despite Russia's vastness, though it left it with proportionately less railway mileage than any major country in Europe.

Russia was reacting in its own way to the intensification of life everywhere that marked the second half of the nineteenth century. Population was skyrocketing, commodity consumption and production shooting up; transport was revolutionized in consequence. The process was solidly embedded in the new techniques. Both economically and socially, the Russia of Alexander II reflected this general expansion of the free-enterprise world.

Of course the lack of culture impeded the assimilation of the new techniques of production and organization; Russian life retained many old-fashioned elements jumbled together with the novelties of the era. Russian free-enterprise developed slowly; the change was slow enough for dynamic lopsidedness to become firmly embedded in Russian life, with consequences still apparent today.

Externally speaking, Russia had made substantial achievements by the end of Alexander II's reign. Its foothold on the Pacific Ocean was consolidated; vast areas in Central Asia as well as the Near East were added to the realm. It had thrown off the restrictions of the Treaty of Paris, the seal of its defeat in the Crimean War, made Turkey powerless, and started a ferment among the Balkan Slavs. To be sure, this was no grandiose march of history but a rather casual tangle of events; ambitious bureaucrats and generals kept encumbering a country already far too large for its population, backward technically and culturally. With wastelands in Asia, men and money were squandered in pointless adventures in the Balkans. The 1877–78 war with Turkey, for instance, was wholly futile from any economic point of view. Russia had never had the slightest business interest in the impoverished Balkans, even more backward and peasant-bound than itself. The war resulted in a diplomatic defeat after a military victory chiefly because the British had been antagonized by feverish and futile Russian maneuverings in Central Asia; the British, overestimating Russian abilities, were nervous about India.

It is true that the Turkish war of 1877–78 has been mythologized very successfully in Russian and Balkan tradition: by injecting into international affairs a novel element of what may be called ethnic sponsorship, the so-called "War of Liberation," as it is referred to by Russians, has had an enduring influence.

But it was, as we shall see, the formation of a new spiritual grouping, the "intelligentsia," that was to have a fateful effect on the world.

CHAPTER VII

THE INTELLIGENTSIA

*W*e have seen what an extraordinary identity of outlook and behavior prevailed throughout Russia until well after the upheaval launched by Peter the Great. Afterwards, Russian society changed rapidly, in its own way.

European influences poured into Russia with the eighteenth century, but they were channelized into the nobility, which found itself elevated into a totally different world. This sharply focused and exclusive cultural impact split Russian society into basically two classes—the aristocrats and the plebeians, separated by a chasm that did not even begin to be spanned until the end of the eighteenth century.

They lived in different universes. Cities outside Moscow and St. Petersburg were no more than big villages. The merchants, with their beards and long cloaks, could scarcely be distinguished from the peasants. Even after becoming rich they did not abandon their old-fashioned manners; they did not become a bourgeoisie until almost into the twentieth century, when industrialization began remolding society at an ever increasing pace. The countryside itself reflected this contrast between the overwhelming sea of peasant humanity and the isolated islets of European manners. Monotonous fields and forests were studded by villages made up of squalid huts; at one end of the village would be found a splendid park, a huge mansion, probably with columns, and elegant people with works of art, libraries, and French tutors. A step away were the peasants, utterly unlike the aristocracy in looks, clothes, manners, and for that matter, language. Pious, respectful, sunk in folk-lore and a life of toil, both exhilarating and exhausting, the peasants remained untouched by the Western currents that had turned their masters into a different race.

It is true that as early as the reign of Catherine II the growth of the public services had given rise to a group that was intermediate between the nobility and the plebeians—the functionaries—but they remained essentially peripheral, a sort of rag-tag-and-bobtail with neither real estate, money, nor influence; there could be no question of their replacing the bourgeoisie Russia was not to develop till much later. This early, diffuse, bureaucratic milieu—described so depressingly by Gogol and Dostoyevsky—never influenced Russian history.

The uneven evolution of Russia, its failure to develop its economic resources and the consequent delay in the formation of a modern spectrum of social categories, created a vacuum. As education developed, however slowly, and the liberal professions increased in numbers, this vacuum became the medium for a class known by the odd name of *intelligentsia,* a word long since incorporated into the international vocabulary.

The intelligentsia was never actually a social class in the sense of a fragment of society distinguished by characteristic roots, livelihoods, or manners. It was actually made up of all sorts of people from all sorts of groups: academic people, students, and lawyers were generally members of the intelligentsia; a great squire or a high functionary might or might not be, while a peasant would not, though his son, if he could become a teacher, might be. A good criterion might be its "world-outlook," an outlook that was rooted essentially in the notion that life was important, that ideas were important, and that the world should and doubtless could be changed.

This is, of course, a fundamentally religious view, and it

may be that the intelligentsia grew from the deep roots of Russian mysticism. The secularization of Russian society effected by Peter the Great and even more by Catherine II had touched only the summit: when education began trickling out of the preserves of the aristocracy into the lives of commoners who, after 1857, began invading the universities, though in pathetically restricted numbers, the mystical element inherent in the people shot up to the surface at once and rapidly coagulated in a new and essentially messianic outlook. It engulfed the most influential stratum of Russian society, and in following the logic of its own development it created by the second half of the nineteenth century one of the most dedicated forces in history—the Russian revolutionary movement, which ultimately destroyed the Tsarist regime and for a time poured its apocalyptic spirit upon the world.

But the distillation of the Russian revolutionary movement happened gradually: the intelligentsia had to mature before it could give birth.

The Decembrist uprising of 1825 had been repressed with great vigor, but a ferment began to work that was to affect the newcomers to the universities. In the University of Moscow we can see its germ: the government, instead of finding a philosophy to justify autocracy, naively shut down the chair of philosophy on the theory that a study of it could lead to no good. This parochial Tsarist error had fateful consequences: the professor of physics undertook to quench the thirst of the student body for new ideas, and physics became exceptionally popular. People began bubbling with ideas; informal groups, united only by a general and often quite personal disaffection and by what Herzen called a "profound feeling of alienation from official Russia," leaped into being and spent their time discussing all sorts of scientific, philosophical, social, and political questions. This element of alienation was to be the imprint of the intelligentsia throughout its existence.

The informal discussion groups, though small, had a disproportionate influence: they included almost everyone of any distinction outside official circles. There was, of course, no program or organization; these passionate debaters flitted freely from one bough to another. In retrospect, however, a general design emerges against the background of the clamor.

The influence of the French age of enlightenment, with its detached rationalism and empiricism, was still powerful, but it was gradually caught up with and overcome by German ideas. The tormented, uprooted Russian Hamlets who, floating about in a social no-man's land, with neither family, wealth, nor position, passionately longing to *believe* as well as to *know,* were revenging themselves on the elegant salon-learning of the Frenchified aristocracy. The scepticism, atheism, and liberalism of aristocratic salons since Catherine II gave way to a yearning for faith and a desire to change the world.

The rationalism of the French Encyclopedists was too cerebral; the romantic Germany that had aroused the imagination of Victor Hugo, Michelet, and Edgar Quinet among the French made a similar and far more profound appeal to the early Russian intellectuals.

German thought was both a rejection of classical French rationalism and a way of bypassing the realities of the police state. A whole cluster of German philosophers, beginning with Schelling and going on to Kant, Fichte, and Hegel, came in turn to dominate the new intellectual universe. Hegel's influence was perhaps the most durable, doubtless because in its profound ambiguity the immense apparatus of Hegelian rhetoric has a splendidly mobile pivot: it can be turned in any desired direction. Radicals, conservatives, and all intervening shades of socio-political affiliation could find justification for anything they wanted in the *camera obscura* of Hegelian discourse.

But though German metaphysics was absorbed with passionate intensity—lifelong friendships were broken by a quibble over a Hegelian nuance—its intellectual remoteness gradually came to be chafed at.

Social studies began being emphasized in contrast with timeless philosophical lucubrations. France, in a different incarnation, was turned to again. The more extremist or radical thinkers began studying Russia herself, past or present, which in turn led to an avid absorption of French socialism—Saint-Simon, Fourier, Proudhon, Louis Blanc.

In the 1840s the tournament of opinion threw up two broad attitudes conventionally described as *Slavophilism* and *Westernism*. Both words are misleading.

The Westerners were basically humanitarians with a Russian tinge: they wanted to believe in a universal European culture and steep Russia in it so that it could transcend its parochial limitations and achieve world significance. "European culture" was of course a grab-bag of ingredients; since the Westerners had no clear-cut principles, they simply took their pick. Entirely heterogeneous in origin, they believed with varying degrees of emphasis in science, constitutional government, liberal values, and freedom of expression, and they were theoretically, though often tactfully, against serfdom. They also deplored the chasm between the Russian masses and the cultivated elite. They were far from committed to socialism; a leading Westerner, Granovsky, opposed it.

The Slavophiles were generally devoted to a glorification of the Russian national past—all quite imaginary. They looked on the West as decadent and enthralled by materialistic rationalism. They also tended to regard the Orthodox Church as the axis of the Russian people and its chief hope for the future.

They came chiefly from the landed aristocracy, and though conservative in the romantic sense were by no means in favor of official government policy, though there were of course points in common. Since they were particularly concerned with Russian Orthodoxy, they were hostile to the Church's *political* subservience, which had been a cardinal trait of Russian history. Politically, they were opposed to the Catholic Slav nations, which they regarded as traitors. For that matter they were also opposed to Ukrainian nationalism: they thought it disloyal to Great Russia, though this was because they regarded the Great Russian state as the incarnation of true Slavdom, and naturally called Ukrainian nationalism separatism. Up to the Crimean War they were not much interested in the Balkan Slavs.

Slavophilism began by having a world-view independent of official policy; in fact it was often highly critical of the government, but it ultimately dwindled in influence by becoming identified with the official regime. A curious instance of how the same institution can be ideologized in different ways was the Slavophile adoration of the village commune as representing the quintessence of Russian congregationalism—a dominant motif in Greek and Russian Orthodoxy. Their insistence on the commune, indeed, is taken by many to be the essence of their doctrine. Later on the village commune was sponsored by the radical Westerners, who thought of it not as a holy Slav institution but as the matrix of a future socialist society.

Perhaps the most attractive and in some ways the most influential of the forerunners of the intelligentsia was Alexander Herzen (1812–1870), a novelist and journalist who was the first of the "penitent gentry." Herzen was one of the principal channels in Russia for the somewhat vague though extraordinarily imaginative views of Saint-Simon. He had been given a conventional aristocratic education, largely under French influence, and at first he was attracted to some extent by Slavophilism. But when the two groups, which though vague about programs nevertheless represented differing casts of mind, fell out in 1844—the climax was occasioned, typically enough, by a series of lectures on the history of the Middle Ages—he struck out for himself, fusing a number of elements in a system of his own, a sort of synthesis of Westernism and Slavophilism that became known as Populism. It was based essentially on an idolization of the common people—i.e., the peasants—and looked forward to the institution of a form of agrarian socialism based on the village commune. Thus he retained the Slavophile adoration of the village commune as the source of all good things, while emphasizing its purely economic and organizational aspect and discarding the ethico-religious emphasis of the Slavophiles.

Herzen detested the complex modern state. He thought of Russia as a federation of free communes, in which the elements of serfdom, nobility, and bureaucracy introduced by the Romanovs were essentially alien to the people. Tsar, peasants, and clergy were all native—everything else was an exotic and generally pernicious excrescence. If Russia simply flung aside serfdom, aristocracy, bureaucracy, and that part of the Church represented by Byzantium, and created a new society based on a partnership between the village commune and the workers, it would accomplish an entirely pacific and unfettered revolution. He thought the modern Russian state resembled Chingis Khan's system plus the telegraph. He loathed modern, liberal, civilized Europe as well as all forms of legalism; he condemned them as engulfing the individual personality, and thrust aside as superfluous the notion of constitutional reforms.

Herzen's attitude toward Peter the Great was twofold. On the one hand he admired him for having broken away from the Byzantine conception of the Tsar as a remote, unknowable figure to be venerated, turning himself and the Russian people into a nation of democratic workers, destroying the power of the Byzantinized church, letting in the light, and wiping out women's Byzantine seclusion. But by elevating the nobility and europeanizing it, Peter also created the cleavage between the serfs and their masters, straddling the divided people by means of a German bureaucracy. Since Peter the Great, accordingly, Russian history was no more than the history of the Tsar and nobility, bridged only by functionaries and parasites. The people had vanished from history, except for a brief upheaval during the Napoleonic invasion. Only the village commune and the fellowship of the workers had managed to hold out. Herzen thought it was this cleavage in the nation that explained the profound malaise of Russian life. There were two Russias: European Russia, or the educated classes, wanted one thing, i.e, Western civilization, and old, religious Russia wanted something else. This was how he explained the stock figure in Russian literature, the "superfluous man," as well as a certain ineffectuality in Russian character.

If Herzen was a prime inspirer of the intelligentsia, its father, so to speak, was Vissarion Belinsky (1810–1848), who exercised great influence not only in publicizing new ideas but as a professional literary critic, the first and perhaps the most important in Russian history.

Belinsky's fame was extraordinary. At the height of his brief career his name was known to every earnest young man in Russia. He was a sort of distillation of the activities of the intelligentsia as a class. Because he was socially unattached—of plebeian origins with no money—not exactly a writer, and not exactly a thinker, but a vehement and dilettantish exponent of others' ideas, he is typical of the intelligentsia's dynamic principle. He knew no foreign languages and actually read little even in Russian: his chief function was conversation. He could never write a book, after a tragic and catastrophically received boyish effort; his literary influence was exerted through correspondence and reviews. He worshipped Peter the Great and Hegel.

Belinsky began as a believer in aesthetics—naturally understood ethically—and as a Hegelian he was also in favor at first of the position taken by Hegel in his celebrated defense of the Prussian monarchy—i.e., whatever is, is right, or at least reasonable (in Hegel's mind, or vocabulary, this was the same thing). He then became a fervent proponent of utility in literature and so became the father of the long line of industrious literary propagandists and moralists Russian literature has become famous for.

Belinsky combined the cardinal traits of the Russian intelligentsia—devotion to "Western" ideals: worship of science; socialist doctrine, however vague, as part of the service of mankind, which in its turn was idolized as a sort of substitute for the mystical emotion of orthodox religion; the powerful expression of the sense of guilt by the longing to atone for the wrongs perpetrated against mankind; philosophizing without knowing anything about philosophy; and above all the infusion of a powerful though nebulous moral emotion into the discussion of everything. From this point of view, the arts and sciences were merely material for the moral emotion to work on. Only an ethical criterion implanted in mankind made any judgment possible at all. This point of view also implied personal asceticism and a dedication to duty—in other words, the suppression of individual life on behalf of the collective ideal. The sum of these attitudes characterized the intelligentsia throughout its existence.

Belinsky ultimately broke with Hegelianism; he and his friends formed the Westernizing tendency described above.

It will be seen that there was a completely matter-of-course interaction between literature and political activity. It is in fact this curious interweaving of the two that may be taken as the hallmark of Russian literature for most of the nineteenth century and later; it is certainly this aspect of it that has been accepted abroad as characteristic. Messianism was the significant element held in common by both Westerners and Slavophiles; Belinsky's attitude was largely accepted by the writers themselves, which is doubtless what gives literature its special importance in Russian history.

The earliest beginnings of modern Russian literature can be traced to the seventeenth century as an imitation of a Polish imitation of French models. But with the second quarter of the eighteenth century, the original source itself was turned to; French classicism became the wellspring of Russian writing, chiefly through the work of the many-sided scholar and scientist Lomonosov (1711–1765). For decades after him, Russian literature was negligible: it is best understood as the digestion of the best of Western writing. Most of the writers were basically schoolmasters and translators who provided the channels for the new ideas and forms that came not only from France but from Germany and England. Russians were familiarized with various currents of German and English pre-Romantic literature and given new models for verse, which finally, in the nineteenth century, laid the foundations of Russian literature in its modern phase. This begins with French classical standards all over again; it was inaugurated by the publication of Pushkin's first book in 1820.

Pushkin, unquestionably the greatest Russian poet, indeed the Goethe and Dante of the Russian language, is both a literary ideal and a symbol of national culture. For Russians his immense charm is not in his being characteristically Russian, as foreigners conceive this, but in his universality, his "pan-humanity," as Dostoyevsky put it. Pushkin thought of himself as a Romantic, but his virtues were harmony and restraint: none of his effects is meant to startle. He is essentially a contained, delicate, classical poet.

Yet though Pushkin had an enormous influence on literary

development, the swift growth of the messianically preoccupied intelligentsia meant his eclipse, at least in artistic content. After its brilliant classical efflorescence in the beginning of the nineteenth century—the epoch of classical poetry lasted scarcely more than a decade—Russian literature slipped into the mainstream of Russian moralizing.

The triumph of Russian messianism, in its two forms of Slavophilism and Westernizing radicalism, meant that after a half-generation of transition following the Golden Age of poetry, the basically dogmatic temperament of the committed intelligentsia suffused literature with purposiveness. Romanticism, which had merely been invoked during the brief classical period of Russian poetry, now made up the content of literature. German influences flooded the literate class, and the clash of political ideas overwhelmed literature. Art became the handmaiden of other ideas.

This was to have immense significance because it was just at this time that Russia emerged from its ancient spiritual isolation. In the nineteenth century the Russian intelligentsia, and above all its writers, left an indelible imprint on the world at large as well as on Russia itself.

The most characteristic effect in literature of the "two heads of Janus"—as Herzen called the Slavophile and radical currents of Russian idealism—was in the creation of the "natural school," a transition in which Gogol (1809–1852) may be considered the pivot.

Gogol's outlook was poetic; his first work was a product of a fantastic imagination quite indifferent to the social background that served as its springboard. It was essentially a lyrical caricature. But Belinsky found a social message in it; he explained to everyone just what Gogol had really meant or what he should have meant. Gogol himself was converted, and though he was not hostile at all to the social order, his choice of material, combined with the interpretation thrust on it by Belinsky and others, persuaded everyone that he was a social satirist. His admirers of 1845 thought him a model of realism.

With the surrender of poetry to prose as the core of Russian literature, the artistic serenity of Pushkin and his disciples was gone forever. The writer now sought some gripping world-truth; if he found anything solid he could cling to himself, he became a preacher. Gogol failed to find anything: for instance, in the sequel to his *Dead Souls,* the characters refused to be tailored to fit a moral purpose, whereupon he flung the manuscript into the fire.

But it must not be forgotten that, aside from content, as a literary genre Russian realism owes its forms to the French, especially Boileau, Molière, and La Fontaine, who were imitated and built on by a long line of Russian fable-writers culminating in the well-known rhymes of Krylov and Griboyedov, author of *Woe from Wit* (1825). Indeed, while the realism associated with Russian literature stems from the messianic commitment inspired by Belinsky and his followers, its language—primarily the absence of stylistic ornamentation—owes even more to the fine prose of the poets Pushkin and Lermontov. Pushkin's stories, to be sure, are pure action, and have none of the character-study the Russian novel and theater have become famous for, but he at least handed on his own form of realism in the classical spareness of his style.

The natural school gave rise to the Russian realistic novel, which, though many distinguished dramas were also written, wholly dominated Russian literature until well into the twentieth century. Gogol, in Belinsky's ferociously tendentious interpretation, became a model for later Russian novelists.

The realistic novel, though its form changed frequently, at bottom constituted a single school of writing, characterized primarily by an overwhelming preponderance of character-drawing over action, an indifference to fine style, and the ethical suffusion mentioned above.

The dramatic effect of Russian novelists on world literature is surely due to their intense concentration on the portrayal of character. There is an absence of any distraction from "real" human beings by superficial storytelling. The converse of this, of course, is a certain narrative sluggishness and a general tendency toward the fusion of fiction and biography.

The indifference or hostility to style was doubtless a corollary of the real milieu Russian novelists chose to describe with painstaking precision. Between Gogol and the symbolists there was no attempt at linguistic adornment, which makes up so much of style in other literatures. Russians were preoccupied by a verisimilitude of detail bearing on the important problems of society as a whole. This was bound to forbid any purely stylistic excursions. The literary critics, whose role in Russia was disproportionate, could be relied on to remind an author of waywardness.

The preponderant foreign influence remained French. Dickens was very popular about 1845, but his influence was minor. Until 1917 France was to remain a deep source of Russian inspiration. George Sand was idolized; Balzac's following, though less extensive, was equally devoted. Tolstoy acknowledged the cardinal influence of Stendhal, most of all, of course, in the analytic method of establishing personality.

Turgeniev, born in 1818, was the first Russian novelist to fix Russian letters in the minds of foreigners. He was far better known than any other novelist of his generation except Tolstoy and Dostoyevsky; for a time his name outshone any other in Russia. He has since been outdistanced in world fame by perhaps the two best known novelists, Tolstoy and Dostoyevsky, in whom, together with Stendhal, the psychological novel of the nineteenth century reached its zenith.

Both Tolstoy and Dostoyevsky were typical of Russian literature as a whole; they were increasingly preoccupied, indeed obsessed by what they considered the essential problems of life—death and God. The various threads in their writing can be disentangled only by disregarding the profound fusion of interest and execution in both of them. In Tolstoy especially we are obliged to endure his lifelong afflictions together with him. It is of course possible to discuss endlessly the ingredients of Tolstoy's art, but even when he was being most purely an artist, before his religious conversion around 1880, the whole of his outsize personality was at grips with the ultimate "reality" he was writing about. After his conversion, of course, his preoccupation became still more explicit, even didactic.

Tolstoy's career, though from a literary point of view it exemplifies the ethical nature of Russian writing, was socially unusual. Born in 1828, he received a purely aristocratic education: he had scarcely any contact with intellectuals at all before attending the university; even there, and for the rest of his life, he never had anything to do with them. Not only are the middle classes and their problems never referred to in his writing, but for all practical purposes they did not even exist for him. The only point of view he was aware of as even possible was his own, that of an aristocrat of independent means, and that of mankind at large, which for him boiled down to the peasants. Of all the Russian writers who became internationally celebrated, he was the least "literary": he was simply a gentleman. His intense nature and idiosyncrasies made him bored or irritated by society, but aside from his writing his life was that of a squire. His external interests were raising his family, farming his estates, and seeing friends of his own class; his artistic interests expressed themselves in stories about peasants and aristocratic families.

It is true that he gave all this up after his religious conversion, but he never became a mere writer. He turned into a prophet, exhorting the human race from the depths of his own discontent. With its patriarchal and profoundly aristocratic traits, Tolstoy's figure was an arresting contrast to the generally plebeian or middle-class atmosphere of Russian literary life. Indeed, his personal distinction, aside from his remarkable talents, was inextricably rooted in his aristocratic outlook: as a writer it made him unique.

Russian literature had a tremendous impact on the international public, but with the death of Chekhov its great period, at least insofar as its world influence is concerned, was practically over. The great age of the novel itself ended about 1880; Dostoyevsky died in 1881, Turgeniev in 1883; Tolstoy's conversion about then also meant the subtraction of his talents from the novel and their application to his hortatory goals.

The growth of the educated classes entailed a general flare-up of activity in other arts as well as literature. In music, especially, Russia made the world aware of itself almost as much as in literature, in marked contrast to its status before. The meagerness of Russian music, as far as the outside world was con-

cerned, had been due to the oral transmission of folk-songs
and the inadequacy of the few transcriptions available. Religious
music had been jealously shielded against secular influence;
since the Russian Church made no use of instrumental music,
there was no way for it to develop as in Roman Catholic
countries. There were actually no music schools in Petersburg
or Moscow; music was taught by private instructors, largely
foreigners. Consequently, Russia had no operatic or concert
music worth mentioning until the late 1830s. The handful
of so-called Russian composers of the eighteenth and early
nineteenth century were either foreigners living in Russia, who
might have been technically competent but had no knowledge
of or sympathy with their adopted country, or incompetent
native Russians.

Michael Glinka (1804–1857) may be thought the first distinguished Russian composer; his characteristic contribution lay
in the application of European technique—he had studied in
Italy, Germany, and France—to the musical themes he had
been familiar with as a child. The result was a combination
of technical competence, originality, and talent. He wrote two
operas, *A Life for the Tsar* (1836), now called *Ivan Susanin*
in the Soviet Union, and *Ruslan and Lyudmila* (1842). But his
reception was so discouraging that he never wrote any others.
The first became part of operatic repertory because of its patriotic subject, in spite of being sneered at by aristocratic audiences
as "coachmen's music"; the second was withdrawn after a year
and never produced again during his lifetime.

Almost every nineteenth-century Russian composer can be
traced back to Glinka's work. Tchaikovsky found the seeds
of the whole of the Russian symphonic school in Glinka, even
though the latter wrote no symphonies.

After Glinka, Russian music made a sudden leap forward,
like so much else in nineteenth-century Russia. A Russian
Music Society was founded in 1859; it revolutionized standards
in everything, both in teaching and music appreciation, establishing branches in Moscow and thirty cities in the provinces
and sponsoring the setting up of conservatories in Moscow
and Petersburg and music schools in a number of major Russian

centers. Symphony orchestras were maintained, and concerts and recitals by Russian and foreign artists were sponsored by the Society. This immense enterprise, which was extraordinarily successful, was launched by Anton Rubinstein (1821–94), the son of a Jewish convert to Christianity. Rubinstein, who started out as a musical prodigy, was a prolific composer as well as a celebrated pianist.

During the 1860s, a group of exceptionally talented composers all appeared at once. Known as "the Five," they were Balakirev, Cui, Mussorgsky, Borodin, and Rimsky-Korsakov. They provided an effective counterpoint to the conservative tradition of Rubinstein and the Conservatory. These five composers, often described as the "Neo-Russian" school, were great admirers of Glinka and of "realism" (they particularly admired Berlioz and Liszt). They thought a composer ought to draw on his national background, including popular songs; they were hostile to the classical school, to Wagner, and to Italian operas.

It is revealing to recall that the only trained professional among the Five was Balakirev (1837–1910), who was a pianist and conductor as well as a composer. Cui (1835–1918) was a general in the Army Engineers, while Mussorgsky (1839–1881) was a Guards officer and later a bureaucrat. Borodin (1834–1887) was a well-known chemistry professor; Rimsky-Korsakov (1844–1908) was a naval officer, though he later taught at the St. Petersburg Conservatory.

The Five did not last long as a group: after the 1860s each struck out alone. Borodin and Balakirev are considered the founders of the Russian symphonic school, while Mussorgsky's *Boris Godunov,* Borodin's *Prince Igor,* and Rimsky-Korsakov's *Le Coq d'Or* have been played all over the world.

Perhaps the most famous Russian composer of the period was Tchaikovsky (1840–1893), whose talents took in every form of composition from romances and chamber music to ballets, operas, and symphonies. Though of his eight operas *Eugene Onegin* (1877) and *The Queen of Spades* (1890) are much more popular in Russia than abroad, his symphonies, especially the *Pathétique,* have been international favorites for years.

Painting made a far less flamboyant debut than either literature or music. The Academy of Arts was the bulwark of the
pseudoclassical tradition; its authority was supreme until the
1860s, when it was successfully challenged by the younger
generation. The only portraits thought worth doing were of
Biblical, allegorical, mythological, and historical subjects. The
realism that swept through literature was severely curbed; the
only landscapes and interiors tolerated were scenes of upper-
class surroundings and of "sunny Italy." Russian themes, unless
entirely romanticized, were unacceptable.

Most painters had been trained abroad in any case, especially
in Italy, where until the latter part of the century they were
supposed to copy the work of Renaissance masters. The Society for the Encouragement of Artists, founded in 1822, was
entirely academic. Consequently, until the latter part of the
century, Russian painting was a pale reflection of Western European art.

In keeping with the general ferment that seized the country
after the Crimean War, however, painting rebelled against routine: a revolt that had long been brewing against the pseudoclassical tradition of the Academy of Arts came to the boil
in 1863. The entire graduating class refused to join in the
contest on a set traditional theme; they launched the Association
of Free Artists. Though soon dissolved, this was to lead in
1870 to the establishment of the Society of Circulating Exhibitions, which lasted until the upheaval of 1917. The cultural
life of the country was at last affected.

Perhaps the chief fault painting suffered from was the social
commitment that now submerged Russian art in the wake
of Russian literature. The young rebels against academic con-
vention also attacked all the old masters on principle: having
espoused the social-message theory of art in a particularly
gross form, they thought art was to be directed at the toiling
masses, who of course never came to exhibitions. All questions
of talent were subordinated to social content. In view of their
general mediocrity, this theory was actually rather well conceived. Even Repin (1844–1930), the most famous painter of
this period, is primarily of sociological interest.

Architecture, because of its collectively symbolic character, suffered most from the narrow-minded constraint of the authorities. Churches, public buildings, and sometimes even private houses had to have government approval. Nicholas I took a great interest in architecture; he considered his taste infallible. The result was that the "Russian Empire" of the eighteenth and early nineteenth centuries, which had a certain charm, succumbed to a vulgar eclecticism rooted in the haphazard mingling of styles borrowed from Western Europe. This eclecticism yielded in turn to a precise counterpart of the official patriotism of the regime: invented by a Professor Ton (1794–1881), it combined what in his opinion were the characteristic elements of Byzantine and ancient Russian architecture. This Russo-Byzantine style was made compulsory for church designs, public buildings, and even cottages in military settlements. The Grand Palais in the Kremlin was one of Ton's best-known works, as was the Church of Christ the Savior in Moscow (renamed the Palace of the Soviets after the Bolshevik putsch in 1917).

During the second half of the nineteenth century, Russian architecture, perhaps in keeping with the dramatic deterioration of taste all over Europe and the United States, produced some of the worst and unfortunately the most durable buildings, which reflected more than ever its absence of genuine tradition and its low technical standards. This period was particularly disastrous because it was just now that cities began expanding rapidly, and wood was uniformly replaced by brick and stone.

These signs of artistic efflorescence were both effect and cause of a general intellectual stimulation based on the growth of education, and above all of the considerable absolute, though relatively insignificant, growth in the actual numbers of educated people. In spite of the various repressive measures of the Tsarist regime, the technology of the nineteenth century did not curb the longing for information and self-expression through the arts, especially since there was no conception of the potentialities of social disruption before the modern totalitarian dictatorships. No attempt was made to extirpate opposition physically, nor even to silence every organ of unofficial public opinion.

Between 1855 and 1861 progressive circles, with the sympathy of the more enlightened bureaucrats, removed the most oppressive restrictions on the universities. The student body no longer had a limit on size; Russian scholars were allowed to travel and study abroad; inspectors could no longer supervise students' behavior off-grounds; undergraduate uniforms were eliminated; philosophy and European constitutional law began being taught again; the general public was allowed into lectures.

But as though to illustrate the provocativeness of repressive measures half-heartedly applied, the universities, especially after the Crimean War, became the scene of disturbances that remained permanent in Russian academic life until the Bolshevik putsch. Undergraduate agitation, the forerunner of student unrest throughout the world today, became a mass movement. At first students merely protested against the vexations of academic controls and living conditions, but the growth of general disaffection throughout the intelligentsia soon gave their protests a political tincture.

The first attempt on Alexander II's life, in 1866, led to another tightening of the screws. A liberal Minister of Education was dismissed out of hand, and his place was taken by Count D. A. Tolstoy, notorious for his hostility toward Roman Catholics and his virulent opposition to the emancipation of the serfs. Tolstoy was in control of both church and schools for some fourteen years; he had an effect on educational institutions that lasted until 1917.

In retrospect, of course, we can see that Tolstoy's attempt to dam the liberal and revolutionary spirit of the universities by police repression—repression, moreover, that in the nature of things could only be palliative—was bound to exacerbate matters. A law promulgated by him in 1871, for instance, replacing a more liberal law of 1864, attempted to exploit in accordance with Tolstoy's views the ancient issue of classicism versus science in the secondary schools. This issue was not, of course, entirely academic, since the teaching of the humanities was used as a method of preventing boys with no money or social status from getting into higher schools, an objective openly proclaimed in 1887. The 1871 law launched a secondary-school regime described as "Greco-Roman bondage." Both classical languages were made compulsory in all secondary schools, Latin with the first and Greek with the third year; each language was assigned six to eight hours per week for the whole course, which in 1877 was extended to eight years. Mathematics and religion were also given more time at the expense of literature, history, and geography.

Of course, even in the classics there was no question of the nature of ancient civilization: the time was spent on boring things like vocabulary and syntax.

These classical courses were designed to fill up the young scholars' time in such a way as to deflect their attention from things closer at hand. In discussing the struggle in Rome between patricians and plebeians, for instance, it was to be "strongly emphasized that both parties displayed moderation and self-control at all times."

The classical secondary schools were a complete failure; very few boys graduated. The schools were not even effective as a shield against subversive ideas: the scholastic regime was so deadening and at the same time so futile that revolutionary and liberal ideas spread like wildfire, even among the teachers, to say nothing of the students and some of the parents.

Despite the restrictions, formalism, and grinding foolishness, education was gaining. Women's education made substantial progress, and in the 1860s and 1870s a genuine beginning, however modest, was finally made in elementary education. On the eve of the emancipation of the serfs there had been scarcely any elementary schools to speak of, but even under Tolstoy's regime a start was made that was to have far-reaching effects. The problem in education generally was not so much the unreasonable measures of the government as the appalling lack of teachers, the general poverty, and the consequent reluctance of the local communities to take up the burden of a school system, which was largely left in the hands of the harassed and incompetent central government.

By the end of Alexander II's reign in 1881, there were eight universities in Russia with a teaching staff of 600, and a student body of almost 10,000, most of them (7,700) graduates of secondary schools. Petersburg and Moscow had the largest universities, with 2,400 and 2,000 students respectively, nearly half of them working toward a medical degree. The women's universities had over 900 students in Petersburg, for instance, and 400 in Kiev.

The elementary school system was still more meager in terms of the population: in 1881 there were 229 county schools, with 17,300 students; 262 municipal schools with 28,100 students; and 22,800 primary schools with 1,207,000 pupils, including 235,000 girls.

These figures are strikingly low, of course; nevertheless, there was a substantial advance over the 1850s in the number of both schools and students.

It was typical of Russia to have an Academy of Science at the university long before there were any elementary or secondary schools. The characteristic anomaly of Russian life had not yet been exorcized: the cultivation underlying civilization—science and the arts—sprang from a foreign tradition and remained exotic.

Nevertheless, in actual achievements, and indeed in talent, the Russian upper class and intelligentsia were proving to be an immense reservoir of intellectual ability and moral dedication. The cultural and technological progress launched by the branching out, however meager, of education after the middle of the nineteenth century laid an ineradicable imprint on the younger generation.

During the 1860s and 1870s young Russians became impassioned students of all forms of science—chemistry, physics, zoology, geology, and everything else, including mathematics. The devotion to science was itself a revolt against the restraints of the established social order, and perhaps even more against the scholasticism and metaphysics that were objects of so much conventional piety. The exact disciplines of science seemed a more effective and rational approach to the comprehension of the universe; in addition, their form was, of course, relatively immune to the probings of the police regime. Here again the

West played a vitalizing role: though the chief centers for the study of natural science were the Universities of Kazan and Petersburg, most Russian scientists of note were trained, at least partially, in the great universities and academies of Western Europe, particularly Germany. Most of them did a good deal of their work under the celebrated German chemist Liebig.

The widespread significance of scientific study is indicated by its extraordinary popularity: not only were learned societies, congresses, and journals produced for the scientists themselves, but as early as 1858 some businessmen built a hall where public lectures were given to packed houses on such subjects as "Galvanism and Its Applications." Some of the most notable names in the scientific Russian tradition that was established then and was to remain characteristic of Russian life were the chemist Mendeleyev (1843–1907), the biologist Mechnikov (1845–1916), and the physiologist Pavlov (1849–1936): they are familiar even to laymen.

The success of the abstruse sciences is of course less surprising than the development of a cultivated intelligentsia as a whole: just because theoretical science lends a role of such importance to individuals, the Russians, even with the small fraction of their population engaged in such studies, were able to develop great gifts.

The extraordinary upsurge of literary creativity during the 1860s and 1870s was accompanied by a great expansion of the periodical press. The grotesque regime of censorship at the end of Nicholas I's reign—Gogol's name was not even allowed to be printed—was relieved after the accession of Alexander II, to the benefit of journalism. Between 1845 and 1854 there were only 6 newspapers and 19 magazines, aside from those issued by governmental agencies and learned societies, whereas between 1855 and 1864 66 newspapers sprang up and 156 magazines. Nicholas I's restriction on political periodicals—only 4 newspapers had been allowed to comment on politics—was removed in 1855.

All in all, though the position of the press remained inherently precarious and the rigors of the censorship remained, complicated by the cumbersomeness of the censorship apparatus, censorship, like other government controls before the twentieth century, was not strong enough to be stifling.

The realism in the arts, with its tacitly assumed concomitant of political radicalism that characterized the general unrest and disillusionment of the 1860s and 1870s, was largely due to the liberalization of the government, however half-hearted and contradictory the process was.

The great event, both political and social, of the latter part of the nineteenth century was, of course, the emancipation of the serfs. It was widely reflected in literature. In particular the landed aristocracy, which had produced the classical literature of the early part of the century, had been decaying on its estates or had floated off to join the evolving intelligentsia. Scarcely anyone but Tolstoy retained a specific class consciousness; nearly all writers and thinkers, even those such as Turgeniev who had patrician origins, became more or less uprooted. By the time of the emancipation, the gentry was completely overhauled: the middle layers were finished off by the pressure of the emancipation and its aftermath; the aristocracy proper was isolated.

Meanwhile, the intelligentsia, which had been in the grip of the two broad currents of Slavophilism and Westernizing radicalism, was being polarized still more sharply. The romantic Slavophilism of the early intelligentsia turned into Russian Pan-Slavism, which simply became a synonym for the ambitions of the Russian state. The sentimental theories formerly held about Slav kinship were exploited to provide the autocracy with pretexts for expansion. From the view that the Slavs as a whole were united by deep ties of culture and psychology, the Pan-Slavists, whose influence grew substantially after the national humiliation of the Crimean War, began to formulate a crude theory that it was the mission of Russia to liberate the Slavs from foreign yokes.

The theory, aside from encompassing irreconcilable differences about all conceivable details, was encumbered by insoluble riddles. For those Pan-Slavists who based their claims of Russia's historic mission on religious grounds, the disadvantage was that it excluded all Roman Catholic Slavs, such as the

Poles, who were loathed by all Russian Pan-Slavists, as well as the Czechs and Croats, unless they recanted their Catholic "heresy," which was highly unlikely. Since by the end of 1906 all the Slavs in the world were thought to number some 150 million, of whom 70 percent were Greek Orthodox and 23 percent Roman Catholics, the remainder being divided into Uniats, dissidents, Protestants, and Muslims, this was a substantial loss for the religiously motivated wing of Pan-Slavism.

The less pious Pan-Slavists disregarded the religious issue and developed a quasi-ethnic basis for Slav unity: the cardinal factor in Slavdom's position in the world was the historic struggle between the Slavs and Western (i.e., German-Magyar) Europe. The conduct of this struggle had to depend on Russia, the only great Slav power.

It need hardly be pointed out that all such claims belong to mythology. This is of course very powerful, but in fact the Russians ultimately failed to achieve anything beyond adding one more element of confusion to the imbroglio of the First World War, from which Russia was to emerge so disastrously. On any rational plane, of course, the comparison with Germans and Italians was fatal: unlike them, the Slavic peoples had never developed any common culture but had simply evolved under the impact of cultures imported from various points abroad. The Poles, Czechs, Croats, and Slovaks, for instance, had been molded entirely by Western Europe and Catholic influences. There is, in fact, no such thing as Slavic civilization in the sense in which the term has meaning for French, Italians, or Germans; hence the opposition of Slavdom to the decadent West was literally senseless.

The interest taken by Russia in its Slavic brethren after the Crimean War was quite novel; beforehand it had been negligible. As for the Russian attempt to involve the Balkan Slavs in the schemes of the Russian state, not many of them were willing to exchange Austrians, Magyars, or even Turks for Russians. They were not encouraged by what had happened to Poland.

Pan-Slavism was not a genuine emotional focus as its more intellectual predecessor, Slavophilism, had been; it was a mere

device of statecraft. Its basic significance lies in its political
role; it became a rallying-point for the Pan-Russian agitation
that preceded the First World War.

At the other end of the spectrum, the former Westernizing
movement also began delineating itself far more sharply. The
fusion between the educated elements of the middle and smaller
gentry and the self-made intellectuals, in Russian the "men-
of-all-ranks," who had somehow slipped into an education,
formed a milieu that was to take its abstract ideas into the
field of action.

An organized movement took up the ancient heritage of
Russian rebelliousness. A sector of the intelligentsia broadened
its messianic perspective to encompass the overthrow not
merely of the political regime but of the whole of the social
order. Simultaneously it organized, for the first time in history,
a movement for the realization of this apocalyptic vision. This
movement ultimately swept the field and created a new society
over the ruins of Tsarism.

To see the movement in perspective, let us glance at its
formation.

CHAPTER VIII

DISSIDENCE ORGANIZED

*T*he revolutionary movement carried disaffection to a logical extreme. Almost as soon as the intelligentsia became conscious of itself as a special group with an awareness of the contrast between Russia and Europe, a desire to do something about it began growing. Ultimately it took an organized form.

It was during the second quarter of the nineteenth century that Russia, for the first time, developed an articulate group of people prepared to criticize the authorities—the foreshadowing of public opinion. Those vitally interested in reform were no longer a handful of people from the social elite, such as the Decembrist noblemen, but represented the plebeian classes. Despite all the efforts at censorship, journalism, literature, and even the theater reflected a state of uneasiness, however veiled, about social affairs. Initially, to be sure, the ferment was limited to the educated few.

In this quarter of the nineteenth century "official Russia" diverged from liberal opinion. Nicholas I began tightening the screws in reaction to the subversive currents agitating Europe toward the turbulent year of 1848. In 1847 Herzen, who had been optimistic about the possibility of working for his ideals in Russia, finally left for good. Having inherited a large fortune, he devoted himself to promoting his ideas. In 1858 he launched *The Bell* in London, a little journal that had great influence for several years; it was smuggled into Russia and reached the topmost strata of the regime.

Though Herzen had no objection in principle to revolutionary action, he thought everything necessary could stem far more appropriately from the Tsar. His special concern was social and economic reform, especially the abolition of serfdom, which at first he hailed enthusiastically.

But when the aftermath of the emancipation shifted the peasant question into a far more serious perspective, Herzen's influence declined. It is true that he gave the nascent revolutionary movement two of its most lasting slogans: in an editorial in *The Bell* of July 1861 entitled "What Do the People Need?" his reply, rooted in his indignant rejection of the results of the emancipation program, was simple—"land and liberty." This motto became a rallying cry for generations.

Herzen had left Russia just before the storm of 1848 made Nicholas's police regime even harsher. The radicalized students and intellectuals remaining in Russia were confronted by a repressive apparatus they could no longer elude, though its treatment of dissident opinion was characterized by a mingling of severity and caprice.

This baffling combination was illustrated, for instance, in the case of Peter Chaadayev (1793–1856) an aristocratic dandy and Guards officer, an habitué of the salons of Petersburg and Moscow and also, curiously enough, a religious philosopher of distinction. Chaadayev had a gift for writing, and after his retirement from the army at the age of thirty he expressed himself vigorously in philosophical letters circulated in aristocratic circles. After abortive attempts at publication, one of the letters finally appeared in a Moscow newspaper, *The Telescope,* in 1836. It was like a gush of cold water on the chauvinistic enthusiasm of official circles; Chaadayev took away from Russia practically everything:

> Hermits in the world, we have given it nothing and received nothing from it; we have contributed not a single thought to the sum total of mankind's ideas; we have not helped perfect human understanding and we have distorted everything we have borrowed from it. . . . Not one useful thought has been born on our soil.

He blamed the Byzantine source of Russian Christianity for Russia's isolation from Western Europe.

But though the article infuriated the French- and German-speaking proponents of Russian grandeur to the point of suspending *The Telescope,* exiling the editor, and sacking the censor who passed the article, Chaadayev was simply declared insane without being put into an asylum. His movements were only slightly restricted; he remained a revered figure in Moscow's aristocratic life. It is more than likely that official patriotism was confined to a small bureaucratic and imperial circle, and that the regime was already beginning to lose the wholehearted backing even of the topmost social stratum.

The "Petrashevsky group" was another example, perhaps the most tragic, of the authorities' obtuseness. Petrashevsky, a graduate of the aristocratic *lycée* of Tsarskoye Selo and a minor official in the Foreign Ministry was an admirer of Fourier, the mildest of the French visionaries. His literary receptions, very popular with the elite, finally aroused police suspicion. When Petrashevsky and his friends started talking, among many other things, of forming a secret revolutionary society, and furthermore held a dinner in memory of Fourier in April 1849, the overexcited police spies thought Petrashevsky and his friends were preaching sedition. Thirty-nine of the group were arrested, though nothing could be proved against them but the offense, nonexistent in the criminal code, of a "conspiracy of ideas." Fifteen were sentenced to death, six to forced labor or Siberian exile.

Nicholas I reverted to a sport he had not had a chance

to indulge in since the Decembrist revolt of 1825: he examined the "ideational conspirators" himself, with the same skill he had shown twenty-four years before. He decided to commute their sentence, but in order to dramatize things he did not inform them of their pardons until they were already standing on the scaffold. In his own hand he prescribed the distances between gibbets, the number of drum-rolls announcing the bogus executions, and the costume to be worn by the chaplain.

Dostoyevsky, whose first works had come out shortly before, was one of the victims: he was sentenced to four years of hard labor, then six years in a Siberian army garrison. (He has left an absorbing record of this in his *House of the Dead*.)

A comparison between the Petrashevists and the Decembrists is revealing: both were futile, but in different ways. If the Decembrists seemed a hold-over from the eighteenth century, with their aristocratic, abstract, purely personal and socially isolated idealism, the Petrashevists seemed to foreshadow the end of the nineteenth century, when the action of plebeians, linked to a collective ideal and informed by a general idea, was to lay an ax to the social order.

A natural reaction to Nicholas I's authoritarianism was its transformation into its opposite. In the 1860s a mood was generated for which the word applied by Turgeniev to his famous hero, Bazarov—Nihilism—has become standard. The Nihilists denied all authority of whatever origin: not merely the state, family, and religion, but science as well, or at any rate absolute Science.

The Nihilists, after replacing the utopians of the 1840s, were succeeded in their turn by the practical revolutionaries. The sentimental philosophizing of the Fourierists yielded to a determination to change society as well as talk about it.

This determination did not bear fruit for a decade. Russia had no revolutionary movement at all during the 1850s: Herzen's *Bell,* published abroad, was the only focus of subversion. But in the optimistic atmosphere surrounding the accession of Alexander II, the winds of radicalism began to blow.

There was some justification for thinking Alexander II's reign the beginning of an era of reform. In the late 1850s, for instance, the surviving Decembrists and the Petrashevists were allowed to return from Siberia. The emancipation of the serfs was hailed even by radicals as the beginning of progress.

Under the Tsar-Emancipator the reins of academic repression and censorship relaxed; young people, mostly commoners, stampeded into the universities. Talk was unconfined. Dostoyevsky's novel, *The Devils,* gives us a glimpse of the excitement of the period:

> They talked of the abolition of the censorship, of phonetic spelling, of the substitution of Latin characters for the Russian alphabet, . . . of splitting Russia into nationalities united in a free federation, of the abolition of the Army and Navy, of the restoration of Poland as far as the Dnieper, of peasant reforms and of manifestoes, of the abolition of the hereditary principle and of the family, of children, of priests, of women's rights.

But despite the relaxation of controls during the first years of Alexander II's reign, the autocracy could not be expected to permit open opposition. The need for secrecy led to the establishment of the underground in Russian life—the revival of secret societies typical of the final phase of Tsarism. Indeed, perhaps the most portentous phenomenon of the Era of Great Reforms was the rise of the revolutionary movement: it is surely significant that the whole of the generation that emerged during the upheaval of 1917 was born between 1870 and 1880.

Broadly speaking, the revolutionary movement was made up of two currents—Populism and Marxism. Populism was launched in a sense by Herzen, though his essentially humanitarian, social-reformist, perhaps sentimental views were swiftly out distanced by the anarchist terrorism interwoven with the fabric of the new movement. In addition to "Land and Liberty," his other rallying-cry, "Go to the people!" (an exhortation written in November 1861 to the students expelled from the universities in a general shut-down) remained magnetic for generations, perhaps because of its inchoate, indeed almost meaningless yet ardent pathos.

The Populist attempt to organize the peasants was based

on the idea that they were intrinsically hostile to the official regime. The desire to "go to the people" did not mean, to be sure, that the people were available. The Populist movement, in fact, developed a terrorist wing that was far more notorious, and indeed effective, than any of its other elements, just because the people failed to respond to the fervent enthusiasm of the youths who found a goal for their idealism in the notion of inflaming the sodden, oppressed Russian masses with a broad vision of a new society.

Herzen lost much of his Russian support by coming out for Polish independence toward the end of 1861, but his major shortcoming in the new era was that he remained essentially a gentleman. His reasons for hostility to the centralized Russian state failed to strike an echo among the younger radicals thronging out of Russia to London, Paris, Zurich, and Geneva in the seventies and eighties.

Herzen was far too rhetorical and humanitarian for them. By 1865, when he transferred the printing press and editorial offices of *The Bell* to Geneva, the center of the new Russian emigration, it was obvious that he had been left far behind by the new developments. After 1863 the circulation of *The Bell,* never more than 3,000 copies in any case, slumped: it was suspended in 1867. Herzen, embittered and characteristically disillusioned, died in 1870.

The men who typified Russian dissidence differed widely in temperament and origins: "Going to the People" was the chief idea they had in common. The idea reflected two distinct emotional states: one was the idealistic, misty adoration of the People—the desire was to sacrifice oneself and serve. The other was due to an exasperation caused by the failure of this deity to respond to the love being borne it. The incapacity of the people for mass action imposed on the frustrated intellectuals a need to express themselves in violence. Thus two emotional currents always carried intellectuals into Populist activity—the folk-worshippers and the idealistic assassins.

All successive movements of dissidence rotated around the same axis of differentiation—the desire to serve the historic process identified with oneself and the eagerness to force that same process to obey one's will.

It is curious to recall that the "Going to the People" associated with the Russian revolutionary movement was also echoed, innocuously, a little later in England, where university settlements in slums became fashionable, to say nothing of the fad of "slumming" itself.

The success of the Paris Commune of 1871 in surviving for several weeks was very encouraging to the "immediate action" groups among the revolutionaries. It influenced their attitudes both in the shake-up of 1905 and in the upheaval of 1917.

One of the most potent publicists of the period was Chernyshevsky, who in 1861 founded the new secret society, Young Russia. Together with his comrade Dobrolyubov, he was a leading figure in the world of "criticism" that molded so many Russian ideas.

Though a Westerner like Belinsky and an agnostic, Chernyshevsky had nothing but contempt for the peasants; he also expected very little from the proletariat. Though unlike Marx in many ways, primarily in his belief in the absolute validity of morality, in contrast with Marx's emphasis on the objective environment as a precondition to the attainment of any ideal, Chernyshevsky resembled Marx in pinning his hopes to the development of society's productive forces through capitalism. This contrasted with the utopian views of those who expected miracles to be wrought by the wooden plough and by small groups of benevolent cooperators. He also, like Marx, stressed the role of the state; above all he regarded socialism as emerging of necessity from the economic situation in and of itself.

Chernyshevsky was disappointed by the emancipation; he had fought for the bestowal of land on the serfs as well as liberty. His imprisonment after the 1866 attempt on Alexander II's life was not surprising. The relative mildness of the Tsarist regime is indicated by his managing to publish, from prison, a novel called *What Is To Be Done?* Though all the ideas expressed in it are to be found in Owen, Fourier, George Sand,

Godwin, and John Stuart Mill, the book had a great influence, not least on the thinking of Lenin, for whom Chernyshevsky was a favorite. A character in *What Is To Be Done?* dreams of a Russia transformed into a paradise of beauty and health by the total subjugation of nature to human needs, with the whole utopian community living in a palace of aluminum and glass (doubtless inspired by the Crystal Palace Exposition of 1851: Chernyshevsky was a great Anglophile). This sort of dream later mesmerized the Bolsheviks; though inspired by utilitarianism, Chernyshevsky was manifestly a forerunner of theirs.

Michael Bakunin (1818–1876), son of a rich nobleman, had fabulous energy and temperament. He was a sort of one-man hurricane; from the age of twenty-five he was the eye of every tornado in Europe. A founder together with Marx of the International Workingman's Association of 1864—the "First International"—he soon broke with Marx and after many violent disputes was expelled from the International in 1872. He died as he was about to try launching a revolution in Italy.

Though something of a Slavophile in his earlier days—he supported Slav federation—Bakunin is known primarily as the father of revolutionary anarchism, a logical extension of Proudhon's idea of the negation of the state. Bakunin combined this idea with one taken from Marx, of collective ownership, and pushed it as far as it could go. His personal glamor and exciting presence made him a symbol for all those who craved action justified by some theory, however obscure and even incoherent.

Despite his diffuse, though flamboyant gyrations, Bakunin made a real contribution to insurrectionary tactics. It was vitiated, to be sure, by a streak of nihilism: he maintained, for instance, that the first thing to do in any outbreak was to set fire to—not seize!—the Town Hall. Herzen cracked a joke about Bakunin's invariably mistaking the second month of gestation for the ninth; he said Bakunin bounded around in the preliminaries of the Polish insurrection as though decorating a Christmas tree. Among the supporters of the autocracy, he was nicknamed the "Old Man of the Mountain," after the chief of the Assassin Sect. Nicholas I remarked that he was "a nice boy, but we must keep him locked up."

The tendency represented by Bakunin was counterbalanced by the allegiance of many other young revolutionaries to Peter Lavrov, who in a series of historical letters published in 1868–69 inspired young idealists to help the peasants by going to their villages to teach and awaken them. Lavrov believed in the simultaneous perfection of the individual and of society in a unity that would avoid the contrast between individualism and socialism. He also believed that ideas were the source of power; hence a society that repressed the creative minority was doomed to stagnation.

The creative minority had to be allowed to do its thinking in peace; accordingly the state's coercive power had to be curtailed as much as possible. Lavrov's social ideal consequently boiled down to a form of anarchy, with the sections of society bound to each other by contractual duties, supervised by the benevolence of a natural aristocracy of the intellect. Though a revolutionary in this sense, Lavrov was hostile to dictatorship, which he thought corrupting; he believed the People alone ought to wield power. He also believed that these ideas of his should be taught gradually, in accordance with a maturing process. He was editor for a time of the *People's Will,* a magazine that advocated terrorism.

Both Bakunin and Lavrov stood for individual, not mass action: both were revolutionary, both were terrorist. The contrast between them was in their long-range aims: the Lavrov group believed in an ultimate transformation of society through gradual ripening processes, while the Bakunin group believed in short-range agitation for immediate insurrection wherever possible. Lavrov thought enlightenment had to come from the intelligentsia; Bakunin believed the elemental instincts of the people were in fact the only source of correct, i.e., insurrectionary action.

Before Marxist ideas had spread very widely in Russia, this belief in long-range and inevitable historical processes gave

the nickname of "Marxists" to the Lavrov group: at this time
Marxist doctrine was still considered gradualist, merely hortatory.

Typical of the new generation was Sergei Nechayev (1847–
1883), a plebeian schoolteacher who was a disciple and friend
of Bakunin's. Nechayev distinguished himself as the first Russian revolutionary to set up a practical outline for a revolutionary program and organization; at the age of twenty-two he
gave the notion of terrorism a principled formulation.

Fanatically devoted to his own cause, he imposed a puritani-
cal code of personal behavior on his followers while at the
same time resorting to any kind of fraud to magnify his personal prestige. Preceding the myth-making totalitarian regimes
of our own day, he personally manufactured his own propaganda, sending out news about bogus arrests and escapes, even
his own death. He was an early believer in the cult of the
leader: on conceiving doubts of the loyalty of a blindly devoted
associate, he personally decided on and carried out his assassination. (The episode is described in Dos·oyevsky's *The Devils*.)
Nechayev was tried and imprisoned for life. While in prison
he kept up regular contacts with his associates and directed
their terrorist activities. A visionary as well as organizer, he
devised imaginative plots for popular rebellions to be provoked
by fictitious imperial manifestoes. His extravagant ruthlessness
led to his repudiation by Marx and Bakunin, but he went
on being venerated by the bloodthirstier branch of the movement. Zhelyabov, who organized Alexander II's assassination,
vacillated between that and setting Nechayev free: Nechayev
insisted that Alexander II be killed instead.

Peter Tkachev was typical of the next two or three generations of revolutionaries; born in 1844, he was first arrested
for subversive activities at the age of seventeen. A radical journalist close to Nechayev, he contributed a characteristic element
of his own that places him directly in the line of Lenin's spiritual
forebears. Under the influence of Auguste Blanqui, Tkachev
developed the view that it was not the business of a political
party to propagandize the masses, but to seize power. This
gave him the reputation of a Russian Jacobin. He thought

Russia quite ripe for a socialist revolution, though too much talk about it would simply play into the hands of the bourgeoisie, who would have the time to organize and thus jeopardize the chances of an insurrection. Tkachev was far from Marxism: he was primarily interested in the peasantry and indifferent to the industrial proletariat. It is his organizational point of view that makes him a forerunner of Lenin.

The general structure of Populism, whose progress we have been tracing from Herzen's writings of the late 1840s and early 1850s through its elaboration ten or twenty years later by Chernyshevsky, Dobrolyubov, Nechayev, Tkachev, Lavrov, Bakunin, and others, rested on the following points: the Russian existing order, which was doomed and had to be overthrown by a socialist revolution, was different from that of other countries. It was this difference that permitted free–enterprise to be skipped over altogether and socialism to be embarked on directly. This conclusion was based on the assumption that a couple of specifically Russian institutions—the village commune and the associations of workmen and craftsmen *(artels)*—were in harmony with socialism; hence free–enterprise in Russia would be a step backward. The fraternal cooperation assumed to underlie these institutions was considered to derive from the character of the Russian peasants, collectively minded by instinct and therefore the authentic force behind the revolutionary movement.

There was, of course, no agreement on just how all these objectives were to be achieved. Optimistic fantasy remained inherent in all Populist assumptions about political affairs; even when it was the general creed of Russian radicals during the 1870s. Its mixture of socialism, national conceit, visionary idealism, and ferocious brutality was not enough to provide the movement with a manual of instructions for bringing about the great overturn.

Perhaps just because its large-scale program was difficult to formulate, the practical echoes of Populism in ordinary life were far from trivial. A long series of revolutionary periodicals began appearing in Russia in the autumn of 1861 and went on until the 1917 upheaval. Secret societies of the modern

kind, after Chernyshevsky's short-lived Young Russia, really
began in 1862 with the establishment in Petersburg of *Land
and Liberty,* the first important one, though it only lasted a
couple of years. Chernyshevsky was in close contact with it.
These were only the first organizational and propagandistic
attempts to arouse opposition to the official regime.

The unsuccessful 1866 attempt made against Alexander II's
life by Karakozov, a member of an extreme radical group who
acted, however, on his personal initiative, led to all sorts of
official harassment of students. They kept being penalized,
and expelled in addition, to such an extent that in 1882 the
Director of the Police, Von Plehve, later Minister of the Interior, thought that it was the excessively harsh police repression
that alienated an enormous number of young men from normal society and practically forced them into the revolutionary
movement.

When women were barred from universities in 1863, as part
of the official repression, Russian girls began flocking abroad,
especially to Zurich, to be drenched in systematic propaganda,
by now becoming dense enough to constitute an entire philosophy of life. It took the government a decade to see the results
of this expatriation of able, idealistic young women. It finally
issued an edict promising the opening of higher schools for
women in Russia and ordering the students home by the end
of 1873 on pain of exclusion from Russian schools and government employment. But though most of the Russian girls came
back, it was only in order to participate in a mass propaganda
campaign among the peasantry that the revolutionary groups
had meanwhile decided on. It seemed as though the government's activities, as usual both too extreme and not extreme
enough, could only help its enemies.

The movement "To the People" assumed an organizational
character in the "crazy" summer of 1874. Thousands of young
men and women, inflamed by optimistic reports that the countryside was about to explode, put on peasant clothing and
invaded rural Russia. Some of them tried to set up fixed centers
for agitation; others roved about preaching. But their ideas

were so far removed from the peasants' experience that though they were sometimes listened to with approval, the strange crusade, watched in any case with great vigilance by the police, came to little. The revolutionaries were arrested in droves; the chief Petersburg organization was eliminated in the winter of 1874–75.

The failure of the attempt to appeal to the People directly and arouse its conscience stimulated the growth of terrorism. The young intellectuals, despairing of attracting the masses to their idealism, decided to fight the autocracy personally, to be sure in the name of the People.

In 1878 an organization was formed in Petersburg that revived the name of *Land and Liberty;* it embodied many of the terrorist principles of Tkachev and Nechayev. A new approach "To the People" was made in 1877–78; now the peasants were cajoled not by the mere preachings of individual idealists but by the revolutionists disguising themselves as important personages, such as storekeepers, trained workmen, and teachers. The peasants remained irremediably apathetic; the only people to pay attention to the movement in its revised form were the police; by 1879 the second crusade "To the People" had evaporated. Its failure accentuated the lethal idealism of the youth.

Sometimes, to be sure, there was a peasant response. A peculiar charade was performed in the Province of Kiev in the style of an amusing anachronism. Some flexible revolutionaries talked a few thousand peasants into joining a clandestine organization sworn to the defense of the autocracy: the ringleaders wrote a bogus manifesto in the name of Alexander II giving all the land to the peasants and declaring the emancipation Acts of 1861 a forgery; they called on the peasants to organize in secret and free the shackled Tsar from the aristocratic and bureaucratic usurpers. This curious modern dress revival of a Pugachov drama was uncovered in 1877; about a thousand people were arrested. The spirited improvisation, however, had nothing to do with *Land and Liberty.*

Though *Land and Liberty* contained views that were both

terrorist and purely educational, the difficulty of establishing effective contact with the peasantry weighted the balance in favor of terrorism, a trend that was strengthened by the celebrated case of Vera Zasulich.

An unsuccessful demonstration had been staged by *Land and Liberty* in December 1876 in Petersburg; the few dozen participants were roughly handled by the police, the leaders arrested, tried, and given long terms in jail. One of them, Bogolyubov, was flogged by General Trepov, Military Governor of Petersburg; the revolutionaries decided to protest by killing Trepov. Vera Zasulich, a twenty-nine-year-old aristocrat who knew neither Bogolyubov nor Trepov but was an active revolutionary who had been imprisoned for two years at the age of twenty, forestalled everyone by firing at and seriously wounding Trepov in 1878.

Her trial symbolized the general indictment of the regime: to the dismay of the authorities, she was quickly given a verdict of not guilty. A huge crowd in the courtroom and outside, including even higher bureaucrats, applauded in rapture. An attempt to arrest her again and set aside the verdict was checkmated; she was slipped secretly out of the country by friends and returned legally to Russia only after the 1905 amnesty.

The Zasulich trial shed some light on the mentality of the upper classes. In the struggle between the Tsarist autocracy and the revolutionaries, the wild applause that greeted Zasulich's acquittal must be taken as a sign that the most solidly established stratum in Russian society was not sure of its moral position.

Political terror was immensely stimulated by the Zasulich case. A great many Populists were impressed by the popular endorsement of terrorism that was thought to be the significance of the verdict. Outrages on the persons of state officials, including, of course, policemen, became rife; logically enough, they led to an attempt on the life of the Tsar.

The issue of regicide divided *Land and Liberty,* which split up in October 1879 after Solovyov, one of its members, fired five shots at the Tsar and missed. Solovyov had used a party gun without authorization; on this the internal dissension came to a head, splitting the party into the *People's Will* and the *Total Partition,* the latter led by the founder of Russian Marxism, George Plekhanov.

Though the *People's Will* used a conventional humane vocabulary revolving around socialism, faith in the people, the overthrow of autocracy, and democratic representation, in fact it concentrated solely on the killing of the Tsar, which after seven attempts it finally succeeded in accomplishing in March 1881. Their preparations testified to boundless zeal, painstaking diligence, and great personal daring, all in the name of an ideal.

Such idealism is perhaps the most impressive thing about the Populist movement: though a few Populist leaders came of peasant origins, most of them were drawn from the intelligentsia of the upper and middle class. Their motives were quite impersonal; one of the things that baffled the police in stamping out the movement, which, indeed, they never managed to do, was just this combination of zeal and selflessness.

The membership of all the secret societies was quite small. Yet revolutionary ideas attracted wide support in the topmost circles of the bureaucracy and the security police itself. The upper-class origins of many of the revolutionaries meant a copious course of funds; many of them, such as Peter Kropotkin, the celebrated revolutionary anarchist, donated their entire fortunes to the movement. The contradictory situation of the Russian upper classes was to account for immense sums of money being made available to all sorts of revolutionary organizations, including the Bolsheviks later on: capital was substituted for membership.

The Populist movement was apparently exhausted by the assassination of Alexander II. The *People's Will* appealed to his son, Alexander III, offering to cut short all agitation in return for a political amnesty and the convening of a representative assembly. By 1883 most of the leaders were either exiled or jailed; by the end of the century the movement seemed moribund.

A final spasm of activity was the abortive attempt in 1887 to kill Alexander III. One of the five young men executed for the attempt was Lenin's older brother, Alexander Ulyanov.

The Populist wing of the revolutionary movement under-went a crisis primarily because of the groundlessness of its two basic assumptions—the political effectiveness of terror, and the indispensable peasant leadership of the revolution. Its basic attitudes were to be inherited by the Social Revolutionary Party, which remained a factor in Russian life until shortly after the 1917 Bolshevik putsch. But toward the end of the nineteenth century the Marxist movement, which had already made substantial progress in Europe, began overshadowing Populism.

Marxism was much later in coming to Russia than Populism, though the first translation of *Das Kapital*, published in 1867, was the Russian version of 1869. Itself a form of idealism, Marxism nevertheless reflected an organic development, the emergence of an industrial proletariat.

George Plekhanov (1857–1918), a convert to Marxism from Populism, broke away from *Land and Liberty* at the age of twenty-two and emigrated to Switzerland in 1880. In 1883 he founded the first Russian Marxist organization, the *Emancipation of Labor.*

There is no need here to enter into the details of Marxism. Perhaps its chief appeal for the Russian intelligentsia, even more than for the intellectuals of other countries, was its combination of a powerful messianic emotion with an appearance of scientific methodology that offered enthusiasts the best of both worlds. Their burning desire to change the world was buttressed by what they took to be sound scientific reasons why this was not only possible, but inevitable.

Marxism in its Russian form may be broadly summed up as the contention that Russian history was a part of universal history. This meant that Russia had to pass through capitalism in order to reach the future socialist society, that neither the peasantry nor its characteristic institutions were conducive to socialism, in contrast with the proletariat, that terrorism must be abandoned, and that the main task of the revolutionary leaders was to create a disciplined working-class party to conduct Russia into the promised land.

This program diverged from Populism on fundamental points, of course, and since for a long time neither group had a mass base, the energies of a small number of intellectuals were expended in arguing with each other. From 1883 on, Marx and Engels were translated, adapted, pored over, commented on, and analyzed, in order to funnel everything they said into the historical conditions of Russia. By 1883–84 small groups of "scientific" socialists were formed, chiefly among university students. By 1887 *Das Kapital* was the most popular book among students.

But despite their hope that the motive force for the revolution was to be found in the nascent Russian working class, these early Marxist students had very tenuous connections with the workers or none at all. The great strikes, for instance, that broke out in the 1880s and early 1890s owed nothing to ideology—they were due primarily to economic grievances, the growing pains of Russian free–enterprise. The police and troops found their repression a simple matter. In the beginning, Russian Marxism was just as detached an intellectual effort as the other products of the intelligentsia: it was essentially a literary discussion group.

Marxism's faith in the development of the objective forces of society protected it from the Tsarist censors: the notion developed in the early eighties that Marxists were actually friendly to capitalism because of their conviction that Russia had to develop a bourgeois society. To Marxists, the capitalist system was *bound* to succeed feudalism, just as it was *bound* to precede socialism; consequently some orthodox Marxists favored capitalism to such an extent that in the calamitous famine of 1891–92 they were against helping the peasants for fear of hindering the growth of capitalism.

In its early days Russian Marxism was also sometimes identified with the Manchester School of economics: this was why for some time the Tsarist government tolerated what was called "legal Marxism." Aided by its antiterrorist character, Marxism in this form could be expressed in the legal Russian press. Until the outbreak of the First World War there was, in addition to an illegal branch of Marxism, a legal one adhered to by many of the new class of business managers and engineers produced by the growing industrialization of Russia.

Until the middle of the 1890s, Marxism was a matter of polemicizing against Populists, not much more: factories and workshops were still too remote. About 1895 the term *Social-Democrat,* already current in Germany, began to be used for Russian Marxism, to distinguish it from terrorist or anarchist opinion by virtue of its theory of social development. 1895 is perhaps best taken as the starting point of the movement that in a little more than twenty years was to find itself at the helm of the Russian state.

Some twenty Marxist discussion and literary coteries in the Petersburg area, under the leadership of Lenin (born Vladimir Ulyanov) and Martov (born Julius Tsederbaum) fused into the *Fighting Union for the Liberation of the Working Class.* Shifting for Union's emphasis to unambiguous agitation among the working class rank-and-file, it combined discussion with practical activity. Moscow and other industrial centers followed suit, and by the end of the century the Marxist movement, though in size still negligible, was a real factor.

But it was still shapeless. A congress, or perhaps a symbolic congress—nine people!—met in Minsk in March 1898 to unify the movement. The nine participants were collared by the police out of hand. They had represented five local organizations and the Jewish *Bund,* a Social-Democratic organization of Jewish workers established the year before. The *Bund* was to play a stellar role in the revolutionary movement for years, but its relative importance declined as Marxism anchored itself in Russian society.

Russian Marxism, despite the scientific methodology it shared with other Marxist movements, was always splintered; perhaps the message of the scriptures was too elusive to be fathomed with precision. The great arch of deviation was studded with factions expressing every form of opinion from mild reformism to the narrowest views of the Dictatorship of the Proletariat. Russian Social-Democracy was always steeped in the most venomous, implacable, extravagantly expressed factional struggle, to the natural accompaniment of denunciations, splits, and excommunications. It would be a hopeless endeavor even to begin to indicate the range of groupings and regroupings that took place, even after the "unification" that finally articulated the movement.

An early—and decisive—grouping had produced a newspaper, *Iskra* ("The Spark"), that first appeared in Stuttgart in December 1900. The editorial board was made up of Lenin, Martov, Potresov, Plekhanov, Axelrod, and Vera Zasulich, the last three of whom were in exile. This initial attempt at unity was succeeded by the emergence of the Russian Social-Democratic Party at the Second Party Congress, the real founding congress, which met in 1903 with a joint program representing twenty-six constituent organizations.

But the program, though adhered to formally by the major groups until after 1917, contained enough ambiguities to allow the factional strife characteristic of the movement to go on even within the framework of a single party. The program was really twofold—maximum and minimum. The maximum program had to do with the ultimate goals of the Social-Democracy—the abolition of capitalism and the establishment via a revolution of a new socialist society under the Dictatorship of the Proletariat. The minimum program dealt with the immediate tactics of the Party and its structure: the overthrow of the Tsarist autocracy, the establishment of a democratic republic, and the eight-hour day; also, the restitution to the peasants of the land they were thought to have been deprived of by the emancipation of 1861. The charter of the Party laid down the conditions for membership and the framework and reciprocal relations of Party agencies. The basic organs were the Central Committee, the council (dropped a couple of years later), and the editorial board of *The Spark,* now the Party's official organ.

It was the staffing of the Party agencies and the general attitude toward Party membership that led to a cleavage in the Party that far surpassed all other factional struggles and was never, indeed, bridged over. Lenin's group had managed to elect its candidates to the editorial board of *The Spark,* and the Martov group had refused to take part in any further relations to or accept a representation in the Party's basic agencies. At this particular moment, among this handful of individuals, Lenin happened to have a majority, on the basis of which his group were called *Majoritarians*–in Russian, Bolsheviks. The converse referred to the Mensheviks headed by Martov. With this inconspicuous beginning these names became fixed by history.

What must seem curious to us is that the profundity of the cleavage, which in the light of past and present history seems to us a matter of course, was unnoticed by any of the participants in the war of words that went on relentlessly in the mini-universe of the Russian Marxist emigrés.

The differences between Bolsheviks and Mensheviks were never really formulated. Broadly speaking, Lenin was distinguished by an organizational preoccupation: he wanted the Party to consist of people whose lives were completely taken up by the revolution—a group of professional revolutionaries. The Mensheviks were satisfied with a much looser concept of "sympathy" with the revolution: they were willing to accept anyone who supported the movement intellectually. The Bolsheviks were for the caucus as the spearhead of the proletarian dictatorship, the Mensheviks for the mass meeting.

Still more broadly, this organizational concept was itself the reflection of a more general view of the dynamics of planned upheaval: all Marxists considered socialism impossible without the establishment of an economy of abundance based on a society with the requisite culture and technological competence to undertake the industrialization that was the only thing that could make it work. They thought such a society could be brought into existence only through capitalist evolution, which would enable the working class to become mature enough to play its role as the midwife of the new society.

The Bolsheviks, however, thought that the Social-Democracy itself could accelerate this historic process and was indeed the sole channel for the revolutionary education of the proletariat. They conceived of their own organizational activity as a sharpened application of "consciousness," i.e., leadership. Just as Marx had reserved a special place for "Philosophy"—intellectuals with the right ideas, or, more precisely, himself—as the guide required even by the cosmic surge of History, so the Bolsheviks emphasized the indispensability of the right party—Lenin's.

Yet none of this was grasped at the time. Indeed, there was no place, properly speaking, for the individual at all in the Marxist schema, in which impersonal forces were thought to be working themselves out independently of human desires. Marxists merely thought they had a Great Key to history; it was the powers of comprehension inherent in "Philosophy," according to Marx, that gave it its special role. His schema, infused with "inevitability," could not be altered by human will.

This combination of general inevitability in the schema as a whole and the unconscious projections of personality no doubt underlay the extravagant factional wrangling and envenomed hairsplitting that filled the lives of the Russian Marxists.

In retrospect we may see that Lenin's distinguishing feature was willpower, doubtless derived from the unconscious assurance that in the expression of that willpower he was—in fact and beyond argument—identified with the working out of an ineluctable force of History. This injected a special element into the wranglings of the Social-Democratic movement, but since all forms of debate were necessarily expressed in scholastic language, Lenin's personal quality was never made manifest, especially since it was precisely this unspoken identification of himself with History that enabled him to be unostentatious, affable, and self-sacrificing. The practical consequences of Lenin's personality were not to be demonstrated until the autumn of 1917.

In 1900 Lenin was only thirty years old and merely one among other Social-Democratic leaders, far from the ikon he has since become. In addition Populism and the romantic traditions of the *People's Will* revived somewhat and, toward the turn of the century, spurred on by the great famine of 1891–92, began growing once again with great vigor. The Social-Democrats still shared the field with the new Populist movement, known at the end of the 1890s as Social-Revolutionaries.

The Social-Revolutionary Party—its name designed to steer a course between the older Populism and the newer Social-Democracy—was formally established in the summer of 1900. In spite of itself its program actually resembled that of the Social-Democracy; nevertheless most of the major Social-Revolutionary groups both in Russia and abroad joined up by 1901. The differences between the S.R. Party (as it was usually referred to) and the Marxists were still great. The S.R.s believed that Russian capitalism was so weak that the collapse of the monarchy would lead automatically and at once to socialism; hence they supported cooperation with the liberal bourgeoisie against the autocracy. They also retained their faith in the peasantry as the motor of the revolution and were hostile to the concentrated bureaucratization they thought inherent in Marxism.

But the most dramatic aspect of the S.R.'s contrast with the Marxists lay in their belief in terror as a means of indoctrinating the public. This, in fact, was the only principle that tied together the otherwise loosely associated segments of the S.R. Party. The Social-Democrats, though they greeted the terrorist exploits of their rivals with a certain amount of glee, thought terror both pointless and pernicious.

In 1901 the Social-Revolutionaries devoted a specific segment of their organization to terror. From 1902 to 1907, when there was a slump in the revolutionary movement and the police were successful in catching most of the terrorists, a wave of S.R. atrocities swept the country. The Central Terrorist organization was extremely secret: its members carried their self-sacrificing zeal to a high pitch. Its membership was drawn from every section of society, including professional people and aristocrats. The best known leaders were Gershuni, Azev, and Boris Savinkov, the last of whom, under a pseudonym, was a well-known novelist and the protagonist of melodramatic exploits of an improbable extravagance. (Churchill though him the most fascinating man he had ever met.)

Azev's extraordinary role typified the complex relations between the security police and the revolutionaries. The heads of the security police were often highly sophisticated; they occasionally sympathized with the idealism of the revolutionary cause, and were fascinated by the revolutionaries themselves. Azev was simultaneously a terrorist and an agent of the security police. It would have been impossible to say whom he was *really* working for: he would occasionally organize a terrorist coup while hoodwinking his police contacts, while at other times he would ensure his credit with the police by denouncing his terrorist associates. He did this with such acumen and plausibility that he survived for years in spite of repeated accusations, dismissed by his comrades as calumny, a slander on the Party honor, etc. He was finally exposed incontrovertibly in 1908 by Burtsev, an emigré journalist and historian. The exposure of Azev was a major blow to political terrorism, which in any case had begun to wane.

The S.R. organization also followed a policy, entirely logical, of carrying out armed robberies for which "expropriations" was a handy euphemism. Regardless of the logic involved, however, the S.R.s were not easy in their minds about these robberies; they claimed they were trying to restrict these expropriations to government funds and not to kill anyone but police officers.

As opponents of terrorism, the Social-Democrats naturally could take a far less crass line, but Lenin himself was involved in a scandal by authorizing some "exes" of his own, successfully carried out by Stalin, among others. The Social-Democrats had no principle to advance in defense of these "exes;" Lenin either denied them vehemently or shifted into one of his incessant attacks on factional rivals.

The interaction between the police and the revolutionaries was so intense that not only were individual agents sometimes psychologically split about their roles, but on occasion even propaganda found its only audience among police spies. Some of Lenin's activities in exile consisted of delivering lectures;

he would spend hours lecturing to tiny classes—perhaps four or five people—most of whom consisted of police spies conscientiously reporting back to headquarters.

The most famous incident involving Lenin concerned a police agent, Roman Malinovsky, who was not only a faithful disciple of Lenin's for years but actually served as the major orator of the legal Bolshevik faction in the semiconstitutional regime that was set up after 1905. Malinovsky was an energetic and talented speaker: he would receive general drafts of speeches from Lenin, go over them carefully with the head of the security police, and then, pursuing a policy decided on by the subtle minds in the security police, exaggerate various points in order to widen the chasm between the Bolsheviks and their fellow revolutionaries. The theory was that if Lenin was made too much of an extremist he would discredit himself completely and thus weaken the revolutionary movement. Malinovsky was vehemently defended by Lenin; his critics, including the generally esteemed Burtsev, were assailed with Lenin's usual lush invective. Malinovsky was not exposed to Lenin's satisfaction until the archives of the security police were thrown open after 1917, when Malinovsky was shot out of hand.

The infiltration of the revolutionary organizations by police agents was given a characteristic defense later by Lenin and his sympathizers on the theory that the facts proved to have been stronger than political espionage and that the revolutionary organizations grew regardless of the role played in them by individual traitors.

The revolutionary movement was hampered for many years by hopeless wrangling and by its exiguous membership. Despite all their devotion, abundance of funds—the Bolsheviks also benefited by the openhandedness of rich patrons—and tireless energy, the revolutionaries remained alien to the peasantry and for a long time to the growing working class. At the beginning of 1905 a claim of a mere 8,000 members was made by the Bolsheviks; to be sure, such figures are inherently unreliable. The strength of the Bolsheviks was not, of course, derived from their dialectics but from the prevalent disaffection.

It gave the propaganda of all revolutionary groups something to sharpen itself on.

It was not until 1917 that, in the case of the Bolsheviks at least, the importance was realized of the modern role of simplified propaganda wielded by a limber and well-articulated organization. Only now in fact can we see the significance of Bolshevik innovations—they were to engender a new world. In the Russia of the time there was no feeling that anything really serious was *happening:* the stability of the regime in a broad sense was unquestioned. However ardent the discussion of the new ideas, respectable society went its own way imbued with an attitude of composure essential for its peace of mind.

What was far more important, on the public horizon of the era, was the upswing in liberalism—the somewhat inchoate desire, generally associated with a constitution, for a softening of the monarchy. The famine years of 1891–92 that were such a stimulant to the Populist and Marxist movements also promoted liberal ideas.

Fixing a specific label on this amorphous body of attitudes, to be sure, is a falsification *per se:* the huge camp between the autocracy and its enemies was filled by the bulk of educated and critical opinion, opposed to the state for its backwardness and arbitrary controls, but not to the point of advocating violent action.

It was the Rural Councils that sustained this pacific, forward-looking movement, which was aimed, broadly speaking, at the installation of some form of popular representation in the central government and also at the creation of a central Rural Council administration. This would have had the effect of supplementing the cumbersome, high-handed central regime by a flexible, decentralized administration. The liberal sentiment that had suffered in the general movement of repression after the assassination of Alexander II cautiously began pushing ahead during the last decade of the nineteenth century and afterwards, invigorated by the ardor derived from the relief work done during the famine years of 1891–92. People were loath to return to the indolence of normal routine.

In addition, by the middle of the 1890s the so-called "Third Element," as the hired employees of the Rural Councils were called—teachers, doctors, nurses, veterinarians, statisticians, agronomists–played an increasingly effective role. This Third Element—the other two were officials of the crown and the elected members of the Rural Councils—was interested in the establishment of professional unions and in discussing issues of the broadest nature at conventions held with the tacit approval of the Rural Councils. The Third Element stemmed, of course, from the radical intelligentsia; many of them were linked to revolutionary groups. But as a body they reached beyond the framework of the Rural Councils proper and came in contact with other classes; the interest in professional unions, for instance, infected professional men outside the Rural Councils altogether.

Agriculture, in the wake of the defective emancipation of 1861, was still functioning poorly. There was another failure of crops in 1897–98 and in 1901; by the end of the century the defects of emancipation were unmistakable. The general agricultural stagnation and the progressive impoverishment of the peasants had their roots in the staggering taxes and in the paralysis due to the communal tenure of the land. Rural mutinies kept breaking out, illustrating the depressing statistics that accumulated about increasing arrears, meager crops, and debased living standards.

In addition, the working class began incubating a persistent malaise: the strikes of the 1890s went on increasing in number and scope. It was not so much their number: the manufacturing, mining, and metallurgical industries employed some 2,200,000 workers in the Russian Empire in 1900, while the strikers in the peak years of 1899 and 1903 numbered 97,000 and 87,000 respectively. It was the novelty of mass organized strikes that proved so disturbing, even though their grievances had not yet found a politically articulate channel.

Student agitation, which kept growing in importance, added a serious factor to the froth. Not only were living conditions still harsh for most students—an indication that the regime's attempts to confine higher education to the upper classes had in fact misfired—but the very juxtaposition of the poverty-stricken students to their elegant, wealthy fellows gave special point to the various levelling theories contending for attention. After a period of relative quiet in the 1880s, student agitation began taking on a more and more truculent character in the 1890s; in 1899 disorders flared up with exceptional violence for causes in themselves trivial. Assassinations carried out by Social-Revolutionary students became commonplace.

There was thus a fusion between the various kinds of opposition to the regime. Individuals with a variety of attitudes united in a common detestation of the *status quo;* though the remedies projected differed in accordance with outlook, the Tsarist fortress found itself besieged from all points in the compass.

Liberalism was established as an organized political force by the initiative of Paul Miliukov, a history professor, and P. B. Struve, author of the Social-Democratic manifesto of 1898, who had shifted over to the Right of the socialist movement. In 1902 they launched the first issue of *Liberation,* which advocated the overthrow of the autocracy and the establishment of a constitutional regime. The periodical, printed in Stuttgart, was smuggled into Russia.

It may be said that liberalism as an organized movement made its entry into Russian politics when the program of the Miliukov-Struve periodical, *Liberation,* was endorsed by the Union of Liberation, clandestinely launched at a Rural Council Conference in 1903 and formally organized in 1904. The Union, which had a network of local agencies, did not limit itself to coordinating the activities of the Rural Councils themselves but also managed to involve substantial numbers of intellectuals and professional men.

Thus lively forces in Russian society were in the midst of reshaping themselves beneath the crust of the autocracy, or rather alongside the obdurate element in the ruling stratum of the country.

At the time the potentialities of these new forces in Russian life could scarcely be assessed; on the official level life seemed normal.

CHAPTER IX

THE EXTINCTION OF
TSARISM

*A*lexander II's assassination in March 1881 did not affect
the regime. The revolutionary mood that had been hoped
for as a result of the regicide did not come about: the only
result was that one sovereign imbued with traditional ideas
was succeeded by another with an even more authoritarian
turn of mind. Nor did Alexander II's murder stir the countryside in any way: the peasants remained indifferent. For all one
could tell, they were utterly apathetic. Some peasants seemed
to think the Tsar had been killed by landowners working off
a grudge.

The new sovereign, Alexander III, was unusually single-
minded. He was indissolubly identified with the old formula,
"orthodoxy, autocracy, and nationality"; the element he emphasized was autocracy. He was profoundly influenced by Constantine Pobedonostsev (1837–1907), who tutored both him
and his son, the future Nicholas II, and who was rightly considered the most powerful man in the state. Pobedonostsev's strategy, while defending the union of the common people and

the throne on the one hand, systematically attacked the corrupt, self-serving bureaucracy, plus all proponents of constitutional reform, on the other.

Alexander III's regime became more oppressive on all the questions that had been agitating Russia. The press was gagged, the schools were thrown back to the regime of the 1830s, when children were supposed to be educated in terms of their social station, and "undesirable" elements, especially Jews, were excluded as far as possible from the educational system, which was forced into the straitjacket of intensified government supervision. Ethnic minorities, local languages, and dissenting religious sects were systematically persecuted (Pobedonostsev's letters to the Tsar overflowed with diatribes against Roman Catholics, Protestants, Jews, and Russian dissenters.) The treatment of the Jews was singularly harsh: Alexander III himself had a special hatred of them based on a naive acceptance of traditional anti-Semitism—the supposed Jewish responsibility for the Crucifixion. Not that anti-Semitism was confined to conservative and orthodox milieux: in the early 1880s the *People's Will* used anti-Jewish slogans.

The Jews were in their classic position—caught between two fires. Their role in dissident organizations (a Jewish woman had participated in Alexander II's assassination) made them the target for conservative hatred, while their prominence in the newly forming business world inflamed the revolutionaries.

In 1881 southern Russia was swept by a wave of pogroms, condoned or even instigated by the police. They aroused public opinion everywhere to such an extent that the government had to promise some sweeping reforms. In the event, however, after receiving a report from a conservative body recommending that discrimination be discontinued, the government did the opposite—it made the treatment of the Jews even more oppressive. The boundaries of the Jewish Pale were restricted still further; quotas for Jews were introduced into secondary and higher schools (1887); Jews were practically excluded from the legal profession (1889) and from the Rural Councils (1890); Jewish craftsmen and businessmen were expelled in droves from Moscow in harsh circumstances (1891); they were excluded from municipal governments (1892) and denied licenses to sell liquor, which made it impossible for many village Jews to make a living (1894). It was even made a criminal offense for a Jew to use a Christian given name.

The severity of this regime naturally increased the vulnerability of the Jewish community to the personal greed of government officials: bribery, renewed exactions, and pressure went hand in hand. But perhaps the chief effect of the treatment of Jews during Alexander III's reign was to kindle a spark among Russian Jews that had far-reaching consequences: the mass migration of Russian Jews to the United States and the launching of the Zionist movement, which began to form in the 1890s and was to establish the State of Israel in 1948. In addition, the brutality assumed by Russian anti-Semitism during this period evoked a powerful reaction abroad, particularly in the United States and Great Britain. The monarchy was creating enemies for itself abroad as well as at home.

In 1894, however, Nicholas II ascended a throne universally considered a rock of stability; to any superficial observer the country would have seemed tranquil. The police appeared to have suppressed all dissidence. The revolutionary movement was decapitated, its leaders exiled to Siberia and abroad. The peasants were motionless; they had not even reacted to the great famine of 1891 in which thousands had perished. The Russian autocracy seemed to have lost nothing as it entered the twentieth century. It looked as tranquil at home as the international outlook seemed secure. Alexander III had been known as the "Tsar Peacemaker"; the international scene was calm. France had taken Germany's place as Russia's ally; relations with Great Britain were much more harmonious.

Then Tsarism was shaken up, for the first time, in the wake of the Russo-Japanese war that broke out in January 1904. Initially the war generated a wave of patriotism that overrode, for a time, the social frictions beneath the surface, but as Russian forces, underequipped and outfought, were struck by one reverse after another, topped by the humiliating surrender of Port Arthur, the national opposition concerted its campaign against the autocracy.

A spectacular incident—"Bloody Sunday"—gave the mounting tension a focus. Underlying it was a convergence of police action and revolutionary enthusiasm. The incident began with a strike that broke out early in January 1905 in Petersburg and spread to some factories with tens of thousands of workers. The strike was directed by the so-called Assembly of Russian Workmen, a group organized and financed by the police themselves. Just as mutinies had been led in the name of the Tsar, so the police had done a certain amount of dabbling in setting up organizations professing concern with the interest of the working class. This one was headed by Father Gapon, a priest in the service of the police.

Whether or not Gapon was playing a role, he thought of appealing to the Tsar directly; he organized a parade of columns of workers flaunting a wide variety of grievances. The parade was peaceful; some of the marchers actually carried sacred ikons and portraits of the Tsar. But the demonstrators were stopped by cordons of troops and fired on when they refused to disperse. Official estimates listed some 130 killed and several hundred wounded. No doubt the casualties were much heavier.

The demonstration and its bloody sequel made a dramatic impression, out of all proportion to the number of casualties. The agitation of the Rural Councils and a variety of other bodies was intensified; in February the Grand Duke Sergius, the Tsar's uncle and brother-in-law, was assassinated in a coup planned by Savinkov under the protection of Azev.

The government reacted irresolutely: from now on nothing it did, including concessions made to liberal opinion, could catch up with the swelling disaffection that flowed in the two channels of conciliationist liberalism and revolutionary intransigence. The government felt itself forced to concede the principle of popular representation in an advisory assembly, but this was no longer enough to satisfy the liberals, who were now intent on securing a constituent assembly based on the commonplaces of political democracy in Western Europe—universal suffrage and a secret, direct, and equal ballot.

By May 1905, when the Russian fleet was annihilated by

the Japanese in the straits of Tsushima, the domestic situation seemed hopeless. Agrarian upheavals, strikes, and political agitation by liberal and revolutionary groups (countered by the action of the autocracy's supporters, aimed particularly at the Jews) strained the situation to the breaking point.

A tardy concession in August 1905, which laid down the procedure to be followed for elections to the State Duma (the consultative assembly announced in February), was greeted by open mockery. The definition of the franchise satisfied no one, conservative or liberal.

The universities were given a substantial degree of autonomy in an unexpected law of August 1905; the manner in which this was worked out against the background of the relentless pressure of public opinion transformed academic lecture audiences into debating assemblies, where speakers safe from police interference could erupt to their heart's content.

The political tension broke at last in the second half of September 1905 in a general strike of printers and bakers. A sympathetic strike was organized in Moscow by a union that was functioning in spite of no official recognition; it spread to the whole network in a few days, involving the telegraph and telephone services and halting almost the entire industrial plant.

Though the strikers at first made the conventional demands for a constituent assembly, civil liberties, and an eight-hour day, they soon added some revolutionary demands—a democratic republic, political amnesty, disarming of the police and troops, and the arming of labor. This program, inspired by the previous decade of radical toil, was endorsed even by the unions of professional people.

The populace was deliriously excited: euphoric mobs roved about carrying red banners and revolutionary posters. Everything shut down—banks, shops, government offices, even pharmacies and hospitals. Newspapers, electricity, gas, and in some places water were all suspended; barricades were set up in a number of cities.

In October things came to a head: the Tsar signed a Manifesto (17 October) transforming Russia into a constitutional monarchy, and the "Soviet of Workers' Deputies," a by-product of the flood of oratory unloosed by the university autonomy decreed in August, met for the first time.

The Manifesto was devised by Witte, a former Minister of Finance recalled from semiretirement to conduct peace negotiations with Japan via the mediation of Theodore Roosevelt. It guaranteed basic civil liberties, promised to extend the franchise of the August law establishing the State Duma, and laid down an "immutable rule" that all laws had to have the sanction of the State Duma, which was also to exercise a control over crown appointees.

The concessions contained in the October Manifesto, a milestone in Russian political evolution, aroused the consternation of the conservatives and a certain amount of skepticism among the liberals. But the public reaction generally was one of unbridled enthusiasm. The conservative response took the familiar form of pogroms against the Jews; during the week after the signing of the October Manifesto, hundreds of pogroms ravaged small towns inside the Jewish Pale and outside, especially Kiev and Odessa.

The government was hamstrung by the fact that the October Manifesto proclaimed principles of liberty that the law still obstructed or limited; this led to a state of paralysis in the government, especially the police. The official censorship ceased operating; the Printers' Union began exercising an impromptu censorship of its own by refusing to print whatever displeased it while allowing scores of radical papers to be printed and to circulate freely.

Though the Petersburg Soviet of Workers' Deputies had only thirty or forty delegates at first, by the end of November, shortly before it was dispersed, it had almost six hundred. In theory, one delegate was supposed to represent five hundred workers, but some deputies were backed by much smaller groups. The elections to the Soviet had been carried out by the revolutionary parties, chiefly the Mensheviks, who dominated the Soviet and its executive committee. It published an organ, *Izvestiya,* which appeared for the first time on 17 October, the same day the Tsar signed the constitutional Manifesto.

The Petersburg Soviet disregarded the October Manifesto by carrying on with a general strike. There was, to be sure, a spontaneous and irresistible back-to-work movement following the Manifesto, but the Soviet had now become a revolutionary tribune; it proclaimed that the proletariat would never lay down its arms until the monarchy had been replaced by a democratic republic. The temporary governmental paralysis, plus the long-range calculations of Witte, who was biding his time, enabled the Soviet to act with a great deal of freedom: it handed out orders and carried on negotiations with the government. A partial amnesty granted a few days after the October Manifesto enabled many political exiles to return and resume their activities.

The revolutionary mood overflowed into the Russian hinterland: over 2,000 manor houses were burned or plundered and their owners killed or expelled.

The government finally pulled itself together; it proclaimed a state of emergency and sent off expeditions to suppress the riots. In November it arrested the whole Moscow headquarters of the Peasants' Union, a clandestine organization led by radical intellectuals, which had held its first conference in Moscow in August. Witte's calculations were bearing fruit.

Now, in early December, as the tide of excitement ebbed and the hold of the Petersburg Soviet over its clientele slacked off, the government finally intervened. In a simple police action it arrested all the leaders of the Soviet and dispersed it. A feeble attempt to replace it proved futile. The following month, January 1906, the government was in complete control again. Order had been restored.

One of the arrested Soviet leaders was Leon Trotsky, who at the age of twenty-six had played a stellar role as orator and writer. As Bronstein, son of a well-to-do Jewish farmer in the Ukraine, he had entered the revolutionary movement at the age of seventeen and had been exiled to Siberia and escaped. In exile he had been taken under Lenin's wing for a while; he had joined with Lenin at the 1903 Founding Congress in Brussels. But Trotsky could not, it seems, fit into Lenin's tight little entourage.

In the turmoil of 1905 Trotsky, under a number of pseudo-nyms, played an independent role; he was, indeed, the only Marxist to become prominent in the democratic arena of the Soviet, of which he was elected chairman. Together with fifteen other defendants from the Soviet, Trotsky was sentenced to Siberian exile for life. By March 1907 he had already escaped and made his way back to Petersburg, but, with the ebbtide in full flow, he emigrated. (He was to return a decade later.)

The Soviet lasted only fifty-two days; it made very little impression on the busy life of the capital. Nevertheless it was, in revolutionary mythology, glamorized at once; it was to be ikonized when reincarnated in 1917.

The 1905 disorders did not, in short, impair the Russian regime. Though the principle of autocracy had been cracked, the monarchy had survived intact; the forces of dissidence seemed quiescent.

Yet the chasm between the summits of society and the illiterate masses was spanned by only two bridges—the intelligentsia, bent on turning society upside down with its abstractions, and the liberal classes.

The liberals were the sole mediators between the monarchy, with its overblown bureaucracy, and the masses of peasants and workers. But with no experience of self-government, no parliamentary skills, and no established parties, the liberals were poorly equipped to cope with the perhaps insoluble problem of providing a representative government for the gigantic, backward, multiracial empire.

Nicholas II, the last Tsar, was sadly outmatched by circumstances. To be sure, even a monarch more acute and with a more flexible character might have fallen short of the demands made by the upsets of the epoch. He seemed unable not only to cope with the inherited situation but to understand what was happening.

His personal diary, which he kept regularly throughout his life, may shed some light on the man. It never fails to mention the weather and various outdoor activities—playing with dogs, rowing, swimming, walking, mushroom-picking. All are faithfully recorded. Shooting was Nicholas's favorite pastime; the day's bag of every hunt was conscientiously listed. When he had no time to hunt, he shot the crows flying on the grounds of the imperial residence, with all results recorded. The cardinal events of his reign—the Japanese War, the 1905 revolution, the creation of the State Duma—are hardly mentioned. He had the outlook of an indolent, good-natured, passive boy. At the age of twenty-six, for instance, he took the trouble to record fighting a chestnut battle with Prince George of Greece; two days later he mentions a battle with pine cones.

His passivity, however, was combined with extreme stubbornness: he remained sulkily unreconciled to the restrictions on his legislative powers imposed on him by the 1905 shake-up. Nicholas was fortified in this attitude by his unbending wife, the former Princess Alice of Hesse-Darmstadt. their intimacy was flawless; they remained utterly devoted to each other until the end.

The Tsarina, whose mother was Princess Alice of England, had been brought up by her grandmother, Queen Victoria; Alice and Nicholas wrote to each other in English. After somewhat reluctantly embracing Russian Orthodoxy to marry Nicholas, she became an ardent devotee of her new religion: her mystical nature felt itself wholly fused with her conception of the union of the "People" with the crown, with a concomitantly virulent loathing of any curb on autocratic power. The Tsarina was both shy and sickly. Her health was impaired by the birth of four daughters, and the desire for an heir to the throne made her and Nicholas turn for advice to adventurers, faith-healers, and quacks. A longed-for heir to the throne was finally born in 1904; when the infant was only ten weeks old, the parents learned with grief that he had hemophilia, an incurable disease hereditary in the males of the House of Hesse but transmitted only through the mother.

The providential savior appealed to by the anguished mother was Rasputin, a semiliterate peasant from the Siberian wilderness. His powerful body, magnetic personality, and unintelligible talk—his "charisma"—had firmly anchored him in a coterie of Petersburg society neurotics. A characteristically Russian self-constituted religious teacher living by his wits on hand-outs from naive believers, Rasputin had an attractive combination of eroticism and mysticism: his creed was based on the logical assumption that forgiveness could only be accorded if there was something to forgive, i.e., the act of sinning. He promised eternal salvation to believers who achieved true humility by way of sexual license.

Rasputin seems to have been trained by a professional medium (according to Beletsky, Chief of the Imperial Police). He was actually successful, according to a number of trustworthy witnesses, in stopping young Alexis's bleedings. His performance of this miracle was enough to embed him solidly in the Empress's confidence. Not only was he the incarnation of her beloved People—rough-hewn and filthy—but he was a divine prop of the throne. She dismissed all rumors of his debaucheries as evil gossip; she sought his advice on matters of state policy as well as the welfare of the imperial family. Rasputin realized the great power given him by his strategic position with the imperial family; his growing influence was exploited by all sorts of bureaucrats, businessmen, and adventurers. In the minds of the public at large, as well as of the summit of society, by the time the First World War broke out he was one of the cardinal elements in the pall that overhung the monarchy.

The beginnings of parliamentary democracy laid in 1905 had had reservations that made its actual functioning difficult. Not only had the government dug in its heels, but the parties that emerged from the shake-up had proved equally rigid with respect to each other. Before 1905, after all, no political party had had any status: the Social-Democratic and Social-Revolutionary Parties that were to play a decisive role in the upheaval of 1917 were basically underground organizations.

The constitutional regime set up after 1905 established a spectrum of political parties that—at a casual glance—resembled their Western models. Opinion organized itself into groups that spread from left to right, beginning from what we should now consider the center. Extremist liberalism was represented by the Constitutional Democrats—known as Cadets, from their initials—a party, led by Miliukov, that had emerged from a campaign by the Rural Council groups. Its program was approved by the first and the second (January 1906) party congress; it naturally represented a compromise of contending views. The extremist demands for a democratic republic and a constituent assembly based on a direct and universal ballot were eliminated; the party as a whole came out for a constitutional monarchy, with the State Duma being given a full-fledged role in the establishment of the new constitution. The Cadets sponsored broad social and economic reforms, including the expropriation of great estates against fair indemnification.

The more conservative elements set up their own parties, the most important of which was the Octobrists, headed by A. I. Guchkov; it was founded in December 1905. Basing itself, as its name indicated, on the October Manifesto, it vigorously opposed the more far-reaching socio-economic demands of the Cadets, especially the expropriation of the big landowners. Conservative extremists joined in the Union of the Russian People.

With the shaping up of the parliamentary regime, the Rural Councils subsided as the expression of liberal opinion; until the abolition of the monarchy the new Russian parliament remained the arena of conventional politics.

The first two Dumas were far more radical than the regime had been counting on. In the First Duma, for instance, inaugurated 27 April 1906 (O.S.), though the peasantry was well represented and was counted on as a traditional bulwark of conservatism, the 200 peasant deputies (of a total of 500) turned out to be unexpectedly liberal; they took an inconveniently intractable line on all land questions.

This Duma was dominated by the Cadets, who were very disturbing to the conservative elements. Though the Duma represented 26 parties and 16 national groups, the Cadets had between 170 and 180 members and were generally supported by the Labor Group, which had over 100 members. The latter was made up of a merger of 10 groups that were even more liberal than the Cadets, especially about the land, but were not socialists or revolutionaries. The ethnic groups, such as the Poles, Ukrainians, and Letts, had about 60 to 70 members; they backed national autonomy and had a generally radical tinge. The Social-Democrats, now legally recognized, had a small separate faction. There were no conservative deputies at all.

The First Duma lasted only a few months. The very fact of its radical composition, as expressed in the demands it made in its program (adopted practically unanimously) insisting on universal suffrage, a one-chamber parliament, and a land reform based on expropriation, implied a rapid demise. By July it was dissolved.

The Second Duma, scheduled for 20 February 1907 (O.S.), was even more radical in composition than the first and just as short-lived; it lasted a little more than three months. Both Social-Democrats and Social-Revolutionaries had taken part in the elections (Lenin had been impressed by the First Duma's propaganda potential); the Second Duma had some 65 Social-Democrats and 34 S.R.s, while the Cadets fell to 92 and the Labor Group to 101.

The surprising radicalism of the first two Dumas pointed up a defect in the arithmetic underlying the theory of representation. The defect was rectified quite simply by reducing the number of deputies to be elected by industrial workers and increasing the landowners' ratio, and so a fairly conservative Third Duma was ensured.

Of the four Dumas Tsarism was destined to see, the Third Duma was the only one to complete its full term. Dominated by conservatives, it lasted from November 1907 to June 1912. The right-wing, moderate right-wing, and nationalist parties had about 150 members, as did the Octobrists. The Cadets had sunk to 53, and the Social-Democrats and the Labor Group had 14 each.

The last Duma—November 1912 to February 1917— was even more conservative: the right wing had 185 deputies, the Octobrists 97, and the Cadets 58. The Social-Democrats kept their 14, while the Labor Group sank to 10.

Both the Third and Fourth Dumas were boycotted by the Social-Revolutionaries.

Witte's return to public life in 1905 had been cut short by his becoming the target of attacks from all quarters—conservatives, liberals, and revolutionaries—and especially by Nicholas II's detestation. Witte's reverence for Tsarism, coupled with his contempt for the Tsar, made it impossible for him to apply his considerable talents to the efficient performance of his duties as President of the Council of Ministers, the equivalent of Prime Minister in a representative regime. His resignation was accepted a few days before the convocation of the First Duma, and his place was taken by an elderly routine functionary, Goremykin (1839–1917), whose career, grounded on obsequiousness to the Tsar, made him an ideal choice, from the latter's point of view, for supervisor of the new constitutional regime.

Perhaps the most distinguished newcomer to the government was Peter Stolypin (1862–1911), Minister of the Interior in the First Duma and later a powerful, able President of the Council of Ministers.

By temperament Stolypin was more of a landowner than a functionary. Marshal of the Nobility for Kovno Province, where he owned a great deal of land, and afterwards governor there as well as in Saratov on the Volga, he combined a high degree of Pan-Russian militancy with far-reaching originality of outlook and a grasp of the peasant problem that led him to embark on a series of agrarian innovations. Stolypin's attempt to revise the communal system of peasant administration was the only serious effort of the government to cope with the imbalance in land relations inherited from the defective reforms of the 1860s.

Stolypin intended to enable the peasants to own land independently of any other institution; he thought this would still the congenital restlessness of the countryside. Stolypin wanted to eradicate once and for all the village commune, zealously preserved in the settlement of 1861, and thus launch for the first time in Russia a class of peasant proprietors. Of course he hoped to benefit by their political influence. The basic part of a somewhat ramified scheme to accomplish this was embodied in a law of November 1906 giving an individual peasant the right, once he had secured the consent of two-thirds of the village assembly, to consolidate his scattered strips in the common fields into single plot, which from then on was to be private property in perpetuity.

Stolypin's legislation did not destroy the peasant commune all at once (in 1917 the great bulk of the peasantry were still being governed by it), but his agrarian reform was in fact spreading in wider and wider circles and laying the groundwork of a new peasant economy. By the outbreak of the 1914 war about a quarter of the peasant households in European Russia had transformed all their holdings into personal property, with about ten percent already consolidated. It would have seemed to be a mere question of time before the process spread throughout rural Russia and radically transformed its entire face and outlook.

Stolypin accompanied this far-sighted transformation of rural Russia by a ruthless repression of radical activity. There had been an upsurge of terrorism after the turbulent events of 1905; the Social-Revolutionaries had managed to arrange the assassination of almost 1,600 people in 1906, mostly officials of all grades, and more than 2,500 in 1907. This wave of murders reflected a general belief, shared by Lenin, that another armed revolt was in the offing.

In August 1906 the Maximalists, a newly formed S.R. group, blew up Stolypin's summer villa, killing thirty-two people, including the bomb-throwers, and injuring twenty-two, including Stolypin's son and daughter; he personally was unscratched. Though the S.R. Central Committee declined to take any credit for this particular outrage, the terrorist movement had frightened the regime; under Stolypin's energetic direction, the government reacted with brio. The security police were given immense latitude; the activities of the terrorists were countered by the lawbreaking of the security organs themselves. The extensive use of *agents provocateurs* directly involved the police in the most extravagant enterprises. Stolypin himself, in fact, found himself indirectly one of the victims of this regime of reciprocal lawlessness: a prison-break was arranged on behalf of one of the Maximalists, Solomon Ryss, who took advantage of the liberty given him by the police to organize the attack on Stolypin's villa. Ryss also organized a lucrative hold-up in the heart of St. Petersburg: it increased the Maximalist treasury by 400,000 rubles.

The wave of terrorism did not last long. The strength of the revolutionary movement at this time was altogether illusory. In 1907 the central S.R. organ was arrested and liquidated; by the end of the year almost all local groups had vanished. The activities of Ryss himself were finally noticed by his police sponsors, somewhat belatedly: he was hanged in 1908. The terrorists who escaped arrest fled abroad. By the end of 1907 the Central Committee of the S.R. Party, which after the amnesty of October 1905 had returned to Russia, was obliged to emigrate again. On top of this the exposure in 1908 of Azev's double-dealing, while highly embarrassing to the government, was even more so to the S.R. movement, which was nearly wrecked by the revelation. The Social-Democracy was also in a bad way. Rent by factional strife, its members arrested in droves, it almost broke up entirely. Even its fitful spurts of propaganda fell on stony ground. After Trotsky, Lenin emigrated in 1907, while Joseph Stalin, arrested in 1908, was deported to Siberia. By the spring of 1908 Russia was practically cleared of the whole of the revolutionary leadership.

The liberal movement, its premature hopes withering, was hard pressed. The conservatives were winning, at all points, including the Rural Councils that had once seemed such promising arenas of agitation. The government, having abandoned its intention of keeping its hands off the parliamentary process, was lavishly providing right-wing organizations with secret funds. The government also openly sponsored the arch-conservative organizations that began springing up with increasing boldness. The most prominent of these was the Council of the United Nobility, though a stellar role was still played by the Union of the Russian People, which split in 1908, producing the Union of the Archangel Michael.

The notoriety of the Union of the Russian People's activities is a striking index of the political corruption of the period between the 1905 upheaval and the First World War. It was public knowledge that the Union of the Russian People was engaged in criminal activities, including the organization of pogroms; its president, Dubrovin, had successfully conspired to murder two Cadet deputies to the First Duma, and he had also made two abortive attempts to assassinate Witte. Nothing was done about these notorious enterprises; Nicholas acknowledged a flood of telegrams organized by the Union demanding the dissolution of the intractable Second Duma by calling the Union the "mainstay of the throne."

Stolypin's Pan-Russian zeal led to an intensification of the nationalist element in his program. In practice nationalism—perhaps inevitably, considering the inherent blurriness of the concept—took the form of persecuting the various minorities of the Empire and of artificially ensuring the predominance of Russians in the quasirepresentative institutions imposed on the regime.

Russian was rammed down the throats of the minorities; it was made the language of instruction in the Ukraine, a special target of government ire. The regime made no secret of its hostility to the Ukrainian nationalist movement, which was suspected, doubtless rightly, of separatist tendencies, fortified by the autonomy accorded Ukrainians in the adjacent Austro-Hungarian provinces.

The qualified liberties the Finns had once managed to secure were nibbled away at. In 1910 the Russian government resumed its authority in questions affecting Finland if the matters went beyond purely Finnish interests, as determined, of course, by the Russians. This meddling involved a variety of issues, such as the assessment of Finland's contribution to the Russian budget, the taxes needed for it, army service, and education, all extremely irritating to the Finns, who were alienated and embittered.

The position of the Jews also deteriorated. The discriminatory regime they had been accustomed to for so long was intensified. In 1906 the Council of Ministers, without going so far as emancipation, recommended a slight liberalization of the anti-Jewish restrictions by the elimination of some measures that led to abuse and were unenforceable anyhow. The Council of Ministers argued that it would be good public relations, in the jargon of today, to ease up on the Jews, who might then be counted on to increase Russian chances of securing foreign loans. Nicholas took a personal interest in the Jews and reacted to these proposals with unusual vivacity; referring to the "inner voice" he had always been guided by, he turned the proposals down in spite of what he admitted was their persuasiveness. The outcome was that Jewish disabilities were reinforced, most flagrantly in a law passed in 1912 restoring the institution of Justices of the Peace, which had been abolished in 1889. Until 1912 Jews, though never appointed to any judicial office under Alexander III or Nicholas II, had never been excluded as a matter of principle; now they were specifically made ineligible. Perhaps the most illuminating indication of Russia's anachronistic attitude toward the Jews was the revival of the notorious ritual murder accusation made against a Jew, Beilis, in March 1911. For more than two and a half years, until Beilis was finally acquitted, and for some time afterwards, the validity of these long-exploded remnants of medieval superstition was vehemently discussed in the press.

By Stolypin's standards his career might have seemed successful. During his regime the revolutionary forces reached their nadir, while his land-program, despite the failure of many conservatives to appreciate its significance—it was June 1910 before the program was passed by the Duma—had effected a comprehensive metamorphosis of rural Russia.

Stolypin was actually considered an enemy by the conservative elements in the government and at court; his boldness and energy, expressed with an arrogance due, no doubt, to his awareness of his superiority, kindled hostile intrigues whose success seemed ensured and that were forestalled, ironically enough, only by his assassination in September 1911.

Stolypin's death was an outcome of his condoning of the police network of double agents, spies, and *agents provocateurs*. His assassin, Dmitri Bogrov, was one of the revolutionaries on the police payroll.

The next President of the Council of Ministers was V. N. Kokovtsov, who had been Minister of Finance since 1904, except for Witte's brief return, and who retained the office while

President of the Council. Kokovtsov was cultivated, complacent, and bureaucratic; he prided himself on the fine speeches he made in the Duma, though his real feelings about representative government were summed up in a famous *mot:* "Thank God, we still have no parliament!"

It was under Kokovtsov that the security police made their brilliant coup of secretly getting Lenin's trusted friend Malinovsky elected to the Fourth Duma. The more visible activities of Kokovtsov's ascendancy in 1911–1914 included the rise of Rasputin and its public repercussions. In spite of Nicholas's efforts to hush things up, there was a series of scandals following the appointment of V. K. Sabler, one of Rasputin's selections, as Chief Procurator of the Holy Synod; the scandals involved all sorts of church figures, including dissolute monks. Rasputin was denounced on the floor of the Duma by so unquestionably reactionary a personage as V. M. Purishkevich, leader of the Union of the Archangel Michael, as well as by Guchkov, head of the Octobrists.

On Kokovtsov's retirement in January 1914, Goremykin, by now seventy-five and somewhat senile, became President of the Council of Ministers. His professional credentials of unquestioning loyalty to the Tsar were fortified by his association with Rasputin; the two relationships doubtless interlocked. It was in Goremykin's palsied grip that Russia was to slide into the First World War.

Apart from the transformation of the peasant villages launched by Stolypin, other structural changes were being manifested. After 1905 the cooperative movement grew with great rapidity. The first Russian cooperatives, some forty years before, had made very little progress, but between 1905 and 1914 the membership of the cooperatives grew tenfold, increasing from less than 1 million to more than 10 million. While not impressive in absolute terms, the potentialities of this movement are obvious.

At the peak of Tsarist prosperity, before the war, the national income per capita was eight to ten times less than in the United States; this is understandable when it is recalled that in 1913 the number of people engaged in all nonagricultural pursuits—

industry, commerce, transport—did not amount to more than one-seventeenth of the whole population, whereas in the United States over two people were engaged in industry for every person engaged in agriculture. Nevertheless there was a great industrial boom in Russia toward the end of the century; it achieved its unusual dimensions precisely because it took place within the framework of Russian backwardness.

The industrial expansion, particularly rapid from 1893 to 1899, slowed down in the first decade of the twentieth century; it speeded up again rom 1910 to 1913. During the 1890s, 15,000 miles of railway, including the Trans-Siberian, were built; this was the chief single cause of the business boom, which then slowed down because of the turmoil following the turn of the century. All in all, industrial production in Russia increased by roughly 100 percent between 1905 and the First World War.

But what was far more important was the character of the industry that sprang up. Russia's very lateness enabled her to dispense with the obsolescent features that hampered the capitalism of older industrial countries.

Thus, although agriculture and peasant life had not risen much beyond the level of the seventeenth century, Russian industry—in technique and structure—was well in the forefront of international capitalism. More important than absolute industrial growth was the density of the production process. This density, already noticeable in the first stages of Russian industrial development, became still more marked in the twenty-five years before the First World War.

A comparison with the United States is illuminating. In 1914, 35 percent of all American industrial workers were employed in small businesses with fewer than a hundred workers apiece; in Russia there were only 17.8 percent. The two countries had about the same ratio of businesses employing 100 to 1,000 workers, but less than 18 percent of the workers were employed in the United States in giant enterprises of 1,000 each, while in Russia the same category took in 32 percent of all workers in 1901 and over 40 percent in 1914. The figure is still more striking in the main industrial areas: in Petersburg,

for instance, over 44 percent of the enterprises had 1,000 workers, in Moscow more than 57 percent. Russian textile and
metal industries were dominated by gigantic plants.

The usual aridity of statistics is relieved in this case by the
realization that the concentration of vast numbers of workers
on the same premises was a political factor of cardinal importance; it was vital in heightening the workers' *esprit de corps*
and discipline—in a word, their solidarity.

The industrial boom, to be sure, was not reflected in actual
living conditions or wages; though there seems to have been
a rise in real wages in the decade before the First World War,
the workers' entire income was almost exhausted on the barest
necessities of life.

A substantial element in the great industrial boom of this
quarter century was the flow of money from abroad. By 1914
foreign companies owned about one-third of the total capital
investment of Russian industry, and the great influx of foreign
money accelerated the industrialization of the south. About
a third of the investments came from France; England contributed 23 percent, Germany 20 percent, and Belgium 14 percent.
France controlled almost 75 percent of Russia's output of coal
and pig iron.

These aspects of Russian capitalism, confined as it was to
a small sector of the population, and even more to the external
world of socio-political affairs, are only one indication of the
evolution of Russian society.

The cultural isolation of Russia from the West, which had
lasted so long, was a thing of the past. The Russian educated
classes were now on a level with their counterparts in other
countries.

In spite of all obstacles, the number of students at higher
schools had increased substantially. In the beginning of 1914
there were 67 higher schools numbering 90,000 students; this
included some 13 women's institutions with 21,000 students.
There were 36,000 students attending universities, 22,000 in
the engineering and other technical schools and 10,000 in specialized institutions such as agricultural colleges.

The secondary schools also showed some progress, and the

primary school system became an object of immense concern even to the conservative Third Duma, which with considerable success undertook a general reform. The general background of the problem, to be sure, remained rather depressing: in 1914, 49 percent of the children between ages eight and eleven did not go to school at all. In its broad outlines, the problem of illiteracy remained unsolved.

Nevertheless, despite the flimsy underpinnings of the educated classes, there was a very lively development of the press and the arts. After 1905 the press was largely free in spite of the censorship regime. The broad spectrum of opinion expressed in the 2,167 periodicals that in 1912 appeared in 246 cities and towns (excluding Finland) took in even Marxist writers, who found it entirely possible to express their views in public. In 1924 the Communist Academy made a survey, which it admitted to be incomplete, of the Social-Democratic literature—Menshevik as well as Bolshevik—that was legally published in St. Petersburg and Moscow between 1906 and 1914: it came to well over 3,000 items. In spite of the government's intensified program of russification, minority languages were used extensively. The periodicals mentioned above appeared in 33 languages, including Polish (234), German (69), Lithuanian (47), Estonian (45), and Hebrew and Yiddish (31). Indeed, from 1906 to 1914 the Russian press was freer than at any other time.

The industrial and political fevers of the turn of the century, as well as the increased freedom of the press after 1905, had a stimulating effect on literature and the arts. The realism Russian literature had become famous for during the 1860s and 1870s was sustained by a group whose leaders were Tolstoy, Gorky, Anton Chekhov (1860–1904), and Ivan Bunin (1870–1953). Tolstoy, in fact, loomed bulkier than ever, perhaps because of his religious conversion around 1880 and his ascetic repudiation of his purely literary writings. Having become a world sage, after working out a highly simplified form of Christianity that he himself considered primitive and that repudiated authority, violence, and all institutions, in short the whole fabric of accepted society, Tolstoy went on living on his estate in Yasnaya Polyana. His contradictory life filled him with growing revulsion, but he finally achieved a certain degree of spiritual consistency by attacking the Orthodox Church until the Holy Synod, which had shown great forbearance because of his name, eventually acknowledged a *de facto* situation and excommunicated him in 1901.

The success of writers in winning Russia a name in world literature was echoed more faintly in other arts. From 1900 on, Russian painters began appearing at international exhibitions. All the movements of contemporary art found their exponents in Russia—impressionism, post-impressionism, expressionism, cubism, and futurism. In the decade before the First World War, Russian art had altogether caught up with Europe. It did not, to be sure, make a particularly original contribution of its own; because of its rapid growth, it was contaminated by many signs of precocity—meaningless, rootless extremism, slavish imitation of foreign models, and so on. At the same time, it had freshness and boldness.

Russian music was now entirely acclimated all over the civilized world; Stravinsky and later Prokofiev were the most famous of the newer composers. The pre-World War generation produced a vast array of celebrated interpretive artists–Rachmaninov, Vladimir Horowitz, Scriabin, Leopold Auer, Ephrem Zimbalist, Jascha Heifetz. Russia, indeed, was one of the most brilliant spots on the horizon of international music-lovers: St. Petersburg had four opera houses, each with a full season; Chaliapin was famous all over the world. Stanislavsky's theater started an international reputation that has survived to this day. The ballet, which had been introduced into Russia in 1672 and had struck root under Catherine the Great, who founded a ballet school modelled on Paris, was finally, by the turn of the century, defrenchified to some extent. A host of Russian ballerinas became internationally celebrated. Fokine, the youthful choreographer of the Petersburg ballet, completely recast its traditions; choosing the works of the most famous Russian composers, Tchaikovsky, Rimsky-Korsakov, Glinka, Borodin, and Stravinsky, as well as Schumann, Wagner, and Weber, he brought about a fusion between dancing and music.

He also laid special emphasis on the role of mass dancing; this increased the importance of the *corps de ballet* in relation to the prima ballerina. All these innovations, framed in splendid new costumes and decor, created by Diaghilev, were introduced in the summer of 1909 at Le Châtelet in Paris.

Before the First World War upper-class Russians were characteristically immersed in intense intellectual activity, as is demonstrated by the extraordinarily wide range of the press of that period and the immense variety of different currents in literature, music, painting, and theater. The court itself was considered rather stuffy, but many grand duchesses and aristocratic matrons had intellectual salons that established a national tone. Outside the circle of the Tsar's immediate entourage, educated Russians tended to be urbanely critical of the existing order; the State Duma, for all its parliamentary imperfections, was the object of absorbed attention in cultivated circles.

Ties with Western Europe were very close; upper-class children were habitually taught to speak French, German, and, somewhat less frequently, English. Foreign literature was widely read, and Russians flocked to all the capitals and resorts of Europe. By the end of the nineteenth century educated Russians were thoroughly europeanized.

Yet this complete assimilation merely pointed up in another way the profound chasm that has been referred to so often. Precisely because of these European influences, the upper classes were alien to the bulk of the country. The cosmopolitan attitudes streaming in from abroad were concentrated socially in the upper middle classes and territorially in the capital. Petersburg, with its splendid embankment and its baroque eighteenth- and nineteenth-century palaces constructed by Frenchmen and Italians, was entirely Westernized, physically and temperamentally: even the court and the bureaucracy were highly accessible to foreign influences. But the farther one got away from the capital, the farther one sank into a quagmire of life altogether alien to Western Europe. Even Moscow had a certain provincialism, and in the small towns the imprint of the West began fading fast; in the remoter cities it was altogether absent. These were cities in name only, actually no more than peasant villages with no modern amenities to speak of. Indeed, 87 percent of the population, according to the 1897 census, lived in the countryside, and from the point of view of any Western European capital, the rural population might just as well have lived on Mars. In customs, way of life and thought, and even language, there was nothing in common between the peasants and the tiny educated class. Unless an aristocrat happened to take a personal interest in his land, the peasants and the upper class had no interests whatever in common.

The egalitarian effects of the vigorous and lively popular press were inhibited by illiteracy, which remained widespread, though by the beginning of the First World War illiteracy was doubtless a little less than the 79 percent recorded in the 1897 census. On the other hand, it must also be recalled that in official reports, *literate* might mean nothing more than school attendance in childhood; a literate Russian might not have had the slightest contact with a book or newspaper since, perhaps not even be able to sign his name.

The Russian Church did not have the cultural or unifying influence of the Protestant or Roman Catholic Churches, a fact that fostered disunity and backwardness. This disunity was further exacerbated by the persecution of all the national and religious minorities—Finns, Poles, Jews, and Ukrainians.

Russia plummeted into the First World War, accordingly, with her ancient lopsidedness still embedded in her institutions. The backwardness of the immense majority and the cosmopolitanism of the upper class were radically out of balance. Russia's profound structural flaws were merely plastered over by her façade of monolithic placidity.

Tsarism had been no more than shaken up by the 1905 revolution. But the First World War had undreamed of consequences for Russia.

There is no need to discuss the causes of the First World War or for that matter the course of its development. Russia was involved in it with the same curious mixture of blindness and irresponsibility that characterized the actions of all the great powers. Europe had not had a war for so long and the technological and organizational background of society had meanwhile changed so profoundly that it proved impossible for even the most astute statesmen to speculate on the conduct of an armed conflict involving the mobilization of millions of men. Not merely were forecasts in detail utterly falsified by events, but the very fabric of society, thought to be fissure-proof, was to be shredded by the war and its aftermath.

The economic and political structure of the Russian state was hopelessly outdistanced by the demands of a modern war. Russian leadership proved to be completely inadequate from both the military and the economic points of view. Having slipped into the maelstrom of a comprehensive conflict even more unprepared than the other great powers, Russia found itself short of armaments as well as of war aims. Two contrary tendencies were embodied in the Tsarist state—the essentially medieval and still exclusive prerogatives of the throne, and the defective but existent popular representation in the State Duma and the scattered institutions of local government. The characteristic wartime concentration of the executive power on the one hand, and the involvement of masses, reflected in the representative institutions, on the other, accentuated both these tendencies.

The authority of the crown was reasserted: the Tsar's personal rule was buttressed by the Empress's personal ascendancy and by Rasputin's backstage role: the cumbersome Tsarist bureaucracy was circumvented. The Duma, the Rural Councils, and the municipalities were called upon to enlarge their functions in order to cope with the magnified tasks of recruitment, supply, and all aspects of economic functioning. These two tendencies collided and helped shatter the whole system.

Politically speaking, the war was supported, though with varying degrees of enthusiasm, by all parties in the government with the exception of the Bolshevik faction of the Social-Democratic Party, which took the intransigent position that the working class ought to fight against the domestic bourgeois and imperialist regime instead of against the enemy's armies. Though this attitude was eventually to help the Bolsheviks, at the time it simply meant the arrest of the five Bolshevik deputies who made up the legal, parliamentary section of the Bolshevik group and their exile to Eastern Siberia in 1915.

One of the major atmospheric elements, so to speak, leading up to the 1917 revolution was Rasputin's towering role. In the topmost circles, Rasputin's power soon became so disturbing that a plot was set afoot to get rid of him. He was assassinated in the palace of Prince Yusupov in December 1916; no action was taken against the assassins, who included a nephew of the Tsar as well as Yusupov himself.

Rasputin's influence had damaged the prestige of the monarchy and helped alienate the most conservative elements in the country from the support of the throne. But it would be a gross extravagance to think of Rasputin as a genuine factor in the 1917 breakdown, whose roots must be looked for in the strain imposed on the administration by the exigencies of a major war.

The crumbling of national morale that led to the events of 1917 took place only gradually. A patriotic fervor swept the capital in the summer of 1914, as indeed it swept every capital that went to war; the fervor was shared by every social group. Huge crowds collected to express their dislike of Germans and Austrians, the mobilization went off smoothly, and the strike movement that in the summer of 1914 had set a record since 1905–6 simply evaporated.

But the façade of orderly devotion to a common cause began splintering at once. the immediate factors in the disintegration of the patriotic mood were the successive defeats of the army, the chaos of the administration, and a growing irritation among the masses with a war that remained entirely incomprehensible to them. The Duma spoke for the bulk of the upper and middle class, but the peasants and workers had no interest at all in general politics; their restlessness began increasing because of perfectly simple economic grievances blamed on the meaningless war.

Prices were going up, and the necessities of life were going down. These facts, plus the overcrowding, naturally squeezed the population, especially the poorer part of it. Except for the better-paid workers in the war industries, wages receded from the already low level of 1915–16. As for the families whose male members were drafted, they were in a desperate situation; the government gave them only enough to buy food and nothing more.

As labor felt the pinch, it began striking. In 1915 more than a thousand strikes took place, involving more than half a million workers. In 1916 there were 1,400 strikes involving more than a million, and the strike movement kept mounting in January and February 1917. These wartime strikes, though somewhat below the figures for the first half-year of 1914 (when the strikes had been, moreover, partly political), were quite spontaneous; they had nothing to do with political perspectives or trade union leadership, except for the class-conscious, relatively highly paid metal-workers. As for the peasants, though economically they were better off than the industrial working class, it was they who had to bear the brunt of the staggering war casualties, which for the First World War amounted, on the Russian side, to more than 7 million men, the bulk of whom, in harmony with the representative quality of a conscript army, were peasants.

The people at large could not grasp the nation's remote aims in the war. Not only did the peasants desert en masse, but entire regiments would panic and flee for the most trivial reasons. In 1915 the Minister of War, Polivanov, was reduced to proclaiming his faith in Russia's "immeasurable distances, impassable roads, and the mercy of St. Nicholas, patron of Holy Russia."

It was primarily the defeatist mood of the peasantry and industrial working class that was to undo the Tsarist regime, immersed in a war it was technologically baffled by.

None of the discontent arising from the wartime conditions was guided by revolutionary centers. The police repressions that had taken place after the strikes of 1914 had exterminated all the clandestine revolutionary organizations, and it was not until the end of 1915 that the Central Committee of the Bolshevik faction resumed some very quiet activities in Petersburg.

None of the revolutionary leaders was in Russia. Lenin was

in Switzerland. Trotsky had made his way to New York after being expelled from one European country after another. It is true that though the revolutionary movement had been decapitated, thousands of its members and sympathizers were scattered throughout the army and the wartime agencies and factories. But their propaganda was limited to the propagation of ultimate aims: there was no question of planning for a revolution.

· The capital was completely calm the week before 23 February (Old Style). The Duma had been convoked on 14 February; on 22 February the Tsar left for army headquarters. The excitement caused by Rasputin's assassination had died down completely during the first few weeks of 1917.

All at once some riots broke out. They seem to have begun among irritated housewives queuing up in front of food shops, spread with incomprehensible rapidity to the working-class suburbs and then flowed back through the main streets and squares of the capital. There was no violence; no hostility was shown by the police and troops; the city authorities were not alarmed.

At some point it became apparent that orders given to troops to stop unarmed demonstrators from proceeding along streets or over bridges could not be carried out. When a commanding officer gives an order that is not carried out and he cannot punish anyone for it, military discipline is at an end. This was what happened to the broad, unguided movement in the streets of the capital during the first few days after the food riots.

The absence of authority was noticed all of a sudden: it was embodied most dramatically in the simple fact that all the policemen had vanished. The feeling of anarchy had found a dramatic symbol.

The Duma session was cut short, but after some vacillation the Duma leaders decided to remain informally in session. On 27 February a Provisional Committee was elected consisting of the leaders of the Progressive Bloc of the Duma plus some left-wing representatives—Alexander Kerensky, a temperamental young lawyer of Populist sympathies, and Nicholas

Chkheidze, a Menshevik. This committee had nothing subversive in mind: it was simply supposed to "restore order and deal with institutions and individuals."

On the very same day, 27 February, in the Tauride Palace, the seat of the Duma, there convened, with no guidance, no mandate, and no plan, the Petrograd Soviet of Workers' Deputies, which on 2 March changed its name to the Soviet of Workers' and Soldiers' Deputies.

During the afternoon, while the Petrograd garrison was *de facto* sapping the foundations of the old regime, some left-wing Duma members, recently released political prisoners, and a variety of journalists, doctors, lawyers, Rural Council employees, and so on, had set up the Provisional Executive Committee of the Petrograd Soviet, which was not yet in existence, and in the evening hundreds of people of unknown antecedents held a plenary session of the Soviet confirming the Executive Committee.

The idea of reviving the 1905 revolutionary assembly seems to have sprung up by itself. No one has ever claimed credit for it; it must have occurred more or less simultaneously to a number of labor leaders and intellectuals. It should of course be emphasized that the Soviet—simply the Russian word for *council,* a word that was retained by the present-day regime of the Russian Communist Party—at that time did not have its present political connotation. In origin the Soviet was a genuinely representative institution, at any rate to a considerable extent.

By 3 March the Soviet had 1,300 members, and a week later 3,000, of which 800 represented factory workers and the remainder various army units, a fact that is in itself significant since there were far more workers in Petrograd than soldiers.

Thus, even before the collapse of the Tsarist regime, the Tauride Palace became the seat of two sources of power that were more authoritative than the former government apparatus.

Thousands of soldiers and civilians began streaming into the vast and stately halls of the Palace; the whole building was turned into an arena for a shabby, headstrong, seething mass, with the more sedate quarters reserved for the Duma and its hangers-on.

By 2 March the Tsar had signed a document of abdication; the following day he was sent off by train with his family to captivity and ultimately death.

In the space of three days the apparently unshakable Tsarist administration had simply been short-circuited. Nothing was left of it—and this was felt by everyone in the capital.

The throngs of people teeming in and around the Tauride Palace had no clear objective. It was the conservative Fourth Duma that was first turned to by many of the upper- and middle-class Russians, who gravitated toward it as the new state authority.

The Soviet, a mass-meeting in many ways, was against the retention of the monarchy with or without Nicholas II. On 2 March, by the time a provisional government had been formed by the Provisional Committee of the Duma after a laboriously arrived-at agreement with the Executive Committee of the Soviet, it was evident that a constitutional monarchy, which had been hoped for by the conservative Duma leaders headed by Miliukov, was no longer a possibility. The insistence of the Soviet had excluded it, and the liberals, who had been hoping for the accession to the throne of the Tsar's brother, who would serve as regent for the Tsar's young son and heir Michael, were confronted by the de facto elimination of monarchism as a principle of government. The ancient Russian historical tradition was extinguished. Thus the Provisional Government, though created by a conservative Duma, was forced by circumstances to be as radical an institution as the Soviet; it was obliged to assume the direction of the state and hence to consecrate the rupture with the past.

Despite the casualties of the upheaval—some 1,500—the monarchy had evaporated with fabulous ease. It had been short-circuited through the spontaneous behavior of the inhabitants of Petrograd, plus the disaffected garrison, and in the absence of any leadership. The rest of the country and the army as such played no role. The overturn of the government was accepted throughout the country, with or without enthusiasm, as an accomplished fact.

For eight months the destinies of Russia were to be played out in an arena of democratic expression against the background of the continuing war. Russia was freer than at any time in its history before or since.

The Soviet leaders, almost uniformly Social-Revolutionaries and Mensheviks, did not contest the authority vested in the Provisional Government that had sprung out of the Fourth Duma. Their own authority had been forced on them long before the authority itself was juridically recognized, which did not actually take place until the eve of the Bolshevik insurrection in October. The trade unions, the industrial working class generally, and the peasants supported the Soviet. The trains would not move, the municipal institutions and the police were paralyzed, and the most basic functions of administration were inhibited unless authorized, sanctioned, or specifically ordered by the Soviet, which according to the official theory of the Provisional Government remained a private body. And despite the theoretical sovereignty of the Provisional Government, its authority was viable only through the grace of the Soviet, which declined to acknowledge its own authority in theory while in fact retaining control of all administration.

The Marxists in the Soviet—Mensheviks and Bolsheviks (the latter being represented before Lenin's arrival in April by Stalin and a young man, Vyacheslav Molotov)—could not take power; their political analysis prevented them. For Marxists, socialism could come about only after capitalism had matured, at which time the proletariat would also have matured sufficiently to be able to establish socialism. It seemed obvious that socialism was bound to fail in a backward, agrarian, semifeudal country such as Russia. Hence, until socialism was on the order of the day as the next stage after the ripening of capitalism under the bourgeoisie, it would be best for a socialist party not to compromise itself politically, in the eyes of the proletariat, by taking any state responsibilities.

During the eight months of the provisional government,

accordingly, the Mensheviks, together with the Social-Revolutionaries, would do nothing to hamper the provisional government representing the bourgeoisie; the Marxists would at most act as the government's supervisors.

Lenin's arrival in April transformed this configuration. A discussion of Lenin now, however, would lead far afield; I shall merely situate him socially.

Vladimir Ilyich Ulyanov (Lenin) (1870–1924) was born into a prosperous family. His father was a professor of mathematics and an academic supervisor who had been given a noble title in accordance with the Table of Ranks. Lenin's mother was the daughter of a well-known physician. Educated by family tutors and governesses, she spoke four languages, sang, and played the piano. In spite of Soviet legend, in short, Lenin belonged by birth to the landowning class.

Until Lenin was twenty-seven the question of his earning a living never arose. Afterwards the combination of family and Party allowances, as well as what he made by his pen, enabled him to live in circumstances that were, materially speaking, perfectly bourgeois, though the personal frugality of Lenin and his wife, Nadezhda Krupskaya, made them indifferent to such questions.

On his return to Russia at the age of forty-seven, Lenin was merely the leader of a small group in the mini-universe of the Russian revolutionaries. No one could have foreseen that in a few months he was to become one of the most influential people in history.

In February 1917, when the food riots broke out, Lenin, together with many other revolutionaries, including Martov, was in Switzerland. The idea was conceived (apparently by Martov) of getting back to Russia via Germany. The German government was approached; it assented and provided the revolutionaries with a sealed train.

The sealed train was instantly notorious. Lenin's return to Russia with the enemy's permission, plus his systematic agitation for peace—i.e., his sabotage of the front—made it seem obvious to many that he was functioning as an agent of the German government.

On the other hand, since other revolutionaries on the train were in disagreement with Lenin, and since it was plain that Lenin could not have returned in any other way, he could be defended on the left side of the political spectrum without much difficulty.

On his arrival Lenin made a switch in Marxist theory to the effect that a Marxist party could take power, after all, *legitimately*. The word is important—Marxist parties must buttress their behavior by theory. Lenin's theoretical switch was a vital prerequisite for his entourage; it immediately made him formidable politically.

The switch itself was based on an analysis generally attributed to Leon Trotsky, though Lenin had, as it seems, come to the same conclusion independently.

Leon Trotsky (1879–1940) was known as a brilliant speaker and a many-sided writer. Since becoming a celebrity amongst the Russian exiles after his precocious role as chairman of the short-lived Soviet of 1905, he had become a more or less full-time journalist with a revolutionary hobby. As a revolutionary he had had a position of his own outside the Bolshevik and Menshevik camps, which he made some futile efforts to reconcile. In effect Trotsky remained a maverick throughout the decade preceding 1917; he was distinguished, moreover, for the implacability of his attacks on Lenin, which he set forth in the usual guise of theoretical differences.

Trotsky's theory—patented, so to speak, as "permanent revolution"—held that the Russian bourgeoisie was too weak to overcome Tsarism alone and reform capitalism adequately before the Russian workers grew strong enough to push it out altogether; hence it was necessary for the working class to take power in order to accomplish the bourgeois revolution on behalf of the bourgeoisie, thus creating a situation in which the proletariat could construct socialism later on.

Lenin took up this theory in April; to the consternation of his comrades, he insisted that the Bolsheviks must take power and waste no more time waiting for the Russian bourgeoisie to reform capitalism.

Lenin arrived in the evening of 3 April at the Finland Station of Petrograd. Though unknown at this time outside political circles, he was welcomed by a huge throng that filled the square. His speech ended with a slogan that at the time was utterly alien to all socialists in Russia, including Bolsheviks—"Long live the socialist revolution."

Sukhanov, a semi-Menshevik journalist and economist who has left us the only full-length memoir of the turbulent eight months of 1917, slipped into the celebration of Lenin's arrival in the Bolshevik headquarters, where he had been driven from the Finland Station on top of an armored car, "holding a service," as Sukhanov says, at every street crossing to gaping crowds.

Sukhanov gives us a vivid description not only of Lenin's oratorical style, but of the emotional impact of his break with socialist tradition. Even though Lenin, while not yet ikonized, had immense authority within his faction, his new theory flabbergasted his disciples—he had to conquer them before acquiring a mass following. Here is Sukhanov's eye-witness account:

> The celebrated master of the order got to his feet. I shall never forget that thunderlike speech, which startled and amazed not only me, a heretic who had accidentally dropped in, but all the true believers. I am certain that no one had expected anything of the sort. It seemed as though all the elements had risen from their abodes, and the spirit of universal destruction, knowing neither barriers nor doubts, neither human difficulties nor human calculations, were hovering around Kshesinskaya's reception room above the heads of the bewitched disciples.
>
> Lenin was a very good orator—not an orator of the consummate, rounded phrase, or of the luminous image, or of absorbing pathos, or of the pointed witticism, but an orator of enormous impact and power, breaking down complicated systems into the simplest and most generally accessible elements, and hammering, hammering, hammering them into the heads of his audience until he took them captive.

Sukhanov goes on to give us some typical reflections of Lenin's opponents:

> Skobelev told Miliukov about his (Lenin's) "lunatic ideas," appraising him as a completely lost man standing outside the movement.

I agreed in general with this estimate of Lenin's ideas and said that in his present guise he was so unacceptable to everyone that now he was not at all dangerous for our interlocutor, Miliukov. However, the future of Lenin seemed different to me: I was convinced that after he had escaped from his foreign academic milieu and entered an atmosphere of real struggle and wide practical activity, he would acclimatise himself quickly, settle down, stand on firm ground, and throw overboard the bulk of his anarchist "ravings." What life failed to accomplish with him, the solid pressure of his party comrades would help with. I was convinced that in the near future Lenin would again be converted into a herald of the ideas of revolutionary Marxism and occupy a place in the revolution worthy of him as the most authoritative leader of the Soviet proletarian left. Then, I said, he would be dangerous to Miliukov. And Miliukov agreed with me.

We refused to admit that Lenin might stick to his "abstractions." Still less did we admit that through these abstractions Lenin would be able to conquer not only the revolution, not only all its active masses, not only the whole Soviet—but even his own Bolsheviks.

We were cruelly mistaken. . . . .

During the eight months of the Provisional Government, all parties, except for the Bolsheviks after Lenin's arrival, supported the war. This burden, inherited from Tsarism, was to undo the Provisional Government and pave the way to the Bolshevik putsch. The war situation was or seemed to be hopeless: the material difficulties kept accumulating, and though there was a certain amount of enthusiasm at times for the Provisional Government, and though Kerensky often seemed genuinely popular, the hardships of war, plus its unpopularity, made the task of the middle-class government, as well as of the Social-Revolutionaries and the Mensheviks who supported it, in practical terms impossible.

There was another factor, in any case, that was to prove crucial. It may be called the secret background of the Bolshevik putsch—unsuspected at the time even by knowledgeable insiders like Sukhanov.

Lenin did in fact have an organic relationship with the German government—if not an agent, he was undoubtedly an ally. Since he was the only Russian revolutionary demanding an end to the war—which to the German General Staff meant the immobilization of the eastern front—it was natural for the German government to support him. Beginning no later than the spring of 1917, the German government had been putting huge sums of money at the disposal of the Bolsheviks.

At a minimal estimate these sums amounted to more than 60 million gold marks, or, in today's currency, about $1,000 million. This sum, staggering by any reckoning, though of course a bagatelle for a regime sustaining millions of soldiers on two fronts, enabled the Bolsheviks to maintain a vast press (forty-one periodicals) that hammered away at public opinion with the simplest of slogans—none of them Marxist in the slightest—and thus made the Bolsheviks both respectable and popular. This ramified press was undoubtedly a factor in the Bolshevik triumph in October. The German subsidy was to be maintained until long after the Bolshevik putsch—until the eve of the German collapse on the Western front in the autumn of 1918.

The subsidies also played a considerable role in Bolshevik politics.

Trotsky had worked out "Permanent Revolution," his own twist on Marxist theory, together with another Russian Jewish Marxist some twelve years older than himself, Alexander Israel Helphand (1867–1923), who had made a name for himself as editor and writer in the German Social-Democratic movement and during the 1905 upset had collaborated with Trotsky, who had the highest opinion of his brainpower. Helphand had gone to the Balkans a few years before the outbreak of the 1914 war and made a fortune as a businessman: he was, no doubt, the only Marxist multimillionaire in history. It was he who had proposed to the German government that it subsidize the revolutionaries, since the interests of the German government and of the Russian revolutionaries were identical.

In July 1917, when in the midst of the unremitting turbulence the Bolsheviks were thought, perhaps rightly, to be preparing a putsch, the news of the German subsidy leaked out in the form of documents that were so puerile as to suggest that they might have been planted on the Kerensky government. Lenin and his top aides bolted immediately. Plainly, they could not afford a full-dress inquiry; it was a question, after all, of high treason in wartime.

Trotsky, not a Bolshevik at the time, was not subject to the same charge as Lenin; Trotsky joined the Bolsheviks while Lenin was in hiding. Using his influence as Chairman of the Soviet, to which he was elected in the autumn of 1917, Trotsky stage-managed the Bolshevik putsch and, moreover, in the teeth of Lenin's violent objections, presented it as a Soviet enterprise. In the event, this rallied the bulk of left-wing and even liberal opinion to the new regime and enabled the Bolsheviks to survive the civil war after the putsch. Trotsky's remarkably successful imposture still survives in the name of the Soviet Union.

Lenin and Trotsky had concurred in a Marxist justification of a socialist party's taking power, even in a backward agrarian country, as a way of imposing a bourgeois revolution on the bourgeoisie. But this required a further justification—it was assumed that once the socialist party was in power in such a country, the revolution that was thought to be imminent in the advanced industrial countries would come to the rescue of such a socialist outpost.

On this point Lenin and Trotsky were equally euphoric—they were both convinced that the big revolution was bound to break out, at the very least in Germany, the industrial heart of Europe. By October 1917 Lenin was transported; it seemed to him that Germany was on the point of exploding. On 7 October he wrote that "the worldwide workers' revolution had begun . . . doubts are impossible. We stand on the threshold of the world proletarian revolution."

It was against the background of this general expectation that the decision was taken at a secret meeting of the Central Committee, on 10 October, with twelve of the twenty-one members present. The discussion (which took place, curiously enough, in Sukhanov's flat, without his knowledge) lasted for about ten hours. Lenin's resolution that the "armed insurrection is inevitable and the time for it fully ripe" was passed by ten to two (Lenin's two intimates, Zinoviev and Kamenev, voted against it).

The Bolshevik putsch proved to be child's play. As Lenin said later, "it was as easy as lifting up a feather." With the Marxist justification of the putsch reserved for the Party elite, the masses were appealed to by the enormous, German-subsidized press on the basis of a broad campaign summed up in three words—peace, bread, land.

In Lenin's absence Trotsky, Chairman of the Soviet since 23 September and moreover Chairman of the Military Revolutionary Committee set up by the Soviet for the "revolutionary defense" of Petrograd, created the strategy of the putsch. The idea was simple, the putsch was led up to through preparations that were presented as a general defense of the Soviet. Though the plan itself—as Trotsky was to admit—was crude, hasty, and improvised, and for that matter publicly discussed beforehand, it was enough: the Bolsheviks' opponents were strangely indolent.

Against the background of civic disintegration, mass apathy, and the incapacity of the Provisional Government to reason its way out of supporting the war or to conceive of either an attractive program or an effective tactic, the Bolsheviks found it a simple matter to implement their plan.

On the night of 24 October the Military Revolutionary Committee sent armed detachments to occupy the key points of the capital's railway terminals, bridges, state banks, telephone exchange, central post office, and various public buildings. Though the troops were apathetic, they were at any rate not against the Bolsheviks, except for a few neutral regiments, including the Cossacks; there was no bloodshed or opposition. The next day nearly all the ministers of the Provisional Government were arrested, except for Kerensky, who escaped abroad. They were taken to the Peter-Paul Fortress to join their Tsarist predecessors.

The putsch was so easy that no one was aware of what was happening. Most of the shops, theaters, and cinemas were open: on the afternoon of 25 October, when the putsch was supposedly at its height, city life looked practically normal.

That same afternoon Trotsky took time off to preside over

a session of the Petrograd Soviet. Lenin, who had been in hiding from the Provisional Government since July, finally emerged to take over publicly the reins of power seized by his Party. After the preceding months of tension, wrangling, and apathy, the mood was now very enthusiastic. Sukhanov reports the scene:

> Long-drawn-out ovations alternated with the singing of "The Internationale." Lenin was hailed again, hurrahs were shouted, caps flung into the air. A funeral march was sung in memory of the martyrs of the war. Then they applauded again, shouted, flung up their caps. The whole Presidium, headed by Lenin, was standing up and singing, with exalted faces and blazing eyes. . . . Applause, hurrahs, caps flung up into the air . . .

Lenin's entourage had undertaken a momentous gamble. A tiny minority, with no control of the population and with no administrative personnel, had embarked on the government of a large, backward, agrarian country. Shortly after the putsch, moreover, the Bolsheviks had dispersed the Constituent Assembly—the dream of generations of Russian revolutionaries, including the Bolsheviks themselves before the putsch. Thus the handful of Bolshevik leaders were to exercise a monopoly.

They had, in fact, replaced the working out of economic forces as analyzed by classical Marxism with political decisions, improvised *ad hoc*. What is more, they took this road alone. The failure of the revolution to sweep Europe—there were a few fiascoes after the war in Germany and Hungary—isolated the Bolsheviks.

A striking instance of Bolshevik improvisation was their promise of land to the peasants. A land decree abolished all private ownership in land, making it impossible to buy, sell, lease, mortgage, or alienate land in any way. This scheme, which revived the most unworkable features of the antiquated village commune, was lifted bodily from the arsenal of Social-Revolutionary theory, which the Bolsheviks had been laughing at for years. Lenin defended this incorporation of his opponents' theories as—expedient.

The Bolsheviks had not, in fact, worked out a plan to remake society. In Lenin's words, "The point is the seizure of power; afterwards we shall see what we can do with it."

Thus the Bolsheviks, intellectually rooted in Marxist abstractions and without practical plans, were determined to maintain their monopoly by reshaping society. The large-scale goals to be lumped together as "Socialism" (now distinct from "Communism," far in the future) amounted to the control by the State—i.e., the Party—of all social and economic activities.

CHAPTER X

THE NEO-BOLSHEVIK STATE

*T*he legacy of the war was disastrous. Russia lay prostrate. Even if the Bolsheviks in making their putsch had had a concrete scheme of social reconstruction, they would have been incapable of implementing it. Their energies were consumed by ending the war with the Germans and defending themselves against the "White" opposition in the civil war and various foreign forces (Great Britain, the United States). The combination of civil war and foreign intervention went on for more than four years.

Before their defeat, the Germans imposed a savage peace settlement on the new Bolshevik regime at the very moment when the Germans were keeping the Bolsheviks propped up to make sure they would not be replaced by a government that might carry on the war. The Bolsheviks were obliged to surrender vast chunks of the national territory; by the time the First World War ended with the peace settlement of 1919 and the German defeat—a god send for the Bolsheviks—the Soviet Union, successor to the Russian Empire, was substantially truncated.

An attempt made by Pilsudski, the Polish dictator, to take advantage of the civil war in Russia by marching into the Ukraine gave the Bolsheviks a pretext for carrying the revolution into Poland on the bayonets of the Red Army. The Polish workers and peasants failed to hail the Bolsheviks as liberators; the Red Army was thrashed outside Warsaw in 1920. The Bolsheviks relinquished for the time being any territorial hopes. The whole of Poland was made independent, as were the Baltic States, Finland, and part of Rumania. A *cordon sanitaire* was set up by the disgruntled Allies to contain the Bolshevik "infection." Thus the Bolshevik Party was to embark on its innovations within a reduced sphere.

Those innovations proved fundamental. The Bolsheviks came to be a unique phenomenon in world history: enthralled by faith in a complex of ideas—the Marxist system—they transformed the society under their control independently of the real-life concerns of ordinary people. The ultimate goal of the Bolsheviks was to transform a living society into an entirely different society—an ideal society.

Strangely enough, however, this goal, though rooted in the Bolshevik faith in Marxism, had nothing to do with Marxism itself. The very circumstances of their seizure of power, the goal itself and the mechanism involved in its pursuit—state power instantly amplified into the largest administration in history—contradicted the main thrust of Marxist doctrine.

Marxism does not, in and for itself, solve any of the problems of a society governed by those who believe in it; the theory might be called, in mechanical terms, a universal joint whose function is wholly verbal, or rhetorical, since one of the features of Marxism—the juggling of words in accordance with the gimmick of the dialectic—can provide any event with an explanation that will be acceptable when enforced.

Marx's main idea—part of his Law of Motion of modern society, viz., the polarization of the population under capitalism into a small group of rich people getting richer and richer, and a huge group of paupers constantly increasing while getting poorer and poorer—implied that the prerequisites for a socialist state would already have been realized *before* the transition;

a society ripe for socialism would merely need a small shift in power at the top, without necessarily much bloodshed. This in turn would lead to what Marx toward the end of his life characterized as the "withering away of the State," for him a natural development, too.

This goal was part of a still larger idea, to the effect that the whole world was destined to pass through the same stages as Russia, i.e., from capitalism to socialism, after superseding feudalism (in the case of backward societies) and hastening on through capitalism.

But once the Bolsheviks seized power in a backward peasant country, and set about installing socialism by force, it was no longer possible to look to Marxism for guidance. Marx had regarded all writers of blueprints for the future as mere idiots; his sole concern had been the road leading to the assumption of power by the proletariat.

Instead, the Bolsheviks, claiming to represent the proletariat, had taken power and set themselves up as a government with the aim of totally transforming that backward society via an administration that encompassed all aspects of life. It was the titanic dimensions of such a project that brought about the gargantuan magnification of its administration.

Thus the Bolsheviks had put themselves beyond Marxism practically by the very fact of their putsch: the tiny Bolshevik nucleus was not obviously the proletariat, nor was it possible to explain from a Marxist point of view their seizure of power.

Their innovations accordingly could not be explained by Marxism at all. At the same time they *had* to be: they were, after all, pious Marxists.

This contradictory situation gave rise to the outstanding phenomenon in the politics of the twentieth century: the consolidation of Marxism as a state cult at the very moment that its fundamental ideas were contradicted. Marxism had proved to be irrelevant to the evolution of capitalism; all its predictions had misfired. It had ignored the two outstanding phenomena of the modern age—technology and the rise of a vast middle class. Marxism was also irrelevant to the problems of Russia under Bolshevism, but the Bolsheviks in power could enforce their own view of Marxism, despite its manifest irrelevance, as the framework of all society and indeed of all life.

The Bolsheviks accommodated these ideological difficulties in their own way by rapidly developing the concept of "Leninism." Lenin, who headed the *putsch* by virtue of his authority over the Party (even though Trotsky had stage-managed it), had been instantly deified, placed alongside Marx and Engels. This gave doctrinal authority to the *putsch,* which was never questioned, and enabled all problems confronting the new state to be handled verbally by an appeal to Leninism.

In effect this merely meant the tactical reactions of the new state to the world at large, authorizing in essence a variety of conspiratorial frauds and deceits, no doubt a part of statecraft in general and merely focused in a special way by the aims of the new power. Leninism could never, of course, be said to supersede Marxism, since that is what all Lenin's writings stem from. Hence any contradictions concerning either facts or theories could be efficiently leaped over via the dialectic.

It was the need of laying down a line to which obedience could be compelled that transformed Marxism, now Marxism-Leninism, into a state cult in which only one interpretation was authoritative. For who, after all, could distinguish between possible interpretations of Marxist abstractions? In the Soviet Union this was almost immediately to be only the faction with the power to do so. This monolithic, quasi-ecclesiastical structure was to dominate the Soviet Union from 1917 on.

The Bolsheviks began with a regime of "war communism" This merely meant the massive expropriation of all the major institutions of the country: the banks, the merchant marine, the grain dealers, the mines, and the oil industry, as well as all enterprises with a capital of between a half-million and a million rubles. Only businesses with fewer than ten workers were left untouched. This first attempt at centralized direction was done so amateurishly, against such a background of devastation, that when the civil war was over, the country was substantially reduced.

Vast areas had been lying fallow for years. The battlefields had been shifting constantly, especially in the Ukraine, where the destruction was general; harvests had been destroyed over and over again. Industry was completely shattered: production was down to a seventh of the prewar figure. Most of the factories were standing idle: many mines had been physically annihilated. Pig-iron production amounted to only 3 percent of what it had been before the war. The stocks of metal and industrial products were exhausted; food and fuel were unavailable. The workers were discontented: wages had been lost by the shutting-down of factories for lack of raw materials and fuel.

Commerce also had been halted. Small as well as large businesses were shut down; private trading was altogether prohibited in 1920. All cash had to be deposited in the state bank, all precious metals surrendered.

A black market naturally arose to take the place of the commercial market. This situation squeezed the workers and the city-dwellers very severely, though of course it favored the peasants. Prices soared: between 1920 and 1921 the price of bread went up 11–12 times.

The early enthusiasm that, despite the immense opposition, had attended the Bolshevik putsch, and the excitement of the civil war had evaporated. The Bolsheviks found themselves at the helm of an utterly ruined country that in addition had lost practically all its educated classes. After the Bolshevik putsch some 2 million Russians, nearly all of them belonging to the aristocracy and cultivated classes, emigrated, leaving the Bolsheviks the immensely difficult problem of finding and training technicians and administrators.

The new role of the state made all economic activities political *ipso facto*. Having replaced the private employer, the state now collected all revenue from production: thus it played the same supervisory role as the private employer before it, with of course, the added advantage of a potent police force. Thus the Bolshevik slogan, "socialization of the means of production," meant in practice a highly centralized network of production subordinate to the governing apparatus and backed by a concentrated police power. This was duplicated, on the consumers' side, by the vast bureaucracy required for large-scale distribution.

In the early part of 1921 the rations of the Petrograd factory workers had to be cut because of the widespread shortage. This action brought about a wave of massive strikes, political in their very essence. They culminated in a first-class insurrection headed by the naval base in Kronstadt, across the gulf from Petrograd. This mutiny was highly political from the very beginning. The sailors had always been among the most militant of the Bolsheviks' supporters; the insurrection marked their disappointment. The uprising was not aimed at the restoration of democracy but called for a revolutionary regime *without* the Bolsheviks—a "third revolution."

The Bolsheviks found themselves outflanked on the left; to defend themselves they ruthlessly shattered the Kronstadt uprising. The Kronstadt garrison—14,000 men, 10,000 of them sailors—was wiped out by March. The survivors of the Bolshevik attack, which encountered indescribably ferocious resistance, were shot or sent to prison camps.

The Kronstadt insurrection was the first of the feuds within the Bolshevik fold. With its dense intermixture of political and economic factors, the insurrection was an obvious danger-symptom; it was clear that a way out of the economic quagmire had to be found. The conclusions Lenin first drew from the Kronstadt mutiny involved a tightening of the security police system to forestall the danger of any further mutinies, but ultimately the mutiny made him turn aside from the program of planning—a national planning commission had been established in the early part of February 1921—and look for a radically different way out of the devastation exacerbated by the chaos of war communism.

The Bolshevik solution was simply a return to capitalism: the regime, still too weak to plan on a national scale, had to stimulate the peasants' interest in producing for a market. It had to ensure the food supply, start up commerce again, and fortify the industrial plant.

The Bolsheviks, while tightening the controls essential for their monopoly, made a bold about-face. In the New Economic

Policy (March 1921) they established a mixed economy; the concerns that still remained nationalized were to compete with reborn private enterprise. The theory was that the socialized sector of the economy would gradually grow at the expense of the private sector, but that this would come about through the natural operation of economic forces, not by political action. The large industrial plants, transport, the banking system, and foreign trade were to remain the monopoly of the state; the rest of the industrial sector and domestic trade were to be open to private initiative. The right to private ownership was restored within limits; the peasants could again sell some of their produce on the open market. Foreign capital was solicited, and foreign firms were invited back to Russia, even into heavy industry. This Bolshevik surrender to capitalism went hand in hand with generally successful attempts, via treaties and trade pacts to restore international relations with the non-Bolshevik world.

The new policy bore fruit, though not at once. The 1921–22 winter was very severe and the harvests quite inadequate during both years; reserves were of course nonexistent. Even if the New Economic Policy could have been effective very quickly, it came too late to prevent the first great Soviet famine, in which some 5 million people were supposed to have died. An international committee directed by Herbert Hoover, later President of the United States, was established after an appeal, written by Maxim Gorky, was broadcast; the Bolsheviks accepted massive aid.

The country gradually recovered: production started up again, in both agriculture and industry, and commerce became much livelier in the money economy restored by the N.E.P. By the beginning of 1923 the country seemed to have weathered the storm; for the first time in seven years the economy began to look viable.

During the first few years after the Bolshevik putsch, indeed, even during the rigors of war communism and the civil war there was an atmosphere of indulgence and relative tolerance.

Academic and university education, severely curtailed during the civil war, began to revive. Education met with the greatest difficulties; Russia's intellectual life had almost collapsed during the years of crisis. Vast numbers of intellectuals, who belonged chiefly to the upper classes, had died in prisons or been killed by hunger and cold. The chief scholars of Russia had joined the huge White emigration. But during the N.E.P., education revived substantially, initially with the collaboration of the bourgeois experts who had managed to survive.

Moreover, there was a great efflorescence of artistic creativity during the first decade of Bolshevik rule. Some original poets became prominent—Yesenin, Mayakovsky, Blok, and Pasternak. In music Prokofiev and Stravinsky were very influential; Shostakovich was perhaps the best known of the younger composers. An immense international impression also was made by the cinema; Eisenstein's films were considered a stunning innovation. The theater and ballet revived once again, to be sure without any novelties. In the arts the tendencies that had been considered decadent were now hailed as expressions of the vanguard.

Even the Bolshevik excesses during the first decade after the putsch exemplified, in the purely social sphere, a utopian enthusiasm. The feeling of fruitful break-up felt by many socialists throughout Europe, for instance, at the prospect of the first socialist party in history actually taking power, reflected itself in a general euphoria among the intellectuals.

The ancient tradition of the family came under attack as a bourgeois institution; marriage and sexual morality were much chuckled over; sexual license, concomitantly, was lauded. Discipline in schools was castigated as the height of reactionary outrageousness. Religion—according to Marx the "opiate of the people"—was of course anathema to all official circles, though the churches, while deprived of funds and generally speaking squeezed and propagandized against, were not actually proscribed.

This relatively liberal situation lasted until about 1928—the watershed in the evolution of the Bolshevik monopoly.

In retrospect we can, no doubt, see that the relative slackness of the first decade of Bolshevik power was merely an era of marking time while waiting for major decisions to take shape.

Those major decisions were, after all, entailed by the fundamental Bolshevik dilemma—how to maintain a monopoly in
a country bound to be overwhelmingly opposed to institutional
innovations.

For some time after the putsch the Bolsheviks were euphoric
about the prospect of the revolution's exploding in Europe.
As late as 1923 Lenin thought his fanatical assurance about
the imminence of the Revolution was going to be backed by
events; in the last year of his life, already incapacitated, he
gave this hope up with the fizzling out of a rather pathetic
uprising in Germany. The question for the Bolsheviks at first,
accordingly, was whether the capitalist restoration of the N.E.P.
was to be permanent, or whether socialism might not be established with the help of some industrial working class elsewhere.

As the Revolution kept failing to appear—the Bolsheviks
never assumed their theories had misled them—and as the Party
tackled the problem of administering a country, differences
of opinion began to spring up about how to cope with the
unforeseen situation. It was obvious that the country had to
be industrialized somehow or other: Lenin's aphorism, that
"Soviet power plus electricity equals socialism," seemed mere
common sense even apart from socialism.

But the scope and phasing of industrialization was a peculiarly elusive problem, intertwined with the general interpretation of the Revolution, the significance of the Bolshevik
monopoly, and more practically the approach to the control
of a hostile population.

Though the new regime was to "justify" everything it did
by references to Marxism, in fact Marxism had nothing to
tell them: all Marxist analysis and prediction stopped with
the seizure of power by the Proletariat whose representatives
the Bolsheviks proclaimed themselves to be.

Divergent views were expressed within the summits of the
Party even before Lenin's death in January 1924. But decisions
were reached not by a process of debate but as a result of
organizational politics—the administrative apparatus, in full
control of Soviet life, became the locus of Bolshevik authority.

The apparatus had, inevitably, appeared overnight. As the

Bolshevik Party, originally a coterie of agitators, conspirators, speakers, and writers, began coping with practical matters, it was transformed into a corps of administrators. And to the extent that Bolshevik controls blanketed the whole country and all aspects of life, both social and economic, the role of the administrators was bound to be all the more comprehensive.

But though it is a Marxist platitude that the material base determines the spiritual superstructure—common sense up to a point as well as Marxism—neither Lenin nor the other Bolshevik intellectuals foresaw this obvious consequence of the inevitable administrative expansion.

Anyone controlling the center of the Party obviously controlled the country, and as the prospects of the revolution faded, leaving the Bolsheviks isolated in a huge country, the specific weight of the apparatus grew by leaps and bounds. Concomitantly, the power of the General Secretary—in charge of all personnel appointments, the allocation of functions, and of government procedure—expanded.

Joseph Stalin had been appointed General Secretary in 1921, while Lenin was still in full vigor. It was Stalin, accordingly, who was to formulate all Party decisions.

Joseph Vissarionovich Dzhugashvili (Stalin) (1879–1953) was born into a poor family in Georgia in the Caucasus; his native language was Georgian. As a student in a seminary of the Greek Orthodox Church in Tiflis, he was swept into politics by the agitation seeping from Russia into her outlying territories. Georgians played a disproportionately large role in the Russian revolutionary movement, perhaps because their rebelliousness was sharpened by a feeling of nationalism. Most Georgians touched by Marxism, however, became Mensheviks; Stalin was one of Lenin's few Georgian recruits before 1917. In his practical way Stalin had conducted some of Lenin's "expropriations."

Stalin's reputation, indeed, was that of a practical man; he was thought negligible as a speaker and writer. But during the civil war his ability singled him out; as General Secretary of the Central Committee, he created, within the space of a year, no doubt the largest and most concentrated government in history. His office, in control of all aspects of administration, inevitably became the hub of the government.

Presenting himself for a time as a mere servant of the Party, attending to Party chores—the government!—Stalin became more and more prominent. As his own faction, i.e., the *de facto* government, had its resolutions passed in all Party institutions—as the dictatorship settled down this was a mere matter of rubber-stamping from the very beginning—all other dissident views soon became proscribed. By 1927 the Bolshevik state was monolithic.

Trotsky's prestige had been enormous after the putsch, even more so after his creation of the Red Army during the civil war. With his oratorical, literary, and organizational abilities, he was the chief man after Lenin, and in the public eye, at least, far more *there*.

But despite his ability and his renown, Trotsky was quite incapable of influencing policy. His real authority within the parvenu regime lasted only a couple of years or so; even before the end of the civil war he had no influence to speak of.

Trotsky was incapable, as it seems, of forming a faction (factionalism was in any case utterly proscribed by the Tenth Party Congress in March 1921). This was partly because of his temperament and partly because his classical Marxism was wildly irrelevant to any realistic assessment of Bolshevik prospects. Moreover, his own shortcomings as an organization man blinded him to the immense power that was bound to accrue to anyone in Stalin's position.

Trotsky, still clinging to the old dogma of Permanent Revolution, his chief contribution to Marxism, was undone by the new dogma, "socialism in one country," linked to the name of Stalin.

The idea that socialism could be confined to one country, however large, would hitherto have been nonsensical to any Marxist. Socialism, as the next higher stage of social organization after capitalism, naturally had to cover at least a substantial section of the world economy, and in any case had to have an advanced industrial base of its own to operate on.

This had been a Bolshevik commonplace up to 1924. In

the early part of 1924, for instance, in his *Foundations of Lenin-ism*, Stalin agreed that the proletariat might seize power in a single country, but could never create a socialist economy. No single country, however large, was enough to ensure social-ism.

However, since the revolution was not, in fact, making its much-predicted appearance, Trotsky's obsession with classical Marxism, plus his temperamental incapacity for rallying sup-porters to his ideas in an organizationally effective form, made him helpless *vis-à-vis* Stalin's secretariat. In a bureaucracy de-pendent on its functions within the vastness of the new, state-controlled society, the theory of socialism in one country was a natural umbrella for the potent role of the General Secretary.

In the records left by the Soviet government and by its internal critics—notably Trotsky—the middle twenties were dominated by a struggle for power between Stalin's central faction and various oppositions. Yet a glance at the actual suc-cession of events will make it clear that there was no struggle whatever. As Stalin consolidated his government through his office of General Secretary, he merely used the influence that was naturally his in order to give all decisions the appearance of institutional support. Since Marxist jargon was the natural idiom of the Party, and since it took a few years before the Bolsheviks outside Stalin's entourage were reduced to silence, it was natural for all activity to be expressed in the conventional idiom. Since this suited both Stalin, for obvious reasons, and his opponents, principally Trotsky, for reasons still more obvi-ous, it has been easy for historians, poring over the records, to be misled.

Stalin throughout his ascension played the role of a moderate, practical administrator. Incarnating the Bolshevik state, and selecting from the Party debates what suited his purpose, Stalin finally, after a decade of Bolshevik power, came to grips with the great dilemma of the regime—the capitalist prosperity of the New Economic Policy. In 1927 Stalin outlined a series of proposals that in their ensemble constituted the true Bol-shevik revolution—a massive reorganization of society. The slogan of "socialism in one country," established as state policy in 1924, was now implemented as the only alternative to the dreaded revival of the peasantry and the restoration of capitalism.

The draft program proclaimed by Stalin in 1927 was ratified by the Fifteenth Party Congress in December. Stalin set two cardinal goals for the Soviet economy—the massive collectivization of agriculture, and the overall, intensified industrialization of the country.

It was the first attempt in history to encompass the entire economy of a nation under one centralized agency in one unified plan that took in the boundless ramifications of retail distribution.

A State Planning Commission was entrusted with the elaboration of the first Five-Year Plan. The collectivization program was initiated in 1928. Involving a vast overturn in agricultural relations, it had a political side: before the program could be implemented, the "rich" peasants–*kulaks*—had to be eliminated. The collectivization drive was launched, in fact, on the official theory that the rich peasants had to be curbed. An "offensive against the *kulaks*" was the slogan of the big drive.

The implications of this titanic project were not clear at first. Stalin seems to have thought there would not be too much resistance. In early 1928 the Political Bureau decreed numerous emergency measures—raids on big farms, requisitions, mass arrests. But the farmers were not yet expropriated. The first Five-Year Plan, presented in late 1928, called for the collectivization of not more than 20 percent of all farmers by 1933; as late as the spring of 1929 Stalin announced that private agriculture would retain a fundamental role in the economy.

An attempt was made by the Party theoreticians to break down the peasantry into 5–8 million poor peasants, 15–18 million intermediate peasants, and 1½–2 million *kulaks,* amounting to a grand total, exclusive of families, of 25 million peasants.

But the collectivization movement built up its own momentum so quickly that private agriculture was soon explicitly proscribed. By the end of 1929 Stalin called for the "liquidation of the *kulaks* as a class"; in 1929 the *kulaks* were wiped out—or rather, to put it more accurately, all those who were wiped out were called *kulaks*.

For some reason the planners thought the middle-income peasants were potentially friendly to collectivization and could be won over. It was assumed that the poor peasants would be mad with joy.

Yet not only the *kulaks,* but the peasantry as a whole, poor peasants as well as the so-called middle-income peasants, fought collectivization tooth and nail. The program turned out to depend for its implementation on the police. The measures taken by the government to overcome peasant resistance illustrate the new factor introduced by modern technology into the handling of this outburst of peasant despair, the latest and most violent in a long line of peasant revolts that had recurrently churned up Russia since the earliest days.

The peasants were determined not to turn over to the government what they regarded as theirs: vast quantities of food were stored away, the cattle scheduled for the new farms were slaughtered, the crops were burned, the tools were smashed. The peasants calculated that such tactics would halt the government's crash program and force it back into a reasonable attitude.

They were sadly mistaken. Since mere administrative measures were futile, the government turned the army loose as well as the political police. Mutinous villages were surrounded by units with machine-guns and forced to surrender. The *kulaks,* both real *kulaks* and those suddenly called *kulaks* because of their opposition to collectivization, were rounded up in droves and deported to Arctic regions by the hundreds of thousands. By the end of 1929, as Stalin said, even expropriation was no longer sufficient: the *kulaks* had to be excluded from the collective farms entirely. Millions of peasants of all kinds were exiled, jailed, or killed.

This violence had been so unexpected that by March 1930 Stalin was forced to modulate the crash program. He did this, characteristically, by blaming the functionaries, who had become "dizzy with success." Thus Stalin gave a modern counterpoint to a traditional theme—bureaucrats were responsible for thwarting the benevolent Tsar!

In any case, by the end of the first Five-Year Plan, 60 percent of all holdings had been turned into independent economic units consisting of large and small holdings, with the land jointly cultivated. The average collective farm (abbreviated in Russian as *Kolkhoz*) had 75 families, who had to work between 100 and 150 days a year. All produce was supposed to be turned over by the *Kolkhoz* to the state, which would thus be in a position to handle the distribution of food to city-dwellers and other workers.

Stalin had embarked on this crash program of collectivization and industrialization on the basis of purely abstract considerations, in the teeth of both Left and Right oppositions. As the great compromiser, he had borrowed from all relevant sources, taken a middle course, and gone ahead with implementation. In the event his program was extremist both in scope and method. The "agrarian revolution from above" that was effected in 1928–30 proved as calamitous for the country as the devastation of the civil war. Some years later—in January 1934—Stalin felt free enough to disclose some figures: of the 34 million horses Russia had had in 1929, less than half were left; some 30 million head of cattle and almost 100 million sheep and goats had been slaughtered. As in the civil war of the preceding decade, vast areas of land lay fallow. Untold damage had been done to farm implements.

This catastrophe created an unprecedented famine. In spite of official silence, the news leaked out; the regime was forced to admit that literally millions of people died of hunger in the governmentally induced famine of the early thirties. After the Second World War Stalin told Winston Churchill that 10 million peasants had been eliminated. He did not mention the vast numbers—hundreds of thousands, according to Bukharin—including women and children, who were machine-gunned by special political police detachments.

The crisis in agriculture was further compounded by its direct repercussion on the industrialization program. The slaughter of the horses meant that the land could scarcely be

cultivated at all: even if it had been customary to use cattle
as draft animals, which it was not, the cattle had, after all,
been killed off, too. Hence the tractors envisaged as part of
the industrialization program had to be provided at once, to
cut short the devastation of the famine. The need for tractors
was all the more vital since Russian agriculture is extensive;
the *Kolkhozes* were spread out over vast areas that could not
even begin to be cultivated without tractors. This of course
had been understood even before the horses had been slaughtered in vast numbers. The speedy implementation of the industrialization program was now literally a matter of life and
death.

Consequently, Russia was thrust brutally into the thick of
a problem difficult to solve even without the attendant crises—
the creation of an industrial working class that could provide
agriculture with the new implements it needed for its mechanization, cope with the increasing needs of the country as a
whole, and above all restore the country's armed forces. Since
the cadres of the industrial working class already in existence
in Russia were exiguous to begin with, the training problem
became particularly acute: people to train people were both
indispensable and unavailable.

To accomplish these tasks, the straitjacket of the political
police became tighter and tighter. Beginning with the thirties,
all the peoples under the neo-Bolshevik Executive were put
through an ordeal doubtless unique in history.

It has been fashionable among students of Soviet affairs,
even those unsympathetic to communism, to praise Stalin for
his ruthlessness in carrying through the crash programs of
collectivization and industrialization. But the amusing thing,
if amusement is to be derived from the macabre, is that Stalin
seems to have been unaware of the probable repercussions of
such a program. He was astonished at the violence with which
the peasants opposed the large-scale projects of the government.

Stalin did not, in short, far-sightedly hack his way through
inevitable difficulties; despite the consensus of countless internal critics—both Left and Right oppositions within the Party

agreed on the dangers of the programs—Stalin showed a curious lightmindedness. His conduct of the crash programs that wrought so much havoc in Russia was a tribute not so much to his intellectual powers, still less to the prescience Marxists claim for themselves, as to the inner composure attendant on Marxist faith.

The successive Five-Year Plans were to become the foundations of the Soviet Union. The vast Russian sacrifices in consumption created a large-scale technical elite and an immense concentration on heavy industry. Stalin was undoubtedly the consolidator, if not the founder, of Soviet power.

In consonance with the concentration of power within the Bolshevik apparatus, the political scene, too, became increasingly monolithic. After a short period of indulgence, the Bolsheviks, having dispersed the Constituent Assembly, began cracking down on all political expression.

As late as August 1920 the Mensheviks could hold a Party Congress in Moscow; both Mensheviks and Social-Revolutionaries were allowed some latitude. But the atmosphere soon changed: by the beginning of 1921 Martov and Theodor Dan, the Menshevik leaders, as well as Victor Chernov, the Social-Revolutionary, had to leave. It was the beginning of the new radical emigration.

A general campaign soon followed, first against the Mensheviks, then against the Social-Revolutionaries; by February 1922 arrests—the first of a long, long series—began to be made against the Bolsheviks' former fellow-revolutionaries. In the summer of 1922 the first political "trial" mounted by the Bolshevik Party took place; it was aimed at the Social-Revolutionaries. The court handed down fourteen death sentences and only two acquittals. The Social-Revolutionary movement, heir of so much agrarian, communizing, and anarchist tradition, was annihilated.

The suppression of all Left-wing, non-Bolshevik currents was followed very quickly by the beginnings of repression against dissident opinion within the Bolshevik Party. The repression of the Workers' Opposition, then the banning of the Left Opposition, in December 1927 (Trotsky, Zinoviev, Kame-

nev), culminated in the suppression of the Right Opposition
(Bukharin) shortly after the onslaught on the *kulaks* early in
1928.

With the intensification of the crash campaign of collectivization, in fact, the Right Opposition, whose polemics had been
used by Stalin in order to manipulate Party opinion against
the Left Opposition, was itself distanced from the Stalin "center." The Right Opposition found itself in exactly the same
position as the Left Opposition before, this time without even
a Left Opposition to counterbalance Stalin's now overwhelming power. By pulverizing both Oppositions in turn, Stalin
was now in unquestioned control of the entire Soviet government.

State power gave a new dimension to the theoretical wrangling about Bolshevik policy. For with Stalin's ousting of all
opponents within the Party, a new institution was created—the
secular cult of Soviet orthodoxy.

This cult, having begun with the anathematizing of opposition during the Party bickering in the twenties, may be said
to have been launched on Stalin's birthday in December 1929.
The Trinity of Party, State, and Doctrine was symbolized in
the person of Stalin, himself perched, so to speak, on the
pedestal of Lenin's cult, engineered by Stalin himself the very
year of Lenin's death in 1924.

In this general ascension, in which Stalin ultimately became
head of the Bolshevik pantheon, the dead Lenin had been placed
on the same pedestal as Marx (to be sure, Marx was never
worshipped in a mass way as Lenin was to be and to remain).
Yet Soviet Marxism was baptized "Marxism-Leninism," meaningless or blasphemous from Lenin's point of view, no doubt,
since Lenin never could have described himself as anything
but a faithful disciple of Marx and Engels.

The Lenin cult served as a stepping-stone in Stalin's ascension; it enabled him to present himself as heir to the legacy
of Marx and Engels, and in the current age as Lenin's heir
and executor.

In full view of his own generation Stalin was glorified beyond all imagining. In the nine years between Lenin's fiftieth birthday in 1920—a very modest affair—and Stalin's in December 1929, the Soviet government, within the Bolshevik strait jacket, had expanded immeasurably. At the very pinnacle of the structure, Stalin, whirled aloft by the process he was instrumental in promoting, became a quasideity—the Godhead of the Soviet Trinity of Party, State, and Doctrine.

During the Stalin era, from Stalin's fiftieth birthday in 1929 to his death in 1953, he was invariably referred to in language hitherto reserved for semidivine personages such as Muhammad and the Buddha, though not, to be sure, Jesus Christ.

Huge portraits of Stalin were pasted on buildings and walls throughout the Soviet Union; his bust was everywhere. All speeches, the entire press, every expression of literary, political, or scientific opinion invoked his name with the most extravagant floweriness. The whole history of the Party was rewritten to establish his prominence from adolescence on. Not merely did he seal the prophetic line—Marx, Engels, Lenin—but he was conventionally hailed as the greatest genius in world history, an arbiter of all questions from linguistics to zoology, the peer of every thinker the human race has known, in short the greatest man in the world past or present.

Framed by the new cult, the Bolshevik state, having weathered the crash campaigns of collectivization and industrialization, might have seemed firmly embedded in the nation. The cult of Stalin the Genius, Locomotive of the World Revolution and Father of the Peoples, had finally stabilized Soviet life, as it seemed, and socialist construction, whatever its content, now constituted the balanced framework of a zealous society busily reworking its destinies. Yet Bolshevik totalitarianism was not yet rounded off. Despite appearances—despite the censorship, despite the monolithic state, despite the repression—the consummation of the Stalin regime had yet to be achieved. The peoples of the Soviet Union were to be put through another threshing machine.

In December 1934 Sergei Kirov, Secretary of the Party in Leningrad, was assassinated. His assassin was said to be a former Young Communist. The assassination triggered a series of arrests, hearings, and executions that culminated in the "Moscow Show Trials" of 1936–38—a unique phenomenon.

There were three such Show Trials, in 1936, 1937, and 1938; differing in some trivial details, they were all frantically publicized and marked the elimination of all the "Old Bolsheviks."

Zinoviev, Kamenev, Radek, Bukharin, and many others were accused of being agents of Leon Trotsky—in exile at the time—in a conspiracy he had entered into with Hitler, the Mikado of Japan, and the British Secret Service to murder the Politburo, dismember the Soviet Union, and restore capitalism.

The Show Trials were characterized, in particular, by the well-nigh complete absence of any evidence and by the confessions of the prisoners vilifying themselves in an hysteria that kept pace with the denunciations of the prosecutor. With a couple of exceptions, all these Old Bolsheviks were executed immediately after their "trial."

The Show Trials, while giving rise to occasional doubts outside the Soviet Union, were accepted fairly unanimously by the world press. Trotsky defended himself as best he could, together with his son Sedov—his "accomplice" in Paris—but despite exhausting efforts he could not counteract the impression made by the Trials.

A few years after Stalin's death, Nikita Khrushchev, one of his successors, in a famous secret speech to the Twentieth Party Congress in 1956, made it clear that the Moscow Show Trials were, quite simply, fabrications.

Khrushchev's secret speech confirmed what in any case had been established by a large literature that had begun appearing in the fifties. This literature, though somewhat fragmented—memoirs of deserters, defectors, and survivors—sketched in the outlines of a remarkable enterprise, nothing less than a broad-gauge scheme for the reordering of Soviet society. Stalin, personally responsible for Kirov's assassination, exploited it for his large-scale projects.

The Show Trials, in fact, were in no sense of the word trials, not even in the sense of being frame-ups. They were actually propaganda cast in the form of charades, contrived by Stalin to achieve certain psychopolitical objectives.

The Great Charades cast as Show Trials served as an umbrella for a process of far broader scope that was carried on relatively secretly, was never admitted to by the Soviet leadership, and has never, in fact, been acknowledged to this day. Outside the Soviet Union this process was known later on as the Great Purge, though here again the word purge was itself an aspect of Stalin's propaganda. It was not remotely a purge of the Party such as the Soviet public had grown familiar with during the expansion of constraints beginning with the early twenties: it was, rather, a Deep Comb-out of the population as a whole, in which millions of citizens, also accused of complicity with Trotsky in his conspiracy with Hitler to restore capitalism, were put through a wringer.

The tidal wave of arrests in the Deep Comb-out that began with the Great Charades of 1936–38 engulfed all former oppositionists of all kinds, former Mensheviks and S.R.s, anarchists, members of the Jewish Bund, Zionists, sympathizers of prerevolutionary Left-wing parties, returned immigrants, Party people whose duties had sent them abroad, everyone who had corresponded with anyone abroad, foreign communists taking refuge in the Soviet Union, members of all religious sects, anyone who had ever been excluded from the Party, any Party member who had resisted the purging process itself, and representatives of all ethnic minorities. All strata of the population were represented, from top to bottom, and all occupations.

Most enigmatic was the decapitation of the government apparatus itself; of the 140 members of the Central Committee in 1934, for instance, only 15 were still free in 1937.

Perhaps the most spectacular aspect of the Deep Comb-out was its catastrophic effect on the armed forces. With Europe dominated by Nazi Germany, Stalin raked out the Red Army. During 1937–38 he cut down the membership of the Supreme War Council by 75 perceent, killed 3 out of 5 marshals, 13 out of 15 army generals, 62 out of 85 corps commanders, 110 out of 195 divisional commanders, and 220 out of 406 brigade commanders. Probably 65 perceent of the officers from colonel up were arrested, numbering, together with those in the lower echelons arrested, some 20,000 officers. Of the 6,000 high-ranking officers, 1,500 were killed; others vanished into various forms of detention.

The slaughter of 1936–38 is conservatively assessed as having destroyed between 5 and 10 percent of the population—perhaps 8.5 million victims. Many think the figure was nearer 20 million.

Trotsky was assassinated in 1940 in Mexico by an agent of Stalin's, a couple of years after his son Sedov's murder in Paris. Unaware of the theological uses his person was to be put to, Trotsky had spent four years in exile in Turkey after his deportation from the Soviet Union in 1929; after flitting about in France for a brief, uneasy period, he found refuge first in Norway and then, after being forced out of Norway by the Soviet government, in Mexico, where he continued his lone, practically unaided fight against the stupefying effects of the Great Charades.

The Great Charades and the Deep Comb-out are generally relegated to the dead past—a grotesque episode blurred by remoteness. Yet this brief period of extravagant bloodshed to the accompaniment of ghoulish elements of blanket betrayal surely consolidated the neo–Bolshevik state.

The practical elements in the Charades and Comb-out—their merely utilitarian benefits—were minor. They provided convenient scapegoats, to be sure, for the grueling hardships and endless blunders of the Five-Year Plans, the crash collectivization campaign, the poor harvests, and the famines. Yet it is plain that they served a far more profound purpose.

The Great Charades and Deep Comb-out consummated a process, initiated in the twenties, that established the secular cult of Soviet orthodoxy. They provided orthodoxy with the counterpoint required, perhaps, by all orthodoxy—its polar opposite.

The disagreements on policy that had beset the Party in the early twenties were emotionalized in the space of a few years. As it became necessary to replace the dogma of world revolution with the dogma of socialism in one country, the verbiage generated by Marxist bickering took on a special theological tinge. The Stalin apparatus, while pretending to take classical Marxism as the basis of decisions, in reality enforced them through the administrative machine.

There was a remarkably steep jump in the intensity of the official reaction to Trotsky's views beginning in 1924. Attacked at first as merely incorrect, Trotsky's ideas were swiftly projected as the reflection of an inherent wrongheadedness; by the mid-thirties they were equated with evil itself.

The theologizing tendency of the Bolshevik apparatus may be seen in the new scriptures authorized by Stalin. The writings of Marx, Engels, and of course Lenin were a natural object of reverence; in 1938, the last year of the Bolshevik massacre, the dialectical materialism underlying, in theory, the Bolshevik state was crystallized in an official textbook—*A Short Course in the History of the Communist Party of the Soviet Union*. All Marxist writings outside this textbook, including the writings of Lenin himself, were in effect proscribed.

Just as the Roman Catholic Church has traditionally forbidden its unguided laymen to read the sacred books of Christianity, so Stalin condensed all Marxism in the new textbook, the only authorized guide to the interpretation of the Marxist scriptures proper.

Essentially, the *Short Course* consummated the total rewriting of *all* history begun with Stalin's justification, in 1924, of the shift from Permanent Revolution to socialism in one country. In the thirties Stalin, obliged to explain how it was that all Old Bolsheviks except Lenin and Stalin had been maniacs and traitors, had to have the entire history of the Party rewritten from top to bottom, as well as all encyclopedias and reference works.

The *Short Course*, plus the satanization of Trotsky, consummated the Soviet cult of orthodoxy. The massacre of 5 to 10 percent of the population engraved that cult in the flesh of the people—if Marxism did not fit the Soviet people, then the people had to be reshaped surgically in order to fit Soviet Marxism. The "proud flesh" of the population—all those who were superfluous, recalcitrant, or potentially so—was lopped off. Others were terrified.

Bolshevik mythology was thus created to justify the existence of the Bolshevik state. The concept underlying the Great Charades and their concomitant massacre—encirclement outside and betrayal inside—was given a theological foundation—the forces of light under Stalin and the true party were contending with the forces of darkness under Trotsky and the hosts of hell. Thus the satanization of Trotsky created a formula flexible enough to encompass all aspects of dissidence and nonconformism, genuine or alleged, within the framework of the all-inclusive concept of "Trotskyism." This ingredient of Stalinism was to survive for decades, even in the agitation for the "reforms" of the 1980s.

The consummation of this theological process may very well have been accelerated by the menace that began looming up with the victory of the Nazi movement in January 1933, when Adolf Hitler was elected German Chancellor. Though at first sight it might seem altogether irrational on Stalin's part to mutilate the Red Army at the very moment a powerful enemy was arming at breakneck pace, it seems plain that the very menace to the Soviet state made Stalin's decision to re-order its inner structure all the more urgent. Stalin's monopoly within the neo-Bolshevik monopoly as a whole had to be ensured at all costs.

Stalin's apotheosis was, of course, the apotheosis of the state he symbolized. The concept of an all-powerful Soviet state replaced the classical Marxist view of the ultimate "withering away of the state" after it had ushered in a socialist society. The "Stalin Constitution" of 1936 manifested the profound changes both in the government structure and in the Party doctrines. Though Marx's withering away of the state was still paid lip service as an ultimate goal, it had to mark time until capitalist "encirclement" had ended. Until then the struggle against capitalism had to be waged by the Soviet state, to which all aspects of life—art, literature, morality, philosophy, law, the civil service—were unreservedly subject. The omnipotence and omnipresence of the state, the groundwork of a new patriotism, now embraced all individuals and all institutions.

During the thirties, the Party itself changed radically as a new elite grew in tandem with the economy. The working class element in it, relatively exiguous even during the twenties, dwindled to less than a third, while the new intelligentsia—Party officials, the upper strata of academic life, executives, managers—came to about half. Since the thirties, the social origins of Party members have been a well-kept secret.

The Eighteenth Party Congress (March 1929) erased even the fictitious pre-eminence of the working class; by promoting the intelligentsia, in the broadest sense, to equality with workers and peasants, the Congress established the social primacy of upper government functionaries. This itself was anchored in the status of the Party as a mass institution: still only 500,000 in 1923, five years after the putsch, it had become a mass organization by 1934 (3.5 million). During the mid-twenties, Stalin in his initial domestic skirmishes, had been diluting the Party with more or less illiterate recruits in order to swamp his opponents: in 1925–26 alone 200,000 new members were admitted. Then the Party was cut back; by the beginning of the Second World War it was somewhat more than 2.3 million. Since then it has been relatively on the increase, discounting the casualties of the Second World War itself.

With the rise of Stalin the bohemianism of the early regime was sloughed off completely; the totalitarianism of the Stalin regime was to survive Stalin's death for decades.

In 1935 discipline and the iron hand of an all-powerful teacher were restored in the school system; report cards and marks, previously the hallmark of bourgeois reaction, were re-introduced. The death sentence was restored and extended to children from the age of twelve on (this seems to have been part of the technique of handling the millions of potential victims during the Deep Comb-out: it was a handy device for interrogators to be able to hold a real law as a tangible threat over the heads of victims).

Not only was the family restored in the thirties as the foundation of the state, but it was buttressed by old-fashioned safeguards. Divorce was made much more difficult; families with many children were subsidized; abortion on nonmedical grounds was declared a criminal offense. (A decision on the question of abortion was actually called for from the population at large, in factories, offices, and collective farms; the government disregarded the popular verdict—overwhelmingly hostile—which it had evidently not reckoned on, and applied the new restrictions with characteristic harshness.)

The armed forces, too, were subjected to an old-fashioned regime of traditional discipline. In keeping with the new Soviet practice of grounding patriotism on the specifically Russian tradition of the past, the military glories of even the Tsarist Empire were assimilated.

The new Soviet patriotism—quite distinct from Marxist ideology—was reflected in the unprecedented subsidizing of the intelligentsia as a class. Having realized, no doubt, that a disaffected intelligentsia is the most dangerous single social element, the Stalin regime simultaneously straitjacketed and coddled its tame intellectuals. Combining the classic incentives of bribery and fear, it created a general mold for the expression of all artistic and intellectual interests.

The effects on literature were of course the most direct, though painting, music, architecture, and for that matter even science, up to a point, were put under the censors. In these fields, as in all others, Stalin's predilections were decisive.

In the arts the mold was to be described simply as "socialist realism." Coinciding with the initial glorification of Stalin, socialist realism became the dominant, well-nigh exclusive trend in Soviet culture. Like the old Tsarist formula of nationality, it is profoundly ambiguous, indeed almost meaningless. For that very reason, no doubt, it is ideal for manipulation by a highly centralized administration; at bottom it can be no more than a synonym for official patriotism. Its projected themes have been simple—construction, team spirit, sentimental heroism, unquestioning loyalty.

This whole period of socialist realism, which succeeded the experimentalism of the soft era of Soviet intellectual life in the twenties, was exemplified in the person of Maxim Gorky

(1868–1936), one of the few talented writers inherited by the Bolsheviks. Gorky had fled Russia in 1921, disgusted, as it appears, by the primitive Bolshevik hostility to bourgeois culture. Aging a little prematurely, and apparently discouraged by exile, Gorky was cajoled by Stalin into returning in 1928.

Internationally famous, Gorky had the unusual charm of looking like a genuine plebeian, moreover the only non-Bolshevik who had been personally friendly with Lenin. On Gorky's return to Russia, Stalin made him an official monument. (Stalin had, it seems, been hoping Gorky would immortalize him in a biography and wooed him for years. But Gorky, though satisfactorily gullible enough about Soviet activities as a whole to be a priceless showpiece for foreigners, balked at glorifying Stalin, who dropped him, accordingly, shortly before Gorky's death in the mid-thirties.)

The growth of the Party since the thirties was far outstripped by the growth of the bureaucracy, especially since the ramifying function of mind-control—propaganda, censorship—was bound to develop a bureaucratic arm to weld the new factor of ideology into the structure of the state. A sort of spiritual lining was added to the administrative apparatus; it took care of cultural affairs, the sciences, and mass media as well as such things as public health education. It was plain that in the Stalin stage of the neo-Bolshevik dictatorship, experts and executives were vital.

The managers of the state economy—*apparatchiki*—increased by leaps and bounds. In 1926 they were numbered at about 2 million, in 1937 9 million, in 1940 11 million and by 1949 between 15 and 16 million. If one recalls that the general tendency of the regime has been to soft-pedal the ramifications of the "apparatus-people," the specific weight of the bureaucracy in Soviet society is obviously substantial.

Concomitantly, the Soviet differentiation in wages became even more acute than in free-enterprise countries, including the United States. Though the apparatus at this time accounted for only 14 percent of the working population, their share of the country's wages was estimated at 35 percent, while the corresponding figures were 33 percent for the workers, who comprise 22 percent of the population, and 29 percent for the peasants, who comprised 53 percent. As for those in the forced labor camps, supposedly about 11 percent of the population, they received only 2 or 3 percent.

These figures are heavily underplayed in official statistics, which also cast a veil over the countless perquisites of government service—motor-cars, houses, railway travel, vacations, and medical treatment—which substantially elevate the real income of the privileged groups, a curious parallel to capitalist regimes in which the expense accounts of business executives have become an important factor in living standards.

The special privileges of the upper strata of Soviet society were consolidated. Until 1932, for instance, 65 percent of all students had to be workers; by 1938, when this requirement became obsolete, working-class students had dropped to 33.9 percent, while bureaucrats' children went up to 42.4 percent. Since then the whole question has been veiled by official silence, in itself, of course, highly significant.

It is plain, in short, that in the space of a couple of decades the neo–Bolshevik decision to wield a monopoly of power in the framework of state planning, with the resultant administrative apparatus, produced an entirely new society, with its own stability, stratification, momentum, and mythology.

In world politics the existence of the Soviet Union was surely a dynamic factor in the preparations for the Second World War, and was, indeed, the vital principle in the organization of Hitlerism—a reaction both to German distress after the First World War and more specifically to the fears of Bolshevism rampant after the establishment of the neo-Bolshevik state.

But the Soviet Executive itself played an altogether minor role in world affairs before the Second World War. The trickles of refugees that followed the initial repression of non-Bolshevik currents in the early twenties had no effect whatever on politics; nor did the Communist Parties that seceded from the Social-Democratic Parties in Europe in the wake of the Bolshevik putsch and were organized in 1919 under the Third International exert a positive influence of their own. Still less did the various Bolshevik oppositions succeed in influencing their handfuls of followers in the European working-class movement.

Whatever had been the apocalyptic perspective of the early neo-Bolshevik regime, it soon evaporated in the light of reality. The political turmoil in Europe, which after the First World War seemed to favor the emergence of potentially insurrectionary situations—Germany, Hungary, Bulgaria—was altogether beyond the powers of the enfeebled and distracted neo-Bolshevik government to influence. Lenin was obliged to forget his revolutionary euphoria by 1923; the neo-Bolshevik regime accommodated itself to its isolation.

As the imminence of an auxiliary revolution in Europe receded, the various local Communist Parties were automatically transformed into instruments of the neo-Bolshevik state. Hence the tactics of any given national party were no longer seen in the increasingly chimerical perspective of a revolution but through the prism of neo-Bolshevik self-interest.

The most dramatic example of this was the celebrated People's Front before the Second World War and its numerous parallels since.

The neo-Bolshevik regime and the Comintern had clung, if not to their hopes, at least to their intransigent tactics throughout the twenties, but after the disappointment of one revolutionary hope after another in Germany, and with the emergence of the Nazi movement, the regime was confronted by an unmistakable foreshadowing of catastrophe when Hitler came to power in 1933.

The Nazi movement had been successful, after all, for two reasons: Stalin's rejection of any collaboration with the German Social-Democrats in order to forestall Hitler, and Hitler's foreign policy of "eastward expansion"—i.e., the destruction of the Soviet Union—which had secured the tacit, but effective, support of influential circles in Great Britain and France.

Hitler's foreign policy was plainly the gravest danger ever faced by the neo-Bolshevik regime, which now completely reversed its intransigence *vis-à-vis* all capitalist regimes and more particularly its Social-Democratic rivals. The Soviet government launched a largely successful campaign to unite all liberal and socialist elements against the growing threat of fascism.

But while the rise of Nazi Germany alarmed Western Europe and even, to some extent, the United States, it did not alarm it seriously enough to give the Stalin regime any assurance against an attack by a rearmed Germany. In August 1939 Stalin abruptly reversed positions and made a pact with Hitler that triggered the Second World War.

What was, perhaps, astonishing in the context of this period was not Stalin's mistrust of the countries that were shortly to become Allies—Great Britain and France—but his serene trust, as it seems, in Hitler's good faith *vis-à-vis* himself. He was, indeed, altogether gullible about Hitler—he greatly admired his brains and dash—and did nothing to alert the Soviet armed forces even when told of an imminent Nazi attack in 1941. Stalin was later to explain his pact with Hitler as a ruse to gain time for military preparations, but the conduct of the war, as well as official disclosures after Stalin's death in 1953, indicate Stalin's guileful boast to have been a clumsy apologia.

The Hitler-Stalin pact led to the partition of Poland, which was extinguished as a sovereign state for the fourth time. The Soviet regime adopted a new role as "gatherer of Russian soil" and the executor of ancient Russian claims. The eastern territories of Poland, part of the ancient Kievan realm, had been regained by Catherine the Great by the first Polish partition of 1772; the territories, a bone of contention during the reign of Alexander I, were forcibly detached from the Tsarist Empire by the First World War, and now they were integrated with Soviet Russia, as were the Baltic States and Bessarabia in 1940. The Soviet Union was creeping back to the old borders of Tsarism; the Versailles settlement of 1919 was nullified.

Hitler intended the pact to secure Germany's eastern flank and thus avoid the terrifying prospect of a war on two fronts, the undoing of Hohenzollern Germanytwenty-five years before. In the event, however, Hitler was bound to perceive that even a successful assault on Great Britain, even after the occupation of France in 1940, would leave Germany defenseless against the Soviet Union. Thus, in the summer of 1941 the German army flung the bulk of its strength against the Soviet Union.

The Stalin regime was now forced to accept Great Britain as an ally, and for that matter France and a little later the United States as well.

In the beginning the German army did remarkably well; by the end of 1941 it controlled about 40 percent of the total population of the Soviet Union in an area containing 65 percent of its prewar coal production, 68 percent of its pig iron, 58 percent of its steel, 38 percent of its grain, and 84 percent of its sugar, as well as about 40 percent of the railway network. Between June and November, Soviet industrial production had fallen by more than half and steel production by more than two-thirds.

In December 1941, however, there was a setback outside Moscow that proved fateful for the Nazi campaign in Russia. The advance on Moscow had been delayed for a month or two by army difficulties in Yugoslavia. It was finally launched in the coldest winter in memory, with the troops lacking even adequate clothing. The German army was halted.

This was its first serious defeat. Within a few days Hitler made two catastrophic decisions: he declared war on the United States and set in train the "Final Solution" of the "Jewish Question."

Militarily, both decisions were incomprehensible: The German armed forces were incapable of affecting the United States, while the attempt to exterminate the Jews required thousands of SS–men, the equivalent of several divisions, and vast amounts of rolling–stock, vital for the army in Russia, to corral scattered, unarmed Jewish civilians and transport them to death centers in Poland. Thus the attempted extinction of the Jews—between five and six million were killed—served a counter-military purpose.

Moreover, the many sources of Soviet disunity—from religious hostility to the Communist regime to the peasants' hatred of the collective farms—were disregarded by the Nazis in the grip of their obsession about the Slavic "submen." The utter inflexibility of agencies such as the Waffen-SS in their treatment of Russians, Ukrainians, and Poles, made it impossible for the Germans to benefit by any nonmilitary factor. The fabulous mass surrenders of the Russian armies during the first six months of the German onslaught, which should have indicated the internal weaknesses of the Soviet regime, were disregarded.

The disastrous siege of Stalingrad in 1942 undid the German forces completely.

By December 1941 the Japanese attack on Pearl Harbor put the United States directly into the war; as the vast amounts of all kinds of supplies were increased still further, the Russians gradually began moving westward again.

Even the staggering losses they were now suffering did not increase the Nazis' flexibility in dealing with the Russians. They were even reluctant to make use of Vlasov, a captured Soviet general sincerely hostile to the Stalin regime, who was eager to lead an army made up of Russians and other ethnic units against the Soviet Union as long as he retained some degree of autonomy. Though the Nazis had almost a million Russians serving in the German army itself in 1943, Vlasov's ambition made them hesitate until 1944, when it was far too late. From the Nazi point of view Vlasov's principal shortcoming was that he was a Russian patriot and hence opposed to the atomization of the Soviet Union that the Nazi geopoliticians took for granted even while their own realm was melting away. Vlasov was finally half-heartedly accepted, and after a meeting in Prague in November 1944, when he was elected president of a committee made up of representatives of the Orthodox Church, of the "eastern workers" dragooned by the Nazis into German factories, and numerous Tsarist emigrés as well as official German delegates, Vlasov's manifesto was proclaimed. Its highlight was a demand to overthrow Stalinist tyranny, "to liberate the people of our homeland from the Bolshevik system, and to give them back the rights they had successfully fought for in the popular revolution of 1917."

The Vlasov army was not allowed more than a few divisions, an indication of persistent German mistrust. Vlasov was smothered in the converging Soviet and American advances. After being interned by the Americans in Prague, he was handed over to the Russians and executed in 1946.

The Soviet Union emerged from the ruins of the war in a commanding international position. Its ability to withstand the German onslaught, even though with the massive aid of the United States and Great Britain, and to make a westward advance with its own armies enhanced its prestige, which was bolstered by the political incapacity of the United States administration and its insistence on fighting the war from a purely military point of view. This astigmatism not only made the American leaders go out of their way to allow the Soviet armies to take Berlin, Prague, and Vienna, but enshrined these artificial military positions in a series of diplomatic accords.

The Yalta Conference in February 1945 granted the Soviet Union a dominant position in the Far East, which an American occupation of Japan could balance only partly, and in the whole of Eastern Europe except Greece. Although some compromises were effected at Potsdam in the summer of 1945, the net result was favorable to the Soviet Union's interpretation of the accords reached in Yalta and in Teheran in the winter of 1943. Soviet territory was extended by about 193,000 square miles; not only were the Baltic countries altogether absorbed, but the Soviet Union also engulfed eastern Poland and Bessarabia, north Bukovina, the northern part of eastern Prussia, and parts of Finland. Moreover, an impressive array of buffer states was established on Soviet initiative. Poland, East Germany, Czechoslovakia, Hungary, Bulgaria, Rumania, and for a time Yugoslavia and Albania immediately became satellites. Soviet gains came to a total of roughly 110 million people.

By 1945 the Soviet regime, propped up by the "bastion of world capitalism," the United States, was at the zenith of its authority—far above its nadir in 1938. Its troops were in Berlin and Vienna, had come as far as the Elbe, controlled a third of Germany, the Danube area and the Balkans as a whole, and had occupied Manchuria.

These spectacular political successes were a dramatic counter-

point to the material devastation of the war, which was on
a scale comparable with the havoc of the First World War
and the subsequent civil war. The total loss of life in the Soviet
Union was estimated at about 20 million, the homeless numbered some 25 million. Countless towns had been levelled;
the housing shortage was catastrophic.

The material losses were made up for by the harnessing
of the industrial power of the satellites. Soviet control of East
Germany secured 36 percent of Germany's 1936 industrial capacity, for instance; the system of reparations between the Soviet Union and the satellites was heavily weighted in favor
of the former. Incalculable assets streamed into the Soviet
Union; German talents of all kinds, including nuclear physi-
cists, were imported wholesale.

Despite American trustfulness, the military coalition with
the Soviet Union collapsed the moment the war was over.
More mistrustful of the West than ever, perhaps through the
contemplation of the industrial might revealed in the American
war effort, culminating in the construction of the atom bomb,
the neo-Bolshevik regime withdrew to a characteristic position
of defensive aggressiveness. Rejecting the Marshall Plan aid
offered by America and mobilizing its Communist Parties all
over the world, the Soviet Executive began systematizing the
ideology of the socialist society as an insurmountable contrast
with the capitalist West. The Third International, buried in
1943 as a peace gesture, was revived in 1947 in the shape
of the Communist Information Bureau; the West, countering
through the American-inspired policy of containment, found
itself projected into a long-drawn-out era of Cold War—an
alignment of sustained confrontation that was to constitute
the international climate for a long time, to be replaced, fitfully,
by hints of détente in the seventies and by a tidal wave of
discussion of reforms, both in the Soviet Union and its satellites, in the eighties.

The Second World War—known in the Soviet Union as the
Fatherland War—greatly intensified Stalin's prewar tendency
to amplify Soviet patriotism through the incorporation of tradi-

tional Russian motifs. In November 1941, in a speech Stalin made to the troops in Moscow under the threat of the German guns, he had struck a note characteristic of the whole Soviet war. Disregarding the Communist pantheon altogether, he had held aloft the "virile images of our great ancestors—Nevsky, Donskoy, Minin, Pozharsky, Suvorov, and Kutuzov,"

Brandishing before his listeners' eyes the ikons of Imperial Russia, Stalin brought Soviet patriotism, kindled during the thirties, to its logical conclusion. He drove the point home at a reception for the Red Army commanders in the Kremlin in 1945; with Germany shattered, he gave a toast, not to the multi-ethnic citizens of the Soviet Union, but to the health of the Russian people—"the outstanding nation among the peoples of the Soviet Union."

This singling out of the specifically Russian strand in the skein of Soviet patriotism was heightened to the absurd by Stalin's explanation of the precipitate Russian entry into the war against Japan, the same day the second American atom bomb had been dropped on Nagasaki. Aside from taking the credit for the defeat of Japan—America's role in the end of the Japanese war has been ignored in Soviet historiography—Stalin described Soviet participation as an act of revenge for the Japanese victory over Tsarism in 1905. "The defeat of the Russian troops in 1904 left bitter memories in the hearts of the Russian people. . . . Our people hoped . . . the day would come when Japan would be defeated and this blemish erased. For forty years we, the men of the older generation, have waited for this day. And now it has finally come."

Surely, from the point of view of early Bolshevism, a magnificent piece of irony! Lenin had hailed the Japanese victory in 1905 as a prologue to the rising of the European proletariat; even bourgeois liberals in Russia had been delighted by the defeat of Tsarism. Yet after the Second World War the assimilation of Russia's national tradition seemed the natural outcome of the ethnocentrism inherent, no doubt, in socialism in one country. As the concept of socialism itself was denatured to adapt it to the specific conditions of Russia, so the Russian national concept was amplified and incorporated in the conservatism of the bureaucracy that was busily fusing all available elements into a new tradition.

The upsurge of Soviet chauvinism, potentially irresistible once the formerly ideological movement was nationalized, became more intense in 1943 with a campaign initiated by an attack of the Party organ, *Bolshevik,* on an apparently harmless volume of philosophy.

This violent attack inaugurated an epoch characterized by the blanket eulogy of everything Russian or Soviet. Russians began to be given credit for everything under the sun, from the invention of the steam engine to radio and penicillin. The movement constituted an indignant rejection of the old charge of backwardness, commonplace among all students of Russian affairs. The new campaign required—under severe penalties—the demonstration of Soviet superiority in all areas of science, art, and literature. The intellectual censorship of the regime was intensified, achieving special notoriety in the Lysenko case that came to a climax in 1948. The imposition of the Party line on the geneticians and biologists who opposed Lysenko's theories marked the entry of the new-style Soviet metaphysics into the realm of abstract science, though Lysenko himself was soon to be discredited and the sciences, too, were ultimately to be safeguarded against such excesses.

The Jewish "problem," which Marxists had claimed would vanish along with traditional society, not only failed to vanish, but even after the conquest of Hitler's Germany was exacerbated and given a specifically "Marxist-Leninist" tincture.

At the end of the forties a campaign was launched by the neo-Bolshevik Executive specifically aimed at the Jews ("passportless wanderers" and "rootless cosmopolitans"). This embedded deep in Soviet life the classical theme of formal, medieval anti-Semitism, a theme that was articulated, amplified and institutionalized in a series of satellite "Show Trials" (in Hungary, Bulgaria, and Czechoslovakia) in the late forties and fifties, where lifelong Bolsheviks, expressly denounced as Jews, and for that matter as Zionists, were stigmatized on the model of the Moscow Show Trials, as agents of a "capitalist" restoration and servants of the principal enemies of the Soviet regime.

In 1953 Stalin was on the verge, as was to come out, of preparing a new Show Trial, heralded by the intensively publicized charges that some well-known Soviet physicians—nearly all Jews, as was equally publicized—were engaged in a plot against him and the Politburo. Then he died in circumstances regarded by many as suspicious.

The death of Stalin, without question the most powerful individual in history, not only marked the end of the era associated with his name—though interpretations of this have been very various—but the end of the Stalin cult as such.

His death naturally led to some backstage maneuvering at the summits of the all-powerful Party. Since there was no legal, still less doctrinal, justification for making the office of General Secretary supreme, there was no institutional framework for the contest between the top luminaries of the Party: this created a vacuum filled by primitive power politics.

The tension during the decades of "Socialist" construction in the Soviet Union, heightened during the last years of Stalin's reign, had made everyone in the upper strata of the Party jittery. For a short time G. M. Malenkov, L. P. Beria, and V. M. Molotov formed a sort of preeminent trio, very soon broken up, however, by Beria's arrest and later execution at the end of 1953.

Nikita Khrushchev, made First Secretary (not General Secretary, still too close to Stalin) of the Central Committee in September 1953, was to oust his rivals and become Party leader a few years later. He attempted some major organizational reforms, with the usual failure inherent in the problem. One of his macrocosmic successes, however, was brought about in May 1955, when he made a trip to Belgrade for discussions with Tito. Whether or not the breakaway of Yugoslavia from the Soviet camp in 1948 had been genuine, after these discussions it rejoined, semi-clandestinely, the Soviet bloc. This may have been linked to a policy initiated by Khrushchev, the formation of an overall disinformation project taking in all intelligence services of the Soviet bloc, for the purpose of allowing some latitude to individual regimes while misleading Western allies by simulations of conflicts.

Khrushchev's outstanding feat in the Soviet domestic sphere was the launching of a process that has remained a basic strand in Soviet politics ever since—"de-Stalinization."

It was necessary for Soviet leaders to distance themselves from the heavily charged Soviet past—the explosion of atrocities and blunders associated with Stalin—without at the same time weakening the Party itself. On the face of it this might have been thought impossible, since it was the all-powerful Party, after all, that had installed Stalin during Lenin's lifetime and with his approval. Nevertheless the attempt to single Stalin out as bearing the entire blame for the disasters in the Soviet Union, an attempt that may be said to have acquired institutional status at the time of the expulsion of the Trotskyites in the twenties, has been made repeatedly, achieving institutional status in the wave of agitation about reform in the eighties.

Khrushchev, at a secret session of the 20th Party Congress (February 1956), officially exploded the Stalin myth once and for all. In copious detail Khrushchev, overcome by emotion, bitterly attacked Stalin's megalomania, sadism, cowardice, and incompetence. For seven hours he aired in public charges that among opponents of the regime had been commonplace for decades. Lay opinion was startled; for a time faithful Communists everywhere were paralyzed by doubt. The pious who had actually believed the illusions manufactured by neo-Bolshevik propaganda were naturally upset by the abrupt annihilation of the orderly mythical world a whole generation had grown up in.

But even the shattering revelations of Khrushchev in February 1956 dealt only with the Party victims: the vast slaughters of the population (in which Khrushchev himself had played a stellar role) were untouched. Khrushchev made much of the systematic falsification of history, which had been written by Stalin personally or on his orders (Stalin had once said "paper will stand for anything"). In short, Khrushchev denounced the whole "cult of personality" but succeeded, characteristically, in slanting his denunciations away from the Party that had brought Stalin into being. (The very phrase "cult of personality"—picked up from one of Marx's letters—is a typical neo-Bolshevik euphemism.)

The 20th Party Congress of 1956, perhaps as part of the new overall disinformation policy, modified a celebrated formula made much of by both Lenin and Stalin: that war between the Soviet Union and the West was inevitable. It was laid down at the Congress that while war was, to be sure, inevitable, it was not "fatalistically" so.

The effects of Khrushchev's "secret speech" and the attendant initiation of a de-Stalinization campaign had intensified general discontent and considerable erosion of the central authority. In the Soviet Union itself many intellectuals and young people channeled their indignation into active agitation that went beyond mere grumbling. The denunciation of Stalin inevitably led beyond Stalin.

Abroad, the Soviet stranglehold on Eastern Europe was shaken: In October 1956 heavy detachments of Soviet troops were hastily sent into Hungary to put down an uprising that was in fact led by Communists acting as workers' leaders. In Poland, too, military intervention, which had been looming, was averted by an accord with Wladyslav Gomulka, who had become leader once again over Soviet objections.

The crushing of the Hungarian rebellion by Soviet troops in October and November of 1956 coincided with an acceleration of the Soviet penetration of the Middle East.

Initially a sponsor of the newly established State of Israel in 1948, the Soviet regime almost immediately changed its tactic and switched over to overt and increasingly dynamic support of the various claims made by Israel's uniformly hostile neighbors.

It was perhaps inevitable for the Soviet Union to take advantage of the internal ferment within the various Arabic-speaking countries bordering the State of Israel. Without doing much more than responding to invitations, the Soviet Executive could intervene massively in the 1956 Sinai War conducted by Great

Britain, France, and Israel against Egypt and in consequence secure a foothold in Egypt, Syria, and Iraq that it could exploit for its own purposes.

Though it acted in concert with the United States in obliging Israel to give up its territorial gains in the 1956 Sinai War, the Soviet Executive soon resumed an independent strategy. In 1967 it backed very heavily a coalition of Egypt, Syria, and Jordan against the State of Israel. When the Israelis managed to withstand and in fact crush the Egyptian and Syrian armies, the very discomfiture of the Arab forces interacted with Soviet discomfiture itself in anchoring the Soviet Executive even more firmly in the Middle East.

This procedure was repeated in the autumn of 1973, when Egypt and Syria were even more powerfully armed by the Soviet Union, which moreover compensated for the astonishingly swift attrition of armaments by fabulously expensive sophisticated armaments of its own. In the Yom Kippur War the difference was that the Egyptian and Syrian forces acquitted themselves far better than in 1967. Moreover, the oil embargo, proclaimed at the same time by the oil-rich Arab states in the Persian Gulf, quickly outweighed the territorial aspects of the war itself.

Under Khrushchev a rupture seemed to take place between the Soviet Union and Red China: the two major components of the vast Marxist-Leninist bloc seemed to be diverging. It is true that relations between the Kremlin and the movement led by Mao Zedong had been ambiguous from the outset. Immediately after the 1917 putsch the prospects of a Chinese revolution seemed very bright to the euphoric Bolsheviks: they were sympathetic to the Chinese nationalist movement, with which a working alliance was achieved after the civil war in Russia. During the twenties, on Stalin's initiative, the Chinese nationalist organization, the Kuomintang, was fully supported, perhaps in an effort to compensate for the disastrous setbacks of the communist movement in Europe. The Soviet Executive agreed not to build up the Chinese Communist Party, founded in 1921, independently of the Kuomintang but to support the Kuomintang directly.

However, after the death of Sun Yat-sen in 1925 and the rise of Chiang Kai-shek, the situation changed abruptly. Chiang Kai-shek, now head of the Kuomintang, broke the pact Stalin had been nurturing against the attacks of various opposition elements in the Party, and by a ruthless massacre of Communists and industrial workers in April 1927 brought the collaboration between the two movements to an end.

When the Chinese Communists, headed by Mao Zedong and Chou En-lai, succeeded, after overcoming the Japanese army and expelling Chiang Kai-shek's forces, in establishing themselves in 1948 as the sole power in mainland China, both Mao Zedong and Stalin disregarded in public their differences of the past and proclaimed their solidarity as Marxists.

Yet the proclaimed identity of doctrine could not withstand differences of basic interests. For the Soviet Executive, the Red Chinese preoccupation, for instance, with the expulsion of the Kuomintang regime in Taiwan was meaningless. Thus the alliance, whatever might have been its substance, did not last much more than a decade. Even though during the Korean War with the United States the Soviet Executive provided the Chinese divisions in Korea with arms and credits—though, not to be sure, in any abundance—relations began to worsen just when China was struggling to carry out an ambitious program of its own—the Great Leap Forward, which almost immediately, and perhaps inevitably, turned out to be a failure.

A split between the two regimes was advertised in 1960 and an open rupture occurred three years later, while Khrushchev was still head of state. From then on relations between the two great states, of which China, with its billion people, was still incomparably feebler materially, seemed to grow more and more hostile, though that may also have been less genuine than it seemed.

The Mao regime was particularly wary of following the half-hearted and essentially propagandistic attempts at de-Stalinization that became fashionable in the Soviet Union after 1953. Characteristically, Sino-Soviet frictions were presented to the world as fallings-out over Marxist-Leninist ideology. The rupture in 1963 between Red China and the Soviet Union may be said to have quartered the world between the United States, the Soviet Union, Red China, and the European Common Market scheduled for 1992.

The condition of the peasants had deteriorated sharply in the wake of Stalin's draconian treatment of the thirties. Their plight was alleviated, very slightly, after Stalin's death, though there was no question of abandoning their de facto enserfment. A few palliatives were put into effect; they did nothing to arrest the decline of agriculture. Khrushchev made an attempt to develop vast lands outside Russia proper—in Kazakhstan and Siberia—but the attempt was substantially a failure.

The rigidity inherent in the problems confronting Khrushchev and other Soviet reformers was highlighted by an experiment tried when he was looking for some specific to cure the neo-Bolshevik system. One Ivan Khudenko, an upper functionary in an apparatus under the Council of Ministers, was authorized to reorganize the labor-wage system at a state farm. He proposed that the work be done by small teams of workers with full economic autonomy: their pay would depend on the results of their work.

The cost of growing grain fell to a quarter of what it had been; wages increased by four; the profits per worker increased by seven. On the basis of this, Khudenko calculated that if his proposal was applied to the whole country, grain harvests would be increased by four and the farm work force (35 million at the time) would go down to a little over 5 million.

Initially well received, the idea was simply dropped when it became obvious that the whole of the economy would be upset, i.e., local initiative would be increased and central planning sharply cut. (Khudenko was arrested and sent to a camp for trying to "damage state property on an especially large scale." He died in prison 14 years later).

Aside from management, it was obvious that what the land needed was repose and fertilization—in short a renewal, but since decisions were necessarily based on needs of the moment, on expediency, etc., the realities of the situation were necessarily disregarded. The shortages in consumption were to remain endemic; they became catastrophically critical by the eighties.

Under Khrushchev an agreement was reached among the Party leaders not to kill each other, and to establish a program of comprehensive disinformation of enemies of the regime that would be integrated with the satellite parties. Thus Yugoslavia was covertly restored to active collaboration with the Moscow Soviet Executive, though the fact itself was camouflaged.

Between 1953–64, attempts were made to rival the United States technically, to realize the deepest longing of the neo-Bolshevik regime, epitomized in the celebrated slogan—"to overtake and pass" America. Stalin, in the last phase of his life, had systematically trivialized the achievements of the West; this was given up, cybernetics was recognized; enormous sums were given to science as well as to its implementation. In the summer of 1953, in fact, the Soviet Executive might well have seemed to be approaching its goal. After having dumbfounded the United States experts by duplicating the atom bomb (with the much publicized assistance of some spies), the Soviet Executive announced the creation of a hydrogen bomb.

The West, headed by American technique, had suddenly lost the nuclear monopoly that had been thought to guarantee its world hegemony. Then in 1958 the Soviet government, obviously advancing in all technical areas, announced that by launching a sputnik it had outclassed the engineering elite of the United States. The Soviet Union seemed not only to have drawn level with America in rocketry—the accuracy required to aim a large sputnik plainly puts the vulnerability of remote spots in a new light—but to have outdistanced her in at least some branches of science, both abstract and applied.

Soviet success in rocketry at last managed to draw the attention of authoritative Americans to what was a matter of common knowledge years before, that the Soviet Union was producing vast numbers of well-trained engineers in addition to the handful of abstract scientists it had already become famous for.

The Cuban missile crisis of October 1962 was the first successful attempt to establish an open foothold in the Western Hemisphere. In 1959 Fidel Castro had overthrown the former dictator, Batista; an attempt made by the Kennedy Administration to remove Castro led to the comprehensive military and political Bay of Pigs fiasco.

The Soviet intervention in Cuba was also the first major deployment of the fundamental threat underlying Soviet relations with the West—i.e., the use of nuclear weapons as a form of blackmail. It created a dilemma that in terms of public relations has retained its force: either submission to various Soviet enterprises, or the horrors of nuclear warfare.

Thus the territorial acquisition of Cuba as a real satellite was highlighted by the Soviet use of nuclear blackmail, while the explanation of the peaceful resolution of the crisis, presented in the United States as a triumph for the Kennedy Administration—as though Soviet missiles had been forced out of Cuba and the risk of war thereby averted—could not conceal the obvious fact that Soviet forces stayed on in Cuba and, in addition, that Cuba immediately became one of the most useful of all Soviet puppets. It was to serve as the springboard for recruiting and managing Marxist-Leninist allies and agents in Latin America, while its reservoir of manpower was to prove an indispensable instrument for Soviet political/military adventures in Africa and Arabia.

In October 1964 Khrushchev was forced to resign. A new collective leadership, led by L. I. Brezhnev and A. N. Kosygin, was set up, though it was obvious that Brezhnev was the real victor; in the spring he became General Secretary, the first time the title was used since Stalin.

Generally speaking, despite the Soviet mastery of the techniques needed for weapons and space flight, as well as iron and steel production, and its technical progress in a wide variety of basic new techniques—notably computers, as well as industrial research—the Soviet Executive remained far behind not only the United States but Western Europe and Japan.

A half-hearted attempt was made under Brezhnev to solve the main Soviet problem of Soviet economy, managerial inefficiency (incentives again), but the problem remained intractable. After dropping all Khrushchev's attempts at reform, the Brezhnev administration swerved back to a more extreme centralization.

Politically, too, problems kept mounting for the Soviet Executive. After Khrushchev's deposition, an actual dissident movement had crystallized displaying three principal tendencies: an explicitly democratic, liberal opposition associated with the scientist Andrei Sakharov; the Christian ideology associated with the well-known writer Alexander Solzhenitsyn, and orthodox Marxism-Leninism, which entails a simple-minded reverence for Lenin as the Redeemer and the rejection of Stalin as the Devil.

The birth of a generalized, though still quite restricted, opposition with these three tendencies mirrors the formation of an embryonic public opinion, which achieved a slight degree of organization because of the relative slackening of repression after Stalin. In September 1965 two writers (Sinyavsky and Daniel) were accused of having had some attacks on the Soviet regime published abroad. They were indicted and eventually given fairly long terms in prison camps. These events were accompanied by the beginnings of nationalist agitation in the non-Russian areas of the Soviet Union. By the mid-1960s national movements had reappeared in the Ukraine, Lithuania, and Transcaucasia.

In January 1968 the emergence in Czechoslovakia of a new leader, Alexander Dubcek, led the "Prague Spring," an optimistic attempt to give communism a human face. By the summer this was cut short: Soviet forces, including East German, Polish, Hungarian and Bulgarian detachments occupied Czechoslovakia, reimposing the iron discipline from the center.

The Czech invasion had two fairly long-range effects—the Brezhnev Doctrine, which meant that the Soviet Union would, if necessary, intervene militarily in the affairs of its satellites, a fact obvious from the very beginning, and it also put a stop to the hopes of détente, the Soviet goal, as it would have seemed, since the mid-1960s; It was to be another decade or two before detente became a serious perspective in relations between the Soviet Union and the West.

The suppression of the Prague Spring intensified repression everywhere; it also took in cultural life. Solzhenitsyn, who had been seriously constricted even before the invasion of Czechoslovakia (his manuscripts had been confiscated and some of his published works withdrawn), was expelled from the Writers' Union in November 1969.

All this seemed to generate a gradual ferment in the scientific and artistic intelligentsia: discontent was obviously spreading. *Samizdat*—presented as a sort of underground press, though it was obviously well-known to the KGB—became a byword.

Events in the Middle East had repercussions in the Soviet Union: the new course of the Soviet Executive in the Middle East, its overt hostility to Israel after the Israeli victory in the Six-Day War of June 1967, led to a general attack not only on Israel but, with particular virulence, on Zionism and on Jews generally. The groundwork for the Soviet version of medieval anti-Semitism, established by the campaigns against Russian Jews at the end of the forties and by the satellite Show Trials of the forties and fifties stigmatising Jews as essential enemies of the regime, was now to provide a motor for dual exploitation, both against the State of Israel and against Jews as such.

The Helsinki Conference of the summer of 1975 sealed the territorial settlement concluding the Second World War, at least vis-a-vis the Soviet Union. It was a clear-cut victory for the Soviet Executive, which got the approval of all powers for its own borders in Europe and Asia in return for its lavishly distributed promises of high regard for human rights and freedom, etc.

In that same summer the Soviet Executive embarked on an extensive military/political program in Africa, beginning in Angola and coinciding with the cooling of interest in the U.S. government, after the disappointing outcome of the Vietnam War, in further involvements abroad.

Making use of the manpower of its wholly-subsidized Cuban satellite, as well as some personnel from East Germany, the Soviet Executive airlifted heavy weapons to Angola, six thousand miles away from its borders, then proceeded to the establishment of strongpoints throughout Africa (Ethiopia, Namibia, Somaliland) and in the Arabian Peninsula (Aden).

In 1973, at a secret conference of Party heads in Eastern Europe, Brezhnev predicted that by the mid-eighties the "will of the Kremlin would prevail throughout the world." On the eve of the massive strategic undertaking, camouflaged for the purposes of the world media by the use of non-Soviet troops and technical personnel, this prediction might well have seemed plausible.

In December 1979 the Soviet Executive, with footholds established in Latin America, Africa, and the Arab world, invaded Afghanistan at the invitation of the local Marxist-Leninist regime to suppress a comprehensive movement of rebellion throughout the country. It was to remain for more than a decade.

In the Soviet Union itself, "real socialism"—the fundamental Brezhnev phrase—had come to mean no more than an economy in constant crisis. Though hailed as a superpower, the Soviet Union was constricted by an exorbitantly expensive arms race as well as by the expenditures inherent in the maintenance of a global network of puppets. The Soviet Executive, at the summit of a huge bureaucracy—self-coopted, self-sustaining and self-justified by various interpretations of Marxism-Leninism—was incapable of solving its economic problems either at the core of its realm or on its fringes.

Leonid Brezhnev, after eighteen years of peace, died in November 1982. He was succeeded by a former head of the KGB, Yuri Andropov, who at the age of 72 set about coping with the red tape, corruption and pervasive inefficiency of the vast Soviet bureaucracy. Andropov died the following year; he was succeeded by Konstantin Chernenko, 76, a bureaucratic routineer.

The second Soviet generation—men in their seventies—had come to an end.

CHAPTER XI

A REVISION OF
PERSPECTIVES

*D*uring the euphoria that attended the victory of the neo-Bolshevik dictatorship over the Nazi regime in the Second World War, the prospect of at last realizing the optimistic slogan of the regime, "to overtake and pass America," might have seemed realistic. Stalin's stubborn rejection of economic aid from the United States, due no doubt to fear of American power, might well have seemed mere prudence.

But such optimism proved to be a chimera. The economy remained incorrigible. By the sixties it was obvious to the Soviet Executive that the economy as a whole was sinking in a bog of shortages, inefficiency, lassitude and exhausting oppression. The Five-Year-Plans bombastically touted since the end of the twenties had proved incapable of enabling the regime not only to meet consumer needs and build up industry but even to maintain agriculture. The notion of even approaching the United States—or by now, even Japan—was merely preposterous.

Still, a tiny nucleus running a great state has many political

resources. Such a nucleus is, after all, immune to social groupings, to a hostile press, to public opinion. For the time being
the neo-Bolshevik Executive, incapable of providing its subjects
with either comfort or even idealism, resorted to a peculiarly
modern specialty—the fabrication of arms and the contriving
of planetary intrigues. This novel, pragmatic, non-Marxist approach found a fertile seedbed in the constellation of forces
that began to coagulate after the Second World War; it was
an ideal background for the flexibility of a tightly-knit executive.

The Soviet Union, unique in history as claiming the support
of an ideal theory for its conduct as a real political entity,
has derived remarkable benefits from that fact alone. While
it would be absurd to maintain that the socialism flaunted
by the regime had any substance, it was obviously effective
for purposes of propaganda. Socialism in an ideal form had
a potent appeal to embryo dictatorships and to elite conspiracies
throughout the former colonial areas of the world—what became known, in the wake of the Second World War, as the
Third World.

The Soviet regime became a model for elite strivers in backward areas. In Latin America and Africa, especially, Marxist-
Leninist, i.e., pro-Soviet recruits drawn from the middle and
upper classes proliferated. In these areas, where free-enterprise
was under the constriction of particularly retrograde parochial
leaders, it was natural for eager young men to be seduced
by the prospect of seizing power under the banner of revolution. All this, following the model of Soviet totalitarianism
itself, was expressed in one form or another of Marxist ideology.

This could transform the abandoned neo-Bolshevik hopes
of conquering the world intellectually into a new hope for
securing power bases in Africa, Asia and Latin America, against
the background of the many communist parties still receptive
to the Soviet Executive and their influence, sometimes decisive,
on social-democratic parties and for that matter on governments in general.

An influential factor in shaping public opinion outside the

Soviet bloc was the remarkable phenomenon of a pro-Soviet shift among important elements of the great Christian Churches. The Bolshevik *putsch* in 1917, which had the appearance of a peaceful victory won by a Marxist socialist party, naturally inflamed opponents, but at the same time the grandiose aim of the Bolsheviks—reform of the world—had an immediate effect on many Protestants and Catholics in the West, despite the notorious atheism of Marx and his followers. After the Second World War, Marxism as such exercised a magnetic attraction for important branches not only of the great Protestant confederations but also of the Roman Catholic Church. Colloquies between Marxists and Dominicans, Franciscans and Jesuits became common; in the sixties a powerful current of synthesis between Christianity and Marxism, known as Liberation Theology, became an international force of some utility to the geopolitical plans of the Soviet Executive.

This convergence of attitudes was rooted, perhaps unexpectedly, in the revival of an ancient idea: the Kingdom of God, which, though it had kindled much socio-religious agitation during the Middle Ages (in various chiliastic movements) might have been thought to be fossilized. Yet it had, in fact, retained its dynamic potential.

Pious Christians could say that though the Church had always put off the Kingdom of God to an unknowable future, while sometimes localizing it in the hearts of men, proper compassion for the poor called for practical expressions of concern in the present. Marxists, for their part, could agree that an accord with the Church on extending compassion to the poor might enable them to disregard mere theology.

By stripping Marxism of its intellectual structure and focusing it on the concerns of the poor—laughable, to be sure, in view of its concentration not on "the poor," but on the Proletariat—Marxists could welcome the offer of Church collaboration in alleviating the lot of the masses. Practically speaking, this meant genuine collaboration both in the West and in the Third World on joint projects of reform. It became possible for Liberation Theologians to say that for them "all four Gospels are Marxist documents," and that they "carry the Cross of Jesus Christ in the name of Karl Marx"—all for the sake of "the poor."

Thus the neo-Bolshevik regime had a vast and variegated milieu in which the conspiratorial expertise underlying the dictatorship could still be effective. Many options, both strategic and tactical, were open to the neo-Bolshevik leadership as it sought a way out of an obvious dilemma: either surrender to the market forces of the world, or combat them politically through overt and covert initiatives.

The political defeat suffered by the United States after its military success in Vietnam had no doubt created a favorable climate of opinion, especially in the American media. It was obvious that an intensification of conspiratorial techniques was the only way out: a vast program of subversion and penetration in Latin America, Africa, and Asia, especially in the Middle East, was implemented with remarkable success.

The absorption of Cuba into the Soviet network created a prop for numerous adventures in Africa, where 50,000 soldiers armed with machine-guns could be a decisive force. The heavy subsidization of the African National Congress, and its presentation as an inevitable alternative to the white South African government, the establishment of actual Marxist-Leninist regimes in countries as far apart from each other as Angola and Ethiopia, the creation of a whole network of puppets indicated the flexibility and thrust of these Soviet initiatives. In the Middle East, too, the Soviet Executive solved the problem of Muslim fronts as easily as it had found Christian fronts in the West.

These Muslim fronts are the principal channel of such machinations in the Middle East. They are all very naturally allied against both the State of Israel and to a large extent against the United States. In this strategy the Soviet Executive enjoys, of course, the support of the many universalist Jews who themselves are willing tools, agents or allies of the Soviet Executive against both Israel and the United States.

On the higher levels of psychological warfare the framework of the contest between the Soviet Executive and the United

States—the Cold War—was grounded in the simple device of nuclear blackmail deployed with such effectiveness during the 1962 Cuban missile crisis. The Soviet Executive found it child's play to exploit the sensibilities of ordinary people by holding aloft these two alternatives: all Soviet geopolitical advances— the puppetization of Cuba, Nicaragua, Ethiopia, Angola, etc.— were submerged in a cloud of misapplied apprehension.

For all these maneuvers to take place unnoticed, eliciting from the major powers, especially the United States, a singular torpidity, what was of paramount, indeed indispensable importance, was a degree of control over what has become a fundamental factor in world politics—the mass media. It is in this area that the Soviet Executive has achieved its most remarkable triumph, whose impact is best assessed by the public's unawareness of it.

In fact, the establishment of key centers of authority in the mass media, their manipulation within the general framework of the communications networks, has proved to be the easiest form of influence the Soviet Executive has achieved.

The media all over the world are staffed to a large extent by natural sympathizers, like the elite in backward countries, of ideals of world reorganization projected by a powerful state with noble ideals. Idealistic voluntary allies of the Soviet Executive sprang up everywhere; material subsidization, while common, was supplementary. These agents have been, in their own way, perhaps, bona fide dreamers, with a unique function to inspire, to shape, to bend, to slant, to concentrate news to make at least part of it propaganda whose most effective camouflage is objective reporting.

By the sixties this form of media penetration was already well-established. Against the social background—the climate of opinion of the liberal milieu, with its acceptance of an ideal despite or indeed especially because of the neo-Bolshevik horrors—foci were established in the world media, and above all in the United States—where they could affect the election of the Congress—that could contrive, without eliciting the smallest attention from the public, a uniquely homogenized treatment singling out, within the torrent of general news, four specific areas: The Soviet Executive itself, Latin America, the Middle East, and South Africa. These four areas, especially the first, are the Soviet Executive's primary concerns. Here piety prevails: puppets of the Soviet government are basically commendable, all else consists of fascism, oppression, starvation, cruelty.

The idealism of these sometimes unconscious Soviet partisans enables them somehow to soar above what, to anyone with common sense, should seem obvious—the real-life concerns of states. The Soviet Executive, after all, has a practical, realpolitik sort of interest in these areas—the unique industrial potential of South Africa, the unique reservoir of petroleum in the Persian Gulf, etc. This form of crypto-partisanship has penetrated the world media. Claiming to be reporting factually from Latin America, South Africa, the Middle East, especially Israel, all the media, including movies and documentaries, unite in lampooning the United States government—especially all aspects of the army, the intelligence services, etc.—while stressing all the themes dear to the Soviet Executive: poverty, oppression, the condition of the blacks, anti-America, anti-Israel, etc.

The success of these neo-Bolshevik initiatives was remarkable. For the first time the American media could become an actual factor of world history. The shifting of Soviet policy over to the making of arms, to global schemes of subversion, and to covert propaganda seemed to be going along brilliantly well.

The success of the media in creating a biased view of the situation in the four areas mentioned above was so complete that it was possible to influence decisively the national discussion of whether or not the United States should aid its own partisans in Central America.

The nuclear competition with the Soviet Executive, against which the United States had spent and was spending astronomical sums, a fact widely publicized as an integral part of the Soviet strategy of nuclear blackmail, was systematically kept distinct from the question of aiding Latin American partisans of the United States; thus the incontestable fact that the Soviet Executive was also spending vast sums in support of the Castro regime in Cuba, exporting weapons to Nicaragua and to countless para-military agents in Latin America, was practically blacked out of public consciousness during the discussion of aid to the United States supporters.

Thus, while on the one hand the need for nuclear arms was not contested even by the Left–liberal element in the government and the media, it remained entirely sequestered vis-à-vis the non-nuclear activities of the Soviet regime, its operations based on puppets and their conventional weapons in Latin America, Africa and elsewhere.

Other campaigns were going equally well: The South African government was besieged as no government had been before. The well-nigh universal disapproval of apartheid—racial segregation in national elections, housing areas, etc.—was used by the Soviet Executive as the basis of a broad campaign to undermine, in its own realpolitik interests, the South African government. The oddity of this Soviet preoccupation with the vote, which Soviet citizens have not had since 1917, has been noticed by few, just as the actual massacres in other African countries–notably Ethiopia—have been paid scarcely any attention at all.

Soviet policy in the Middle East was highlighted from the sixties on by a simple objective—to get the United States out of the Persian Gulf. For this the Muslim fronts were indispensable. All the Muslim fronts, by taking hostages well-nigh at random, by inciting genuine massacres that made the whole area comprising Syria and Lebanon an impenetrable jungle of murderous intrigues and butcheries, were aimed at this objective—to convince America that the Middle East is utterly unmanageable, and that the only practical thing to do is to get out.

By the end of the eighties, in short, it might well have seemed that the neo-Bolshevik Executive, relentlessly squeezing its people, had established itself as a superpower by creating an impressive nuclear arsenal on the one hand, and on the other an equally impressive network of allies and agents whose allegiance to Marxism-Leninism was buttressed by self-interest.

Thus, on the very model of the Bolshevik *putsch* of 1917, once again the Soviet Executive had flouted an elementary Marxist axiom that economics determines everything. In the eighties, the global enterprise of the Soviet Executive looked formidable. The Marxist-Leninist regimes in Europe, Asia, Africa and Latin America occupied more than a quarter of the planet's land area, with about 40 percent of the world population.

Still, though economics does not determine everything, it obviously cannot be ignored indefinitely. The phases of the economy under the neo-Bolsheviks can be summed up handily: The frenzy of war communism in 1918–1921; the New Economic Policy (capitalism) in 1921–1929; the crash program of collectivization and high-pressure industrialization from then on. Politically, the regime, after the shake-up of the great slaughter of the peasantry during the collectivization campaign, was consolidated under Stalin's control in 1936–39, on the eve of the war with Nazi Germany.

The neo-Bolsheviks in Russia had left a grim legacy: The peasantry had been for all practical purposes wiped out; the forced collectivization at the beginning of the thirties, after killing off millions of peasants, had been followed gradually and then after the Second World War torrentially by a mass exodus to the towns and cities.

The older generation could no longer do the hard work of farming, the middle-aged and younger people had largely left. Very few people were there; the greatest granary in the world, up to the Bolshevik *putsch,* could no longer feed itself. In sum, a total of tens of millions of people had been killed for political reasons during the decade 1929–39. These losses, plus the absence of what would have been their progeny, have brought about a shortage in the Soviet population, since the last published census at the time of the First World War, of ca. 100 million.

From the Second World War on the economy was merely tinkered with; minor concessions were made, withdrawn, made again, etc. The problems of the economy seemed to be linked to the very fact of state management in economies that by and large remained stubbornly backward. The quarter-billion people under the Soviet Executive—together with the billion-plus under the Chinese Communist Party—could no longer, it seemed, be held down by the bureaucracy: three-quarters of a century of regimentation in the Soviet Union, half a century of the same in China, had proved incapable of suppressing discontent. The fundamental inability of these state-run economies to provide anything in the way of consumer goods had finally, in a seismic surge, forced its way into the awareness of the self-appointed leaders.

Hope for a real change sprang up once again. Since Stalin's death in 1953, to be sure, this hope had been springing up regularly; each and every successor of his gave rise to a state of euphoria in the throngs of the hopeful and in the great media of the West. The disappointment would be followed, again and again, by a reformulation of projected mini-reforms. Still, all sensible people knew the Soviet system—a cluster of blockages—could not accomplish anything in the way of normal economics, hence it was only natural to assume it would eventually have to change.

By the eighties, with the intensification of technological advances in the wake of the Second World War, the neo-Bolshevik regime was entirely eliminated as a contender in the competition of the great centers of the world—the United States, the looming European Common Market and Japan, and even the smaller free-enterprise states of Eastern Asia—Taiwan, South Korea, Singapore.

Nor could its outdistancing be concealed from its subjects: the unavoidable necessity of educating its population made it impossible to make the Marxist-Leninist cocoon of ideas watertight: intelligent people at universities could not be immunized against the flood of information of all kinds permeating all the technical fields of the modern world—electronics, computerology, sophisticated engineering of all kinds.

By the end of the eighties, in fact, it had become clear that the Marxist-Leninist regimes could not maintain their congealed bureaucracies. The dissatisfaction was so pervasive that it was no longer possible to govern even by means of the bloodshed the population had got used to in Russia in the twenties and thirties. The military cadres could not be counted on for any large-scale repressions; the ardor of the nucleus itself was contaminated, perhaps, by deep doubts as to the point of it all. The simple-minded fanaticism, plus desperation of the early neo-Bolsheviks had been corroded beyond recall.

At the same time it was obvious that the success of the Soviet policy of worldwide subversion and infiltration could not serve to eliminate the United States as an obstacle to Soviet world hegemony. The achievements in Latin America—Cuba, Nicaragua—and the strong-points established in Africa and Asia were peripheral, after all.

In the middle of the eighties, accordingly, a new course was laid down for the Soviet bloc that electrified world politics.

The new course was embodied in a rising star, Mikhail Gorbachov, who in March 1985 became head of the Soviet government. The fanfare in the media focused on the reforms implied by his key concepts—"perestroika" and "glasnost'" (roughly "restructuring" and "openness").

The immediate background of the Gorbachov reforms, which were to change the status of the Soviet satellites and to affect some parts of the Soviet Union itself, lay in the restiveness that had become endemic in Poland.

Poland whose economy had been devastatingly exploited by the Soviet occupation and which had absorbed, to no avail, tens of billions of dollars from the West, began to express some forceful disaffection.

In the summer of 1980, Lech Walesa, an electrical fitter who had been dismissed by the Lenin Shipyard in Gdansk, started a strike (over a fellow-worker's dismissal) that soon mushroomed into a national movement calling for blanket reform— free trades unions, freedom of information, access to the media, civil rights.

The movement—"Solidarity"—was strong enough to force the government, apparently yielding to these demands, to sign an agreement on 31 August. Hundreds of thousands of Polish Communist Party members surrendered their cards; a million members thronged into Solidarity, which seemed to be contesting the Soviet Executive as well as the puppet Polish government.

Walesa's strategy had been rooted in his insistence that Solidarity remain a trades-union movement, without reforming the Soviet system as a whole. Even though he occasionally expressed his hope that the Soviet Executive would restore Polish independence, he never tried to realize his hope.

It was quickly obvious that the Polish government had signed the agreement of August 1980 for tactical reasons: in February 1981 the Soviet Executive put General Wojciech Jaruzelski, a docile agent, in power; at the end of the year (13 December) a "state of war" was declared. There was a massive crackdown throughout the country. Many thousands of people were taken from their beds and arrested; tanks roved about in the capital and elsewhere.

The crackdown was so successful that those arrested were soon released; the regime had demonstrated its power. In October 1982 Solidarity was dissolved; in December the "state of war" was shelved. In the summer of 1985 Jaruzelski put on civilian clothes, a preliminary to his becoming president.

All this took place against the background of an economy that had been steadily deteriorating from an already moribund state in 1970.

The upheavals that had been racking Poland were now echoed throughout the satellites. In 1989 all the other eight countries occupied by the Soviet Executive as part of the Second World War settlement publicly began agitating for some degree of independence of the Soviet Union: Esthonia, Lithuania, Latvia, Czechoslovakia, Hungary, East Germany, Bulgaria and Rumania.

Borders were opened between East and West Germany, as well as between Austria, Hungary and Czechoslovakia; the Berlin Wall was opened up and torn down; people began moving about more or less freely. All the satellite governments began appointing non-Communist members; free elections were held out for the fairly near future.

The media hailed these events with joy; still, the process was not so straightforward as it appeared.

If the free elections were not yet held, while non-Communists were already being "appointed," it was blatantly obvious that those doing the appointing were the Communists themselves.

It is obvious, in fact, that the Soviet Executive had instructed the various satellite Communist Parties running the governments to slacken restraints. The tumultuous elation that ensued was entirely foreseeable.

(There was, to be sure, a brief hitch in the conduct of the Ceausescus in Rumania: their own private apparatus had been built up massively enough for them to risk contravening the directive from the center. But since this contradicted the histrionic objective of the mass rejoicing, they were eliminated as expeditiously as possible, no doubt by the KGB and its local agents. If some legitimate reformers had killed the dictator they would have ostentatiously proclaimed their action.

This was why the first media accounts were ignorant of the identity of the actual killers.)

On the face of it, the two catchwords—*perestroika* and *glasnost* (roughly "restructuring" and "openness")—contained volatile elements of danger. While "restructuring" might be taken to imply a complicated administrative overhaul that could be extended indefinitely, the newly proclaimed openness could easily run into insoluble problems: it could risk exposing the various neo-Bolshevik claims to legitimacy. For instance, the publication (in mid-1989) of the secret clauses of the Hitler-Stalin pact, which outlined the arbitrary occupation of the Baltic countries and led to the Second World War, gave instant justification to demands for independence of the three Baltic states. Similarly, publication of the material demonstrating the vast German subsidy to the Bolshevik Party in 1917 might effectively annul the legitimacy of the government itself. The slightest examination of the background of Trotsky's sudden ascension in the Bolshevik Party in 1917 would incur just the same risk: it could be explained only as a consequence of Lenin's flight outside the country during the preparation of the October *putsch* to avoid the likelihood of a trial for high treason in wartime. Once again, the German subsidy would loom up, nightmarishly, over the Bolshevik pretense of representing anyone.

The complexities confronting Gorbachov were obvious. In the broadest possible perspective, the neo-Bolshevik superstructure could not simply be dropped, even at the end of the twentieth century. A mere glance at the reforms touted by Gorbachov and his countless adulators in the media indicated their rhetorical quality: all the reforms were to be carried out, as before, by the Party—indeed the pro-reform candidates for the usual sort of Soviet elections, were, in fact, all members of the Party.

Despite the ubiquitous harping on "democracy," in short, there was never any question of implementing the word even in an attenuated form. The Party nucleus represented by Gorbachov never suggested, for instance, an organic base for a "democratic" government: no one even proposed an answer to the fundamental question implied by the word: "What is the source of the government's mandate?"

This manifest short circuit of the idea could be maintained only because the media outside the Soviet Union, presumably free to express themselves, slavishly followed the misuse of the word and the concept that was, of course, *de rigueur* in the Soviet Union itself, despite the amplified freedom of expression, which soon boiled down to the resumption of an ancient Soviet theme—blame Stalin.

The positive aspects of loosening the censorship—the amplification of access to information—indicated no "democratization" of the Soviet Executive. Since there was no real prospect of diluting its power, its decision to allow more discussion was actually a sign of strength: in contrast to the desperate attempts of the Stalin regime and its successors to control

areas that were basically irrelevant—history, philosophy, architecture, sculpture, music—the Soviet Executive under Gorbachov could be more flexible. In spite of everything it was
still secure.

From the point of view even of pragmatic reform, Gorbachov's first major speech in Moscow (3 November 1987) was
entirely disconcerting: at the very moment of sounding what
was evidently meant to be a clarion call for reform, he embarked on a lengthy excursion into the dinosaur past of the
neo-Bolshevik Party—a denunciation of "Trotskyism." Thus
the great achievement of Stalin's statecraft—a powerful formula
for satanizing all forms of dissent—was resurrected a half-
century after its purpose had been achieved. This seemingly
eccentric exhumation of a fossil aroused no comment outside
the Soviet Union: it arose out of the very depths of the confusion in the minds of the would-be reformers headed by
Gorbachov.

The project of creating a fairly free market while clinging
to the institutions that had sustained the neo-Bolshevik dictatorship for three-quarters of a century was an attempt to square
the circle. The gargantuan bureaucracy paralysed market forces;
a freeing of the market would have entailed the elimination
of the dictatorship.

That is the simple explanation of why all the clamor about
"freedom" and "democracy" remained no more than rhetoric
as long as the implications of the words were evaded.

Gorbachov's statements rotated around a fundamental contradiction, soared over by the media and most commentators.
While agreeing that Soviet society could realize its potential
only by opening itself up to "freedom" and "democracy," he
also kept saying flatly, at various times, that while freedom
and democracy would be striven for there would be no return
to large-scale private property, that the Party monopoly would
not vanish in the play of pluralistic politics, nor would "communist principles" be abandoned.

Through the turmoil in the satellites and in the Soviet Union
it was evident that the long-range goals of the Soviet Executive
remained untouched. The lavish subsidies propping up Cuba,

as well as the subsidy to the African National Congress, simply went on. Dropping, or suspending the use of the Sandinistas in Nicaragua may be considered the prudent sacrifice of a pawn to sustain the desired impression.

It was evident, indeed, that the Soviet Executive's original objective, epitomized by the abandonment in the sixties of the slogan "to overtake and pass America" and its replacement by planetary subversion through penetration and proxies, had survived the uncontrollable collapse of the economy. The very fact of conspicuous economic incapacity was turned into a strategic-diplomatic instrument for the ultimate circumventing of America. The public-relations campaign carried on by Gorbachov and his colleagues, if successful, would persuade the West that the elimination of any danger of war, long since superseded, entailed a natural prospect for peaceful reconstruction on all levels.

The aim of the Gorbachov reform movement, in short, was to present a plausible picture of its economic problems and secure a political benefit from them by persuading the United States government that even though Soviet armaments, throughout all negotiations about "arms control," had grown more formidable than ever, the *intentions* of the Soviet Executive were now transformed.

By the beginning of the nineties this became the leitmotif of world affairs. It was buttressed by the media, particularly in the United States, which from the very outset moulded public reception of the theme by constant repetition of a few basic concepts, absorbed by the government as well as by the public.

The demonstration of this change of heart in the Soviet Executive revolved around the claim that the agitation against the Communist government of the Soviet satellites was a spontaneous upheaval of the masses, provoked by the universal yearning for the creature comforts denied them so long by shortcomings of the planned economy. The corollary of this was the thirst for democracy.

And the crowning proof to this change of heart was the good grace with which the Soviet Executive had accepted the spontaneous upheaval, and even endorsed the same goals.

The transformation of intentions in the Soviet Executive was illustrated by countless reports that the Soviet economy itself was on its last legs: reports of commodity shortages, notorious since the Bolshevik putsch in 1917, surfaced again in force. The impression was given that the authorities, yielding to the craving for consumer goods, were now obliged to rectify the economy.

Yet to make this view plausible a very obvious fact had to be bypassed—that the agitation for goods, for democracy, for freedom of movement, had in fact been instigated by the Soviet Executive itself, and would, indeed, have been inconceivable otherwise.

Countless clichés ran riot in the wake of the Gorbachov talk about reforms: "Communism is crumbling . . . Marxism is dead . . . the Soviet Union is feeble . . . the planned economy is a shambles . . . the Soviet Union needs help . . . armaments can now be cut back . . . peace will bring its dividend . . ."

Yet the plausibility of these clichés was undermined by two confusions: one was that the Soviet authorities were preoccupied by consumer deprivation, the second was that Marxism was an integral element of the neo-Bolshevik state.

It is true, of course, that the ideological underpinnings of the neo-Bolshevik dictatorship have always been rooted, officially, in Marxism. In the name of this dogma hundreds of millions of school-children were subjected after the 1917 putsch to the complex of Marxist themes ("dialectical materialism" etc.).

But even at the very outset, when the neo-Bolshevik leaders no doubt still believed, in some sense or other, in the unique validity of Marxism as the framework of all thought, what this meant, practially speaking, was that the regime, while concentrating its activities on its goal of world hegemony, routinely claimed the sanction of Marxism.

As belief in the value of Marxism evaporated, except for purposes of rhetoric, in the exigencies of realpolitik, so the theory itself and its countless believers were merely integrated with the arsenal of the dictatorship and its goal of world hegemony. The socio-political reality was that the small core of leaders, within the vast apparatus, had become a factor of world politics.

The aim of world hegemony had little to do with consumer needs. If such needs were taken seriously they were put off until the attainment of the final goal.

The purpose of the huge charade set in motion by the Gorbachov coterie can be grasped merely by discerning its penultimate goal—to demonstrate that the formidable dimensions of its armaments were irrelevant because of the change of heart of the regime.

Essential to this notion was the role of Germany, whose unification and eventual exit from NATO were not only the key operation in the Gorbachov campaign but no doubt its very lever.

The aim of the Gorbachov reform movement was to clear the way to the acquisition of all forms of Western technology, as well as of massive amounts of capital, in order to fortify the economy of all the satellites and ultimately of the Soviet Union, too.

This illustrated the application of a profound, simple idea: the intensive exploitation of technology is more effective than the accumulation of territories.

Thus the Soviet Executive had decided to switch its policy from territorial expansion to the military-industrial overhauling of the economies under its control, a control scheduled to encompass Europe by the end of the century.

This enterprise, with all its immense potential, was modeled on Finland, which since 1945 has been safely encapsulated within the Soviet orbit while carrying on its affairs in a tranquil, democratic manner.

It can be seen in retrospect that the cardinal consequence of the First World War was the creation of the neo-Bolshevik state. For the first time in history a country was ruled by the exponents of an idea they thought powerful enough to enable them to sweep the world via the transformation of all other states. And indeed, the neo-Bolshevik state proved to be a catalyst for social change: combining both the resources of a great country and the glamor symbolizing a utopian ideal, it had material power as well as primordial attraction for the elites of all underdeveloped countries. When the first Marxist-Leninist state survived the Second World War, it brought about a whole universe of Marxist-Leninist states and the incalculable spread of the ideology conceived of as underlying them all.

By the beginning of the nineties the Gorbachov regime, by shifting the former Soviet satellites into a more or less free-market economic mode and by discussing democracy even within the Soviet Union, seemed to have created a different framework for the conduct of world affairs.

Yet the goal of the neo-Bolshevik nucleus remains the same: to survive—and to win. The Gorbachov manoeuvre could surely be considered an exemplification, on an immeasurably grander scale, of Lenin's aphorism about allowing the "capitalists" to sell their enemies the rope to hang them.

The immediate goal of emasculating NATO via the exodus of a unified Germany, and the longer-range goal of peaceably absorbing the technology of the West, including the Common Market, marked a new phase in the policy of the Soviet Executive. But it was a new phase in an old struggle—to defend its very existence by subjugating most of the world, thus isolating and ultimately paralysing the United States.

The risks inherent in this grandiose enterprise were evident. The multitudes buffeted by the new propaganda might take it at face value; uncontrollable forces might be set loose. Despite all manoeuvering, a new conjuncture might transform the Soviet Union, and with it the world.

★   ★   ★

BIBLIOGRAPHY

Baykov, Alexander. *The Development of the Soviet Economic System.* Cambridge: 1946.

Buchanan, G. *My Mission to Russia.* 2 vols. London: 1923.

Bunyan, J., and Fisher, H. H. *The Bolshevik Revolution 1917–18.* Stanford: 1934.

Carmichael, Joel. *Stalin's Masterpiece.* New York and London: 1974.

———— *Trotsky.* New York and London: 1974.

Chamberlin, W. H. *The Russian Revolution.* 2 vols. New York: 1960.

Conquest, Robert. *The Great Terror.* London and New York: 1968.

Dan, Theodor. *The Origins of Bolshevism.* Translated by J. Carmichael. New York and London: 1965.

Dubnov, S. M. *History of the Jews in Russia and Poland.* 3 vols. Philadelphia: 1916–1920.

Florinsky, Michael T. *Russia: A History and an Interpretation.* 2 vols. New York: 1947, 1953.

Gankin, O. H., and Fischer, H. H. *The Bolsheviks and the World War.* Stanford: 1940.

Golitsyn, Anatoliy, *New Lies for Old,* New York: 1984.

Grebing, H. *Politische Studien.* Munich: 1957.

Haffner, Sebastian *Anmerkungen zu Hitler,* Munich, 1978

Heller, Mikhail, and Nekrich, Aleksandr M., *Utopia in Power, The History of the Soviet Union from 1917 to the Present,* New York:, 1986.

Katkov, George. *Russia 1917: The February Revolution.* New York: 1967.

Kerensky, Alexander. *The Catastrophe.* London: 1927.

Kliuchevsky, V. O. *Kurs russkoi istorii (Lectures in Russian History).* 5 vols. Petrograd: 1904–21. Republished Moscow: 1936.

Knox, A. *With the Russian Army, 1914–1917.* 2 vols. New York: 1921.

Kovalevsky, Pierre. *Manuel d'histoire russe*. Paris: 1948.

Lenin, V. I. *Sochineniya*. Vols. I–XXXV, 4th ed. Moscow: 1941–50.

Lockhart, Bruce. *Memoirs of a British Agent*. New York and London: 1932.

Ludendorff, Erich. *Meine Kriegserinnerungen, 1914–18*. Berlin: 1919.

Martin, Malach; *The Jesuits*. New York: 1987.

Masaryk, T. G. *The Spirit of Russia*. London: 1918.

Maynard, J. *The Russian Peasant*. London: 1942.

Milyukov, P. N., Seignobos, C., and Eisenmann, L. *Histoire de Russie*. 3 vols. Paris: 1933.

Milyukov, P. N. *Ocherki po istorii russkoi kul'tury (Essays in the History of Russian Culture)*. Rev. ed., 3 vols. in 4. Paris: 1930–37.

——— *Istoriya Vtoroy Russkoi revolyutsii*. Sofia: 1921.

Mirsky, Prince S. D. *Russia: A Social History*. London: 1931.

——— *Contemporary Russian Literature*. 1881–1925. New York: 1927.

Nicolaevsky, B. I. *Power and the Soviet Elite*. New York: 1965.

Orlov, Alexander. *The Secret History of Stalin's Crimes*. London: 1953.

Rauch, Georg von. *A History of Soviet Russia*. New York: 1957.

Sadoul, Jacques. *Notes sur la révolution bolchévique*. Paris: 1919.

Schapiro, Leonard. *The History of the Communist Party of the Soviet Union*. 2nd ed. New York and London: 1970.

Seton-Watson, Hugh. *The Decline of Imperial Russia*. London: 1952.

Shub, David. *Lenin*. Pelican Edition: 1966.

Stählin, K. *Geschichte Russlands*. 4 vols. Berlin: 1939 (completed).

Sukhanov, N. N. *Zapiski o Revolyutsii*. 7 vols. Berlin: 1922–23. Translated, abridged, and edited as *The Russian Revolution 1917*, by J. Carmichael, London and New York: 1955. New ed. 1975.

Sumner, B. H. *A Short History of Russia*. New York: 1943.

Trotsky, Leon. *History of the Russian Revolution*. 3 vols. London: 1932–33.

Tsereteli, I. G. *Vospominaniya o fevral'skoy revolyutsii*. 2 vols. Paris and The Hague: 1963.

Vernadsky, G. and Karpovich, M. *A History of Russia*. 2 vols. New Haven: 1943–48.

Welter, G. *Histoire de Russie*. Paris: 1949.

Wolfe, Bertram. *Three Who Made a Revolution*. New York: 1948.

Zamoyski, Adam. *The Polish Way*. New York and Toronto: 1988.

Zeman, Z. A. B. (ed.). *Germany and the Revolution in Russia, 1915–18*. London: 1958.

Zeman, Z. A. B., and Scharlau, W. B. *The Merchant of Revolution: The Life of Alexander Israel Helphand* (Parvus). London and New York: 1965.

Index

MORE RUSSIAN TITLES FROM HIPPOCRENE:

HIPPOCRENE INSIDER'S GUIDE TO MOSCOW, LENINGRAD AND KIEV *by Yuri Fedosuk*

Written by a native of the USSR, this guidebook covers the three Soviet cities most frequently visited by Western tourists. Extensive historical and physical descriptions of all the main sights are enhanced by "inside" tips on getting the real feel of each place.

256 pages   ISBN 0-87052-805-X $11.95 paper

HIPPOCRENE COMPANION GUIDE TO THE SOVIET UNION *by Lydle Brinkle*

One in a series of Hippocrene guides written by American professors, this book goes beyond routine information by incorporating both practical details of use to the tourist, and the historical and geographical background, to explain the significance of the sights and the cultures which he or she will encounter.

224 pages   ISBN 0-87052-635-9 $14.95 paper

HIPPOCRENE RUSSIAN-ENGLISH/ENGLISH-RUSSIAN PRACTICAL DICTIONARY *by O.P. Benyuch and G.V. Chernov*
8,000 entries each way.   ISBN 0-87052-336-8 $9.95 paper

HIPPOCRENE RUSSIAN-ENGLISH/ENGLISH-RUSSIAN DICTIONARY *by W. Harrison and Svetlana LeFleming*
25,000 entries, with a grammar summary. ISBN 0-87052-751-7 $9.95 paper

DICTIONARY OF RUSSIAN VERBS *by Daum and Schenk*
20,000 verbs, fully declined. ISBN 0-88254-420-9 $22.50 short discount